I0584596

ESSENCE OF GLUIC

Thorik Dain's Journey, Book 3

A.G. Wedgeworth

Anthony G. Wedgeworth

Copyright © 2010 by Anthony G. Wedgeworth

Written by A.G.Wedgeworth

Front Cover Artwork by Elartwyne Estole

Illustrations by Steve Ott

Editing by Deborah Murrell

ISBN: 978-0-9859159-4-0 Paperback

Library of Congress Control Number: 2010910873

All rights reserved.

No portion of this book may be reproduced in any form without written permission from the publisher or author, except as permitted by U.S. copyright law.

Altered Creatures

Epic Fantasy Adventures

Historical Date 4.0650.0622

Series: Thorik Dain's Journey

Book 3, Revision 3.0

Essence of Gluic

www.AlteredCreatures.com

CONTENTS

MAI'BUSS RANGE
CUEV'IARU MOUNTAINS
MAI' BUSS LESSOR RANGE
UPPER CANINES
Fesh Forest
Gort Glade
Del'Ona
E'Rou'e
DOOMA
BADLANDS
Eryauthian Lake
Ergrauth
OSSUARY RANGE
Del'Grauth
Chuny Range
Lower Canines
Co'Avell Corridor
Corrock
Ro'Yolney
Trewen
Northwall
Spirit-water
Coliseum O'Sid Fields
EVER DUNES
EASTLAND Rapt
Ki'Yolney Lake
Ligona Falls
Della Estoria
Go'ta Gorge
Surod
KIRI DUNES
Yolney River
Pith
Prevail
KIRI DESERT
SHI'PEL PEAKS
EverSpring
Ovia'Mathuus
Solan Ridges
SOLANN MOUNTAINS
DOR'AVELL RANGE
River

Bakalor
Darkmere
Gluic
Bryus
Thorik & Avanda
Santorray
Grewen

PROLOGUE

Thorik's Log: 22nd day of the 6th month of the 650th year.

Our attempt to stop Darkmere from sacrificing Ambrosius' son, Er-
icc, at the Temple of Surod has ended in tragedy. It was far worse than I
could have expected and more distressing than just the temple crumbling
down upon the feuding parties. The soul of my grandmother, Gluic, has
been captured inside an enchanted dagger. In addition, my arm was
broken during our battle, but our new companion, Bryus Grum, used
one of his spells to repair it. The only positive outcome of this venture is
that the relationship between Avanda and me is finally on the mend.
However, I'm concerned about Bryus teaching her magic and what she
will do with such powers. Nevertheless, we require his talents to find the
spell which will free Gluic.

Chapter One

END OF THE LINE

"She's dead, Thorik!" Brimmelle's fists shook uncontrollably. "My mother is dead because she followed your lead. This is all your fault," he accused his nephew.

Thorik lifted the dagger, Varacon, out toward his uncle. The small dagger had multiple blades that twisted to a sharp point. Two red gems in the hilt swirled from beneath their surface and gave off a slight glow. "No, she's not. Gluic has been captured inside this spellbound dagger."

"I saw her lying on the floor, dead. Her life's blood was pouring from her body. Her eyes had rolled back into her head!" Brimmelle shouted. "You told me Grewen would save her!" He firmly pointed at the giant who accompanied them.

Grewen lowered his eyes at the verbal jab; even though the giant mognin stood nearly three times the height of Brimmelle, he came across as much less threatening than his size would indicate.

"There wasn't time. The ceiling collapsed and crushed her body." Still facing him, Thorik stepped between Brimmelle and Grewen. "Uncle, you must understand that her body has gone, but we've saved her essence."

"Says who? Who knows this to be true?"

"Bryus Grum," Thorik replied. "Haven't you been listening to him? He's been explaining this ever since we left the temple."

"You trust this buffoon?" Brimmelle jerked his head toward a lanky man in old torn clothes. "We don't even know him. For all we know, he could be working for Darkmere."

"I seriously doubt that, seeing that he was Darkmere's prisoner when we arrived. We even heard the Dark Lord give the order to kill Bryus."

"Sounds like one of Darkmere's tricks to fool us."

"Tricks?" Thorik was perplexed at the thought. "Darkmere doesn't care about us. He seeks revenge on Ambrosius and his family for preventing his conquest of Terra Australis. He cares not of Nums from Farbank and a few traveling companions."

Brimmelle scoffed. "He's been using us to get to Ambrosius, his son, and whoever else he wishes to destroy."

Thorik shook his head. "Darkmere didn't even know we were going to be showing up at the temple. In fact, we wouldn't have gone there at all if it hadn't been for our attempt to prevent Avanda from reaching the temple to save Ericc. How could he have prepared for such unpredictable actions?"

Brimmelle scowled at Avanda, who was a few years younger than Thorik. "That's very true. She's constantly out of control."

Thorik watched Avanda recoil from Brimmelle's threatening posture. "Hold on, Uncle. This is not about Avanda, nor is it about Grewen or Bryus. If you want to blame someone, blame me."

Brimmelle stepped up close to his nephew and placed his face inches from the young man. "I do." The cold, harsh words made it clear to Thorik that his uncle, Fir Brimmelle Riddlewood the Seventh, the spiritual leader of their community of Farbank, had reached his limit.

Thorik knew that ever since they had left their small village of Farbank, Brimmelle had begrudgingly followed him in an effort to protect his mother, Gluic, from harm. But now that she was gone, his uncle had no incentive to follow him one step further.

Thorik's initial reaction was to back down. Years of training to yield to Fir Brimmelle influenced his judgment. However, this time he composed himself and stood straight and firm against his uncle's stance.

The two stood on the rocky mountain, halfway between the demolished Temple of Surod high above them and the base of the Go'ta Gorge. The bridge had been destroyed, so they were forced to travel down to the bottom of the gorge. Subterranean vent holes slowly released clouds of steam, which lifted just over their heads before dispersing out into a ceiling of fog-like clouds.

Grewen, Bryus, and the young girl, Avanda, stood nearby and watched the altercation. Bryus' intense curiosity was focused on Thorik's dagger instead of the two arguing Nums. His facial tic pulled his cheek back and his eye closed. It had been doing so ever since being attacked by Darkmere's minion. Bryus' own magic could not prevent it from pulling uncontrollably on his face.

Grewen shook his massive head in disappointment at Thorik and Brimmelle's struggle to get along. Clasping his hands together, each one half the size of Thorik, the giant sighed at the sight before him.

Avanda stepped forward and spoke with concern and respect in her voice. "Please, Fir Brimmelle, don't blame Thorik. It was my fault as much as it was his." The swirling dark lines on her skin, also known as soul-markings, faded in color as she held her breath waiting for Brimmelle's response.

Brimmelle's deep stare never left Thorik's eyes.

Standing his ground, Thorik waited for his uncle to speak.

Fir Brimmelle took in a deep breath before responding. "We left Farbank with six Nums. Emilen betrayed us, Wess died trying to save Avanda, and now my mother, your grandmother, is dead." His tone was dry and intense. "I'm heading back to Farbank with Avanda. You are no longer welcome there. Do not return."

Thorik's eyes gave away his heartache. Brimmelle had previously taken away his responsibilities as one of the village's hunters. He had also threatened to strip his spiritual title 'Sec' from his name, which would bring shame to him upon returning. However, to forbid the younger Num from returning to the only home he had ever known was beyond Thorik's belief.

"No!" Tears instantly filled Avanda's eyes. She lunged forward and grabbed onto Thorik's arm as though he was being torn away. "I won't return without him."

Thorik continued to stand strong with his face just inches from his uncle's. "Gluic is still with us." He held up the dagger near their faces to visualize his point. "We can still save her."

"Stop it!" Brimmelle grabbed the dagger from Thorik and backed away several steps. "This is a dagger, not a living being!"

"Brimmelle." Thorik's voice vibrated with great fear. "Please... hand me the dagger, Varacon."

"No. You need to stop believing these illicit tales of the supernatural." Brimmelle waved the dagger about as he talked. "The Mountain King gave us the words to follow and nowhere did he sanction such nonsense."

Thorik's right hand moved out into a begging position. "Please, Brimmelle. Don't wave that about. It was a virgin dagger before striking Granna Gluic. If it strikes again, we may lose her!"

"Hogwash!" Brimmelle claimed, still waving it about. "These are the kind of fables which have caused you to forget your roots and your faith."

Watching the dagger nearly slap the side of a boulder, Thorik panicked. "In the name of the Mountain King and everything he stands for, give me that dagger before you kill my grandmother!"

Brimmelle was shocked. "How dare you use the King's name to serve your personal needs?" With that, he purposely slapped the side of the boulder with the dagger, causing sparks to fly from its blades.

"NO!" shouted everyone as they all rushed toward Brimmelle. But a second slap of the weapon hit before Thorik could leap across and knock his uncle to the ground.

Avanda was the next to jump on as she grappled Fir Brimmelle for the dagger. The three Nums stumbled in their reaching for the item, and they began to tumble down the mountainside. Cooking tools and travel gear flew from Thorik's pack, as well as his spear and his wooden coffer. Avanda's entire pack was ripped from her body as the Nums barreled in a tangled mess down the steep incline.

Bryus yelled at the sight. "Be careful!" The thin old man rushed after them before stopping at Thorik's spear. Picking it up, he quickly inspected it for dents with his brown eye, and then scratches with his blue one. "Are you damaged?" he asked the weapon as he brushed the dirt from it.

Grewen lumbered past Bryus and attempted to follow the trio, but he couldn't keep up with the out-of-control Nums, who whirled and bounced off boulders and loose rocks until they rolled into one of the vent holes and out of view.

Grewen trudged his bulky mass toward the small entrance as quickly as his body would allow him. He wasn't a fast runner on a flat surface, let alone down a mountainside. That said, he was going fast enough to cause him to skid past the hole while trying to stop.

Once he returned, he peered over the brim of the hole, only to find Brimmelle partially blocking the entrance. He had hit his head and been knocked out from a short fall to a small ledge as his legs spanned the hole, resting on the far wall. The enchanted dagger was still firmly in his hand, but the other two Nums were nowhere to be seen.

Straddling the steaming vent hole, Grewen leaned over and used his oversized dual-thumbed hand to pluck Brimmelle off the ledge and set him on safe ground before returning to the hole.

"Hello?" Grewen yelled into the vent, hoping the other two Nums had only fallen to a lower ledge.

There was no answer.

Grewen cupped his hands on both sides of his mouth and called a second time down into the vent hole. "Can you hear me?" Again and again he tried, but the giant's tiny ears couldn't hear any response.

"No respect!" Bryus eventually approached Grewen, who was now lying on the ground, reaching deep into the hole. "Did you see what jeopardy they put the Spear of Rummon into?" He spied the dagger still clutched by Brimmelle and added, "As well as Varacon."

"Right now we have more important matters to deal with," Grewen replied.

"Surely you jest," Bryus laughed as he held up the spear. "Do you realize the sacrifices that were made to create such a finely crafted piece of art?"

"They pale in comparison to one of these Nums' lives." Grewen strained to reach his hand deeper into the dark vent in order to feel around.

"Nonsense." Bryus walked over and pulled the dagger from Brimmelle's hand. "The Varacon dagger was forged out of love. A tragic story of two people who desired to be together, but only in death would they achieve this." Holding the dagger in front of his own face, he admired it. "It's a shame they never used it." His cheek twitched a few times as he gazed at the sight. "We have two of the most amazing enchanted items ever created, and you're worried about Nums."

"Your lack of humanity toward the living is amazing." Grewen continued to stretch his arm as far as he could. "Your precious weapons are safe. Now, how about helping me save Thorik and Avanda?"

Bryus nodded in agreement and waved a hand, shooing Grewen out of the way so he could look down. While the giant mognin dislodged himself from the hole, the Alchemist stored his newly acquired items.

Kneeling next to Brimmelle, Bryus began searching through all of the Num's pouches until he found some fishing line and a hard nut. He quickly removed the items and walked over to Grewen, who had finished rolling the rest of the way out of the hole. "Slap me up," he said to the mognin.

Grewen was confused. "What's that?"

"You know, back side of the head. Give her a tap." Bryus then turned his back to Grewen and began tying a knot into the fishing line.

Grewen blinked a few times, unsure of the reason for the request. "I don't believe in hurting others."

"Just a nice solid tap. Nothing bone-crushing. Perhaps a nice thump on the back side."

"But I—"

"Come on, you big lug, do you want my help or not?" Bryus placed the nut in his teeth, cupped his hands below his chin to catch the nut pieces, and then waited.

Hesitantly, Grewen finally reached over with his massive hand and thumped Bryus on the back of his head.

Bryus' head violently snapped forward. His teeth slammed shut, crushing the nut into hundreds of small pieces. At the same time, the jolt from the powerful thump caused his left eye to pop out of its socket, break from the skin that held it, and flop into his hand.

Bryus screamed in pain as he turned to show the mognin what damage he had done. "Why so hard?" he yelled. "I said a tap!"

A chilling wave rode up Grewen's back as he realized what he had done. The idea of purposely hitting someone and then knocking their eyeball out was horrifying. "Bryus, stand still. We'll figure a way to fix this."

Bryus held his brown eye out in front of him with straight arms. "How? How can you fix this? What have you done to me?"

"I'm sorry, Bryus. I didn't realize I hit you that hard."

"Oh, come now, I've had little puffins hit harder than that." Bryus didn't attempt to hide his sarcastic tone.

Perplexed at the comment, Grewen stopped suddenly as he tried to understand what was going on.

Bryus started laughing at Grewen's bewildered facial expressions. "What a ruse." The man chuckled again before chewing up the nut pieces in his mouth and swallowing with a sigh of enjoyment.

Then, ignoring the giant, Bryus tied his detached eye onto the end of the fishing line. "Shall we have a look-see?" His voice was back to its normal tone.

Dangling the line over the vent hole, the eyeball twisted and turned as it prepared to see what was below. A patch of muscles still clung to the backside of the eye and hung limply below. Bryus proceeded to slowly lower his own eye into the hole. "I can see a second shelf below."

"Are they on it?" Grewen asked.

"No." The Alchemist continued to feed more length to the line.

It was a long and slow process as Bryus had difficulty seeing out of his detached eye in the thick mist of the vent. But eventually he was able to find something. "Ah, there it is. Right there." He then gave a sigh of closure.

"What do you see?"

Twirling up the line quickly, Bryus was silent about what he saw. Once it was fully removed from the vent, he untied the knot on the line to free the eyeball, and then carefully placed it back into his eye socket.

"Well? Did you find them?" Grewen asked.

A twitch pulled Bryus' cheek to the side. "No."

"Then what did you see?"

"The mark." He struggled to get his eye in straight.

"What kind of mark?"

Resolving his eye corrections, he chuckled at the mognin. "Do you not know where we are? We are standing above the underworld, Della Estovia. You know, where the dead roam. The demon Bakalor's realm." His laugh had turned slightly insane in tone. "Bakalor's mark was in that vent hole. Who else would mark his territory with the skulls of the ancient Notarians?"

Grewen sat quiet at first as he began to plan. "I doubt that Bakalor would even know they have entered his domain. There is still time."

"Time? Did you get thumped on the head as well? Bakalor doesn't take kindly to visitors from the surface. People don't casually enter his lair and return to be with the living. It's not a vacation spot. They're gone. There is no escape for them."

Chapter Two

DELLA ESTOVIA

The vent hole slowly curved to the side as Thorik slid and tumbled his way down the tunnel. Rolling head over heels at times, he fruitlessly attempted to protect his head and face from any injuries.

Avanda rolled and bounced behind him until a fork in the tunnel split them up. Her path, down a new tunnel, was longer than Thorik's and finally opened onto the floor of a large cavern, where she skidded to a halt on her stomach.

Thorik's travel through the tunnel ended with a short drop onto the top of an enormous pile of loose grains coated with a thin layer of small pebbles. Pulling his arms in tight, he rolled his way down the massive pile for what felt like minutes before reaching the bottom.

Once he had come to a stop, his first duty was to determine where he was and where Avanda had landed. He was coated with debris from the pile, and his body now itched, as though a thousand tiny pins were pricking him. His arm, which Bryus had recently repaired, was throbbing in pain and needed attention as well. He immediately began brushing off the debris while his eyes slowly adjusted to the low light.

Thick crystals were embedded into the walls and lit the caverns with a soft, bluish glow. Scraggly vines covered large sections of the light-blue crystals, absorbing light and warmth from them as well as moisture from the thick, humid air. It only took a few seconds for Thorik's eyes to adjust to the darker surroundings.

The pile that Thorik had tumbled down was in fact a pile of guano from the tens of thousands of bats hanging from the ceiling. Bats, however, were the least of his issues. The pile's outer layer, which he had assumed was pebbles, was instead a layer of predator roaches and centipedes eating the guano.

As hideous as the sight was, the realization of his own body still covered with the them finally sunk in. Guano was in every pocket and had stained his clothes, while the roaches and centipedes crawled up his pant legs, under his shirt, and into his hair.

Panicking, he began to quickly disrobe in an effort to get the insects off of him. He felt millions of little feet moving up his legs and across his back. Frequent bites pinched Thorik as the insects attempted to burrow their heads into his skin.

Ripping at his clothes as quickly as he could, he screamed from the pain as he stumbled away from the pile of guano and bugs. But the pain was just beginning. Now that he had removed the free crawling insects, he needed to uproot the ones that had latched themselves onto him.

The first one he pulled off his stomach snapped in half, its head still buried in his skin and working its way deeper. There wasn't much left to grab on to; he would need to dig into his own skin to grasp the head for removal.

Thorik pinched his skin around the head and forced the head back out, but the insect's pinchers still held tight. Using his other hand, he grabbed the insect's head and yanked it out of his body. Skin tore, blood spilled, and the poison from the insect burned like acid under his flesh, but at least it had been removed.

It was at this point that he realized the severity of his situation. Dozens of these insects had burrowed their heads into his stomach, arms, and legs. Each one was eating its way through his body as though it were in a race. Each one was extruding an acid-based poison into his system. Each one was looking for a nest to bury its offspring in this fresh new host.

The Num screamed from the pain as he grabbed one after another in an attempt to rid himself of them. His face was covered with tears as well as a few of these insects, one of which burrowed its way through his cheek, falling into Thorik's mouth.

An instant gag reflex caused the Num to spit up the insect along with a shower of vomit. Thorik fell forward to his hands and knees as fluids dripped from his mouth. The insects on his chest and stomach hung like fish on hooks, flapping back and forth as they attempted to grip his skin with their feet.

The poison from the bugs caused him to be lightheaded and dizzy. He pinched another insect out of his arm and screamed from the pain. He then pulled another from his leg. But his eyes were giving him visions of the insects flying and changing shapes. Reality blurred into a hazy unreal world where there was no pain.

Thorik collapsed onto the cavern floor as he viewed what appeared to be a giant insect, nearly the size of him, approach from the distance. He watched helplessly as it ran past his backpack and stood up on its back legs before it pounced on him.

Thorik tried to kick. He tried to roll away. But it was no use. He had lost control of his body. He would now lie powerless as he watched himself being eaten alive.

Chapter Three

Avanda

Avanda looked into Thorik's fearful eyes, as though he saw her as some type of beast. "Thorik! Can you hear me?" she asked as she quickly began removing the insects from his limp body. "Don't you dare leave me!" she shouted, turning him over to see a dozen more insects buried in his back.

Instead of his friend, Thorik's imagination saw her as a giant insect attacking him. Fear and poison raced through his body as he started to fade away.

The sight of the clinging insects caused a wave of emotions through her. They were literally devouring her friend and companion, let alone the Runestone teacher she had emotionally fallen for. These vicious bugs were harming the one she loved, and her fear of his death intertwined with an uncontrollable revengeful rage against them.

Her anger at the insects drove her to aggressively dig out every last one of them. Her hands bled from the insects fighting back and biting at her. At first, she tossed them to the side, but it wasn't long before her fury caused her to squeeze and crush their heads after taking them out. The popping sound gave her satisfaction in repayment for their attack on Thorik.

One after another, she ripped the insects from his back, legs, arms, stomach, and chest. She continued to increase her speed as her anger grew and her concern for self-injury disappeared. Again and again, she cursed them as she plucked them out.

Before she knew it, she had removed them all. She searched his body one more time to ensure she hadn't missed any. Standing up, she then stomped on any full or partial insects within a few yards of Thorik. She didn't know how to stop her desire to fight something, anything, just to relieve the anger that had built up inside her.

Frustrated, she turned to Thorik. His naked skin dripped blood from small holes throughout his body. His injured arm was twisted under his chest, and his legs were wrapped around each other. His face, normally ever so sweet to Avanda's eyes, was now locked in a state of pain and fear.

Her heart melted at the sight, and her anger soon faded. Avanda's feelings for him had grown ever since he became her Runestone teacher several years ago in Farbank. Back when life was simple and fear of death was not a daily concern.

Thorik's body trembled, snapping her out of her momentary daydream. Avanda quickly covered him up before creating a safer place for them to rest.

After dragging Thorik's unconscious body into a side cavern, near one of the soft, glowing wall crystals, which had vines clinging to them, Avanda gently set his head on a pillow she had made from his backpack. She had removed the contents from the pack and filled it with guano to create a soft resting place.

Grabbing his flint and a handful of vines, she started a small fire. Afterward, she collected his clothes and placed them on the pile of his pack contents.

Avanda had also found fresh water dripping down through the walls and ceiling. Using Thorik's only remaining cooking pan, she collected enough for them to drink and for her to wash out the insect bites.

Once he was cleaned up, her concern turned to keeping the campfire going. This was their only source of heat and light, although a very faint glow emanated from the thick crystals.

Exhausted, she took a moment to lean up against one of the crystals, only to find it caused her to relax. Even though it gave no heat, it warmed her insides and washed away any remaining aggression from the event.

Hours passed as Avanda cradled Thorik's head, and she gave him sips of water each time before she took a sip for herself. She repeatedly washed his body to keep his wounds clean. When she became tired, she cuddled up against his back under his blanket, sharing her body heat with him. Then her hand wrapped around his side and lay upon his chest so she could tell if he was still breathing.

This went on for days as she waited to be rescued. Never wavering and rarely sleeping, she constantly checked his breathing and fed him water. She became obsessed with keeping him alive.

Over time, she had learned that the centipedes could be eaten, and the roaches burned like pieces of coal, so she made frequent trips back to the guano pile to keep the fire bright. Each time she did, she rushed back as quickly as possible, always fearful that something would try to harm Thorik while she was away.

Her imagination began to get the better of her as she became convinced that the little critters were plotting to take him. She could hear them whisper in the distance. Knowing they were watching her, she staggered her timing to collect water and roaches so they couldn't plan properly.

She had dreams of fighting off creatures to save Thorik's life. In her state of malnutrition and sleep deprivation, she struggled to tell the difference between dreams and reality. In her mind, she had saved his life a dozen times. She was losing her sense of reality.

On the other hand, Thorik slept. He breathed and his heart continued to beat, but he did not wake.

Preparing to sleep, Avanda pressed her chest up against his back and softly played with his hair. "Thorik, I promise to take care of you. You're safe with me here."

After so many days with no one to talk to, she had become used to talking to Thorik while he slept.

She pulled him in tight and sighed. "I know you've been alone since your parents died. And I also know how Emilen tempted you with love and then used it against you. I knew she was never right for you, anyway." Avanda scowled at the thought of Thorik's prior love and how she deceived him into falling into Darkmere's trap. "Emilen is the reason Ambrosius is dead, and why you are here fighting for your life."

"But I'm here now. I've always been there for you. I…" she paused and reached her lips near his ear before whispering, "… I love you, Thorik Dain of Farbank."

And with those words, Thorik blinked and his lips began to move. Still in his sleep state, he managed a single reply before passing back out. "I love you too, Emilen."

Avanda froze. Her body went stiff, and she felt her heart miss a beat. Her body instantly broke contact with his as she rolled away. She then stared at him in disbelief. "No," she muttered. "NO!" she shouted.

"It's not fair," Avanda argued with the sleeping Num. "I've always loved you. Emilen pretended to love you, only to use you." Standing up, she wobbled from lack of sleep and food as she glared at Thorik. Her head was foggy and her thoughts were a mess as anger built up inside. "Emilen left you for dead, while I stayed at your side to keep you alive!

"Why? What's so special about her?" Avanda waited for an answer, which she knew she wouldn't get.

"Would you prefer if I was ruthless and conniving? Perhaps if I lied to you. Or is it her looks? Is it?" Her voice was loud and angry as it echoed throughout the caverns. "Why won't you love me instead of her? What's wrong with me?"

Avanda's mind raced from topic to topic, trying to make sense of it all. "What did I do to you that was so wrong, making my love for you so distasteful? I deserve to know that! Don't you think you owe me an answer?" Tears poured down her face as she yelled at him.

Thorik continued to be silent.

"Emilen. Emilen? How can you say her name, yet be unable to say mine?" And with that, she grabbed the pot of water and flung the liquid out toward him in an emotional outburst.

The water splashed against his face, causing him to start choking.

Avanda immediately realized that she had let her self-pity get the best of her. She quickly snapped out of it, dropped the pan, and ran to his side, hoping she hadn't drowned him. "Thorik! Can you breathe?"

"Yes," he said as he coughed.

He was awake! He had made it through the insect's poison and had regained consciousness.

"Oh, Thorik, I thought I had lost you. You've been passed out for so long that I didn't think you were going to come back to me." She leaned over his face with a smile that verged on becoming a cry.

"Avanda, you pulled me through. You did it. You saved my life."

"You would have done the same for me."

Thorik looked deep into her tearful eyes and nodded. "Yes, I would."

Chapter Four

PACKING

Realizing that no help would come for them and the vent shafts were too steep and smooth to climb back up, Thorik rested and recovered as long as he could until the need for food overwhelmed the desire to wait. The little protein they had obtained from eating the nearby centipedes simply was not enough to survive on. They needed more.

Thorik created an arrow on the ground out of rocks, which indicated which way they would travel. He still held out hope that Grewen, Brimmelle, and Bryus were on their way to save them.

Untying a pouch filled with Runestones, which had survived the fall into the caverns, Thorik removed the Runestone of Belief. Taking in a deep breath, he traced the ridges on its surface and closed his eyes as he allowed himself to fully relax.

Tingling along his fingertips worked its way up his hands, arms, and then his chest before completing the circular flow of energy that moved between him and the stone. As he did so, the red gem in the center of the Runestone began to glow and light up the cavern. With additional concentration, he could also cause the Runestone to give off heat, but it was a taxing endeavor and required more focus than

Thorik was willing to give at the moment. Light to guide the way would be good enough for now.

Over the past few months, he had become quite skilled at activating this Runestone, although he hadn't yet determined the powers of most of the others.

Thorik opened his pack. His head dropped and he sighed at the sight of the guano within it.

"It packed in nicely." Avanda grinned at the idea of him sleeping on bat droppings for the past week. "It was the best pillow you've had in months."

"I'll never get the smell out of my hair." He gave off a slight chuckle as he dumped the guano out of his pack.

"How's your arm?"

Thorik scooped out the guano so he could use his pack again. The thick consistency clumped between his fingers and on his forearm. "It still hurts." Finishing the unpleasant task, he tried to shake the rest off of him.

"I know that. I was just wondering if it feels broken."

"It hurts bad when I use it, but Bryus' spell to fix the break seems to be holding. The insect bites are currently more sensitive." He scratched at the sores on his neck. "They still itch as well."

"I'm sorry I couldn't heal you. I did the best I could."

Stuffing his items back into his pack, he glanced up at her. "Avanda, you did great. You kept me alive. How could I ask for anything more... especially at your age?"

"What do you mean?" Her voice had turned cold and lower than normal.

Thorik continued to pack with his stronger arm. "Nothing."

"I'm not a child anymore."

"I didn't say that you were." He tried to end the conversation by standing up.

"I'm less than three years younger than you."

"I know. Are you ready to head out?"

"My parents have nearly six years between them."

"That's wonderful."

"So we are close enough in age to be together."

Thorik was realizing where this was going, but didn't feel that it was the proper time to discuss it. "Yes, we are. It's a fine observation, but right now, we need to be talking about getting back to the surface."

Avanda wasn't willing to let it go that easily. "What are you afraid of?"

"Afraid? I fear many things. Those predator roaches for one, bad tempered blothruds for another. But most of all, right now, I fear where this conversation is leading."

"Why? Why can't you talk about us?"

Thorik finished with his pack and lifted it up on his shoulder. It still smelled terrible. "Avanda, now is not the time."

"Now is the perfect time. It's only you and I. No one else is here to disturb us."

"Let's start walking."

Avanda grabbed his sore arm to stop him.

"Ouch!" he yelled from the pain of her grasp, even though it hadn't been more than a squeeze. It did, however, get him to stop and listen to her.

She looked him square in the eyes and waited for him to return the eye contact. The gentle light from his Runestone gave her soft pale skin a glowing appearance. She would never be as beautiful and voluptuous as Emilen, but Avanda had a strength about her that softened when she looked Thorik in the eyes. "Thorik, I need to know if you have feelings for me."

Thorik shrugged his shoulders. "Of course I do."

"No. I mean genuine feelings. Like you did for Emilen."

She had caught him off guard, and he stared while blinking at her. Just Emilen's name made his heart flutter.

"I see," she said softly.

"Avanda, I love you... like a little sister."

She pulled her eyes away, followed by her head and shoulders. Grabbing her items, she kept her back to him. "You must think I'm a fool to expect you to desire me."

Rubbing his brow, Thorik sighed at the situation. "I don't think you're a fool. In fact, I think you're the brightest Num I've ever met. You're courageous, intelligent, and honest. Perhaps even too honest for your own good. But I love that about you."

Turning back to Thorik, she studied his face. Her eyes appeared to be searching for the truth in his expression. "Then what is it about me that prevents you from being mine?"

Thorik bit his lip for a moment as he tried to muster the words. "Emilen..."

Avanda's shoulders drooped again once she heard her rival's name.

"Emilen," he started over, "stole my heart. I would have done anything for her. I practically did. At times, I forgot who I was just to satisfy and please her. In a way, I compromised my core values to please her. And then I came to find out that she was deceiving me. Leading me on, like some grazer on a rope."

Avanda relaxed her shoulders and posture as she listened to him.

"I don't know what kind of spell she had over me, and my concern is it was no spell at all, but instead, it was nothing more than love. If that is all it was, then I fear falling in love again, for I may lose who I really am, what I stand for, and most importantly, the mission I am on to free my grandmother."

"But Thorik, I would never—"

"I know," Thorik interrupted. He stepped up to her and placed his hands on her shoulders. "I know you wouldn't intentionally do this to me. But that is not to say that it wouldn't happen anyway. And right now I can't afford to take that chance. I have to maintain my focus on keeping you alive as well as saving Granna." Looking deeply into her eyes and thinking about more pleasant times, he smiled. "Once we get back to Farbank, I can let my guard down. Not until then."

Although Thorik could tell that she still disagreed with his concerns, he watched her softly nod in agreement.

Chapter Five

TUNNELS

Crystals as thick as Grewen's waist jutted up at awkward angles from the cavern's floor and up through the ceiling. Just like the crystal they had set up camp next to, these occasional pillars gave off a faint glow, helping the two Nums negotiate their way through the maze of tunnels.

They were lost, and no matter which turn the Nums made, the path always led to further subterranean depths. Hope of finding a way back up to the surface was giving way to a desire for an underground river which would lead them out of the Shi'Pel Mountains and to the Volney River.

It had been days since they had eaten. "Even an insect would taste good at this point." Avanda's lips cracked as she spoke. Her body was bruised and cut from the various sharp rocks she had bumped against and fallen onto. Dark circles were now around her eyes from lack of sleep. She was exhausted. "Is there no end to these caves?"

"We'll get through this." Thorik's voice and mannerisms were always optimistic, even when he wasn't. "Just a little farther." He shone the light from his Runestone deeper into several tunnels to decide which one to select.

"You said that yesterday."

"It was only a few hours ago."

"No." Her voice was agitated, and her stomach moaned from lack of food. Insects simply weren't enough to survive on. "We've slept since then."

Thorik tried to recall, but the hours and days were all blending together. Without seeing the sun rise and fall, it was difficult to know just how long they had been away from the surface.

Avanda shook uncontrollably from the cold, damp air of the caverns. This seemed to happen more frequently as time went on. It always started lightly and then became uncontrollable for what felt like an hour before it subsided.

Thorik pulled her in tight to share his body heat. He was worried about her and knew he had to save her from these cold, dank caverns before she became ill. "It'll be all right." They continued to walk together down a new tunnel. "We'll stop soon so I can activate the Runestone for heat."

"Why can't you do that now?"

"Because we'd have to stop."

"Then let's stop so you can warm us up. The Runestone stays warm long after you get it going."

"True, but I don't think you understand how much it takes out of me. I'm already struggling to keep this one activated to shine our way. I'd have to rest after focusing my thoughts enough to generate heat from within it."

"Then let's rest."

"Soon. Just a little farther." Thorik knew that the more often they stopped, the more likely they would die in the caves from lack of food and water. "Besides, I have a good feeling about this tunnel. It smells fresher."

Avanda raised her nose to sniff before disagreeing with him. However, she noticed something different. "Is that water I hear?"

Thorik stood still for a moment. "Your ears are better than mine. I think you're correct." Focusing his thoughts, the gem in the center of his Runestone brightened the path before them as they began walking down it. It wasn't long before they approached a fast-paced underground river with a glowing crystal rising from it in the far wall.

Racing over to its shore, they both began scooping up handfuls of water to their dry lips. The icy water nearly burned as it went down their throats. Handful after handful filled their stomachs until they felt refreshed.

Standing back up, Thorik nodded his approval at the river while helping Avanda back up to her feet. "This is our best option." He had a renewed sense of hope, which came across in his voice. "This river will take us out of here."

Avanda's soul-markings turned nearly white as her heart pounded and her head shook back and forth. "I don't see a path along its side for us to walk." Nervous cracks in her voice were heard over the rushing water.

Holding back a chuckle at the idea of a conveniently placed path alongside the river, Thorik knew they wouldn't be that fortunate. He also knew her fear of the water was overwhelming her. "I'm an excellent swimmer. You can hold on to me."

The idea of drowning paralyzed her in her tracks. In the past, he had talked her into crossing rivers, but at least in those circumstances she could see the riverbanks. This river forced its way into a tunnel with nothing more than a small air gap at the top. "No."

"Avanda," Thorik said warmly. "This is our only option."

"No, it's not. We can try another path."

"For how many days?"

"For as many as it takes."

"We don't have many days left. We're starving to death. Waiting for the perfect situation is not an option for us."

"You know I can't swim."

"I'll do all the swimming. All you have to do is hang on to me."

"And if you go under?"

"Hold your breath."

"WHAT?"

"We're going to hit a few areas in any river that will pull us under for a few seconds. Just hold your breath until I can get us back up to the surface."

Avanda's arms were crossed as she stood in defiance.

"Listen, we're lost down here, and this is the only opportunity we've seen to get to safety. I need you to trust me."

"I trust you. I just don't trust the water." Avanda watched the river lap at the rocks as it sped past them.

Thorik stepped between her and the water and softly held her hand before looking square in her eyes. "Avanda, trust me."

She looked at him and back at the water several times before closing her eyes and nodding her approval. But it was obvious that she did not like it.

Thorik took advantage of the moment and quickly secured everything in his backpack, and then pack onto his body. He tied her to him with a few yards of twine, to make sure that they didn't get too far separated in case she was to let go.

Leading her over to the water, he gave her very little warning, fearing that she would back out. "Here we go! Take a deep breath!" He grabbed her and jumped into the water.

The cool water engulfed them and immediately knocked them against sharp rocks near the bottom, where they tumbled out of control, unable to determine which way was up.

Chapter Six

DARK RIVER

Caught in the violent swirls of the lower part of the raging river, Thorik and Avanda rolled head over heels in different directions until they both were jolted to a stop. The twine that connected them together had become snagged around a rock at the base of the river.

Like two kites on a windy day, the Nums flapped around in the rushing waters. The pitch-blackness of the cavern prevented them from seeing each other, but Thorik knew Avanda would be panicking by now. He had promised to hold on to her, and he currently wasn't. The jolt had pulled them apart.

Thorik fought off the instinct to panic and fight his way free. Instead, he reached for the twine and climbed it. After a few very difficult pulls upstream, he reached the area where the twine had been lodged. Reaching around the sharp rock, he attempted to lift the twine over, but the twine's pressure against the rock was far too much for him to overcome.

Thorik then pulled himself against the river to climb around the far side of the rock. But once there, the water pressure forced his chest firmly against the rock, preventing him from easily getting his hands in place to remove the twine. After working his fingers down along the twine to locate the point of the snag, he realized that the twine was wedged far too deep into a crack for him to jar it loose. It was stuck.

His air was depleting, and he knew Avanda may have already lost hers. His actions needed to be swift.

Reaching past the rock, he grabbed the taut twine, which held Avanda. Kicking off, he allowed himself to be taken by the river straight toward her. He tumbled forward.

Thorik's body slammed into Avanda. They both flopped about at the bottom of the river. Immediately unbuckling his leather belt, Thorik fed the leather through her belt, and buckled it back up. Then he removed his hunting dagger and cut both twines which held them captive.

The two Nums flew like a cork popping off a bottle. They spun, and rolled, and twisted until they finally reached the surface.

Thorik gasped for air, not knowing how long it would last. Fortunately, they were now riding along the surface of the river.

"Avanda!" Thorik yelled, realizing she hadn't taken a breath yet.

Her head was limp on her neck, and she showed no signs of life.

Moving her into a position to ensure her head was above water, he began working his way to the side of the river. He hoped to find a ledge at some point to pull her to safety.

It was then that an unseen rock from the low ceiling cracked against Thorik's head. Lights flashed in Thorik's eyes, and he felt himself pass out.

He didn't know if it had been seconds or minutes, but when he regained consciousness, Thorik noticed the river had slowed. It had widened as it entered the side of a large, hot, dry, boulder-filled cavern with a few glowing crystal columns. The faint blur of the crystals' glowing light in an open area was all he needed to escape the river.

Finding a handhold, Thorik rolled Avanda and himself out of the water. His head bled from the cut created by the unseen rock, but he wasn't concerned about himself. Avanda wasn't breathing.

"Don't you dare die on me," Thorik ordered the lifeless girl before him.

Still unbalanced and dizzy from his own wound to the head, he spun Avanda onto her front and began pressing on her back to get the water out of her mouth. His grandmother, Gluic, had taught him many healing techniques, which he had hoped he would never have to use.

She still wasn't showing signs of life, causing Thorik to shake with fear of losing her. "Avanda! We made it out of the river. Wake up!"

Grabbing his sack of Runestones, he reached in and selected the Runestone of Health before flipping Avanda onto her back. Gluic had also taught him how to know what each Runestone felt like, so he could tell them apart without requiring light to see them.

Setting the Runestone of Health onto her forehead, he placed his hand on it and allowed himself to become one with it. This was difficult to do in his dizzy and panicking state of mind. Focus, he told himself.

The gem in the center of the Runestone glowed as he felt Avanda's thoughts. She was still in there. She was still alive. But for how long? He could tell she was drifting away. She couldn't pull any air into her lungs. She was dying.

"NO!" he shouted in anger.

Thorik knew he had to get her to breathe. Holding the Runestone firmly on her forehead, he took in a deep breath and placed his lips against hers and tried to breathe life back into her. His thoughts still focused on the Runestone to understand what she needed as he took another breath for her.

"Please don't leave," he said between breaths. "I need you."

The Runestone allowed him to know that she was coming back with each breath he gave her. The process was slow, and by no means was she safe yet. He resolved he would breathe for her for all of eternity if that was what it took to save her, and he began with the conviction to only stop when she could do it on her own.

"Come on, Avanda!" he yelled before the next breath. "I know you can do this. Come back to me." Another breath was given. "I believe in you."

Avanda's body jerked once and then a few more times before she rolled onto her side and began coughing up the rest of the river water, which had clogged her lungs. She was alive.

Thorik comforted her and patted her back while she continued to be sick. The rush of anxiety from nearly losing her suddenly kicked in, and his heart beat so hard that it hurt his chest. It overwhelmed him with the joy of her survival, and he dropped his forehead against her shoulder.

Avanda eventually turned over and leaned up against him, resting her head in the crook of his arm. She looked up at him with exhausted eyes. "I told you the water was a bad idea."

With tear-filled eyes, Thorik chuckled and nodded as he wiped his face clean. "I should listen to you more often." He then hugged her tightly, knowing how close she had come to leaving him forever.

And with that, it was decided to rest for a while before determining the next course of action of their escape plan.

Thorik created heat and additional light from one of his Runestones. Because of his depleted strength from malnutrition, the Runestone never lasted long after he let go, so he would frequently pick it back up to recharge the stone with his own energy.

Once rejuvenated, Avanda ripped some cloth from the base of her dress and tied it around Thorik's head to stop the bleeding, before she started exploring for alternate routes out. She refused to get back into the river. "I think this is our way out," she said to Thorik over the noise of the river.

Thorik looked across the boulder-filled room and spotted Avanda's silhouette standing in front of an angled crystal column. "Why do you say that?"

"Because I don't see any water this way."

Thorik grinned. He knew she would taunt him for years to come about his great escape plan, which had been a disaster. But he gladly accepted her teasing over her not surviving the river. "This time it's your decision."

Impatient to get out from the caves, she walked back to the warmth of the Runestone and crossed her arms. "Can't one of your Runestones just show us the way out of here?" Her tone was slightly agitated as she wished for a door to magically appear to allow them to leave the dark underground.

Thorik thought about it for a few seconds. "I'm not sure. I only know what a few of them do. I really haven't had time to try the others."

Even in the hot, dry air, Avanda's shivers raced across her body because of the wet clothes. "See if one of those will conjure up something to eat as well." A smirk crossed her face before she walked about the cavern again.

Sitting cross-legged, Thorik pulled the Runestone of Trust from his sack and closed his eyes. Relaxing the way Gluic had taught him, he closed his eyes and focused his thoughts and energy to allow the Runestone's powers to work their way up one arm and then back down into the other arm before returning to the Runestone. It felt as though miniature electric eels were coursing through his body as he waited for something to reveal itself.

He patiently waited as the sound of the river lowered in his ears before ending his intense focus. Opening his eyes and looking up, Thorik watched Avanda move at a fraction of her normal speed as she walked around the cavern. On the other side of him, Thorik watched the river move at a pace far too slow for water and too fast for ice. Standing up, he moved closer to the river, reached out, and then scooped up a handful of the odd moving water, only to find the liquid he touched suddenly move normally. After flowing out of his palm, it slowed in its descent back to the sluggish river.

Time appeared to be affected by this Runestone when activated. However, time was not the only thing affected. Thorik's body was being depleted of strength as his legs wobbled and his head spun. Unlike the other Runestones he had used, he could not use this one for more than a few moments at a time.

Allowing his thoughts to return to the real world, the rush of the river's noise returned along with the movement.

"Didn't that one work?" Avanda asked as she glanced back at him. "Try a different one."

Giving himself a few moments to shake off the effects from the event, Thorik put the first Runestone away and pulled out the Runestone of Courage, hoping again that this would be the one they would need to help them escape the caverns. He took in a deep breath before relaxing his shoulders as he exhaled. The Runestone texture slowly faded from his fingertips as he felt past the smooth rock and into its internal powers. Closing his eyes, he became an extension of the Runestone and acted as a conduit for it to release its energy.

Avanda gasped, causing Thorik to open his eyes and look at her.

There, in the caves, were hundreds of ghostly figures. Shoulder to shoulder, they walked through the cavern as they all headed in from a passage and then out the other side. More filed in behind them in a continuous, slow and steady march. Sounds of footsteps and moaning filled the room, even though most of the apparitions' feet never even touched the cave floor.

Standing up, Thorik moved over to Avanda and then turned toward several semi-transparent figures coming toward them, while Avanda pushed her shoulder blades against his to watch his back.

The spirits walking toward the Nums proceeded past them, keeping their distance from the Runestone, which Thorik held out in front of him. Their faces sagged like candle wax in the hot sun, yet it was apparent that there were spirits of multiple species in the group. Human, Polenum, Del'Unday, Ov'Unday, and even Fesh made up the slow-moving crowd.

Avanda watched the procession move past them. She eventually reached out with her hand and softly touched the arm of a female gliding past. A tingle ran down Avanda's arm as though the energy of her own body was flowing out of her and into the spirit.

The mist of the ghostly woman's arm turned dark and solid. Her skin became visible and warm as it spread up her arm and toward her chest. Gasping suddenly, the woman turned and looked at Avanda in astonishment.

But the energy needed to bring this woman back to life was being stolen from Avanda, who felt sick and looked pale. Lightheaded, she removed her hand from the woman.

The ghostly lady, with one solid arm, immediately panicked. Feeling life again for the first time in so many years, she wasn't about to let it slip away so easily. Reaching out, she clutched onto Avanda's wrist to absorb the energy she so desperately needed.

Avanda fell to her knees as she felt drained of her life. Her skin turned a light gray, and even her normally colorful hair lost its luster. She was being depleted of all her life forces.

Thorik's shock at the sight of the oncoming ghosts had worn off before he had realized Avanda had fallen behind him. In turning, he witnessed the attack of the semi-solid woman on Avanda. There was no time to spare as his young friend mouthed the word help, unable to make a sound.

Kicking the woman's arm away from Avanda, Thorik stood between them and held out his Runestone to get a good look at her.

But the woman craved what the Nums had; life. Reaching out to touch Thorik, she suddenly stopped. The Runestone prevented her from passing. She tried to touch either of the Nums again and again, each time being blocked by the Runestone's power.

As the woman proceeded, the solid structure of her arm slowly bled out into the rest of her body, causing the ghostly image to become more visible. Along with that, her arm softened and became transparent again. She hadn't received enough life force to keep her with the living; however, she had already stepped out of the realm of the roaming souls.

Her body struggled between the two worlds as parts of her body attempted to become solid, depleting other areas. She let out a hideous scream of pain as the vapor-like parts of her vanished and the solid parts fell to the floor before they quickly dried up, cracked, and crumbled apart.

The woman's spirit continued to change from white vapors to a solid mass as she gave off a high-pitched shriek, which echoed within the caverns.

Both of the Nums covered their ears to minimize the sound, but upon doing so, all the other ghosts disappeared. Thorik's concentration on his Runestone wavered, breaking their ability to see them.

However, the woman and her scream were still present. She looked at Avanda as her face became solid and asked one simple question before it was over. "Why?"

Avanda didn't have time to respond before the woman's head cracked and crumbled into grains of sand before falling to the floor.

Avanda sat in shock. Her body was weakened from the assault, but she slowly regained the color in her skin and hair.

"Are you hurt?" Thorik asked, reaching down to help her up.

Lightheaded, she grabbed his hand, carefully stood back up, and shook her head.

"What happened?" Thorik asked.

"I don't know." Avanda felt terrible. She had not intended to cause the woman any pain. "I just wanted to see what a ghost felt like."

"Well, don't do that again."

Ignoring his comment, Avanda swiveled her head and searched the cavern. "Do you think they are still around us?"

Peering around, Thorik nodded. "I would assume so. We just can't see them without the glow of the Runestone."

Avanda shivered and wrapped her arms around herself. "Do you think they can see us without the Runestone being used?"

"I don't know."

"Can they grab us again?"

"I don't think so. Somehow, the Runestone allows us to see and touch each other. But they can't touch the stone itself." He looked down at the stone still in his hand. "Without the Runestone's powers being activated, they could be walking right through us."

They both stood silently to listen for any noises or to feel any sensations. An occasional footfall or moan was heard, but always at a distance, and the direction was difficult to isolate.

Avanda continued to tremble from the ghostly woman's assault. "Do you think they can hear us without the Runestone being used?"

"I don't think so." Even with that said, Thorik felt a cold sensation on his arm and shoulder. Shivers immediately ran up his spine and then over his head to his temples.

"You don't belong here," a voice whispered into Thorik's right ear.

Thorik quickly covered his ear with his hand and jumped out of the way, expecting to see someone, but he didn't.

"I heard it as well." Avanda's eyes became excessively wide as she scanned the room.

"Bakalor will come for you," the voice said again.

Avanda grabbed onto Thorik's arm as she searched for whoever was talking.

Thorik began to activate the Runestone again, but his nerves prevented his ability to concentrate.

"Who is Bakalor?" Thorik asked.

"You will become one of us, Dain," the now familiar voice announced.

Shaking his head to dismiss the idea, Thorik continued in his attempt to become one with the Runestone. "We will heed your advice. Can you show us the way out?"

Without warning, the cavern shook from a tremor deeper down into the cave. A soft, ill-green light emerged at a distance and exposed the silhouette of a ghastly giant beast stepping into the mighty cavern.

Avanda's grip on Thorik's arm increased as she watched the events unfold.

"It's too late," the voice said as it trailed off.

Thorik ignored everything except the Runestone as he felt its energy flow through him. Knowing it was working, he looked up to see the spirits running the opposite way from where they had been walking earlier. The one who had been talking to him presented a distorted smile on his melted face.

Before they could talk again, the spirit in front of them blended into the rest of the misty vapors that were hurrying away from the approaching yellowish green flaming beast, as it grabbed handfuls of spirits and tossed them into its mouth. Its touch caused them to instantly become solid masses filled with life, and they screamed in pain from his sharp teeth biting down on them. Their sudden return to life was abruptly over.

The screams of horror were deafening, and the crunching of bones, along with the tremors of the beast's movement, put Avanda into a state of panic.

She grabbed Thorik and pushed him into a safe hiding place surrounded by boulders. But by doing this, she broke his concentration on the Runestone. The ghosts were now gone from their sight, but the beast remained.

Chapter Seven

BAKALOR'S LAIR

Bakalor, the demon of the underworld, advanced toward Thorik and Avanda from the far end of the cavern. Rock and mud made up the demon's bones and muscles. Crystals filled in for teeth and long, sharp nails, and diamonds the size of Thorik's head were inset in his eye sockets. Standing on two legs, he shoveled handfuls of the dead spirits into his mouth. Once swallowed, their souls were lost forever, never to have the chance to reincarnate into a body of a future person or creature.

Thick flaming oil dripped off the demon's body, acting as a lubricant to allow his various parts to work together. Subtle, oily flames rippled out from every crack as they illuminated his entire body.

Thorik and Avanda peeked out from the confines of the boulders they hid among. They were silent, but their blood pulsed through their bodies at a fast pace as they realized that the new threat was more than they felt they could deal with.

Towering in size, the demon stood at a height easily twice that of their giant friend Grewen. But this was no clumsy moving creature. He moved within the cave as if he were an extension of the rock and earth. Walking into a cavern wall, he would be absorbed into it before exiting the far side.

After shoveling several more handfuls of the dead into his mouth, he finally came to a stop and searched about for something amiss. Feeling the cave's vibrations through his feet, he could sense something was wrong. "Heartbeats? Here, in Della Estovia?" The voice was booming and coarse.

Thorik and Avanda ducked back down behind the boulders, hoping to evade detection.

"This place is not for the living," Bakalor announced, shaking the walls with his voice. "You have trespassed into my domain. Who are you? And why have you come?"

Thorik and Avanda tried to communicate to each other with hand signals, attempting to plan an escape from the cavern. Neither did an adequate job in relaying their message.

The cavern floors acted as extensions of Bakalor's feet, and he could feel the warmth of the Nums' bodies behind the boulders. Reaching an arm down into the rock below him, his palm sprang up out of the rock across the cave directly below the Nums. Oil quickly saturated the ground near the Nums' feet as the boulders they hid between transformed into Bakalor's fingers.

The giant hand, which had emerged from the cave's floor, closed onto the Nums and encased them in rock before lowering back into the cave's floor.

On the far side of the cavern, Bakalor pulled his hand up out of the ground near his feet and then opened it up near his face. Rattled by the abduction, the Nums in his palm looked back up at him in awe.

The center of the demon's face sagged down over the front of his mouth. His steamy breath smelled of sulfur, and the texture of his skin was abrasive and composed of several types of minerals.

"I am Thorik Dain of Farbank," the Num announced as he held his hand out to deflect the burning hot air from the demon's nostrils. "We fell into your caves by accident. We are here only in search of our way out."

Bakalor's hand lifted them closer to one of his diamond eyes as he inspected his captured prey. "Your name sounds familiar. Thorik Dain of Farbank?"

"Yes," Thorik answered hesitantly. The giant diamond rotated inside the demon's eye socket as it studied the Num. The thick, flaming oil drained out of the socket and into the beast's mouth.

"After all these years? Could it be? Yes, I believe it is. I know you," Bakalor finally announced.

"You know of me? Has someone told you about us?"

"Don't toy with me," the demon growled. "I know you, just as you know me!"

"But how?"

"You are the reason I am here!"

Avanda shot a look at Thorik, who was just as perplexed.

"Me?" Thorik asked sheepishly.

Ignoring the question, Bakalor closed his fingers around the Nums again, sealing them in tight before walking into a nearby wall. The wall absorbed the majority of the demon's body, while a few stray rocks slapped against the wall and rolled to the floor.

The Nums could hear the grinding and slamming of rock as the demon traveled through the earth's solid crust between each cave. Bakalor traveled in a straight line. Cavern walls were just as easy to pass through for him as open caves, much like a Num walking from one room of a house to another through walls made of rice paper.

The difference, however, was that the demon's body transferred from rock to rock along the way instead of pushing a solid form all the way through. This was also the case for his hand within which the Nums sat. The rocks continued to move past them, opening up and separating at just the right time to maintain a consistent shape of the inside of the demon's palm. The only part of Bakalor that traveled with him was the thick oil, which seeped through cracks and acquired new rocks for his body.

Thorik and Avanda bounced around inside the giant fist for quite some time before it finally stopped and the rock fingers opened up. Once their eyes adjusted, they surveyed their surroundings.

A cavernous terrain, miles in every direction, lay before them with a maze of tall pumice walls and several ancient buildings constructed on bridges that spanned the rivers of lava. The cavern's ceiling was nearly a quarter mile high and covered with arching rows of stalactites where cracks in the limestone had existed. Flames shot up from rivers that tumbled down various falls and rapids throughout the open cavern.

In contrast to the red flowing magma rivers, giant light-blue crystals jutted up from the floor at odd angles, reaching up and embedding themselves in the high ceiling. Resembling columns of sunlight breaking through dark and dangerous clouds, the crystals gave the Nums a sense of hope that there was freedom just beyond this hideous place.

But their attention needed to be on where they were and not where they wanted to be. This mighty cavern was a hot and dry landscape, which smelled of sulfur and acid. Even if the demon set them free, they would struggle to survive in such a place for long.

"The underworld," Thorik said under his breath to Avanda. "This is where the dead roam in their afterlife." They had both heard the fables of such a place, but had never given the stories any validity until now.

Bakalor tilted his hand, dropping the two Nums onto the flat top of a rock column, which he had silently called upon to grow from the floor just moments prior. The demon then sat down in his enormous throne and reveled in his accomplishment.

Screams of pain could be heard; however, the bodies they came from could not be seen. The Nums searched in every direction for the owners of the voices, but they found none.

"This…" Bakalor opened his arms, "… is what I have created from my humble beginnings. I nearly perished during my first century down here. Eventually civilizations grew above ground and brought corruption, greed, and malice. These were the tastes I learned to enjoy."

As he listened to the demon, Thorik pulled out the Runestone of Courage, which he had used earlier to see the dead souls. "Avanda, keep him occupied," he whispered.

"It wasn't long before my children began to bring the essense of the dead to me in droves. I no longer need to hunt on the surface during the dark of night." Bakalor straightened the enormous spear and mace next to his throne. "Bitter to my taste were their souls at first, but I learned to tolerate them. The sweet taste of the noble and pure of heart is so rare. However, the crystal columns usually take most savory before I find them."

Avanda trembled as she followed Thorik's instructions. "Bakalor, is it?"

"It is."

"What happens to the souls down here?"

"I eat most of them and they are forever lost. A few are pulled into the crystal columns and whisked away to some higher plane. The rest walk endlessly in my caverns, at least until they are called upon to live again." Bakalor coughed at the idea. "Doesn't seem to make sense. They live life after life, making the same mistakes and always ending up back down here. There are only a few that actually learn from prior lives and are granted access to the columns."

Thorik had been ignoring the demon. Instead, his focus was on the Runestone. It wasn't long before the gem in the center glowed and the light illuminated the hundreds of thousands of ghostly figures which moved among the giant cave's maze.

The dead walked the underworld in an endless search for peace. All species and all ages slowly paraded in lines, hoping they could find any end to their fruitless existence.

"We do not belong here," Thorik said to Bakalor.

"Nor do I," the demon said spitefully.

"No, you don't understand. We aren't dead yet. Only those who have died are allowed in Della Estovia."

Bakalor leaned forward and reached out to poke Thorik with one of his enormous fingers. "You are correct. But I will resolve this issue, slowly, for livestock is a rare treat for me. Your plump, juicy flesh is much to my liking, regardless of your innocence or sins." Bakalor firmly pressed a single giant finger against the Num and held it there.

Thorik's body went rigid as he felt the heat rush away from his body. The gem in the center of his Runestone instantly dimmed and the view of the ghostly inhabitants disappeared.

Bakalor's body jerked at the influx of fresh life-force. "So sweet is the taste, I nearly forgot." He arched his head back as he sucked in the warmth. "You will come to fear me... every minute of every day."

Waves of warmth flowed from the Num, each slowly removing months and even years from his life as his body showed the signs of the attack. Thorik's youthful face was quickly becoming a man's as each year of his life was raped from him. In addition, the process induced muscle seizures and stinging sensations across his skin. His heart quickened, his lungs squeezed tight, and his head felt as though it was being drained of blood.

Bakalor breathed in with quivering lips, as though the sensation of receiving the Num's life-force was erotic in nature. His eyes rolled back in his head as a grin of pleasure crossed his face.

Confidence and courage drained from Thorik's body as well, leaving doubt and fear to fester in his mind. Bitter thoughts from his past sprang forth to suppress the times of joy and love. Good was slowly being devoured by hate and fear.

Avanda grabbed Thorik to pull him away, only to find herself caught in the vacuum effect caused by the demon. Heated waves of energy now pulled from her chest and flowed out of her body and into Thorik's before they continued out into the demon. Thorik's pain was now Avanda's, and they screamed from their suffering.

The agony was stifling for Avanda. She could feel the demon's presence on her, in her, and within her own thoughts. It felt as though the demon had climbed into her body and was using it as a toy as he selected the best parts of her memories to pilfer.

Bakalor was now breathing heavily with ecstasy from his tasty treat of energy from non-dead life forms. His enjoyment caused him such pleasure that he eventually fell back and collapsed into his throne, releasing his contact with the Nums.

A burst of flame erupted from the oil that covered the demon's body. The heat fanned against the Nums as intense fire shot high into the air for several seconds before dissipating to its prior soft flame. Upon returning to normal, Bakalor sighed with pleasure and closed his eyes. The ordeal had literally exhausted his own body, causing him to pass out from a pleasure he had not enjoyed for decades. The spirit of the Nums had been more than he had expected.

Sobbing from the pain, the Nums held onto each other as they dropped to the surface of the column. Fear of another attack caused them to shake and cry, for they had never felt so helpless to defend themselves.

Thorik looked for a way to escape as he held Avanda tight. Her body continued to tremble, and her skin was cold against his. "I'll get you out of this."

Avanda's lungs hurt so much that it was difficult for her to speak while crying and gasping for breath. "We aren't going to make it this time."

Thorik instinctively agreed with her before realizing that the thoughts placed in his head by Bakalor were clouding his judgment. Looking directly into her eyes, his now aged face gave her a stern look. "Don't talk like that. Never give up hope."

She shivered uncontrollably. "It's over, Thorik. We can't beat him."

The words made emotional sense, but Thorik fought off the temptation to give into Bakalor's thoughts of defeat and fear. "Don't say that!" Thorik searched frantically for a way down off the column where they sat. There was no way to climb down, and the jump would easily break their legs. However, there was another option.

"Avanda, stand up." Thorik helped her to her feet and turned her toward the sleeping demon. "We can jump over to his throne and climb down from there."

Shaking her head as she regained her strength, Avanda had no desire to jump toward the demon. The horror he had implanted in her mind swayed her thoughts. "He'll wake up."

"Not if we land on the throne's armrest without touching him."

It was a risk, seeing that Bakalor's arm covered over half of the throne's armrest. On a good day, Thorik would feel very comfortable about the leap, but in his current state, he wasn't sure he could do it. He knew Avanda stood even less of a chance.

Bakalor snarled and growled in his sleep, causing both of the Nums to cower slightly. But the demon's noises only lasted a moment.

Thorik rubbed his hands up and down on Avanda's arms to warm her up. "I'll go first, then I'll catch you when you jump." It was easier to say than to do. The demon had embedded such fear inside him that it was difficult for him to look directly at Bakalor's face.

Avanda stared in a terrified trance at the demon instead of replying.

"Here I go." He stepped back to get a few steps of a running start. Crouching down, he paused before launching himself forward and stretching his body out to make the distance.

Flying through the air, his legs kicked a few times before he landed on the armrest and rolled toward the demon, sliding to a halt just before touching the sleeping giant. He had landed so close that the oily flames on the demon's body dripped onto Thorik's back. Thorik scooted away and rolled on his back to put out the flames before rising to help Avanda. He dared not look over his shoulder to see if the demon was aware of his presence, for fear of cowering once he saw Bakalor's peering eyes.

Avanda had cringed as she watched Thorik's near-fatal leap and roll. Now she paced on the small surface of the column, trying to gain enough confidence in her ability to jump the span. It was uncommon for her to doubt herself, but the demon had struck a nerve she had only felt once before, when she was nearly raped in Southwind. Both aggressors had both made her feel vulnerable and violated, a feeling she hated.

"Jump!" Thorik held out his hands, ready to catch her whenever she jumped.

The sight of the demon caused Avanda to lower her head and her feet to back up. She didn't know why the sight of him caused her such tremors of fear down her spine, but she eventually realized that she wouldn't be able to make the jump if she looked at him. Even the thought of him caused her to become unsure of herself.

Thorik watched her pace. He knew their window of time was limited and Bakalor could wake up at any moment. They had to move quickly and quietly. If caught, a second attack would surely drain them of any energy or desire to attempt such a daring escape. "Hurry!"

Focusing on Thorik's face, a bit of strength came back into her body. "I can do this." She then stepped back before making a three-step jump.

Bakalor coughed and swung his arm off the armrest and onto his stomach while in his dream state.

Thorik fell flat onto the armrest to avoid being hit by Bakalor's arm, but Avanda panicked while taking her last step in leaping across.

Avanda flew across with arms and legs flailing around before landing on top of Thorik. Grabbing him the moment she landed, her out-of-control tumble pulled him off the armrest and onto the seat of the throne before rolling off and landing on the cavern floor.

Thorik landed first, on his back, while Avanda's strong clutch of his shirt kept her on his front.

Lying face to face on top of each other, they moaned softly from the pain of the fall, still hoping to escape before the demon was awoken. The silence that followed convinced them they hadn't woken Bakalor up.

Avanda knew she couldn't have done it without Thorik. She needed him. He had saved her more than once. Without giving it another thought, she gave him a quick, unexpected kiss. "Thank you."

Thorik was slightly unsure how to respond. "Not now." The serious jeopardy they were still in required their full attention. Looking at her disappointed response to his words, he realized he could have said something more tactful. "We're not out of this yet. I'll give you that kiss when we're actually free."

"Agreed." She rolled off of him, and they immediately ran from the demon's throne and into the maze.

Chapter Eight

ESCAPING THE UNDERWORLD

Della Estovia was a vast terrain of rivers and falls of flaming molten rock with ruins of ancient stone buildings and bridges. The dry, bitter air was hard to breathe, and predator roaches periodically covered the ground. Worn trails looped around the entire open cavern in an endless maze of sharp-edged pumice walls preventing the short Nums from climbing up to see a way out.

Running on and off for nearly an hour through the rock labyrinth, Thorik pulled Avanda around yet another corner. "Keep moving so we don't have bugs climbing up our legs."

"I am," she replied as the crunching of insects under her feet made it obvious that she was keeping up a quick pace. "But we're going around in circles. We'll end up right back where we started."

Thorik made a quick decision on the approaching junction as they ran toward it. "No, it just seems that way. We're getting close to one of the bridges I saw before we escaped the top of the column."

"Don't you have a Runestone that can help us find our way out?"

"We don't have the time to try them all right now."

"Then use the Runestone of Courage so we can see the ghosts."

Thorik led them around the bin at the junction. "What good will that do us?"

"We can ask them how to get out of here."

"If they knew that, they would have already used it to escape."

Avanda realized he was right, but she also knew they couldn't keep running forever. "Then let's ask them what path leads back to the caves so we can hide until we figure out a better plan."

"It's too risky."

Avanda pulled her hand free of his. "The risk is mine to take as well. I haven't eaten in days, and I can't run forever. We can't go on like this, Thorik. We have to try something else."

Turning, Thorik watched her slow down to a fast walk. He knew she wasn't going to run any longer. "You're right. It could take us days just to find our way out of this maze, and possibly weeks to get to the surface. We can't survive that long without food and water." He then slowed to allow her to catch up. "Staying here won't help either. Let's at least keep walking."

"Why does it always have to be your way? Didn't the river teach you anything?"

"It's not always my way. Besides, the river would have worked if the undertow hadn't dragged us on the bottom and snagged our line."

"Stop justifying your actions. You always think you know the best way to do things. You don't take my suggestions seriously. The ghosts might be able to help us."

Reaching his hand out to her encouraged her to keep moving. "Once we get to the bridge, we'll be able to see over these walls. If we can't determine a path at that point, we'll try talking to the local souls."

She nodded in agreement. "My ideas are just as valid as yours, Thorik. You need to take them seriously."

"I know. I'm trying."

"Well, try harder." The sharpness in her tone was clear.

Thorik didn't respond. Instead, he led her around several more bends in the labyrinth before it opened up to a raised stone bridge which spanned a wide river of flowing red liquid rock. In the center of the thick bridge was a circle of tall marble columns holding up a heavy, and once impressive, roof structure. It appeared to be the remains of a large temple, with most of its walls now rubble. Only a few internal walls still stood, as well as several columns leading up to the building.

Both Nums showed signs of fatigue as they climbed the tall steps leading to the bridge. The lack of food was taking its toll as they dragged their feet while they passed several freestanding columns on their approach to the center structure.

Thorik noticed carvings in the columns, which he had seen before. They were the markings of the Notarians. These were the original species of this land that created all Altered Creatures. And they were the ones that the Mountain King had fought against to free all species and races from them. Only a few of these extremely powerful Notarians survived. They were known as the three Oracles.

Blocks had fallen from the ceiling of the center edifice, hiding the writings and symbols along the floor tiles. A thick metal ring had been placed in the center of the floor, surrounding a hole a few yards in diameter. Within the hole, flowing lava could be seen.

Thorik stepped up onto the highest block of fallen debris to see as far as possible. In the distance, he could see the mighty Bakalor passed out on his enormous throne. In the opposite direction, he could see the edge of the cavern. Its walls were littered with tunnel openings, but which one would grant them access to escape?

Leaning one way and then the other, Thorik attempted to see beyond one of the large ceiling-high crystals, which blocked his view. It stood just beyond the other side of the bridge, at the base of the steps, and was as wide as the Bakalor's shoulders.

Avanda looked for an escape route as well. "What do you see?"

"A maze with no obvious end." He felt slightly defeated. "But if I could just see past that crystal, there might be something I'm missing."

"Thorik, you promised to try asking the spirits."

"Only after I've tried this first."

"You tried. Now let's move on."

"But I can't see past the crystal. Maybe if I climb over to the side," he said to himself.

"Thorik! Why is there is always one more thing you're going to try before you do what I suggest?"

Snapping him out of his thought, he knew that tone in her voice. She was about to become unmanageable. "Don't get upset. I was just thinking out loud. I was getting ready to try your idea."

"Sure you were." Her arms were folded tightly in front of her.

Thorik climbed back down off the fallen ceiling blocks and removed his sack of Runestones. The close proximity of the glowing light-blue crystal column made it easy to find the Runestone of Courage. With few distractions, he was able to merge his thoughts and energy with the Runestone, causing the center gem to light up. However, his lack of nutrition, water, and sleep made it difficult to keep the link between them under control.

It had been over a week since they had eaten anything other than bugs, and sleep had been in the form of passing out for a few minutes at a time due to exhaustion. If it hadn't been for nearly drowning in the river, they wouldn't have had any water either.

Avanda had moved closer to Thorik, to ensure none of the spirits would touch her. However, she had nothing to fear, for though thousands of spirits appeared throughout the surrounding maze, none were on the bridge.

Thorik opened his tired eyes from his meditation. "Avanda, hurry! Find out if they can lead us to an escape tunnel."

Avanda knew that meant leaving the safety of the bridge and returning to the pumice walls. "Why do they all avoid the bridge?"

"I don't know. Perhaps spirits can't climb steps." He forced a smile.

"But insects can, and they aren't up here either. Everything seems fearful of this bridge. Perhaps we shouldn't be on it."

"It's the safest place we've found so far. Avanda, I don't have the strength to hold this all day. Find out what they know."

Avanda pulled at him to follow her, but his weakened condition caused his movement to reduce their ability to see the spirits. She was only able to move him to the top step before he sat down from exhaustion.

"Just go to the edge of the steps. If they can't approach us, then you'll be safe from their touch. I need to sit and rest if I plan to keep this Runestone active." As difficult as it was to keep a Runestone performing its task, it was mild compared to the initial activation. Thorik wasn't sure if he had the capacity to reactivate it closer to the bottom step if he were to lose his connection on the way down.

Apprehensive about heading down the steps alone, even if this was her idea, Avanda slowly moved toward the passing semi-transparent figures.

"Hello?" She looked for a kind word in return. Instead, she noticed a look of fear in their eyes.

"Get off the sacred aerie!" one spirit shouted. Another repeated the warning.

"I don't understand," she replied.

"He'll see you!" one of them yelled.

"The birthplace of his children cannot be disturbed," moaned another.

Avanda shook her head. "I don't care about that! I need to know how to escape. We shouldn't be here. We need to return to the surface."

"Leave the sacred nest before it's too late!" another spirit warned. "Crystals are the only freedom."

"What does that mean?"

"The bridge is his children's birthplace. Stay clear!"

Avanda refused to leave without an answer, so she continued to ask them for assistance.

Meanwhile, Thorik sat on the top step as he concentrated on the Runestone before him. It seemed like he had been focusing on it for hours, even though it had only been a few minutes. Craning his neck back and then to the side, he stretched it a few times before opening his eyes, hoping to see his companion returning with the information they needed.

Instead, what he saw caused him to lose full concentration on the Runestone.

The spirits disappeared.

Avanda looked up the steps at Thorik, who now had a horrified expression on his face. Climbing the steps as quickly as she could, she reached the top step and turned around to see what had struck him with fear. "What is it? I don't see anything."

Thorik pointed out in front of them. "There, beyond that third crystal column, is Bakalor's throne."

"Yes, I see it. So?"

"He's not in it."

It took a moment for his concern to register in her mind. "He's awake!"

"And looking for us!"

Both of the Nums immediately stood up and started racing across the bridge in hopes of hiding in the far maze before the demon made it this far.

A thunderous crack exploded from behind them as rocks scraped against each other and snapped under tremendous pressure. Bakalor lifted out of the ground at the bottom of the steps to the bridge, as rocks flew in every direction. "Get out of the nursery!" he yelled with such force that it shook the bridge.

The Nums evaded the falling debris from the eruption of Bakalor's entrance as they headed into the structure in the center of the bridge to hide from him. As fruitless a plan as it was, their only other option was to jump over the edge into the molten lava. Hiding was obviously the preferable choice.

Bakalor gave chase, stepping quickly up onto the stone bridge. Flames increased across his body as he approached the building in anger. "Get out!" he demanded, swinging his arms in frustration.

Thorik realized the demon couldn't reach up through the ground and grab them as long as they stayed on the bridge. In fact, it appeared that he couldn't manipulate the stones of this bridge at all, perhaps because it was built by the Notarians. Then again, that wouldn't matter much if the demon knocked the structure down on top of the Nums.

Bakalor was outraged at the Nums' invasion of his sacred place. The columns were just close enough to each other to prevent the demon from coming inside without destroying it. Grabbing one of the stone columns, which led up to the temple, he ripped it from its foundation and swung it like a club at the roof. His intent was to scare the Nums out of his sacred place. However, he had underestimated the remaining strength of the building.

Cracks spread like lightning across the ceiling, and chunks of stones fell near the Nums. The structural integrity of the building had been compromised, and a second attack could finish it off.

"Run!" Thorik yelled to Avanda, pushing her toward the far side of the bridge.

She did what he asked, as the bridge shook from the demon's feet pounding on the other side. Racing across to the far steps, Avanda turned, only to realize that Thorik hadn't followed her. He was standing just inside the building, taunting the demon in an effort to keep Bakalor's focus on himself.

Nevertheless, Bakalor noticed Avanda's escape beyond the building's walls. Instead of hitting the roof again with his column club, he leaned over the side of the bridge and threw it at her. The stone column twirled through the air toward the young Num.

Leaping off the top step, she dove and rolled down the bridge's staircase just as the weapon struck. Crushing the top of the stairs, it cracked and bounced before one end crashed near her as the other side slammed into the thick crystal just beyond the steps.

Fragments of crystals sprayed in every direction. Light blue shards coated Avanda's body as she covered her face to protect herself. Then the stone column broke into several large pieces before coming to a rest near the base of the crystal column.

Slowly opening her eyes, Avanda looked at the damaged glowing crystal, which went all the way up through the cavern's ceiling. The inside of the crystal was hollow and gave off a pleasant and inviting light. Brushing off the dust and crystal fragments, she rushed toward it.

Peeking her head up inside, she saw a bright light which, surprisingly, didn't hurt her eyes. In fact, it felt good and refreshing as she sensed family within the light inviting her in. Her hair flapped in her face as she gazed upon the light. A stiff breeze was pulling her into it. So much so that she had to brace herself in order to prevent herself from being sucked up into the crystal.

"Thorik!" she yelled over her shoulder. "I found our way out!"

Thorik couldn't hear her over Bakalor's growling, which caused the walls to quake and the Num's body to vibrate.

"If you want me out of here, you're going to have to come in here and get me!" Thorik taunted. His hopes of riling up the demon could pay off if the heavy ceiling crashed down on Bakalor and killed him, or at least knocked him out long enough for the two Nums to get away.

Not used to anyone threatening him, the demon took the bait and entered. His shoulder hit the columns instantly, and debris rained down from the ceiling.

Bakalor stopped and watched the sight before glancing over at Thorik, who was poised to leap out the other side of the building once it began to fall.

Slowly pulling back, the demon gained control of his anger. "Clever. I forgot how deceptive you can be."

Thorik was so close to his plan working that he refused to give up on it. "What? Has a mere Num outlasted the mighty Bakalor? How will you ever live with such a defeat? Come and strike me down now, or are you too much of a coward?"

Bakalor paused, took a deep breath, and then laughed. "You have no idea where upon you stand, do you?"

"It doesn't matter where I stand. What matters is that I stand, defying you and laughing at your inability to defeat a Num."

The demon fully composed himself and then grinned, knowing he had the upper hand. "Let me show you where you are." Reaching down, he grabbed one of his stone toes and, with a quick twist, he snapped it right off. The demon screamed in pain for a moment before recovering. He then took the toe, about the size of Thorik, and rolled it into the structure.

Thorik moved back behind a column. He assumed the demon was rolling the giant toe at him, but it quickly became apparent that he was not the target.

The boulder of a toe rolled into the center of the building and into the open metal ring. As it fell into the hole, the metal ring flashed a molten red and gave off a misty vapor that settled across the floor. The toe fell through the ring and into the flowing river of magma.

Thorik looked up at Bakalor's pleased face, unsure what the demon was planning.

"I have just given you the privilege of seeing my son's birth. I shall call him Grub. Isn't that what you Nums call your meal? Because that is what you are about to become. So, in a sense, I've named him after you."

Thorik felt he had lost the upper hand and slowly started backing away. His timing was wisely planned.

Spraying up from the river and back through the metal ring was a large glob of glowing magma. Bakalor's toe had been heated into a molten ball. Landing just to the side of the ring, it started to form.

The round glob of molten rock began to cool and form common features. Soon, he stood the height of a Num, on two massive legs, with long, sharp claws on his feet. Four thick, muscular arms extended from his round torso, one pair set at his shoulders, the other set just above his hips. Nevertheless, his arms were not his oddest feature, for he had no neck or head on his shoulders. Instead, an enormous gaping mouth opened up in his stomach. Dozens of sharp teeth extended from outside his mouth while a second set could be seen inside the creature's mouth. "I am here for you, Your Grace," it announced to Bakalor as its teeth from a significant underbite formed.

The heat emanating from the demon's son was so intense that Thorik felt the hair on his arms burn despite his distance.

Thorik turned from the sight and ran toward Avanda, knowing that once the creature received his orders, he would burn him alive.

"Grub, kill the Nums!" Bakalor pointed at Thorik before stepping away from the structure and back down onto the ground where he had originally erupted from.

Rolling forward, Grub set off in pursuit.

Avanda had pulled herself away from the broken crystal and was on her way up the stairs when she saw Thorik jumping down them. "The crystal!" she shouted, turning herself around to head back down.

Grub arrived at the top of the steps, and Thorik could feel the creature's heat on his back as he grabbed Avanda's hand to pull her to safety.

Avanda pulled back. "No! Climb into the broken crystal. We'll be safe there."

Thorik had no time to argue. He followed her lead toward the large, hollow crystal.

Grub rolled down the stairs with ease as he caught up to them.

The Nums leaped from the bottom step and landed on the ground long enough to make one last jump to safety inside the broken crystal column. As they flew through the air, they knew that this was their only chance of survival. Fortunately, they were on course to land inside the hollow column and succeed.

Just before the Nums landed inside the crystal, a giant stone hand sprang up from the ground. Bakalor's hand reached up and caught them both in midair before closing its rock fingers around them. Again, the Nums were back in Bakalor's palm.

Their escape had failed.

The Nums bounced around inside the demon's hand until Bakalor eventually pulled his arm out of the ground while standing on the far side of the bridge. Opening up his palm, the demon grinned at his prisoners before closing his fingers again. "Grub! Cover that hole in the crystal with some molten rock before any more souls escape. Afterward, introduce yourself to your siblings before returning to my throne."

Bakalor sank into the rocks and traveled below the cavern floor, carrying his cargo of two Nums. A few minutes later, the demon's palm reopened, dropping Thorik and Avanda onto the column near his throne once more.

"Your courage will be removed and you will learn to fear me," Bakalor announced. "This I can ensure." And with that, he pressed them both down under his enormous fingers and started stripping years of life from their youthful bodies.

Chapter Nine

BATTLE PLANS

Thorik and Avanda's bodies had aged over a decade from the two attacks. Muscle spasms and aches filled their bodies, while their minds were groggy and confused. This time Bakalor had made certain to hurt them enough to prevent a further escape.

Lying limp on the top of the stone column that stood before the demon's throne, the two Nums reached out to each other to let the other one know they were still alive. Their bodies had betrayed them and left them without the strength to sit up. A handful of fingers interlacing would be all the physical reassurance they could give one another as they watched Bakalor sit on his mighty throne.

"You are not to be consumed like the meal of a frenzied thrasher." Bakalor produced an evil grin. "I will savor you two, enjoying each and every moment of life you have to give me."

"I can't try again," Avanda coughed out between cries of pain.

"One more time," Thorik said through his teeth, tightening his fingers entwined with hers. But her fingers loosened. "Avanda, don't leave me. I'll get us out of here."

"Not this time." A tone of defeat was in her soft voice.

"It's not over." Thorik spoke despite the pain he felt in his lungs every time he did so. But his body was not living up to his words as his fingers slowly unraveled from hers.

Avanda could feel him slipping away. Unsure if this would be that last time she would talk to him, she attempted to move her head in order to look into his eyes. Fatigued, she was successful on her third attempt. She could now see his face as his eyes struggled to stay open. Knowing what her last words needed to be before she closed her own eyes and drifted off, she said, "I love you."

A loud crack of thunder came from above as storm clouds rolled along the ceiling of the cavern and an intense white light grew from the center of the cloud. Lightning flashed again as thunder snapped hard enough for Thorik and Avanda to feel the powerful vibrations against their bodies.

A dark mass emerged from the center of the cloud, followed by a trail of nearly transparent figures. The long train headed down and then toward Bakalor.

As they approached, it became apparent that the long procession line was a parade of new souls, brought down to be enslaved by the demon. But it wasn't clear what was leading them down. The dark mass was more of a swirling of ash and debris, constantly changing its shape and form.

Bakalor leaned back and relaxed in his throne as the new souls were dropped into the already overcrowded cavern, turning completely invisible to the Nums as each spirit distanced themselves from the dark form which had led them there. The demon waited patiently as the dark mass floated down near his throne after dropping off its cargo.

Avanda's face went rigid, staring at the object descending toward them. She had finally recognized who the mass was.

"What is it?" Thorik felt the pain of each word in his chest.

"The Death Witch," Avanda said in a somber tone.

The swirling mass advanced until it hovered over the arm of Bakalor's enormous throne. Once stopped, the shape of the witch became obvious. Her long hair and flowing robes continued to blow from an unseen wind, and her body was a whirlpool of floating burnt debris, but Avanda could identify her, nonetheless. The Num had witnessed her once before when she, Irluk, had taken her uncle, Wess.

"Irluk." Bakalor's right rocky eyebrow raised. "You continue to keep my halls filled and my stomach full."

"These days are soon to end," Irluk replied.

"Really?" The demon leaned forward with interest. "What news have you heard about our plans?"

"The living are fragmented. Bonds between cities and species have broken down. There is no cohesion nor unification."

"Excellent." Bakalor's thin eyes looked into the distance as he plotted his next move. "When will this opportunity be taken advantage of?"

"War is mounting. Ergrauth's armies are on the move to attack the west."

Bakalor grinned at the thought. "I wish I could be on the surface to watch the end of days. So little remains before my triumphant escape from this prison."

"Our kingdom is near," she said.

"When will Lu'Tythis Tower be ready to fall?"

"It is a strong tower. Everyone you have sent is working on it."

Bakalor looked over the side of his armrest, as an area of rock flooring transformed itself into a replica of Terra Australis. Miniature mountains rose under Bakalor's powers as the grand Lake Luthralum Tunia sank down a bit.

Hanging his finger over the lake area, Bakalor allowed the thick oil from his body to pour down until the lake bed had been filled. Aside from color and clouds roaming over it, the miniature landscape was a perfect replica of Terra Australis. Triangular in shape, the replica ranged from Farbank in the northwest, to the Southwind Mines in the south, and back up all the way through the Ergrauthian Valley of the Del'Unday in the northeast.

Snapping his rock fingers, he produced sparks that flew down and ignited the pool of oil. The sickly green flame from the miniature lake caused the entire map to come alive with colors, clouds, and blue water in the other lakes. It appeared to be Australis in every way except size and the life that lived there.

Thorik and Avanda craned their necks to see the cause of the new bright light. But once they managed to, they couldn't believe their eyes. The oil they had once used from the Mountain King Temple had also been used to create Bakalor. Or was it the other way around? Perhaps the ancient Nums had retrieved the oil from Bakalor's body. Regardless, both Nums had seen this rare oil bring stone objects to life when it was lit as it gave off its ill-colored greenish illumination.

Bakalor and Irluk scanned the map. The tip of Lu'Tythis Tower gave off tiny bursts of lightning, and the demon nodded his approval. "It appears you have already fractured it. This needs to be ready when the war is underway."

Slowly nodding in agreement, she watched the lightning flair out from the crystal on the top of the tiny tower. "Understood. However, we need more forces to make sure it falls down in time."

"Agreed." He then turned his attention beyond the living map. "Grub!" he called out to his youngest son.

Silence followed until the rocks near the landscape replica began to quake and bounce, followed by the surface blasting up and out of the way to reveal the demon's son, Grub.

Cooling quickly on the surface, the glob crusted over before four arms and a mouth emerged from its headless round body. Dirt and rocks rolled off Grub, displaying his crusted skin, which exposed internal hot magma between the cracks. "Yes, Your Grace," Grub said to his father.

"Have you met your siblings yet?"

"Yes, as you instructed."

"Good. How many can we send to Lu'Tythis Tower?" Bakalor asked as he studied the moving map.

Grub had no eyes to see what his father was looking at. The vibrations in the rock led him to where he needed to go. "They have informed me that most of my siblings are already at the tower. There are four of us here in Della Estovia. We await your call, Your Grace." Heat exited his mouth each time he talked, as though the door of a furnace opened.

Bakalor glanced up at Irluk to see if four more of his servants would be enough.

Irluk was also reviewing the map, plotting her own moves. "Three for sure. Four would guarantee it."

"Grub?"

"Yes, Your Grace."

"Take the rest of your siblings to the Lu'Tythis Tower. You are my guarantee."

Grub leaned forward in a bow and held it, waiting to be dismissed.

"No excuses, Irluk, I have given you everything you requested. This had better be precisely executed."

Irluk bowed her head in respect, but quickly released it and looked the demon in the eyes. "With these additional resources, I will be ready by the time Ergrauth leads his army beyond the Guardians and reaches River's Edge. They prepare to leave as we speak."

Focusing on the living map, Bakalor caused a small red-colored ripple within the miniature Ergrauth Valley to move out of the City of Ergrauth and toward the peaks of the Guardians.

Plotting each move out again to ensure he hadn't missed anything, he questioned her about each task she was to perform. "Have you revealed the location of the Winds of Conquest?"

"Not only revealed, but the demon Ergrauth has awoken them."

"Well done. Where is Darkmere?" the demon asked.

Irluk pointed at the map. "He has left the Temple of Surod and is heading toward Corrock."

Under the demon's influence, a small dark point jutted up from the map, located near the city of Corrock. Bakalor wanted to see where each of the pieces were sitting in his game of war. "Will Darkmere have the human armies of Doven moved to north Woodlen when Ergrauth's army attacks Doven's wall?"

"He will. The southern Woodlen walls will be unprotected." Her voice was calm and confident. "He will also have Corrock ready to destroy the city of Trewek."

"Excellent, Irluk. Now, I must know, what did you do with Ambrosius after you killed him?"

Irluk did not answer.

"You did kill him, didn't you?"

"We fought at Weirfortus but I was unable to take his soul. Now he is in hiding. Something prevents me from finding him."

"How many attempts will it take for you to finally remove him?"

"He had unexpected help. I will not underestimate him again."

"Perhaps he is still more powerful than you. You obviously can't contain him," Bakalor jabbed, peering over at her body of flowing burnt particles. "He did turn you into what you are. Perhaps he has regained what he once had." Nodding in agreement to his own words, he added, "I believe he is still stronger than you."

The speed of her whirling debris immediately increased. "Perhaps once, but not anymore! I will take his soul before the end of this war!"

"You had better," Bakalor said bluntly. "Otherwise, he could destroy everything we've worked for."

Irluk pondered her plight. "I must find his weakness." She glanced over at the Nums, still lying on the rock column, dazed and half-conscious.

"You!" The Death Witch floated over to Avanda and Thorik. Her charcoal hair flailed about over the Nums' heads as her face continued to break apart and reform from the ashes that made up her skin. "I've seen you before. You're friends of Ambrosius." She moved in closer for a better look. "Avanda? Is that you?"

The Nums didn't know how to respond, so they held onto each other's hand without saying a word.

"Bakalor," Irluk said in an unusually canny way, "I would like to take these two back up to the surface."

The demon sat up and looked away from his map. "No. This Num holds responsibility for my imprisonment down here. He needs to suffer!"

Thorik was confused and failed to reply before Irluk did.

A devious smile grew upon her face and then she spoke in an ancient language the Nums couldn't understand. "I only mean to borrow them. I need worms for the end of my hook. Besides, I'll bring him back down here afterward whether they live through it or not. They deserve the suffering you plan to unleash upon them."

"The Num needs to suffer for what he did to me. I want to be the one who sucks the life from him."

"Understood. But you've waited many years for your revenge on him. I think you can wait a little longer. He's not going to leave Terra Australis, and he must die eventually. If all goes well, you will rule the land above the caves soon enough, anyway. So he will be yours no matter how you look at it."

Bakalor sighed at the witch's logic. "What is your plan?"

Irluk gathered her thoughts before replying to him in a foreign tongue. "Have Grub follow them back to the lake valley. Once these two Nums are in jeopardy, Ambrosius will come out of hiding to save them. And once he does, I'll be there to end his life."

"What would you have me do to them if no jeopardy strikes on its own?" Grub asked.

"I don't care. Kill the ones they travel with and put these two in peril. Once it's serious enough, the old E'rudite will show himself to save his friends. It's his weakness."

Grub bowed his body forward and turned to the demon. "I await your orders, Your Grace."

Bakalor contemplated his options and licked his lips at the idea of having another taste of Num. But in the end he agreed with Irluk. "Grub, send your siblings to the Lu'Tythus Tower. You, on the other hand, will follow these two Nums until Irluk's trap snares success."

"Yes, Your Grace."

Unsuccessfully, Thorik and Avanda attempted to understand what was being discussed. But even if they had had a grasp of the odd language, they were in no condition to intervene. Nodding at Avanda, Thorik assured her that everything would be fine as he held her hand tight. What else could he do but give her hope, even if he didn't have any himself?

Swirling her ash-filled body above the column, Irluk quickly surrounded the two Nums before lifting them into the air toward the cavern ceiling. Thorik and Avanda's bodies met, and the two Nums gathered enough strength to grab onto one another. Again, clouds formed in the center of the cavern's highest point, while lightning flashed and thunder boomed around them.

Wind tossed them back and forth, but they continued to hold each other as tight as possible, even locking their legs together to prevent them from being torn apart. All was pitch black aside from the blinding bright flashes of the lightning.

Rain drenched the Nums as they continued to roll and spin out of control until they had lost any perspective of time. Their sense of balance was skewed, and they had no concept of which way was up. The rain became so severe that it nearly drowned them.

It was at this point that a large set of hands grabbed them and tried to pull them apart. Their grip was nearly impossible to break as they clutched onto each other even harder. But again, the hands pulled at them, this time breaking their tight bond.

Chapter Ten

REUNION

"What are you two doing?" Thorik and Avanda heard from a familiar voice.

"I'm telling you, they look older," a deeper voice said.

"Nonsense, they are just weathered by their journey," replied the first voice.

Both Nums opened their eyes in the cloudy evening sunlight. Thorik's uncle, Brimmelle, was standing with his arms crossed while their giant friend, Grewen, was holding the two younger Nums in his hands after plucking them out of the river.

Brimmelle spoke up again. "We've been searching endlessly for you, only to find you two playing in the water." He could now see that their faces looked older than he remembered and Avanda's soul-markings had expanded around her neck, but he quickly dismissed it as poor sleep and nourishment. "And apparently you two need a reminder of the Mountain King's words on personal health. You look terrible."

Thorik didn't care what Brimmelle had to say. They had traveled to Della Estovia, been attacked and nearly eaten by insects, and then captured by Bakalor who had the intention of keeping them in damnation for all eternity. Thorik grabbed Avanda's head, pulled it in, and kissed her hard on the lips, giving her the passionate kiss he had promised after their fall from Bakalor's throne. Pulling back just as quickly as he had pulled her forward, he shouted, "We're alive!"

Brimmelle was stunned at the unexpected kiss, while Grewen grinned at the sight. Pleasantly surprised, Avanda took it with much more meaning than was intended.

They were free from the underworld, and Thorik couldn't recall a time he was more relieved. Jumping down with excitement from Grewen's hands, his weakened legs nearly buckled under his weight before he hugged his uncle. Thorik's soaking wet clothes squished against Brimmelle's already dirty robes, turning them into a muddy mess.

Brimmelle quickly pushed free and attempted to brush the water off of him. Slightly taller than Thorik, the robust Num's thick soul-markings running down his arms and across his body were darker than normal, due to his emotions. Standing firm, he was proud of his markings, because of their wide and long patches, unlike the whimsical lacy markings on Avanda or the lack of soul-markings on Thorik. "Have you gone insane?"

"Acting a bit batty, are we?" Bryus Grum walked up to inspect them. "I like you a lot better this way." Thin and lanky with messy hair and torn clothes, Bryus was the opposite of Brimmelle when it came to personal care and hygiene.

Avanda sat calmly in Grewen's oversized hand as she watched Thorik smile and laugh like the teacher she had fallen in love with back in Farbank. Tracing her lower lip with her finger, she played back the kiss he had just given her. It was more than she had hoped it would be.

Grewen watched her reaction as she fell softly onto her back against his forearm. He could tell that she had taken the kiss seriously. His thick, leathery skin wrinkled on his bald head as he smiled at her with wide eyes. Cupping his dual-thumbed hand, he cradled her around her waist and wondered what he had missed while they were underground. "Your age, as well as your relationship, has advanced since we've seen you last."

It wasn't long before Thorik began telling the story of Bakalor, but then he stopped so he could start the story from the beginning, when they landed in the cavern of Num-eating insects.

"Wait just a minute." Brimmelle strummed his fingers a few times. "Demons? Death Witches? It's more likely you fell down that vent hole, landed in an underground river, and washed up on shore. Della Estovia may truly exist, but I don't believe you have what it takes to escape from such a legendary place."

"Uncle, I'm not making this up."

Fir Brimmelle puffed up his chest and felt his nephew's forehead as though he could make a medical diagnosis. "You're burning up. You must have a fever, causing you to hallucinate. In addition, you have a bump on your noggin where you were hit fairly hard. You're lucky you survived the fall after attacking me the way you did."

"Attacking you?" Thorik couldn't believe what he was hearing. "We were trying to save Gluic. Is she harmed?"

Brimmelle was appalled by the question. "Of course she is, Thorik. She's dead!"

"No, I mean the dagger, Varacon. Is the dagger intact? Has it been damaged?"

The name of the enchanted weapon caused Bryus to perk up. "Varacon damaged? Fortunately, no." Pulling it out from a pouch, he carefully removed the cloths he had wrapped it in. "You see, Num, Varacon can't be spoiled so easily. The most experienced tradespeople created this masterpiece from the finest metals. I would assume its birth was in the sacred city of Derivate."

Bryus was a skinny human who wore rags for clothes and an old leather belt with a talon from a claw on one end. On his feet he had thin leather sandals, which exposed his crusty dry heels and cracked wrinkly skin between his toes. He had a personality that flopped back and forth between a jester and a bitter old hermit, neither of which was enjoyable to be with, nor was there any warning of the shifting of attitude. It was a far cry from what Thorik expected from an Alchemist. His two different colored eyes didn't help, nor did the awkward-looking woven pack Avanda had made for him before she had fallen into Della Estovia.

Bryus walked on his bony legs like a drunken bird, and he constantly bumped into the others as they traveled. Thorik assumed the attack by Darkmere's forces had scrambled his brain so much that he was fortunate just to be alive. And lucky for Thorik he was, for he needed Bryus to locate the book of Vesik, which held the spell required to save his grandmother.

Thorik approached the Alchemist and reached for Varacon, but Bryus pulled it away as he spoke about the dagger's assumed birthplace with great enthusiasm. "It is the original home of the Notarians, you know. Pwellus Dementa was the first city created. The original plans for our world were made there."

Nodding, Thorik thanked him for the information and reached for Varacon a second time.

Pulling the dagger away again, Bryus continued to tell his story after a twitch in his cheek. "Plans were developed to make this land into a heaven like no other. I believe the Great Oracle, Ovlan, ruled over the Notarians at that point. She created the Myth'Unday, you know. They are dangerous little critters. Stay clear!" Bryus' arms were straight out at his sides as he warned Thorik of such dangers.

Unclear how his question of the dagger turned into a warning about Myth'Unday, Thorik interrupted as he reached out toward the item held by the Alchemist. "The dagger, Varacon, may I see it?"

"Of course you can see it," he shot back with surprise. "We can all see it. It's no figment of our imagination. It is a genuine artifact. It is a piece of art, most likely crafted by Horib himself. Oh, but Horib was a wicked one, wasn't he? The way he always placed more into his art than what was requested. Never did they suspect what was really lurking in his masterpieces."

"Bryus!" Thorik shouted. He was getting tired of the tangents that Bryus continued to go on. "Please hand me the dagger."

"Well, of course, dear boy." Smirking, he hesitated before giving it up. "Why didn't you just ask?" Spinning the dagger around in the cloth, which still lay in his hand, he handed Varacon to Thorik hilt first.

"Gluic?" Thorik asked softly as he pulled the dagger from the man and lifted it near his own face. "Are you still in there? I hope so. We've survived Della Estovia and have come back for you. I'm going to prevent you from having to see that place."

Brimmelle crossed his arms as he glared at Thorik. "You've gone absolutely insane, Thorik. Are you even listening to yourself anymore? You're saying that your grandmother is trapped inside an old dagger and you fought off a demon and the witch of death to climb out of the underworld where only the dead can go."

"That's only partially true." Thorik held the dagger near his chest, trying to feel any energy inside. "We didn't fight our way to freedom. They let us go. I don't know why."

"Well, that sounds more reasonable." Brimmelle's words were thick with sarcasm. "You stumbled upon a mythical place forbidden by all living beings, and the ruler of the dead just returns you to the surface because you are the almighty Thorik Dain."

Thorik thought about his uncle's comments as he looked the dagger over for any scratches. Realizing there weren't any, he began wrapping it up to place it in his own pack. "You know, I think you're right."

Brimmelle was stunned by the answer. "What?"

"I don't know how, but Bakalor knew me. In fact, he hated me and blamed me for his rule over the underworld. To add to my confusion, I don't understand why he would free me if he loathed me so?"

Brimmelle muttered to himself in disbelief. "The boy's fall must have caused more damage to his head than what is visible."

Thorik continued to talk over his uncle's words. "And then we learned that there's a war coming. It hasn't started yet, but it will."

Brimmelle sighed as he sat down. "Wonderful, Thorik can now see into the future."

"And the only one that can stop it is Ambrosius."

"Well then, why didn't you bring him back up with you? His soul should have been wandering around down there someplace."

"Because he's not dead," Thorik said.

"Of course not. Even though you watched him die."

"Apparently, he still had enough strength to fight off the Death Witch."

Brimmelle dropped his face down into both of his hands as he chuckled at the insanity of it all.

Thorik looked past his uncle and spotted his weapon, the Spear of Rummon, tied to Bryus' pack. He hurried over to it. "Thank you for finding Rummon."

"Wait one minute, Num." Bryus turned in a circle to keep his back away from the Num. "This is no toy. This is the Spear of Rummon."

"Yes, I know." Thorik continued to chase the spear on the man's back, frequently reaching for it without any luck.

"Do you understand that the life force of the most powerful dragon that ever lived is trapped inside of it?" Bryus kept spinning to keep it out of Thorik's reach, causing himself to get dizzy. "He is a demon! Fear him, for he will try to communicate with you and conquer your willpower." His words were getting loud and theatrical, with large gestures of his arms. "He is our enemy, Thorik. He's the murderer of your sacred Mountain King. Do you have the internal strength to handle Rummon's words, should he choose to speak them to you?"

"Yes, we've communicated more than once." Thorik's voice was flat and serious.

Bryus stopped spinning around and became slightly disappointed as well as very dizzy. "You have? Could I have a word with him? I've been trying to communicate with Rummon for days without any luck."

"Perhaps later." Thorik removed the spear from Bryus' back and placed it into the loops of his own pack before looking around at his surroundings. "Where are we?"

They were no longer in the Go'ta Gorge. Instead, they stood near a large river, upstream from an ancient marble bridge spanning it.

"I think I'm going to be ill." Bryus sat down from all his spinning as he fought off the self-induced nausea.

"Volney River." Grewen was still amazed by Thorik's stories. "The Lagona Falls drops off just past the bridge. Where did you think you were?"

"I would have assumed we were still in the gorge." Thorik quickly pulled the facts together. "You gave up on us in the gorge. You left us for dead?"

Brimmelle instantly shot Grewen a look of irritation. "If it was up to me, we wouldn't have left!"

In his usual calm baritone voice, Grewen corrected the husky Num. "If it was up to you, we would have starved to death up on that mountainside staring down into a vent shaft, which we couldn't fit through."

"Bryus was thin enough to fit through it," Brimmelle protested.

Bryus' cheek twitched. "I told you, as plain as the ugly is on your face, that I'm not willing to pass the barrier into Della Estovia to save a few Nums. It's a death sentence. Once I saw the markings, I stopped, and if you were intelligent enough to understand their meanings, you would have as well."

"But this wasn't a request to find treasure," Brimmelle protested. "And these weren't just a few Nums. These were members of my village."

"Listen, you self-righteous little toad, I might have considered going down there for the right historical artifact, but I had only met your companions a few days prior to the incident. The incident where you put their lives in danger and then turned around and expected me to risk my life to save them. I think not!"

"They've been at each other ever since Brimmelle regained consciousness after being knocked out from your tumble," Grewen told Thorik and Avanda as Brimmelle and Bryus continued to spar back and forth. "I tried to lower your uncle down several times, but was unsuccessful. He became stuck on several attempts, and at one point, he was jammed in a spot for several hours. We weren't sure if we were going to get him back out."

Thorik turned his back on the quibbling travelers as Brimmelle puffed up his chest and stood his moral high ground while Bryus cut him off at his knees with logic and sarcastic remarks. "Grewen,"

Thorik said, "we tried to climb back up, but it was too slick and steep. I was nearly killed by insects. We were starving and freezing to death, and yet we waited for you. You never arrived. We couldn't wait any longer."

Grewen nodded with a slight smile. "You did the right thing, little man. There are times you must look after yourself, for as hard as I tried, we couldn't reach you. Eventually, I agreed with Bryus to seek out others that could help us. We thought it would be best to head to Trewek, where there are Ov'Unday who can search underground much more effectively than we can."

Thorik didn't know how he felt about being abandoned when he had been so sure that they would come after him.

"We never gave up on you, Thorik," Grewen handed the Num his wooden coffer and other items that had been flung from his pack before he fell down the vent hole. "We only changed our plans once we realized we could do no more. To his credit, your uncle never wished to leave. However, following his lead most likely would have killed us as well."

Thorik nodded as he looked over the items while returning them to specific locations in his backpack. "Thank you for your efforts. Fortunately, Avanda and I had each other to get us through." Thorik turned and winked at Avanda. "It was an experience I wish never to repeat, but we pulled together, and now we're free of that place."

Avanda realized how right he was and smiled at his last statement. "We're better Nums for it."

Tossing the backpack on, Thorik tightened his pack's straps and stood up straight with confidence. Not overconfidence, but after seeing certain death, life was such a welcome adventure. He looked ahead at the open road before them with an enthusiasm he hadn't felt since they left Kingsfoot.

"So," Grewen said, "where are we off to?"

Bryus stopped his bickering with Brimmelle in mid-sentence once he heard the question. "Govi Glade, of course, to find the spell book Vesik. The spell within is your only hope to free Gluic from Varacon."

Thorik looked over the bridge and toward the northwest. "We must save Granna, but we must also notify others of Bakalor's pending war along the way. They will be destroyed if they are not alerted and prepared."

"And who is going to believe a Num such as yourself?" Brimmelle puffed up his chest as his soul-markings turned nearly black. "Who do you think you are? The Mountain King?"

"I think that's what I've finally come to realize," Thorik said over his shoulder. "I don't need to be the Mountain King to get things done. I just need to believe in myself and take action. Others will listen to my words and see my confidence in what I say."

Grewen grinned. "Well said, little man, but just because they will listen does not mean they will act."

"Grewen, if I've learned anything from you, I've learned that I can only control my own actions and reactions, not those of others. I must do what it takes and hope that others will do the same."

Brimmelle's markings faded back to their normal hue as he shook his head in disgust. "I know the end of the world is near when Thorik becomes responsible for saving it."

Chapter Eleven

CAMPSITE

Thorik's Log: 4th day of the 7th month of the 650th year.

Avanda and I have returned from the fiery depths of Della Estovia, yet we do not know for what purpose. Bakalor had us at his command and was showing no mercy as he stole over a decade of our lives. Regardless of why he released us, we are just thankful to be out of there and back on our way. Before we head to the Govi Glade to find the spell book to free Granna, we'll head north to Trewek to alert them of the pending war. But for tonight, Avanda and I plan to eat, drink, and rest. Three simple pleasures that we have desired for so many days. May tomorrow bring us opportunities, and may we never forget how fortunate we have been, even if those opportunities are not to our liking.

After sunrise, the group collected fresh water for their trek across the desert. The water was warm but drinkable. It was a mixture of Shi'Pel glacier runoff, the rains along the Spirit Tower Range, and hundreds of small desert valleys along the eastern Volney River Valley. It was old water that had slowly traveled through thousands of miles of rough, dry lands, and it tasted of every mile.

In order to head northwest, they first had to cross over an ancient stone bridge which spanned the mighty Volney River. It had held up well for thousands of years, with only minor damage and erosion. Once the water traveled under the bridge, it fell thousands of feet into the Ki'Volney Lake valley. The mist from this mighty Lagona Falls transformed the lower desert into a forest of life, breathing oxygen back into the water before it traveled west to Lake Luthralum.

While crossing the bridge, Thorik and Avanda stopped for a few moments and looked over the falls and across the open land below. The scene was majestic and filled with the colors of life as various rivers ran into clear blue lakes. Beyond the initial forest, tan sand dunes spread across the lower desert like waves on an ocean. Desert lakes were trimmed with green vegetation, as were the mighty mountains, often rising to white peaks.

Taking in a deep breath, Avanda clung to Thorik's hand and absorbed the vastness of the entire landscape. "I never realized how beautiful our land was until we almost lost the chance to see it forever."

Thorik squeezed her hand. "I couldn't have done it without you, Avanda. You saved my life."

"And you mine." She then let go of his hand. "Don't move," she requested as she searched through her pockets. The rest of the travelers had already crossed and were continuing on their way.

Thorik gazed out onto the miraculous scene while waiting for her. It felt wonderful to be alive.

"Here." Avanda handed him a light blue crystal shard.

Thorik looked at it for a moment before realizing where it had come from. "This is from Della Estovia. Is this one of shards from the crystal that Bakalor shattered?"

"Yes. When the crystal was hit, it showered me with debris of small pieces. I want you to hold on to it and think of how we feel right here, at this moment, as we look over the valley and realize how bad it could have been, and how we worked together to make it through alive."

"Thank you, but this is too important of a memory for you to give to me."

"I'm not."

"You're not?" He was obviously confused.

"No. This is ours to share. When times are difficult for one of us and we need strength and support, all we will need to do is hand this to the other." She closed her palm over his, covering the shard before cupping her other hand below his. "No words will be needed; we'll know what it means. Even if we become angry with each other, this will be the symbol of how we felt about one another while standing here on this bridge. It will be the symbol of our true feelings."

"Thank you," Thorik said softly. "But—"

"I know. You need to stay focused on saving Gluic." She nodded. "You'll know when it is time to give me the crystal back, and I will be there for you when you do."

A silent nod followed as the two scanned the horizon for a few more minutes before leaving the bridge and catching up to the others.

The travelers followed the long, sharp edge of the plateau north for the entire day. Looking down over the western valley, the plateau and the valley below slowly merged into the same elevation far to their north, near the southern base of the Ossuary Mountain Range. They still had a long trek ahead of them before this joining of terrain, but night was settling in, and traveling in the dark could lead them right over the cliff. It was time to stop and rest after a long day's walk.

Words from the Mountain King's scrolls quickly filled the air as Brimmelle recited them as he did every night while Grewen cleared the area for camp.

Thorik prepared camp bedding for the night with the help of Avanda at his side. Although he was still in slight denial, a special bond had been created between the two during their time together. They had saved each other's lives, they had warmed each other in the freezing caverns, they had suffered violent pain, and they had nearly died together. It was only natural that deep emotions would come from it. But he questioned if there was enough depth of emotion to last outside of Della Estovia, in the real world.

Grewen moved several large rocks into place for fire containment, as well as some for sitting upon, while Bryus established a secondary campfire for himself.

Helping the Alchemist set up his campsite, Avanda noticed his belt. "What kind of animal talon is that which holds your belt tight?"

Bryus looked down at his leather belt and the clasp made from a claw. "It's just from a Fesh'Unday's claw. A pet of mine." He talked in a low tone and turned his head, making it obvious that he didn't want to discuss it. "I can finish up my camp; you should help with your own."

He wasn't in a talkative mood, so she shrugged her shoulders and left just as Thorik approached Bryus. The two Nums winked at each other as they passed ways.

"Why don't you sleep near our campfire?" Thorik asked Bryus.

"I prefer my own space. Gives me time by myself to think," he replied.

"Time to think? You spend all day by yourself, never adding to any of our discussions. How will you ever get to know us if you don't join our conversations?"

Bryus' eye and cheek twitched at the comment. "Who said I wanted to get to know you?"

"Well, no one. But since we're traveling together, it would be nice to know a little about you."

"Is that necessary?" he replied with a grimace.

"Yes. The only conversations you've had with us are about enchanted relics and ancient symbols. It seems to me that you care more about things than you do people. Surely that's not true."

"It might very well be. I don't know you. And to be truthful, you don't really know each other as well as you may think. Given the right circumstances, most people are willing to abandon or double-cross each other."

"I don't believe that to be true, especially with us. We are what the Ov'Unday call a family pod. We aren't related, and we may bicker from time to time, but we are a family of sorts, nonetheless. We are there for each other and always will be. Do you have any family?"

"Family?" The word seemed to have struck an emotional cord.

"Yes, family or close friends." Thorik's hesitation was caused to the man's reaction.

"Do you not understand who I was? I was the Prominent of Ever-Spring, until that..." He paused as he placed a hand over his eye to keep it from twitching. Emotionally and powerfully, he let loose on Thorik with his background. "... I ruled EverSpring until my friends' fear of Darkmere was greater than our own relationships. Those that I trusted conspired against me and helped the Dark Lord overthrow my power. They turned me into an enemy of my own province, enslaved my family, and imprisoned me in an effort to force me to help him sacrifice Ambrosius' son."

Dropping his head for a moment, Bryus regained control of his facial tic. "Friendship is based on convenience and the need for something from someone else. Once that need is gone, so is the relationship!"

"Surely they didn't all just turn their back on you," Thorik said to Bryus before turning to Grewen for conformation. "People wouldn't give up on their close friends so easily, would they?"

Grewen tilted his big, bald, leathery head. "It is an unfortunate truth for many. Trust takes years to embed in the hearts of others, but only moments of doubt to rip out, regardless of any proof being provided."

Bryus nodded in agreement with the mognin while looking at Thorik. "And people like you have the nerve to question why I care more about enchanted items than people. It's because I know where I stand with these objects. They don't discriminate or judge or change based on threats of greed or cowardice."

Thorik was not expecting the lecture and wasn't sure how to respond.

"Tell me, Num. Do you feel better knowing that I have lost everything and don't even know where to look for the ones I love? My family is locked away, not knowing of my fate or their own. I don't know of my wife's health or my daughter's pain. Have they been tortured? Have they been violated? These are the thoughts that fester in my mind when you say the word family. So, are you pleased with yourself for bringing up such a painful issue?"

"No, of course not."

"Then why the hell do you want me to set all that aside and become one of your happy family pod members so we can save your grandmother? Again, the hand of friendship is reached out to me, as long as I help you get what you need. Tell me that I'm wrong!" he said skeptically.

"Well—"

"Well, what's my other option?" Bryus flung his arms in the air as he spoke in a loud, demanding voice. "I can't return home to my province without being captured again, and I don't know where my family is being held, so I might as well help you until I figure out what I'm going to do next."

Thorik nodded, as though he was accepting Bryus' request to stay with them.

"But I'll tell you this, Num. You need me more than I need you. Therefore, if I want a second camp set up so I can keep to myself, then I expect to have one."

Agreeing with him, Thorik stood there silently as he watched Bryus return to his private campsite.

Grewen leaned forward and grabbed Thorik's head from the back in order to stop his nodding in agreement. "Is it me, or do you get the slight impression Bryus wants to be left alone?" The mognin let out a slight chuckle.

Darkness arrived, leaving the rising moon as the only light source.

Brimmelle had continued to recite the Mountain King's Runestone scrolls from his memory. Thrashers had destroyed his actual scrolls when they had first left Farbank, but his exceptional memory and a lifetime of teaching them enabled him to recall each scroll to the very letter.

In the soft light, Thorik stood silently and watched his companions. He noticed that Brimmelle's telling of the sacred scrolls had changed since they left Farbank from his once dull and dry monotone readings. His presentation skills had improved as he now added examples and short stories to teach the laws, according to the Mountain King. He was slowly becoming interesting to listen to and much easier to understand.

The night was relatively calm aside from Brimmelle's readings and Bryus whistling to catch beetles.

Grewen sighed in relief as he plucked stones from the bottom of his enormous feet. The thick hide on his soles took a lot of abuse, seeing that he didn't wear any sandals or other protection. Then again, most mognins didn't.

Flicking stones out of his skin, the mognin made a game of it and shot them out in the desert to hit various objects. He missed more often than he hit, but he had nothing else to do other than feeding his face with whatever shrubs he could find.

Thorik chuckled at the sight of his giant friend. He never seemed to have a care in the world. Nothing ever got under his skin, figuratively or literally. There was only one other person in his life that lived so carefree.

"Granna," Thorik said softly to the dagger Varacon, which was completely wrapped up for protection and tied solidly to his belt, "I'm going to bring you back, no matter what it takes." Placing his hand firmly on the dagger's hilt, he thought about her. Thorik missed her deeply as he recalled the many times when she got him out of trouble or into trouble, as so often happened with her. He closed his eyes and smiled at the memories.

A second hand was placed on top of his, which still held the dagger's hilt. This one was soft and slightly smaller. It belonged to Avanda. "Can you tell if she is well?" she softly asked Thorik.

He shook his head as he opened his eyes. "No, I can't tell anything."

She slid her fingers in between his so she could touch the cloth covering the dagger. "I'm sure she is fine."

The palms of his hands began to sweat, and his ability to form basic sentences seemed to be impaired by her soft touch. "What makes you... um... say that?" His voice was soft, as it cracked with nervousness.

"Do you know anyone more likely to be trapped in a dagger and still survive?" A shy smile grew upon her face.

"No," was all he could muster.

"Close your eyes." She moved in closer to him. "Breathe softly and call to her in your mind." Watching him for a few minutes, she finally asked, "Did you hear anything?"

"Yes."

"Really? What?" she asked quickly in a soft voice.

"Fir Brimmelle's words from the scrolls, Grewen chewing on local weeds, and your breathing in my ear."

Avanda laughed sweetly at his response. "Come on, it's time to cook some dinner."

Brimmelle opened his eyes and looked up from his absent congregation. "Haven't you started working on lighting a campfire yet? What have you two been doing?"

Thorik shrugged his shoulders like a child would when asked about missing treats that resembled crumbs on their face. Avanda's soft touch and voice had affected him more than he had expected.

Avanda squeezed his hand, stopping him from answering before she did. "We were so taken with your readings, Fir Brimmelle, that we failed in our duties."

"Duties need to be maintained." In spite of his words, Brimmelle easily accepted the excuse and returned to his hour-long sermon.

Avanda winked at Thorik, giving him permission to exhale and move. Even he had to chuckle with her. She knew how to make him feel good and smile.

"Sorry I kept you from your responsibilities," she said.

"It's all right. It doesn't really matter." Not willing to receive a second warning from Brimmelle, they both laughed it off as she left to collect more brush for the fire.

Bryus Grum interrupted their soft laughter as he walked into the main camp to collect a handful of leaves and twigs for his own fire. He was still struggling with the twitch he had acquired during Darkmere's attack on him in the Surod Temple. "It's good to see that you finally understand."

Slightly confused, Thorik started pulling out his cookware. "Understand what?"

"That it doesn't matter," Bryus replied.

"What doesn't matter?"

Bryus chuckled as he looked at the young Num. "Anything."

"Nothing matters?" Thorik asked Bryus to clarify as he attempted to light the fire.

"Exactly."

"Why do you say that?" Thorik started his duties while they talked, before Brimmelle looked over at him.

"For it will all end in disaster, anyway. So why even try?"

Thorik didn't like the sound of that. "You mean Bakalor's War? We may still be able to stop it from happening."

Bryus laughed. "It's already written. There are no other options. We are at the end of this cycle. The fourth age of Australis will come to its climatic finale in this war."

Opening his backpack to remove his cooking spoon, his face crunched up from the Alchemist's comment. "We are? By whose words? The Mountain King never wrote about such things."

"Wyrlyn. The greatest E'rudite of all time. His ancient prophecy speaks of these last days, when the dead rise from Della Estovia and return to the land of the living."

"Sounds dreadful. How would he know of these events to come?" Thorik took a moment to think about the name. "Who is this Wyrlyn? I've never heard of him."

Bryus looked shocked at the news. "How is it possible that you don't know of him? He has influenced everything in everyone's life. Aside from the Oracles themselves, he was the supreme architect of our world."

Removing the wrapped dagger from his belt, Thorik placed it snugly in his backpack before attempting to light the campfire. "I'm a little surprised at your respect for him. It was my understanding that Alchemists and E'rudites have been at odds for thousands of years. However, you have nothing but praise for an E'rudite that has informed you of our doom."

Avanda returned with a handful of dead shrubs for the fire. But before she could toss them near the future campfire location, Bryus grabbed specific plants from the bundle within her arms.

"Clovik Ty," Bryus told her as he held up the first plant. "Dunge-lier." He held up the second plant as his face twitched.

Avanda stared at him, confused as to what he was doing.

Bryus turned back to Thorik as he began ripping the branches into long, thin strips. "I used to be a single-minded spellcaster."

It was an opportunity for Thorik to understand him better, so he kept pressing the conversation forward. "What caused you to be single-minded?"

"Higher magical academics," he spit back. "They gave me the basics, but along with those lessons they planted seeds of their own vision of how the world should work. Their own version of what truth really is."

Thorik continued to struggle to light the campfire. Prior to their arrival, the mountain rains had bled over into the desert valley and drenched the land, so nothing was dry. "Isn't that why you went? To understand how magic works?"

Bryus laughed as he ripped more strands off of Avanda's plants. "That's not what I'm referring to. It's the philosophies of those who are right and wrong in our world that were inserted during our normal lectures."

Thorik was confused again.

Bryus handed the strips of Clovik Ty branches to Avanda. "Tie them end to end." He then ignored her as though she wasn't even there.

Avanda didn't appreciate being ordered around, but, with a wink from Thorik, she began tying the ends together. The branch strips were coarse and rough to her touch, but she learned how to handle them without cutting up her hands.

Again, Thorik tried to create a spark for the fire, but failed. "Why is identifying wrong and right actions bad?"

"What?" Bryus asked while tearing strips from the Dungelier plant.

"Your academic seeds of right and wrong," Thorik repeated.

"Who's to say what's right?" Bryus looked confused as a series of twitches erupted on his face.

"I thought you said you had single-minded thought when it came to spells."

"Oh, not anymore. Not since I accepted the words of Wyrlyn. Once that happened, the headmasters of Alchemy tossed me out on my ear. Lucky for me, they didn't strike me down where I stood. Brave are those who search for new truths, but fools they are called by the educated leaders, for the brave put in question what the leaders have taught. Therefore, they put into question those who have taught it."

Thorik thought it was comical how candid Bryus was about the fact that they could have killed him. His contained laughter worked against him as he crouched on his knees while attempting to ignite the wild grass. "How did you get involved in the teachings of Wyrlyn?"

"Ambrosius Dovenar told me about them," Bryus said to Thorik before addressing Avanda. "Now, tie these Dungeliers from end to end like you did on the Clovik Ty and then weave the two plants together."

Avanda had just finished the first set and wasn't looking for more work to do. Nevertheless, she grudgingly took them from him and began her next task, although she didn't know what he was trying to accomplish.

Bryus turned back to Thorik. "Once I accepted the science of Wyrlyn, everything seemed to fall into place."

"Let me get this straight, you gave up on being an Alchemist, and now you are an E'rudite?"

Abruptly, Bryus sat straight up stared at Thorik for several uncomfortable seconds as one long twitch shook the side of his face. "An Alchemist does not just give up spell casting. It is my faith. It is what I believe in." His voice was loud, and his words were sharply pronounced. "Can I not just add the teachings of the E'rudites to what I already know to be true? Why must it be one or the other and never a combination of the two?"

Thorik suddenly felt like he was under attack from something larger and more menacing than the frail man who sat next to him. The man's change in demeanor was always so sudden that Thorik could never prepare for any extensive discussions.

Bryus roared with anger over Thorik's original question. "I am proud to be an Alchemist! How dare you assume otherwise? I studied my entire life to achieve and master the most complex spells of our time." Pointing at Thorik, he continued in a thunderous voice, "Do you have faith in your Mountain King? Have all new ideas ripped away at the fabric of your beliefs, or are you capable of adding to them?"

"I don't know. I've been questioning my faith for quite some time now. The stories we've heard from other cultures tend to be in conflict with the writings of the Mountain King. Instead of being so quick to dismiss my own culture, perhaps I too need to be proud of what we have, while accepting what others have as well."

Thorik looked at Bryus for some level of approval.

A twitch on his cheek and a few blinks later, Bryus replied very casually, "Doesn't matter much to me. It's your life."

Bryus then looked directly at Avanda and smiled from ear to ear. "Excellent work." She had weaved the two long strips of plants into one thick one. Placing the ends in each of her hands, he had her allow the strips to sag into an upside-down arch. "Now spin them around like a barrel rolling down a hill."

Avanda did as she was told. She was concerned about Bryus raising his voice like he had to Thorik. Once she had the strips spinning so fast they were difficult to see, he told her to pull her arms apart, thus tightening the spin in front of her. The smaller radius of the spin caused the strips to speed up even more.

"Now loosen," Bryus instructed her. And as she did, the spinning strips slowed and became wider. "Now tighten again. Back and forth while saying the word 'Jungere' as you do it."

She did as she was instructed, pulling the spinning strips in tight and then back out again several times as she said the word he had given her. Her hands were now getting hot from the friction.

"Faster," Bryus ordered. "Yell it out!"

"Jungere!" She screamed as the heat increased and her arms tired. "Jungere!"

The strips ignited into flames as they spun around in front of her. "Jungere!" she screamed even louder.

Bryus laughed as he watched her. "The spell is over. You don't have to do it anymore."

Feeling foolish, she stopped the spinning and tossed the flaming strips onto the pile of campfire kindling, where they instantly ignited the rest of the shrubs that she had already stacked.

Bryus clapped his hands before rubbing them together. "So, what's for supper?" His demeanor was oddly light and friendly, as though he had been invited over for tea.

CHAPTER TWELVE

BRYUS' STORY

A distant red ember of light flickered in the wind a few miles from the Nums' camp. Bakalor's son, Grub, patiently waited for Ambrosius to appear. Half buried in order to feel every vibration made at Thorik's distant campsite, the lesser demon could track the footfalls of each individual in the camp. None, however, were created by the visitor he waited for.

Well-prepared roots had been eaten, and the travelers had got settled in for the night. Thick clouds rolled in over the desert, preventing them from seeing stars or even the location of the moon. Yellowish flames from the crackling campfires were the only light source, as shadows of the group flickered against the dry prairie.

Small gusts of cool air frequently blew down from the heavy clouds, fanning the campfire flames and kicking up dirt. The smell of fresh rain was present but not yet seen or felt.

Grewen regularly stoked the fire, Thorik cleaned up the camp, and Brimmelle complained about his lack of comfort. It was their routine, which took place every night at camp. In a way, it gave them comfort and a sense of security to have a predictable pattern, especially seeing that nothing else in their lives right now was stable or reliable.

After making notes about their journey and placing the papers in his coffer, Thorik closed the wooden box and walked over to Bryus and Avanda at a smaller second campfire. "Why don't you join us for a little while?"

Glancing past the Num at Grewen and Brimmelle, the Alchemist dismissed the idea. "Not in the mood for socializing," he said before noticing Thorik's coffer. "Nice prattle box. I gave a set of those to the king when the twins were born."

Thorik looked down at his coffer, which he had always thought to be unique, only now to find out that others had the same thing. "Thanks."

Bryus quickly returned to showing Avanda the insides of a large beetle he had cracked open. "This is his poison sac. It is especially useful for many charm spells on Del'Unday."

Avanda was very attentive to what he was teaching. She had been so limited in the past with only what she had taught herself using the magical items from within a found purse. It was extremely liberating to know she wouldn't be restricted to those enchanted objects any longer.

Thorik stood silently and watched the lesson. He was unsure which bothered him more; the concern that she was more interested in learning from the Alchemist instead of himself, the distrust that was building due to Bryus' lack of interest in becoming part of their group, or the fear of Avanda learning more magic. His former Runestone student had caused more problems than assistance when casting her limited spells. There was also the fact that Thorik had become enamored with her, whether he wished to admit it or not. And these feelings were affecting his judgment.

"Avanda, I'm not sure you should use magic." Occasionally, Thorik would speak in a fatherly tone, and this was one of them.

Tilting her head, her shoulders sank at the thought. "What? Why not?"

"It's dangerous," he replied, holding back his desire to give in to her needs. He battled his emotions to display himself as the leader he wished to become, instead of giving in to the kindness he wished to show to make her happy. Nevertheless, he knew this was the right thing for everyone.

"I've saved us several times with my spells." A sour look appeared on her face.

"You've also nearly cost us our lives twice as many times," he said sternly.

"But now, with Bryus teaching me, I'll be better." Her tone was solid, and her words were evenly paced. She was standing her ground.

Thorik knew her words to be true, and it concerned him that she would have such magical powers. "I'm sure you will, but I just don't think it's right for you to wield these types of forces."

"Why? Because I'm a girl? Because I'm younger than you?"

Danger signals flashed in Thorik's mind as he quickly determined how he was going to prevent himself from looking like the villain in this conversation. "That's not what I said. I mean you, as well as myself and all other Nums. We aren't supposed to be using mystical powers and casting spells. It's just not our way. I don't think we can control the elements of nature safely."

"Oh, I see." She abruptly stood up and brushed herself off. "We Polenums shouldn't be dabbling in things outside the norm... like using a Runestone to see the souls of the dead."

It was now Thorik's shoulders that softened and rolled forward. "That's different—"

Quick to interrupt, Avanda continued. "And we would never harbor weapons that have unnatural strengths and powers, such as the Spear of Rummon."

"I needed it to save our lives—"

Avanda walked toward him, forcing him around the small campfire. "Nor would any of our kind travel with Del'Unday or Ov'Unday, for that would be wrong as well."

Stumbling past Bryus, Thorik continued to walk backward as he kept a healthy arm's length from her. "You can't suggest that it was my idea that we—"

Smiling, she was confident she had the upper hand as she continued to stop him in mid-sentence. "And how safe would you say it is for us to be traveling to the underworld and back while in search of a magical book to give us the spell to free your grandmother from an enchanted dagger?" Stopping at the end of her long and pointed question, she stood rigid with her hands tightly on her hips.

Thorik tripped and fell to the ground as he continued to stare at her. "I'm just telling you what Ambrosius told me. He warned us that magic was dangerous and we should stay clear of it."

Crossing her arms, she stood at his feet, eyeing him down.

His words caught Bryus' attention. "Ambrosius?"

Thorik raised himself from his back up onto to his elbows as he caught wind of a way out of Avanda's verbal trap. "Yes, Ambrosius," he said to Bryus. "You knew him. His words carry significant weight, wouldn't you say?"

Bryus' cheek twitched at the name of the old E'rudite. "Powerful man. He has a lot of questionable ties. But when it came down to it, he could find the most elusive artifacts."

"Artifacts?"

"Ah, yes. The treasure of Joral, the pearl of Wespee, Hesek's belt, and many more were reclaimed by him. He was quite the scavenger when it came to rare antiquities."

Thorik squinted his face, perplexed by the comments. "He isn't like that. He had a larger look at the world. He had no time for trinkets, enchanted objects, or treasures from the past."

Bryus' grin made Thorik feel very uncomfortable. Nearly evil in appearance, the man's face seemed to morph before the Num's eyes as the light from the flames added to the effect. "Ambrosius is one of those treasures from the past."

Feeling uncomfortable, Thorik scooted away and stood up next to Avanda. Suddenly, she seemed safer to him.

"Don't you know who he is? Don't you know the story?" Bryus' voice was rougher and slower than normal, adding an extra element of strangeness to him.

"Of course, I do. He's Ambrosius Dovenar. The rightful king of the Dovenar Kingdom."

"He gave up that right!" Bryus corrected loudly, followed by a severe twitch to his cheek.

"Yes. I know. But only because he felt that he and his brother, Darkmere, were tearing it apart."

Placing his hand over his cheek and eye, Bryus pressed firmly to stop his facial tic. "They have been, ever since they were children."

"Yes, and Ambrosius didn't feel E'rudites should rule a kingdom. Hence, he created the Grand Council to rule the land in his stead. This council was—"

"Don't tell me about the council, Num," Bryus broke in. "I was once on the council. I know what really happened there, not you!"

"I wasn't implying that I did. You had asked me if I knew who Ambrosius was."

Bryus grunted. "What a weak attempt to describe a man who helped design this land and all the history that followed."

"I admit, he was... is," the Num corrected himself, "a great man to whom we owe many a gratitude, but he himself told me of his birth into the kingdom's royal line. He's far younger than you make him out to be."

Bryus jumped from his seat, grabbed a rock, and charged toward Thorik.

Thorik pushed Avanda back out of the way before crossing his arms in front of his face in an effort to block the rock from hitting him. But instead of being hit with the object, Bryus pulled Thorik's arm forward and slapped the rock hard into his palm.

"What is this?" Bryus pointed to the rock he had just given Thorik.

Bewildered at the emotional instability of the man, he cowered slightly as he looked at what lay in his hand. "It's a rock."

"And where do rocks come from?"

"The ground?"

"No, you fool. Larger rocks. That rock used to be part of a larger rock before time had its way with it. Perhaps it sat up high on one of these mountains before it broke off and rolled or washed down into the valley. Do you understand?"

Thorik nodded. "Yes."

Bryus smiled, for his point had been understood.

"But what does this have to do with Ambrosius?"

Bryus' eyes popped wide open with disbelief. "I just explained it to you."

"Well, maybe you need to do it without using a rock."

Bryus snatched the rock out of the Num's hand and held it uncomfortably near Thorik's face. "This is Ambrosius." He then pointed up toward the peaks of the mountains. "That is Wyrlyn."

"Are you saying that Ambrosius is a descendent of Wyrlyn?"

"You're getting closer."

"Surely you're not saying that he once was Wyrlyn?"

"Oh, you're a quick one, aren't you? Figure that out all on your own?"

Thorik ignored the condescending tone from Bryus. "How can one person who lived several thousand years ago become a man who was born a half a century ago?"

Bryus was stunned. "You honestly have never heard this tale?"

"Honestly!"

A grin of questionable intent gleamed across his face. He seemed mad with excitement over the opportunity to discuss such matters. "The story of Wyrlyn and Irluk." His hands waved about for effect.

Avanda got excited as well. She was enjoying the nonsensical ways of Bryus. "Irluk was involved?"

"No questions!" Bryus snapped, as he fluttered his fingers in the air while preparing for the story.

"Wyrlyn was the greatest E'rudite, as well as the first. Taught by the Notarians themselves, he was granted special privileges to help design Terra Australis once the ocean waters were removed from the valley. The Notarians had little interest in structures or devices outside of the Weirfortus Dam, the Lu'Tythis Tower, and a few others. It was Wyrlyn and his apprentice, Irluk, who developed the rest."

"His apprentice?" Thorik asked.

"No interruptions!" Bryus ordered. "Wyrlyn and Irluk created magnificent structures and enchanted items that survived long after the Mountain King War and the murder of most of the Notarians."

Thorik and Avanda were shocked at the comment but a swift open hand from the storyteller alerted them to remain silent.

"After the war, Wyrlyn and Irluk went their own ways and began teaching others in their own methods of controlling the forces around them. Irluk took on a spiritual view of these forces, realizing that nature's energy was not a series of random elements, but life-umbued sources to tap into. She created a new thought and practice of casting spells, which allowed those not as privileged to still perform E'rudite-style acts. Her followers became known as Alchemists."

Avanda smiled at the newfound knowledge. Thorik, on the other hand, was starting to understand where the story was leading, but was unsure how it would get there.

Flailing his arms around, Bryus continued. "Two separate cultures evolved. The E'rudites, who believed the powers should only be accessible to those few who have been taught over countless years to control them with disciplined techniques, and the Alchemists, who believed that all people should benefit from nature's powers. A deep chasm of disagreement and resentment grew between them until it exploded in a war between the two. But unlike any other war, this one affected time and space. It tore at the fabric of all things they had learned to control. The Govi Glade was never the same after that battle."

"The battle may not have lasted long in their time, but it lasted over a thousand years for the rest of Terra Australis. As far as I know, all were killed except Wyrlyn and Irluk. They continued to battle on, both being crippled and deformed from the magnitude of each other's attacks. Eventually, Irluk was removed from the living, but Wyrlyn could not fully eliminate her."

"Wyrlyn had suffered as well. Unable to mend his own deformed body, he traveled to the Dovenar Kingdom and found a host for his essence: a young princess with a child yet to be born. Wyrlyn allowed his broken body to die as his spirit implanted a second child within her."

Bryus finished his story. "And so, Ambrosius was born only moments prior to the original child, Tarosius, thus taking on legal rights to the kingdom."

Never one to hold back, Avanda blurted out her conclusion. "That's why Irluk talked Bakalor into letting us go. She wishes to finish her fight with Wyrlyn, who is now Ambrosius. They let us go so we could lead her right to him."

A moment of confusion crossed Bryus' face, followed quickly by a smile. He nodded approval at her comment, without giving away whether he had himself come to the same conclusion.

Thorik's eyes darted back and forth as he thought about the story and Avanda's keen observations. "Why didn't Ambrosius tell me?"

Relaxing his theatrical arm movements, the Alchemist sat back down in front of his campfire. "He has no memory of who he was as Wyrlyn. Only his powers prevailed in his leap into his new mother."

"Why didn't you tell him?"

"I did. He didn't believe me."

"If he didn't believe the story, then why do you believe it?"

Bryus' face twitched, and his half-formed smile made him look insane. "Because I don't have a better theory. Do you?"

Chapter Thirteen

BRIMMELLE'S ACT

Distant howls called to the thunderstorms and raging winds that hung tight along the northern mountain peaks, but the desert campsite was now still, all except for Brimmelle, who tossed and turned on the hard sand. The sleeping venue was bad enough, but what kept him awake was his mother's death and the disrespectful way of remembering her.

Thorik's obsession with the dagger, Varacon, was outrageous in Fir Brimmelle's mind. How could Thorik believe such fantasy? Especially about his own grandmother. Why couldn't the young man just accept her death? He had. Then again, Brimmelle still blamed Thorik for her death. Perhaps that's why the younger Num wasn't willing to accept her being gone. Thorik couldn't face the truth of his own doing.

Brimmelle finally sat up and looked around at everyone sleeping around the campfire. Thorik and Avanda slept quietly, unlike Bryus, who talked in his sleep. Grewen had fallen asleep while eating, as a handful of weeds still hung out of his mouth. All were oblivious to Brimmelle's insomnia.

"Thorik must accept the fact that she is gone," he muttered to himself as he spotted a set of small rocks placed in a swirling pattern near his feet. Assuming his nephew had placed them there to honor Gluic, he quickly disrupted the pleasant design. "Once he accepts this, we can return to Farbank."

Brimmelle sat and thought long and hard about his mother's death and what the right thing was to do about the situation. His conclusion always ended in returning home to let the villagers know of her plight. It never led down a path of telling his people that they had turned her into a hand-held weapon.

What a disgrace he would feel to tell other Nums that his mother was a twisted blade, which couldn't even carve up dinner properly. Gluic was a Num with a soul, not a piercing dagger. People would think he was out of his mind if he introduced them to his mother, the kitchen utensil. He might as well tell them his father was a spaded shovel and his grandfather was a doorknob. Where would this line of thinking end?

Brimmelle shook his head at the thought. "Unacceptable."

But what was he to do? "Thorik wouldn't give up on his quest to save her, unless..." Smirking ever so slightly, he constructed a plan to resolve the issue before him. "It's for his own good," he whispered, justifying his own thoughts. "Yes, this will be best for everyone."

With that, he tossed off the blanket and quietly walked over toward Thorik, stopping short near his gear. Reaching down, Brimmelle kneeled for balance as he slowly opened his nephew's backpack. Untying the top, he reached in and pulled out Thorik's coffer. Disappointed at the sight of the wooden box of worthless notes, he set it aside to reach back in for the dagger.

It wasn't long before he felt the cloths wrapped around spiraling blades. After ensuring Thorik was still asleep, he pulled out Varacon and unwrapped it to validate he had grabbed what he came for, and he had. Setting it aside, he stuffed the rest of Thorik's items back into his pack.

Lifting the dagger from the desert floor, he stood up and walked out of camp to find a place to hide it. He distanced himself from the camp, wanting to make sure that Thorik didn't find it while searching the area. Thus, he walked for a few minutes before stopping at the cliff, which overlooked a great void. During the day he would have seen the great Volney Lake valley, but the cloudy night made it difficult to see beyond the cliff's edge. This actually worked to his advantage, for the light would have allowed him to see how high he was, causing him to shudder with fear.

"He'll miss it at first, but then he'll come to accept that it is gone. We will then head home." Standing on the ledge, he raised the dagger over his head to toss it straight out into the blackness.

"It's about time." Bryus' voice resonated from the darkness before him.

The voice frightened Brimmelle. Losing his balance, he slipped and fell, dropping the dagger as his legs swung out over the ledge.

Bryus walked out from the darkness as though he was walking on an invisible glass which extended from the ledge. Calmly approaching, he watched Brimmelle kick and twist to pull himself back up onto the desert floor. "You obviously don't want Thorik to have Varacon, and I obviously want it. I suggest you stay quiet about giving it to me, and I'll forget that I saw you stealing it from him."

Brimmelle couldn't understand how the man was walking on air, but his immediate attention had to be on climbing back up on the ledge. "Don't you threaten me. I'll tell him what I want."

Bryus' cheek twitched as he thought about the Num's argument. "You are probably correct. So, to prevent that from happening, it would make sense to take Varacon from you and then allow you to fall off the cliff to your death."

"What?" Brimmelle panicked in his climb back up. Slipping in his haste, he caught himself at his armpits. He now hung onto the ledge with his arms straight out and his fingers grasping onto rocks, just inches from the dagger. "How dare you! I'll tell him everything."

Bryus walked directly over him and placed the bottom of his foot on top of the Fir's head, slowly pushing him down off the cliff. "Thank you for warning me of your planned actions."

"If I go, I'm taking the dagger with me." Brimmelle quickly slid one of his hands out and grabbed the hilt of the blade. But in doing so, he lost his grip on the ledge and slid off the cliff.

Bryus stomped his foot forward onto the Num's free hand, which was scratching the desert floor as Brimmelle fell toward his death. The Alchemist's weight, however, was enough to hold the Fir's hand firmly onto the ledge as Brimmelle's feet dangled below. "We can't have that now. I really must have Varacon."

Hanging from one hand under Bryus' foot, Brimmelle held the other hand out with the dagger on display. "I'll make you a deal."

"Excellent! You're in such a suitable position to do so."

Brimmelle's hand was in terrible pain from being crushed, even though he knew he had to ignore it. "Help me back up to the surface… and then safely to camp, and I'll give you Varacon. I won't tell Thorik anything about the dagger. I haven't seen it. And to be honest, I never want to see it again."

"Deal." Bryus removed his foot, allowing Brimmelle to fall.

The scream and fall were short, as the Num fell to an outcropping of rocks just below his previously dangling feet. Falling flat and then taking in a deep breath, Brimmelle watched the Alchemist walk down steps that didn't exist. Once he arrived on the outcropping, he reached out his hand for the dagger, which was grudgingly given to him.

Brimmelle rolled to his knees and then stood up. "I don't understand. Why do you want it?"

"It's old magic. There is so little of it left."

"Old magic?"

Bryus inspected the dagger closely with his eyes and fingertips. "Yes, this is history. It is more valuable than any of us. We are but a blink of an eye. This, my little Num, is a true legend that is timeless. It will exist long after we are gone."

Chapter Fourteen

SEARCH FOR GLUIC

Thorik opened his eyes as the sun began to rise and turn the mountains to deep shades of red with veins of black. The mountain storms had moved on and left pockets of fog clinging to small valleys. It was a beautiful view to wake up to. All was peaceful and seemed right, except for an odd red light pulsing in the distance.

Rolling to his side, Thorik stretched his back and neck before preparing to investigate the red light. However, his plans changed when he noticed his weathered backpack. The sight caused him to sit up quickly and his eyes to grow abruptly large with concern.

Brimmelle stoked the fire in order to warm himself up. "What's the matter?"

Thorik grabbed his pack, opened it quickly, and looked inside. "Someone has been in my gear."

"What makes you say that?"

"It wasn't tied correctly."

"You have a specific way you tie it?"

"Yes."

"You must have just been tired last night and did it wrong."

"No, I've never tied it differently." Thorik reached into his pack to move things around. "And items are out of place."

"Thorik, things shuffle around as we walk."

"True, but I reset them every night before I sleep. I set everything I have in a specific place." Pulling out the coffer, he opened it up to ensure his notes from the travel were still inside. They were. Then he pulled out one thing at a time and inspected it. He found no damage, but something was missing.

Frantically, Thorik emptied the remaining contents and searched the surrounding ground. "Where is it?"

Brimmelle kept his eyes on the fire. "Where's what?"

"Varacon! Where's Granna?"

Never looking at his nephew, Brimmelle fired back a planned response. "We've been through this. Your grandmother is dead. She's gone. Accept it."

Thorik was rattled. "Uncle, I'm serious. The dagger is gone. Someone has stolen it."

"For what purpose?" his uncle asked.

Thorik didn't have an answer as he looked within every cloth and under his own bedding for the dagger.

"When was the last time you saw it?"

Thorik extended the search to the rest of the camp and around the bedding of Grewen and Avanda, waking the younger Num, but not the giant. "I know it was here last night."

Grewen stayed in his relaxed slumber while Avanda stretched and blinked her eyes in the morning light.

"How do you know?" Brimmelle asked. "I didn't see you take it out."

"Well, I did. And I recall having it last night. In fact, I remember feeling it under its protective cloths before I placed it in my pack last night."

Avanda yawned and rubbed her eyes as she began listening to the conversation.

Brimmelle made his way over to Thorik's gear, secretively tossed a few things inside of his backpack, and then walked over to Thorik, who was attempting to roll the sleeping mognin off his bedding to check underneath it. Brimmelle lifted the pack near Thorik. "Is this it?"

Thorik turned with excitement and grabbed at the pack. Inside, he felt a dagger's hilt and blade under several layers of cloth. "You found it, Uncle!" Pulling it out, Thorik tossed off the cloth layers to reveal one of his throwing daggers, which he used to hunt. The sight of it crushed him.

Brimmelle patted him on the back. "It appears that you lost it during yesterday's travels."

Thorik turned back to see the long desert path they had traveled. "Then we need to go back."

"Not likely. Even if we did, the wind has prevented us from retracing our footsteps. If we walked just a few yards from our original path, we would easily overlook it. It would be a wasted journey."

"No! We can't give up on her."

"We didn't. She is in a better place. We have to accept that fate has taken her from us, and now we must move on."

By this point, Avanda was up and looking for the dagger as well. Trying to push Grewen on his side to see if he was sleeping on it, she called over to Thorik. "I'll help. Don't worry. We'll find it."

Grewen eventually rolled to his side, allowing the Nums to check his bedding. A few live scorpions and a small lizard escaped from under his robe after the movement, but the mognin himself never fully woke up.

"I can't give up that easily." Turning from his uncle, he continued to pull the campsite apart in his search. However, after another hour of searching the camp and the surrounding area, Thorik eventually fell to his knees. He had failed to protect his grandmother. "I should have looked beneath the dagger's wrappings to ensure it was Varacon. How could I be so irresponsible?"

Fir Brimmelle puffed up his chest with a deep breath, much like he used to do before teaching his flock the daily sacred writings. "You and I have had this conversation before. You continue to keep your head in superstitions and unnatural beliefs instead of the solid and proven words of the Mountain King. Perhaps this will wake you up and force you to focus."

A slight grin crept into Fir Brimmelle's mouth as he watched the look of defeat grow on Thorik's face. Turning from his nephew in order to hide his satisfaction, he walked away to collect his own items for traveling. The sooner they left the camp, the less likely Thorik would change his mind and start looking for the dagger again.

Covering his face with his hands, Thorik was too deep in grief to fully pay attention to the Fir's words. The cool morning air finally registered on his body, causing him to shiver as he started to cry.

Avanda had listened to enough of his conversation with Brimmelle to understand what had happened. Seeing Thorik mourn the loss of Gluic, she approached him and covered his back and shoulders with a blanket before leaning over and hugging him. "I could have sworn you had it last night," she said softly to herself.

"I can't believe it. She's gone," Thorik finally whispered in disbelief.

"I know." Avanda's voice was kind and gentle.

"I'm responsible. She'll be forever entrapped in a dagger, lost in the desert."

Avanda thought about the issue as she leaned her head up against him. "What if she can help us find the dagger?"

A confused look crossed his face, warranting her to elaborate.

"What if she can venture a distance from the dagger? Last night, Bryus was telling me how souls are trapped in objects. Some enchanted items embed souls, while others act as portals. Because of Varacon's ability to absorb her soul on its own, perhaps this one is a portal. We know she was stabbed, causing her soul to be captured, and we'll need the dagger again to release her. But in the meantime, perhaps it's more of a home for her than a prison. Maybe she can wander away from it."

Thorik listened to the intriguing idea. "She always was one to wander off."

"Right," Avanda continued. "Perhaps she continued to walk with us after you dropped the dagger."

"And how do you expect me to ask her where it is?"

Avanda's right eyebrow raised, as if it was a foolish question to ask.

But Thorik was still fighting off the grief of losing his grandmother and needed a slight prod.

Walking over to his gear, which was uncharacteristically scattered across the ground, she picked up his pouch of Runestones and tossed them to him. "It worked for us when we talked to the spirits in Della Estovia. Let's see if Gluic can do the same."

Catching the sack, Thorik immediately understood the plan, but was less optimistic about it. "You realize that this will only work if your assumption is correct, and she followed us instead of staying with the dagger?"

Avanda smiled at him. "I know. But we won't know until you try."

"Agreed."

Thorik quickly dug into his pouch to remove the Runestone of Courage before setting the rest near his feet. Closing his eyes, he held the ancient stone out and touched two of the three smaller external gems.

"What's going on here?" Fir Brimmelle asked. He had been preparing to leave when he noticed Thorik standing at the edge of the camp with the Runestone in his hands.

Avanda blocked his path. "It's okay, Brimmelle. I've seen him do this before."

The Fir attempted to sidestep the young lady, but he was quickly cut off. He could knock her down if he wanted to, but his desire was to interrupt Thorik, not hurt Avanda. "Thorik, this is the foolishness we just talked about. You must not take part in these rituals. They are against the Mountain King's beliefs."

His words fell on deaf ears as Thorik lost himself in meditation, while Avanda continued to prevent the Fir from reaching him. But after only a few more attempts, Brimmelle stopped trying. In fact, he stepped backward in disbelief.

Avanda turned away from the Fir to see what was happening. Extending from the third small gem on the Runestone was a thin ribbon of vapor as the light in the center gem glowed brightly. The darkness of the Della Estovia caves had hidden the vapor's view, but its purpose was now apparent as it circled Thorik and prevented any spirits within the ring. This had been why the souls of the underworld parted ways when they saw them.

Thorik extended his arms toward the prior day's path in hopes of seeing Gluic standing in the distance. Unfortunately, there was no one there.

"Hold it high over your head," Avanda suggested. "So she can see it. Perhaps it will lead her here."

Thorik held the stone as high and far as he could, while facing it forward. But again, nothing was to be seen.

Avanda ran over to Grewen to wake him up. "Get up! We need your height. You need to lift Thorik high in the air as a beacon for Gluic."

Grewen blinked his eyes a few times and smacked his lips as leftover desert weeds fell from his mouth. "What happened?"

"Thorik needs to be high in the air in order to signal Gluic." Holding one of the mognin's eyes open, she peered into it.

"Right now?"

"Yes."

"Can I get something to eat first?" Grewen mumbled.

"No," the Num, a fraction of his size, ordered.

Grewen nodded, sat up, and shook the sleepiness out of his head before standing up and walking over to Thorik. Stretching one last time, he scratched his chest and asked for the purpose again. "Why am I doing this?"

Avanda was taking charge of this situation. "Just pick him up!"

"Whatever you say, little one." And with that, he grabbed Thorik with his massive oversized mognin hands and raised him high into the air as though he were a torch.

Thorik concentrated all of his efforts into the gem as the light in the center shined brighter against the sun's morning gleam. Prying one eye open, he looked out at the desert to see his grandmother or any other sign of her existence. If not her spiritual vapors, a reflected shimmer from the Varacon blade itself would more than suffice.

Avanda watched intently, changing views from the desert to Thorik, waiting for a sign from either.

Nevertheless, neither of the Nums could see anything out of the ordinary. It was nothing but dry lands and weeds.

Several minutes went by before Grewen spoke up again. "Avanda?"

"Yes?" Avanda responded quickly with renewed excitement. "Do you see her?"

"I believe so."

Avanda tried to force her eyes to look harder. "How can that be? Nums have much better vision than mognins."

"That may be true, but sometimes it's less about your eyesight and more about where you look."

Looking at the giant, she followed his line of sight toward the smaller second campfire where Bryus was still sleeping. Sitting near him was the translucent figure of an elderly lady placing small rocks in swirling patterns."

"Gluic!" Avanda screamed with delight.

Thorik quickly panned down from Grewen's hands to Avanda and then to his grandmother. He was immediately overjoyed, and in doing so, he lost his complete concentration on the Runestone. She was suddenly invisible again.

"Set me down!" Thorik yelled as his excitement got the better of him.

"Up, down, make up your mind," Chuckling, he set Thorik back on the ground.

Running over to Bryus' camp, Thorik held out the Runestone to allow them to see her once more.

"Stop!" Fir Brimmelle ordered. "This is wrong. It is blasphemy to bring the dead back to life. We cannot do this without corrupting our morals."

"She isn't dead!" Thorik fought back.

"She is!" Brimmelle yelled louder. "Even if her soul is adrift and here with us, it is not normal to be conversing with it. This is to be shunned and feared, and not attempted. This is wrong!"

"Why would we fear Gluic?"

"It's not just my mother. You have no idea what you are unleashing with that Runestone. Demons and other evil might be freed to cause us harm in your efforts to speak with the dead. These are not trivial things we talk about, for your knowledge has no more wisdom than mine on what gateways you may open and what dangers can come of this."

"Then let's ask Gluic if it is safe."

"If it is your grandmother. When you start playing with the un-known, you are easily misled into believing what you want, even if it's not real. She could be a beast from Della Estovia in disguise."

"But she isn't."

"How do you know, Thorik? Prove these facts to me, right now."

Thorik started several sentences to do just that, but stopped each time during the first words. "I can't prove this any more than you can."

Brimmelle's face showed signs of being fatigued from the fight. No longer did he attempt to intimidate. Instead, he begged Thorik in a genuinely sincere manner, which was uncommon for the uncle. "Then why take the chance? Why risk this? My mother is dead. Let her rest in peace. I'm asking you to respect your grandmother, as well as her son. If this was your mother, I would grant this to you if you so asked." Brimmelle shook his head slightly as he continued. "Don't contact her again. Please. I can't bear it."

Thorik's natural instincts were to stand up to his uncle. But mem-ories of Bakalor tugged at the Num each time he summoned the courage to say something. It was as though he were fighting against both Brimmelle and the demon. All the fear and self-doubt that he had worked so hard to rid himself of suddenly reappeared. Bakalor's wrath and curse were still affecting his judgment, despite being free of Della Estovia.

Avanda looked at Thorik and waited for him to activate the Rune-stone, regardless of his uncle's words. But he lowered the stone and glanced at the newly awoken Bryus before turning from the sight. Reaching around his waist, Avanda accompanied Thorik back to the mess he had made at the main campsite.

"Thank you," Brimmelle said softly to Thorik as he watched them walk away. Turning back to Bryus, he could see the man was impressed with the Fir's ability to prevent the finding of the dagger in the Alchemist's gear.

CHAPTER FIFTEEN

PYRAMIDS

Thorik's Log: 10th day of the 7th month of the 650th year.

Gluic is gone. I have lost her in the desert, and now our journey has come to an end. Today we will reach the City of Trewek, home of the Ov'Unday, and rest before we make our long trek back to Farbank. War is coming to this land, and we should leave before it sweeps us away with it. The only thing we have left to offer the kingdom is the Spear of Rummon, which I would gladly give to Ambrosius if I should ever be so lucky to see him again. Perhaps he will visit Farbank a second time, but this time under better conditions.

Thrusting up out of the center of a massive sinkhole along the dry desert mountainside, a city of rich brown and green bamboo towers appeared before them. Deep below the desert, surface water rushed out from underground caverns into the sinkhole, flowing past the many green vegetative islands that connected the city towers together through a series of creatively engineered bamboo bridges. Plant life grew with vitality in the humid environment that filled the sinkhole and the surrounding caverns.

Even though the recessed waterway was several hundred feet below the desert floor, the city was prominently displayed above the surface with dark brown towers covered in thick vines. The towers were giant bamboo stalks nearly half a thousand feet high, and multiple holes in the sides allowed light into the hollow center.

Above the city, on the desert floor, were nearly a hundred white tetrahedron pyramids placed in a circle surrounding the sinkhole opening. Each of these three-sided structures was set several hundred feet from the opening and stood twice the height of Grewen. All had markings of the Ov'Unday and a doorway on the only completely vertical wall, which faced the center of the sinkhole. The other two walls of the pyramid angled down into the desert floor, much like a two-sided tent would if the front side was raised and the back side touched the ground.

Grewen approached the closest structure along their path and started reading the carved markings. For several minutes he inspected the door, which was large enough to drive a wagon through. Stepping back away from it, he shook his head. "This is not our way in."

Bryus walked up to the sand-pelted doorway. "Well crafted, although I've seen better. It wouldn't take too much to unlock it."

"No, it's only a distraction." Grewen calmly turned away from the door and glanced back and forth at the other pyramids on either side of the current one. "We'll find the actual entrance. I suppose it doesn't matter which way we work our way around. The odds of finding the right one are the same."

Brimmelle scoffed at the comment. "I thought your people were open and trusting. Why the locked doors and all these games?"

"Trewek is isolated out here, and it's only a few days from Corrock. It is wise to keep the Del'Unday from being tempted to attack."

By this point, Bryus was working on a spell to cause the stone slab of a door to slide open. His interest was less about entering and more of testing his own knowledge.

After giving the door a half-hearted push, Brimmelle dusted his hands free of sand. "Why didn't they construct a wall instead of these games of misrepresentation?"

"Walls have a way of working both ways. They keep others out, and you can also become your own prisoner. It simply isn't the Ov'Unday way."

"The Ov'Unday way? You say that as though it is superior to all other ways. From what I've seen, you are far from it. Your hygiene, for starters, is far less than exemplary."

Grewen grinned at the Fir's misguided perception. "It's not surprising that you would take it that way. You tend to fear what you don't understand."

"Fear?" Brimmelle challenged the notion. But before he could continue, Bryus interrupted him.

Bryus had just stepped back away from the pyramid. "Success! It's unlocked." He was obviously pleased with his skills of deduction. "Ingenious design. It took me several attempts to crack it. I would assume most Del'Unday wouldn't have a chance."

"This is not a good door to enter Trewek," Grewen informed them. "We must be patient and find the proper one, which is connected to the ramp below, leading us down to the city."

Pushing the heavy stone double doors open with a wave of his hand and a few verbal magical commands, a ramp appeared before Bryus. It led down under the desert floor and then turned to the left.

Curious, Avanda grabbed Thorik's hand and led him down to the bend in the ramp. They found that the underground hallway abruptly ended with a fall hundreds of feet to the cavern's floor.

"Grewen, I'm confused," Thorik called back to Grewen, who remained at the doorway.

The giant grinned. "What doesn't add up this time, little man?"

"Why would they build this pyramid if this wasn't a real entrance? It's only a decoy, with no safe way down."

"But it is an entrance." Grewen chuckled at the Num's confused look.

"You told us this wasn't our way down to the city," Thorik replied as Avanda and he walked back up and exited the pyramid.

"That is correct. As you can see, this path ends with a fall to our deaths."

"Now I'm more confused than before. Why am I not understanding you?"

"Thorik, you're going to find out in life how important it is to ask the right questions, not just the first one that you think of. Most people ask questions and resolve that the answer they get is the answer they were looking for. But, in fact, it isn't. If you're confused about the answers, perhaps it is best to ask a more specific question."

Thorik thought about this for a few moments. "What is the purpose of these pyramids?"

Grewen grinned. "Excellent question, little man. All of these pyramids are an entrance to Trewek. However, only one of them is used at a time. This prevents outsiders from quickly approaching and attacking. And to ensure the secret of which one is the valid entrance, a different pyramid is periodically selected."

"How do they change from one pyramid to the next?"

"The ramp in the cave below us is frequently moved so that it fits up tightly to the bottom of a ramp inside one of these pyramids."

Thorik glanced back down the ramped hallway. "So this is an entrance, just not our entrance at this time."

Grewen nodded as he headed to the next pyramid. "So we need to find out which one is attached to the movable ramp. It will take some time to review each and every pyramid, but patience is a virtue."

"How can we help?" Thorik asked.

"Can you read ancient Ov'Unday script?"

"No."

"Then I think you'll have to be patient with me."

Avanda didn't care for the idea of slowly walking all the way around the city, checking each of the nearly hundred pyramids one at a time. There had to be a faster way. "How about if we went to the edge of the sinkhole and looked inside to see where the lower ramp fits up to the pyramids?"

"Be my guest, little one. It might just keep your urge to be active under control. And who knows, there is always a chance it may help." The giant gave her a slow wink to send her on her way.

Avanda smiled proudly at Thorik. She loved being the developer of a great idea. Grabbing Thorik's hand again, she led him toward the rich brown and green towers rising from the distant sinkhole. The hard, flat, tan desert of the immediate area was an extreme contrast to everything in the sinkhole.

Meanwhile, Bryus had climbed up toward the top of the pyramid as he looked for additional writings. "Ovlan," he yelled back down to the party. "She helped create these structures."

Grewen looked up into the blistering sun before replying. "The Nums are heading toward the sinkhole. I'm going to investigate more pyramids to determine which one leads us safely down."

Bryus squinted out toward the sinkhole and the spires rising from within it. "Nothing of interest out there. I'll go with you. I've read these writings before."

The idea of looking down into the sinkhole was far from appealing to Brimmelle. His ankles and knees tingled and became weak at just the idea of looking down over the sinkhole's ledge. "Agreed. I'm not heading out there. I'll stay here with you."

"Excellent," Bryus fired back sarcastically. "Your complaining will surely improve our effectiveness."

Chapter Sixteen

THORIK'S FATE

Brimmelle rested his back against the side of yet another pyramid while Bryus attempted to determine if it was the way into the city. Grewen had already moved on to the next structure to speed up the process, as he and Bryus were taking every other one. The Num had stayed near the pyramids due to his fear of heights. Just the thought of approaching the sinkhole made his stomach churn.

Hot and bored, Brimmelle closed his eyes and recited the ancient words from the scrolls he had lost so long ago. Standing in the pyramid's shade, he envisioned his followers back in Farbank all listening with great interest, hanging on to each and every glorious word he spoke. The Mountain King would have been so proud of him to see how he protected his writings. Oh, how he wished he could have met the king in person.

Over time, Brimmelle had started actually listening to the stories within the Mountain King Scrolls, instead of just reading the words. This revelation inadvertently caused his voice to fluctuate when he told it. It no longer was dry and monotone; then again, he was far from being a great bard. His pacing remained that of a drummer playing a death march.

The readings agitated Bryus, who was already struggling to concentrate on the ancient language. It was more difficult than he had let on. Working on a vertical side wall of the pyramid, he finally called out around the corner to Brimmelle, "Hold your tongue, Num, or I'll cast a spell to prevent you from using it."

The comment was inappropriate in Brimmelle's mind. "These are not just any words. These are the exact words handed down from the Mountain King. They are the foundation of the Rules of Order."

"I don't care whose words they are."

Brimmelle was astounded at the lack of respect. "How can you not care?"

Bryus never looked away from the glyphs he was working on. "Because I don't need you preaching to me about something I have no interest in."

"Well, you should. The Mountain King saved our land from the Notarians." Brimmelle walked around the corner to confront the Alchemist.

Bryus ignored him. "Good for him." His response was flat and unemotional.

Shocked at the candor, Fir Brimmelle puffed up his chest to defend his king. "Good for you, as well! If it were not for him, you wouldn't be free. We would all still be slaves."

"So you say."

"No, these are the facts!" Brimmelle corrected. "They were recorded and handed down generation after generation. He fought for freedom. He did this for all of us, including both you and I."

Bryus had hit his limit. "Listen, you pompous little fat Num. Don't stand there on your moral high ground and tell me what's right and what's not. You weren't there, nor was I. I don't owe him anything. He doesn't even know me, so how could he possibly have done anything for me?"

"This…" Brimmelle's hand shook as he pointed it at Bryus. The thick soul-markings across his body turned a deep shade of red as his blood accelerated through his veins. "This is why your land is at war. This is why you humans, Dels, and Ovs can't live in peace. You disrespect the one who has granted us all freedom. You disregard him and shun him from your beliefs. Even when we freely give you his words to live by, you ignore them. Your species will never survive. Eventually, you will all end up killing each other, and I hope you all end up in Della Estovia, assuming it really exists."

Bryus finally turned from his glyph. "You ignorant Fesh-faced blow-hard. Don't cram your beliefs down my throat and expect me to thank you for sweetening the dung you fed me. Your thoughts are old and outdated. They don't serve our land any longer. Your perfect world of the Mountain King doesn't fit into real-life situations."

"It did in Farbank!"

"Then go back to Farbank and leave us alone!"

"That's exactly what I've been trying to do!"

"Then we agree!" Bryus' voice was still raised and agitated.

"Yes, we agree," Brimmelle announced as though he had won the discussion.

A long silence followed as the two didn't know how to move forward from the point they had ended. Eventually, Brimmelle added onto his thought. "And because we agree, we need to get rid of the dagger."

Bryus' face twitched at the comment. "Listen up, little Num. By the fate of some odd fortunes, Thorik ended up with the enchanted Varacon dagger as well as the mighty Spear of Rummon. Either of which I would give my right arm for. But yet, the naïve Num doesn't tap into the powers of either of them, nor does he wish to give them up, while you wish to toss them away as though they are trash. It makes no sense!" Shaking his head quickly, he attempted to unscramble the thoughts in his head. "I will wait for the opportunity to take Rummon off his hands. Until then, I plan to keep Varacon well hidden."

The thick and messy eyebrows on Brimmelle's face moved inwards and down. "I may have convinced Thorik to stop trying to reach Gluic for now, but my nephew is known to change course and strive for his original plans. And if he tries to reach my mother again with his Runestones, he will again find a potentially deadly vaporish spirit next to you. The boy can be foolhardy, but he is not stupid. He will quickly realize that you have the dagger."

With eyes thinning, Bryus glared at the robust Num. "I plan to keep Varacon. You'd have to be ignorant or stupid to not realize this by now."

Brimmelle puffed up his chest in defiance. "Are you calling me stupid?"

"No, I gave you two options to choose from," Heavy arrogance filled his tone.

Flustered, Brimmelle didn't know how to respond.

Bryus grinned at the Num's frustration. "The key for both of us to succeed is to prevent Thorik from using the Runestone."

"How?" Brimmelle was apprehensive of the Alchemist's plans.

"I could make a spell to break his fingers so he couldn't hold them. Or I could just poison him and resolve the entire issue."

"I think those are a little drastic."

"That means so much from a Num who recently wished my entire species would go to Della Estovia. We're talking about one insignificant little Num, one that never grew any soul-markings. What's wrong with him, anyway? Is he diseased or something? I've never seen one of your species without your markings."

"He's odd, but not ill." Brimmelle was slightly embarrassed about one of his family members looking or acting wrong. He felt it was a reflection on himself.

"Pity, I thought he might pass away on his own, resolving our issues. And honestly, who would miss Thorik?"

Brimmelle didn't say a word. He never thought he'd be in a conversation where he would have to defend his nephew. As much as he grumbled about Thorik, he knew the younger Num was always trying to do good, even if it wasn't within the words of the Mountain King's writings.

Bryus continued after a surprised scoff. "You would miss him? You complain about him all the time. Your life would be so much better off without him. You could return home and all would be well. This sounds like too easy of a solution."

"You're not going to kill my nephew or any other Num if I have anything to say about it. Nor will we hurt the boy. It's wrong to even think about it. Your solutions are extreme. Does morality escape you completely?"

"Listen, most people are just in the way of progress. They're either idiots or naïve and exist only because they have a framework of civilization that allows them to. If they do their job, they can survive. Few can survive without it. Fewer still have the capacity to establish the framework in the first place."

Brimmelle crossed his arms. "Where are you going with this?"

"The masses are expendable. They are easily replaced and are a waste of my time. There are really only a few of us that make life livable for the rest. This Num folklore Mound King of yours—"

"Mountain King," Brimmelle quickly corrected.

"Yes. Fine. Whatever. He sounds to me like one of those few who could establish the framework needed for your people to live. But let's be honest, beyond this king of yours, there haven't been more than a few Nums that have made any serious contribution to these lands."

"I have!"

"You have spoken his words and tried to enforce them." Bryus chuckled at the thought. "If you hadn't done it, someone else would have been there to do it. You're just one more drone in the Mountain King's framework, doing what you were told."

"I'll have you know I play a key role in the upbringing of Farbank's children."

"Really? Do they all look up to you and come running down the street to thank you for changing their lives? Do they go out of their way to be with you and learn more from you? I seriously doubt that."

The words hit hard. Fir Brimmelle had always been very distant from the villagers. In fact, it was Thorik that would have met Bryus' description long before Brimmelle. "This conversation isn't about me. It's about preventing Thorik from finding the dagger."

"Really? I thought we were discussing the mating rituals of the Chuttlebeast." Bryus turned back to the glyph on the pyramid wall. "Get rid of Thorik and we solve the problem."

"I'm not going to allow you to kill my nephew."

"Well, I'm not getting rid of Varacon. Therefore, you'll have to destroy the Runestones so he can't use them."

Brimmelle had never considered the idea. "Destroy the Rune-stones?"

"Yes, unless they are ancient and powerful. In that case, I want them."

"They were found by his parent. It doesn't matter how old they are or who owned them, they represent the Mountain King symbols, which we live by. The idea of destroying anything in the form of a Runestone is sacrilegious."

Bryus shrugged his shoulders. "Then eliminate Thorik. There you have it. Two great options to keep that little brain of yours thinking for the next few days."

Brimmelle had no comeback. He had been outsmarted on every verbal assault he had tried. So, to avoid any further abuse, he slowly walked quietly away from the Alchemist and around the corner of the pyramid.

"Idiot," Bryus mumbled to himself before shouting out instructions to the Fir. "Brimmelle, bring me my water. I need a drink." He was confident that the Num was beaten down enough to take orders. Bryus always enjoyed adding a little salt into the wound.

Dazed, Brimmelle walked over to Bryus' gear and reached in for a water skin. But in doing so, he accidentally uncovered Varacon. Staring at it, he considered stealing it. But he hesitated as he thought about the Mountain King's words against such acts. Then again, he had already stolen it from Thorik, and then Bryus had blackmailed it away from Brimmelle. Perhaps this act was not stealing, but was instead an act of reversing Bryus' unethical act. The Fir's own ethics were in turmoil as he studied Varacon and questioned Thorik's and Bryus' thoughts about the dagger. "Do two wrongs make a right?" he asked himself. "I started this, and I need to end it." Snatching the weapon, he covered it with a cloth and hid it inside his shirt.

Eventually, Fir Brimmelle returned around the corner and handed Bryus his water.

"It's about time," Bryus said.

Brimmelle nodded and moved out of view with a slight grin on his face. "Fool," he mumbled under his breath.

"Idiot," Bryus said again as he finished deciphering the glyph. "Well, this isn't the correct entrance. At this pace, we should have it figured out by the time they change the ramp to a new pyramid."

"Bryus," Grewen shouted from two structures away. His baritone voice rumbled across the desert as he called out to the Alchemist. "I found our way down."

Chapter Seventeen

SINKHOLE

Avanda had led Thorik to the edge of the sinkhole's rim before realizing how thin the ground was near the desert's boundary. Below them, the ground tapered back underneath them and thickened as it approached the countless caves in the sinkhole's walls.

Thorik quietly absorbed the enormous size of the hole and the city within it. Built in the center of the opening, which was easily over a mile across, the towers were out of reach from any attack. The cavern below the opening went back several miles in every direction and was comprised of homes and farms.

"Amazing," Avanda commented as Thorik approached from her side. "It reminds me of the hollow insides of a gigantic pumpkin, but instead of pumpkin guts, it has green vines clinging to the cavern walls and ceilings."

Thorik chuckled at her assessment. It was crude, but mostly true.

They could see a long ramp under the far ledge as it extended in a wide arc around the exterior of the city. Creatively engineered bamboo columns held the sturdy bamboo ramp as it worked its way up from the cavern floor in an enormous spiral underneath the Nums. Towers and bridges between them prevented the Nums from seeing where it finally reached up and hit the surface of the desert.

"Hold my feet," Avanda quickly dropped down on her stomach and leaned over the edge of the sinkhole.

"Wait!" Thorik jumped for her legs to ensure she wouldn't slide too far over.

Grabbing the edge of the desert floor, Avanda stretched her neck down to see what was below them.

She found that the desert was only a few feet thick at the very edge but increased in thickness the farther it was from the edge. "Thorik, lower me to my waist so I can see where the ramp leads to."

"I don't think that would be safe."

"Come on, Thorik. Where's your sense of adventure?"

"It was pushed aside by my responsibility to ensure your safety."

Pulling her head back up, she shot Thorik a look of disapproval. "I want to go lower."

Thorik's instincts told him to stand his ground, but his ability to tell her 'no' seemed to have vanished. He suddenly felt fearful of causing conflict if he didn't do what she requested. It was a relationship that he had slowly been allowing into his heart and he didn't want to damage it.

Avanda changed her expression from a pout to a smile and coyly batted her eyes at him. "Please? It will only be for a few seconds." She didn't have to wait long to determine if her game had worked.

With a deep sigh, Thorik gave in and repositioned himself behind her to ensure she couldn't fall. Sitting down, with his legs straddling hers, he gripped the ground with his boots and held her ankles with his hands. "I've got you. You should be able to lean over far enough to see the top of the ramp now." He prayed that he would not have to use his left arm to pull her back up, for it hadn't fully recovered yet from being broken at the Temple of Surod.

Spinning around, she leaned over at her hips to see beneath them. Avanda allowed gravity to stretch her down as far as she could go. And there it was; the top of the ramp ended on a platform surrounded by two tall guard stations. These were the only military-looking structures in the entire city. They appeared to be designed to stop invaders.

"I can see it!" Avanda began pushing herself back up. Unfortunately, the ground she pressed against gave way, sending a shower of sand to those below her in the city outskirts.

"Time to come back up," Thorik shouted as he clung to her ankles.

Avanda grabbed a firmer hold and pushed herself upward. Again, the rocks and sand loosened up and fell away. "Thorik, you're going to have to pull me up. I can't get a solid grip."

Thorik repositioned his feet to pull her back up. "Try to push while I pull," he instructed. "And... Push!"

Thorik pulled as Avanda pushed, only to find she had loosened a large rock on which she had been lying. Her hands fell free along with the rock, just as Thorik pulled her up to safety on the desert floor. He then let go of her ankles in order to grab his own arm in pain. The sudden jerk to save her had shot thousands of tiny painful spikes through his injured limb.

But the safety was short-lived, as the ground under her began to break away. The fallen rock had caused the ground under them to loosen, and it was all starting to crumble apart.

Avanda screamed and swiveled around toward Thorik. However, she was too late, and her body fell from the ledge.

Reaching out, Thorik grabbed her wrist with both of his hands, causing her fall to snap to a halt. His legs were now spread out around the new opening, braced firmly on the desert floor that remained after the center section of ground had broken free. Thorik screamed in pain as his left arm took the brunt of the jerk.

Dangling below him, Avanda gazed hundreds of feet down toward the city. The only thing preventing her from certain death was Thorik's grip. "Help!" She reached up with her free hand to grab Thorik's arm and kicked wildly.

Residents of the city were starting to notice Avanda's high-pitched screams above and several rocks had fallen into a garden, just outside the islands and city towers.

Adrenaline raced through his body as Thorik dug his heels into the desert on both sides of her. He leaned backward and pulled her up slightly.

Avanda desperately reached out in an attempt to pull herself up. Her hand scratched and clawed at anything she could reach as she continued to thrash about and scream.

"Stop kicking!" Thorik struggled with her movements, as he himself was fighting his own pain. Her violent behavior was causing him to lose his grip as she jostled about.

Unfortunately, she was beyond reason. Her only thought was to grab anything to prevent her from falling.

And as Thorik had warned, her kicking caused her to slip out from his grip. It was a moment of horror for him as he felt each of her fingers slide away from his own fingers. The moment was devastating. He wished it away, hoping it hadn't really happened. But, unfortunately, it had.

Free of his grasp, Avanda's other hand grabbed onto Thorik's belt, nearly pulling it down below his waist. Thankfully, his legs had been spread out to span the gaping hole, where she still hung.

Thorik instantly grabbed her wrist with one hand and used his other to help pull himself away from the ledge. Pressing with his heels and pulling with his free hand, he slowly moved himself to safety while dragging Avanda out of danger. Again, pain shot through his previously injured arm as he used it without caution to save her.

Once they were a few yards from the opening, she released his belt and he released her wrist.

"I knew this would happen!" Thorik's agitated voice was shallow as he gathered his breath and clutched his arm in pain.

"You did not!" Avanda replied, struggling with her own breathing. Her emotions were still running very high, even though she was on safe ground. His agitated words caused her to reply in the same tone.

"Yes, I did! I shouldn't have let you talk me into it." Thorik was upset about the situation more than at her. In fact, he was furious at himself more than anything for doing something so foolish. He knew better.

Avanda had crawled slightly farther away from the sinkhole before picking her head up enough to question Thorik, who was now resting next to her. "I talked you into it?"

"Why do I let women affect me so?" he scolded himself, for he knew better than to attempt such a foolhardy act, especially with a bad arm. He had stood up to dragons, the undead, and other various beasts, but he struggled to stand up to those who he loved, always afraid of losing them in an argument. Nursing his arm, he continued, "I need to learn to stand my ground."

"Stand your ground? All I did was ask for your help. You could have said no if you felt it wasn't safe."

"I couldn't. Once you gave me that look and that smile..."

"You put my life in danger because I smiled at you?"

"No, you didn't let me finish." The adrenaline from the event was fueling both sides of the conversation.

"I don't have to. I love you, Thorik Dain, and you love me whether you're willing to admit it or not. I expect you to protect me from anything that can harm me, even if it's from myself."

Thorik blinked in confusion. "I tried to stop you!"

"Not very hard. I can't believe you allowed me to risk my life when you knew I shouldn't."

"Hey, this isn't my fault," he fought back. "You're the one that felt the need to lean over the ledge in the first place."

"Fine! This is all my fault." She abruptly rolled onto her side with her back to him.

"That's not what I said."

"You were very clear. It isn't your fault. Those are your exact words. Therefore, it must be mine."

Thorik bit his lip in frustration. "Avanda…"

"No, I will never coax you with my smile again. I don't want to be accused of causing you any more pain. I'll continue to learn enough magic so that I don't need your help, or anyone else's, for that matter."

Thorik sighed and rolled on his side, facing away from Avanda. "I don't need this. This is why I can't have a relationship right now."

"What relationship?" Her words were bitter and to the point. She had just severed any relationship that had been started.

"What happened to 'our love'?" he fired back at her.

"I'm questioning the same thing."

Bryus eventually made the trek over toward the sinkhole in order to notify the Nums that Grewen had not only found the entrance, but also been granted clearance for all of them to enter the city after speaking with the guards at the top of the ramp.

When the Alchemist arrived, he found the two Nums lying on the desert floor, back to back.

Bryus chuckled at the sight. "Must be some kind of Num ritual." A series of face twitches followed before he continued. "Either of you Nums want to join us? We're heading down to the city."

Chapter Eighteen

TREWEK

Passing the guard towers at the entrance, Grewen led the group down the long ramp, which rotated around the perimeter of the city. Easily twice the width of Grewen's wide shoulders, the ramp and its railing were designed for simplicity and functionality, as well as subtle elegance.

Despite its width, Brimmelle struggled with the ramp's height and fell twice from disorientation. During one of his bouts, he fell and landed against the trim of the walkway. Taking advantage of the situation, he pulled out the cloth-covered dagger and dropped it over the edge. The Fir watched Varacon unravel from the cloth and plummet to the muddy fields below as his stomach rolled and his head spun from the height. The deed was done. The dagger would be lost forever.

Bryus watched Brimmelle just lie on the ramp and stare down at the fields below. "Stand up, you old fool, and keep your feet about you."

Avanda eventually assisted Fir Brimmelle to his feet and then with the rest of his descent down the ramp.

The base to the entire lower ramp rested on a pontoon-style bamboo platform that floated in a wide and very deep water-filled ditch among the city's farms. This ditch had been dug out in a perfect circle around the city and through the cavern-filled farms and fields so that the ramp could be rotated in order to line up with any of the pyramid ramps above them. A dirt path followed the exterior side of the ditch, as horizontal bars were embedded in the base of the ramp every few yards. It appeared to take hundreds of Ov'Unday to work together and push these bars in order to rotate the ramp to a new pyramid.

The fields reached back miles from the city toward the dull cavern walls. Various crops were in season, while other land was being plowed and seeded. They had carved trenches out to carry water from the underground river into the fields to water the land.

"Did you have any issues getting permission for us to enter?" Thorik asked Grewen as he gazed out at the festive city below them as the high water levels ran slightly over its banks.

"No. I have been here before. Nums are not feared, and Bryus looks too old to cause much trouble, even for a human. Had he been a Del'Unday, we surely would have been rejected."

As the travelers made the long walk down, they observed the city and its surroundings. The city itself was a marvel to behold. Grand bamboo towers rose hundreds of feet in the air; several even extended above the desert floor in the center of the opening. Walkways between them resembled branches, while bridges between the islands contained creative open and covered bamboo designs.

Rising out through the openings and above the desert surface, the tallest towers had been designed to capture the sun's rays and send them down the center of the enormous shafts below the desert floor before dispersing them to meet the city's needs. Bright arrays of light beamed out of well-planned holes within the towers, coating the subterranean fields with the rich sunlight they needed.

Farther away from the sinkhole opening, fewer plants existed. The far walls of the sinkhole were bare, aside from a littering of cave holes, some carrying water into the city area, some carrying the water out. Many of the caves did neither.

The aroma of freshly baked goods and sweet fruits filled the air. Low-pitched water-chimes gave the entire city a background noise that put everyone at ease. These pleasant, soft-sounding metal water-chimes were periodically accompanied by a few higher-pitched wind-chimes. The native music was calming and relaxing. Even Brimmelle was able to walk the lower section of the ramp without gripping tightly onto Avanda's hand.

Once they reached the bottom, they worked their way through the farming community toward the central city. The Ov'Unday were a collection of gentle races. They consisted of many different species; some on four legs, some on two, and others with none as they slithered or flew. An endless variety of colors and skin types covered the many different types, which ranged from the giant mognins down to the mouse-sized quix with their six legs and large eyes.

Passing a garden, Avanda noticed a large rock had crushed a row of plants. Explaining the ordeal that had taken place above with Thorik and herself, she easily convinced Grewen to reach into the garden and remove it.

Children ran up and down the streets and played various games of tag, enticing Avanda to play as well. The adrenaline rush from her near-deadly fall from above had subsided, and she had slowly begun talking to Thorik again. Her interest in playing with the locals was deferred with a soft nod from him to keep up with the group as they traveled inward toward the towers.

Thorik watched the playing as they walked along before making any reference. "Grewen, these children seem very happy. It reminds me of Farbank."

Grewen nodded and grinned. "Yes, they are happy. But they are raised far differently than the children you know."

"Why do you say that?"

"You have restrictive ties to your children. Parents oversee and control their raising."

Thorik thought that it was an odd observation. "Yes. So?"

"Once Ov'Unday are capable of moving about, they become the community's children. All adults are now their parents, and they must protect all young and help guide them."

"That's ridiculous," Brimmelle spoke up. "They couldn't possibly all give the same advice. The children would become confused. They would have no foundation."

Grewen stopped a child running in the street. "Don't run near the river. It's overflowing, and the streets are slick."

The child looked out toward the river and then at Grewen. "I'll be careful." He then headed off to catch up with his friends.

"You see," Grewen continued, "We believe if young minds are exposed to many ways of thought, it stimulates their ability to reason and judge for themselves what is right and wrong."

Avanda was amazed. "I want to live here."

"Oh, no you don't." Fir Brimmelle grabbed her by the hand to ensure she didn't wander away. "This kind of thinking leads to chaos."

Thorik naturally wished to prevent any arguments. "If that was true, then it would already be chaos."

"To a degree, it was at first." Grewen recalled historical stories of the time. "A wise mognin named Trewek started our culture believing that a level of chaos would be required for us to gain the internal salvation we needed."

"That makes no sense." Brimmelle scoffed at the idea.

"You must be willing to be open to all thoughts and ideas before you can select the ones you wish to adhere to. If you only know of one option, you can never be enlightened enough to know if you are following the right path."

Brimmelle shook his head. "This is wrong and confusing for children. It is the parents' duty to have them understand the truth."

"Isolating them in Farbank to give them only one point of view prevents them from knowing if it is the right one." The mognin smiled with anticipation at the expected response from the Fir.

"But it is the right one. Why fill their minds with things that are wrong?"

"Wrong in your mind, but not to others."

"Are you suggesting we should teach our children in ways that we don't believe, even when we know they are harmful?"

"I'm not suggesting that you do anything. I'm only stating that we Ov'Unday allow our children to question everything and make their own decisions."

Avanda continued to watch the wonderful sights. "If I lived here and did something wrong, who would discipline me if everyone is considered to be my parent?"

Grewen chuckled. "I can understand why you would want to know such a thing before moving here. However, we do not provide discipline or punish others. Trewek did not believe in it."

Even Thorik was surprised by the answer. "So you can get away with anything you want?"

"Acting out against your fellow Ov is a sign that something is wrong. We come together as a community to try to help these individuals. We counsel them so they understand what they have done, how it has affected others, and how they could handle the challenges better in the future."

Brimmelle scoffed. "You mean to tell me if someone committed murder, you wouldn't throw them in prison?"

"We have no prisons. This is a concept that only the humans and Polenums share."

"Don't be lumping us in with humans." Fir Brimmelle puffed up his chest. "The human we have with us should show you our differences."

Looking back in order to see Bryus, the group realized the Alchemist was no longer with them.

"We need to find him." Thorik was disheartened that they would need to take the time to do so.

Grewen softly nodded to Thorik to ease his concerns. "He will find his way. We are nearing the bridges to the city. He knows you will plead your case to the elders to warn them of pending war. I'm sure he will catch up to us."

Crossing a bridge to the first island, Thorik was impressed by the craftsmanship and attention to detail on the railing. Not nearly the detail of the Kingsfoot carvings, but definitely more artistic. Nothing had been constructed haphazardly; it was all done to provoke thought and awareness of the surroundings.

They walked across island after island, linked by the bridges, until they arrived near the center where the tallest of the towers rested on one of the largest islands.

Grewen then approached a large sloth-like creature known as a gathler. This specific gathler stood before the entrance of the tower and wore forest green robes. Grewen's conversation with him continued for several minutes as he pointed at Thorik while explaining what they came for. With an official nod from both of them, Grewen turned around and walked back to Thorik.

"The next meeting of the elders is not scheduled for another month."

"What? We don't have a month," Thorik argued.

Grewen held up his hand to stop the Num from getting upset. "However, they will be making a special meeting here in a week."

Brimmelle was skeptical. "That seems a little too nice for them to do for a few unknown outsiders."

"True. However, we are the second request they have received in the past two days to speak to the elders of pending war. Apparently, there are others who know about this."

Chapter Nineteen

OV'UNDAY ELDERS

Thorik's Log: 18th day of the 7th month of the 650th year.

Today we will meet with the Elders of Trewek to warn them of Irluk and Bakalor's plot to take over the land. It has been a slow, restless week, as I can't for the life of me figure out who else could be here to warn of the same matters. The only advantage of this past week was the care I received for my injured arm from the locals. It's never fully healed from being broken at the Temple of Surod and is a constant reminder of the event and the stabbing of my grandmother. Bryus, however, is still missing. Then again, what do we need him for now that the dagger has been lost?

"Hurry up, Avanda." Thorik wished to be on their way to the elders' meeting. After impatiently waiting days for the event, he certainly didn't want to miss his opportunity to speak.

They were already running late due to Avanda's new interest in playing a local ball game. She had been playing the game for nearly a week and had become very good at it. As always, she became obsessed with the idea of becoming the best at it.

A large circle of brown and white pins was near the perimeter of the field of play. Most of the white pins were still standing up, while only one brown one remained upright. Normally played as a defensive game, where each team member stood near their pin to protect it, Avanda had bewildered her opponents by playing an aggressive offensive strategy. Leaving her pin unprotected, she ran around the field knocking over her opponents' pins with the ball. The one-on-one ball play worked to her advantage, as the rest of the players feared to venture away from their own pins, in spite of the fact that they had already fallen.

Keeping her eye on her next opponent, Avanda prepared for her next shot. "We're almost done," she shouted to Thorik. Then, taking her final shot, she kicked it past a young mognin and knocked over the pin behind him. "Yes!" she cheered with her hands in the air, followed by her team members quickly congratulating her.

"I'm leaving without you. I'm not going to miss the entire meeting," Thorik warned.

"I'm coming, I'm coming." She finished up the last few congratulatory hugs with her new friends and then ran over to Thorik. "Why the rush?"

"The elders' meeting has already started."

Keeping up with his pace, she ignored his concerns and skipped along in a carefree manner. "So? You're not scheduled to be the first to talk, anyway."

"I'm curious as to who else brings warnings about war and what they have to say about it."

"Why? This isn't our war."

Thorik shrugged his shoulders. "It might very well become our war."

"Why would anyone want to fight Nums? What have we ever done to them?"

"They don't think that way. They want to rule everyone, regardless of whether we have issues with them or not."

Walking past a market, Avanda stopped for a moment to take in the sweet smell of the freshly baked bread. "We could always live here. We're safe in Trewek."

"No one will be safe as long as Bakalor and Darkmere wish us harm."

Avanda turned from the bread and quickly caught up to him. "But if we leave them alone, they'll leave us alone."

"I wish that was true."

"You don't know that it isn't." Stepping up to a vegetable and fruit stand, she smiled and looked over the produce. The Ov'Unday tending the stand winked at her and handed her a small bunch of grapes. She thanked him and ran over to Thorik.

"There are others that wish to see us dead if we don't follow their ways."

Pulling a grape from the stem, she popped it in her mouth and enjoyed the sweet, rich taste. "Then we'll just follow their ways."

Thorik stopped and looked at her. "How can you say that?"

Plucking another grape, she held it out to Thorik. "These are fantastic. You should try one."

"Avanda, I'm serious. How can you say that you don't care?"

Realizing he didn't want the grape, she ate it herself. "Easy. I didn't follow Fir Brimmelle's rules most of the time, and nothing ever came of it. What do I care what rules others put in place?"

Thorik grabbed the grapes from her. "What if I said that you could no longer have grapes?"

"That would be mean. Why would you do that?"

"I'm not. Our new rules may say you can't have them."

"That's just silly." She quickly reached out for her grapes.

Thorik pulled them back. "No, you are no longer authorized to have them. Now, what are you going to do?"

Trying to grab them again, she missed as he moved them away. "I'm going to take them, anyway."

"Such acts under our new leadership could cost you your freedom or your life."

Avanda grabbed his arm in an effort to pull the grapes toward her. "Stop it, Thorik. I'm hungry."

"The new rulers don't care. You have one purpose, and that is to serve them."

Avanda let go of him and crossed her own arms. "I don't serve anyone." Her lips tightened, and a hint of a scowl appeared.

"You will have to if we don't all stand up and help fight this threat to our freedom."

Avanda stood silent as she gave Thorik an evil eye. The grapes were now high enough above his head that she couldn't grab them. "Enough with the lesson. I'd like my grapes now."

Thorik smiled. "See, it doesn't feel good to have others in control of you."

Avanda felt he was pushing the point too far. Stepping out, she quickly stomped on his foot, causing him to drop the grapes, which she caught in mid-air. Popping a grape from the stalk, she crushed it in her mouth. "I'm guessing that you would know how that feels better than I do." A sly smile faded onto her face.

After a few hops from the sore foot, Thorik laughed. He only wished that he were half as self-assured as she was. "Okay, you have your grapes, this time. Let's hope that I can always be allowed to give them to you. But for now, we must hurry on to the meeting."

"After you." She nodded with a silly smile, showing him grape juice between her teeth.

A few minutes later, Thorik and Avanda reached the tall tower where the elders were meeting. A crowd of Ov'Unday stood outside in the foyer discussing the various issues that had been slowly leaking out of the meeting chamber.

Grewen and Brimmelle were waiting for Thorik to arrive so they could all walk in together. Grewen calmly chatted with several Ov'Unday as Brimmelle impatiently leaned against a far wall, wondering what was taking the young Nums so long.

"Sorry we're late," Thorik said to Brimmelle.

"Wouldn't surprise me if you end up being late for your own funeral." Brimmelle moved from the wall and walked with them up toward the main door where Grewen stood.

"I don't understand why you even attended this with us, Uncle. You have no interest in Ov'Unday affairs."

"True, but I do have an interest in us leaving here so we can start our journey home. And you tend to say things that get us involved in events that we shouldn't be in. So, I'm here to remind you to keep your words to a minimum. Say what you need to and then let us be on our way."

Rolling his eyes in protest, Thorik shrugged his shoulders innocently. "That's all I plan to do, dear Uncle. I have no plans to get involved."

"Just like all you planned to do was help lead Ambrosius from Farbank to Kingsfoot. That ended up with us here, on the far side of Australis, with two dead Nums and a bounty on your head for escaping the Southwind mining prisons."

"Understood. I've learned my lesson," he said as they approached Grewen at the tower's entrance.

Just outside of the building's main doors was a faralope with reins and a saddle strapped onto its back. Only humans rode the two-legged faralopes, so this was an odd sight in the Ov'Unday city. It was then that they entered the building to address the elders.

The main hall was filled with various species of Ov'Unday disagreeing with one another with a civil temperament. In the center of them stood a tall human with blue robes and a Dovenar crest on his chest plate.

Thorik was amazed at the strength in the man's voice. The speaker didn't need to be loud or aggressive in order to be commanding. Inching his way through the crowd, the Num finally poked through and realized who the man was. Thorik had seen him before, once in the coliseum in Woodlen, another time in Southwind's city of Rava'Kor, and then again in the O'Sid Fields when Thorik and his party were captured by the Eastlanders.

"Truth be known, Asentar, high knight of the Dovenar Kingdom." The leader of the Ov'Unday elders spoke loudly, attempting to clear the air of side conversation so they could focus. This specific Ov happened to be a gathler, which resembled a giant hunched-over sloth in its form and slow movements. "Have you walked in here as a self-appointed liaison to your kingdom? Am I to understand that you don't even have approval from all the kingdom's provinces to speak on their behalf?"

Asentar's rugged facial features didn't flinch at the obviously devastating words of truth. "That is correct. But I do speak on the behalf of the kingdom's people."

"And for these people, you are asking for our assistance to fight against an aggressor who has neither threatened us nor caused us harm?"

"I'm asking for your support to unify our land. We are fractured and easy prey for those who wish to see us fall. And make no mistake; our aggressor is cunning. He only makes enemies with a few of us at a time to reduce his battlefronts."

One of the elder mognins entered the conversation. "But to support your efforts, we would have to go against our very beliefs. We shall not shame the teachings of Trewek, especially here in his namesake city."

"I am not asking you to give up your culture; I only ask that you be willing to fight for the freedom to continue to have it."

The mognin shook his head. "We will not fight."

"Then you will be killed or enslaved. Your civilization will be washed from this land, and your enlightened ways will be forever lost."

"You cannot possibly foresee this," the mognin replied. "You only speculate based on your fears."

"The Grand Council members have been murdered, the provinces within the Dovenar Kingdom have been taken over by local leaders, and communications with the Del'Unday have all but ended. We are now broken as a civilization." Asentar's voice was firm and powerful. His conviction was relentless.

The Grand Council had been the one hope for all species to work in peace. The notice of its destruction was grave news to the Ov'Undays. Their sense of safety within the city of Trewek suddenly was in question.

After allowing the elders time to absorb the severity of the situation outside of their enormous sinkhole, Asentar continued, "Tremors of war have been heard from the east side of the Guardians, Darkmere rallies the Corrockians, and the Terra King breeds hate into the hearts of mankind. We are on the verge of the fight for our lives, whether you care to participate in it or not."

"No, you have it wrong." Thorik had been so caught up in the moment that he had spoken up before even realizing it.

In spite of Avanda's smile at Thorik's outburst, Brimmelle shot Thorik an angry look for speaking up out of turn.

Thorik held up a soft hand and nodded at his uncle to assure him he would not go any further than needed, but his self-confidence wavered once he looked away from his uncle and over at the other faces in the room.

All eyes had moved to the Num, who now stood in the front of the crowd. It was enough to make Thorik feel unnerved, but it was the reaction of Asentar glaring down at him that made his knees weak.

"Truth is in question. Step forward and speak your name," commanded the head elder.

Thorik stepped cautiously forward as he waited for Asentar's approval as well. The Dovenar Knight was intimidating because of his size as a man, but more so because of the self-confidence that emanated from him.

Asentar nodded to the Num, giving him the floor to speak.

"Thorik Dain of Farbank."

The gathler elder leaned forward. "Greetings, Thorik Dain of Farbank. May truth be your ally. Do you have knowledge to discredit what we have heard here today?"

"Yes. I mean no."

"Well, which is it?"

"Asentar is correct about Darkmere and the Terra King. But what hasn't been told is that they are both the same person."

A moment of confusion rolled across the crowd and elders before the Num continued.

"Darkmere has been preparing the Del'Unday army to attack the Dovenar Kingdom, which will be very easy seeing that he is also swaying the kingdom's tactics from within the Dovenar walls disguised as the Terra King."

"How do you know this?" Asentar asked.

"We traveled with Ambrosius after the destruction of the Grand Council."

"Impossible. All of the council members were killed."

"Not all. Ambrosius survived, barely. I nursed him back to health. Then we traveled to Woodlen, where we met the Terra King. He escaped, but we caught back up with him later and prevented him from destroying the entire Dovenar Kingdom."

"If this is true, then why have we not seen Ambrosius?"

"Because he sacrificed his life to save the kingdom. I was there."

The gathler's voice came across sad when he spoke. "Truth be heard, he is truly dead."

"Well..." Thorik was uncertain how to reply. "Maybe not."

Brimmelle dropped his forehead into his palm as he hid his eyes from the embarrassment.

"Thorik Dain of Farbank, do you enjoy confusing the situation?" the gathler asked.

"No sir, just the opposite. I prefer things to be nice and orderly, but I'm finding out that real life isn't fitting into this mold."

"Then spit it out and tell us why you now question his death," Asentar said.

"I overheard Irluk saying that he still lives."

"The Death Witch?"

"Yes."

Another elder spoke up with a condescending tone. "Do you have conversations with Irluk often?"

Several in the crowd snickered until the gathler elder raised a hand to silence them.

"No sir. In fact, I've never talked to her," he replied to defend himself. "She was talking to Bakalor."

After a fraction of a second of quiet, a roar of laughter quickly erupted from the crowd. Grunts and snorts and the sounds of hooves hitting the stone floor monopolized the hall.

By this time, Thorik was feeling very sheepish. However, he noticed that Asentar hadn't changed his demeanor toward him. The man stood respectfully as he waited for him to continue.

"I hope you can support these claims," Asentar spoke softly to the Num before the elders began the discussion again.

An elder mognin stood up tall and clapped his enormous hands together to silence the crowd and regain control. The impressively loud single clap did its job, and the gathering quickly came to a hush. The mognin remained standing as he gazed down at the little Num. "You, Thorik Dain of Farbank, have had acquaintances with Bakalor?"

"You might say that, sir."

The elders cautioned the crowd to control their noises based on his answer before continuing.

"Little Num, do you know where Bakalor resides?"

"Yes, Della Estovia."

"That is correct. You obviously couldn't have met him unless you traveled into the underworld."

"I know. That's where he had his conversation with Irluk."

"Honestly, do you expect us to believe that you have traveled to the underworld and back without getting caught by Bakalor?"

"No. We were caught." Thorik was getting tired of this line of questioning. "And I overheard them saying that Ambrosius was alive. They're also working with Darkmere to cause hostilities among our people. They plan to have Ergrauth's army attack our weak defenses. And most importantly, Bakalor himself plans to return to the surface."

Thorik had everyone hanging on his every word until the final one.

Asentar shook his head. "Bakalor can't return to the surface, even if all creatures would perish in such a war. He simply can't survive in the sunlight."

"Apparently, he doesn't believe that to be true. Irluk and Bakalor are playing us like pieces in a game, and we're going along with it. So, the question is, do we allow them to continue, or do we take control of our own movements?"

The hall fell quiet as the crowd waited for the elders to ponder the Num's concerns.

Asentar watched Thorik as the Num stood firm to his words. Smirking slightly from one side of his face, the Dovenar Knight patted the Num on the back and winked at him. Regardless of whether he had convinced them or not, Thorik hadn't backed down.

One of the mognin elders finally spoke out to Thorik. "Proof! Evidence is needed. This is superficial conjecture. We don't know that any of this is true."

Thorik sighed. There was no way to validate his story.

Asentar realized that the elders had finally opened up to discussing the idea of taking a stance, if he and the Num could provide something more. "Tell me, then, if I could bring proof to this chamber, would you consider joining with us?"

The elders looked back and forth at each other before the gathler replied. "Truth be said."

Asentar was pleased with their answer. He knew the odds of having the Ov'Unday on the side of the Dovenar Kingdom were slim, but the likelihood had just increased. "Excellent. Then we shall return with proof."

"We?" Thorik and Brimmelle both said, confused about the knight's statement.

"Thank you for honoring my request to speak with you today." Asentar bowed to the elders. "I can only hope that I am wrong about the pending war, but it is a good sign that you are willing to discuss the option if I should unfortunately be correct."

"Willingness to discuss this topic does not ensure our support in your efforts," the gathler said.

"Understood, high elder. We will bring evidence back to substantiate our story or put an end to it once and for all. Is this acceptable?"

"Truth be heard, truth be said."

Nodding his head one last time in courtesy, Asentar turned from the elders and guided Thorik out of the main hall and into a busy foyer. Once there, he stopped and sighed as he peered down at the Num. "You had better be right on this. I'm taking a risk that your story holds water."

Brimmelle was stuck next to Avanda and Grewen in the crowd. It would take them a few minutes to fight their way through the crowd and follow Asentar and Thorik. "He better set that man straight!" Brimmelle complained.

"He'll do just fine," Avanda replied as they followed Grewen out of the meeting room.

Meanwhile, Thorik pulled on his pack's straps to straighten it up. "Why would you rest your success on me?"

"Because..." The knight struggled to admit the truth behind his reasoning as he pulled him farther from the room. "Because I have no other options at play here. I need the Ov'Unday to join with us before it's too late. You are the first one I've met that has overheard the planning of this new war. Seeing that I need evidence to convince the elders, you will help me find it."

"But I have no evidence. I only overheard parts of their plan. I am of no help to you."

"You were in Della Estovia?"

"Yes."

"Then take me there so we can acquire the proof we need."

"I won't be going back to that place! Why would I do such a thing to help you?"

"Are you not the same Num who I held at bay in Southwind along with the blothrud, Santorray?"

Thorik wasn't pleased that the knight recalled his face from that night in Rava'Kor. "Yes."

"You travel with dangerous companions."

Chuckling lightly at the observation, Thorik straightened out his pack again as he watched his companions arrive. "You have no idea."

"The two of you were arrested and placed in the prison mines, only to later escape."

"Again, you are correct. Are you wishing to arrest me?"

Brimmelle was shocked at the discussion he came upon. "Don't let him intimidate you," he said to Thorik, who ignored his uncle's comments.

"Perhaps, if I have to. But, more importantly, I will tell you that your life is most likely in danger. The Matriarch controls the province of Southwind, and she does not take kindly to prisoners escaping, and she took even less kindly to you killing her men, those she sent out to retrieve you."

Thorik shot a look at Avanda. "Lucian?"

Avanda recoiled from just hearing his name, recalling the man who had killed her pet and attempted to rape her.

"Yes, Lucian was taken back to the Matriarch. I know not of his fate, although if he still lives, it is a meager existence for survival. His return without Santorray and yourself most likely caused heated emotions. I'm sure the Matriarch has sent out a platoon of her best men to capture you, or even worse."

Thorik's pale skin faded to an even lighter shade as he realized his past was catching up to him. "Worse?"

"Yes, she may have hired assassins to eliminate you."

"If I understand your offer correctly, you'll protect me from the assassins as long as I take you to Della Estovia. If I don't, you'll turn me in?"

"Thorik, this is not about me or you. This is about saving an entire kingdom. We need to find some evidence to back up our claim that war is coming."

"I cannot lead you to Della Estovia." The Num glanced over at his uncle. "I couldn't even if I wanted to. We were lost when we were captured by Bakalor, and I have no idea how we escaped."

Asentar crossed his arms and scowled at the young Num, uncertain of Thorik's integrity. He had based his case on the Num's story, which was starting to lead to dead ends.

Thorik cocked his head to one side as an idea came to him. "However, there might be another way we can gather what you need without traveling there."

"And how is that?"

Thorik glanced at the crowd of Ov'Unday walking past them. It made him uncomfortable continuing the discussion with so many ears around. "Let's take our leave of this place before we discuss it."

Chapter Twenty

ASENTAR'S MISSION

A sentar reached over and grabbed the reins of his faralope and led Thorik and his friends out of the congested part of the city.

As they paraded away, Avanda hid a few grapes just inside Brimmelle's pack. She was curious to see if the faralope could sniff them out. To get things started, she bit one grape in half and fed it to the Fesh'Unday beast to tempt its taste buds.

Once they had left the main public market area, Thorik explained his thinking to find evidence. "You see, going to Della Estovia will only allow Bakalor and Irluk the opportunity to capture us, and even if we eluded them, they would know we know about their game. We will have tipped our hand and allowed them to change plans, if needed."

"Let go!" Brimmelle complained as he tried to shoo the faralope's snout away from the back of his neck.

Avanda snickered at the sight of the slobbery mess the Fesh'Unday was leaving all over the Fir's pack.

Asentar tugged on the reigns of his faralope to keep it from bothering the Nums. His mount returned to following the knight but occasionally veered off to chew on Brimmelle's pack. "What's your suggestion?" the knight asked Thorik.

"Would it not be better to let them play out their plot so we can be a step ahead of them?"

"It would. But I lack sufficient information to carry this out. The facts you have provided seems too general to establish a plan. Is there more that was said by Bakalor and Irluk?"

Thorik taxed his brain to recall everything he could from the terrible ordeal. "They talked about trying to take down the Lu'Tythis Tower."

Asentar shook his head. "Concerning, but I don't know how that remote tower plays into launching a war."

Warm, moist air blew across Thorik's face as he continued to reenact the scene in his head. "Ergrauth has started moving his troops to the Guardians, and then he'll move them to River's Edge."

"Already?"

"Yes. Ergrauth has also awoken the Winds of Conquest."

Asentar slowly removed his gloves and folded them while in deep thought. His movements were now slow and methodical. "Then he has found them."

"The Winds of Conquest? Do we really need to fear wind?"

"What? No. They aren't really wind. They are lesser demons. Twins, in fact, with the birthright to rule the skies above the battlefields."

"Why have I not heard of them before?" Thorik asked.

"They were captured a long time ago by a great hero, who magically burnt them down and placed their ashes in an urn. They were condemned to an eternity of sleep, never to be released or awoken. A spell was cast on the urn to prevent it from being opened. It was then hidden in order to prevent anyone from trying to revive them. It has long been said that they would be brought back to life in order to fight in the final war of Australis."

"So, they found the urn and have brought them back to life?"

Brimmelle fell back as the faralope grabbed his backpack again.

This time Avanda burst out laughing as the Fesh'Unday ripped a chunk of fabric out of the pack, exposing the grapes.

Asentar tugged hard on his Fesh'Unday's reins, freeing the Num and ignoring him at the same time. "Yes, they may have been revived, if what you heard was correct."

Thorik sighed at the lack of planning he was able to bring forth. "But this again changes nothing. We still need evidence to prove they are on their way."

"This changes everything," Asentar announced. "They will rule the battlefield skies when they attack us. Our arrows and catapults will be useless. Our air attacks will be for naught. We will have to fight them hand-to-hand. And without the strength of the Ov'Unday, we will be quickly overtaken."

"But..." Thorik quickly began to create an alternative plan. "What do you suspect happened to the urn after they were released? Would they have kept it?"

"What? The urn would be useless. It's possible that they may have saved it as a reminder of their imprisonment, perhaps as a symbol of Ergrauth's power to release them. Dels tend to be superstitious about those types of events. Why?"

"If we were able to find the urn, would that not be valid proof that war is coming?"

Asentar nodded in agreement. "You are correct, Sir Num. I must travel to the city of Ergrauth to retrieve this."

Thorik reached out and shook the knight's hand. "I hope our paths pass again someday."

"If we don't cross paths again in life, the stories told of our triumphs will pass long after we are gone. For it is not how long you live, young Num, but what you have done to change the world in the time you were given."

Asentar mounted his faralope, waved farewell, and rode off down the street.

Thorik watched the Dovenar Knight ride around the corner as he wondered if they would truly ever meet again. "Grewen." He then glanced up at his friend. "I'm assuming this is where we part ways as well. With Gluic gone, we must return home to Farbank."

Grewen smiled. "Nonsense, little man. I'll at least accompany you to the safety of the King's Valley before we say our farewells."

It warmed Thorik's heart to know he was not on his own to make the long trek. However, his thoughts quickly changed as he spotted Bryus walking down the street toward them.

Carrying a large pouch filled with items that bulged the fabric at its seams, Bryus was covered with mud up to his waist, and it appeared he had made no attempt to clean any of the clumps off. His sleeves from the elbow down were also coated with the brown soil. Despite that, the old man strolled down the street as though there was nothing out of the ordinary.

Brimmelle's face turned shades of red and his soul-markings darkened as he watched the Alchemist leave a trail of mud clumps down the street.

Thorik half laughed at the spectacle. "What happened to you?"

Bryus walked up to the group, handed Avanda his pouch, and then proceeded to shake his hands and sleeves clean of mud as the Nums covered their faces from the thick flying brown specks. "Nothing. Why do you ask?"

"Maybe because you look like you've been rolling around in the fields for the past week."

Bryus stared at Brimmelle instead of Thorik when he answered. "Why would I do something that insane? Can you think of any reason, Brimmelle?"

Thorik watched his uncle's face continue to turn a brighter red. "Why is he asking you, Uncle?"

"Yes." Bryus scooped mud from his side and tossed it onto the street. "Why would I be asking you?"

Brimmelle's response was cold and emotionless. "I don't know."

Bryus laughed at the response. "Hypocrite."

With tight lips, Brimmelle said nothing to his defense.

That wasn't going to stop Bryus. "What happened to your Rules of Order and sacred words to live by? Does that only apply when it's convenient for you or works in your favor?"

Avanda stepped forward and asked the obvious question, "What are you two talking about?"

Seeing Brimmelle stiffen at her question, Bryus stepped up next to the elder Num. Reaching over behind his head, he placed his arm over Brimmelle's shoulders before pulling him in tight against him. Mud slid down off of his sleeve onto Brimmelle's back, neck, and shoulders. "You see, Avanda, when people make promises to me while explaining how righteous they are, it annoys me. But when they go back on their promise and take it back away from me, then I get upset. And then when I notice them throwing it off a ramp into a muddy farm where it could take months to find, then I get outright vengeful."

Avanda looked at Fir Brimmelle for a response. "What did you do?"

"Yes." Bryus was overdramatic as he pulled him in tighter. "What did you do? Why don't you explain it to everyone?"

Mud continued to drip down Brimmelle's neck, under his shirt, and down his back. His clothes were stained with the brown mud, and Bryus made sure to wipe his boots off on the Fir's pants. "I made a promise which I realized I couldn't keep."

Moving his muddy hand off Brimmelle's shoulder, he placed it on top of the Num's head and wove his filthy fingers through his hair. "Yes, that is what happened."

To the surprise of the others, Brimmelle allowed the Alchemist to cake mud in his hair, as the Num steamed from the disrespectful and embarrassing event.

Brimmelle growled through his tight teeth and lips before speaking. "But the question is, did you find what you had lost?"

"I found mud, you fool. Endless rows of wet mud."

Bryus stepped away from the Num in order to scoop up a clump of mud from his leg before preparing to press it into Brimmelle's face.

Grewen had watched the scene with great interest, but the humor of it all was about to turn violent. Reaching down, he blocked the smashing of mud into the Fir's face. "Not here, boys. We will not bring violence into the home of Trewek."

"We're not done with this," Bryus snarled at Brimmelle as he took his large pouch back from Avanda.

"You are for now." Grewen grinned. "Our stay here is at an end. We'll pack our gear while you two clean up. As soon as you're ready, we'll head up the ramp and out of the city…" He paused and thought about it for a moment before continuing. "… after we eat one more meal."

Avanda laughed. "Always thinking with your stomach."

"Not always... Just when I'm awake." His baritone chuckle echoed down the street, leading their party forward.

CHAPTER TWENTY-ONE

ASSASSIN

With the city of Trewek behind them, the travelers walked west for days along the vegetative desert, which bordered the mountains to the north. Small flashes of red light flickered from the sparse tree- and brush-covered foothills. Always appearing as a single light near a hilltop, the red glow seemed to follow the travelers to the west.

"Do you see that?" Avanda asked Thorik.

"Yes, I've seen it several times since we left Trewek."

"What do you suppose it is?"

Attempting to see farther, Thorik squinted without any luck. "I don't know. I think someone might be following us."

Avanda followed his lead and squinted at the distant light. "Do you think so? Could it be one of those assassins Asentar told you about?"

"Possibly, but they are traveling in a very difficult way. It appears they are climbing up and down those sharp ridges in order to go from peak to peak."

The two Nums continued to watch the light until it faded from one location, only to show up at a distant hilltop moments later.

Avanda shook her head in disbelief. "How are they doing that?"

Waving the mognin forward, Thorik kept his eyes on the distant red glow. "Grewen?"

Slapping his huge bare feet onto the scorching desert floor, Grewen was enjoying the walk. "What do you see, little man?"

"It's a light up on the foothills that seems to jump from peak to peak in only a few moments. But I never see it leap. Instead, the light fades and then reappears at the next location. We're being followed, although I don't know what it could be."

Grewen glanced out toward the mountains. "A dragon? It could be flying from foothill to foothill and then give off a fiery blast upon the crest of each."

Thorik agreed with the logic. "Scout? Or is it spying on us?"

"It's more likely to be a scout, seeing that we have nothing to do with the pending war. And even if we did, Del'Unday are more likely to attack us and get it over with instead of watching us from a distance."

The flame faded as they all watched and waited for it to reappear. But this time it did not.

"Odd." Avanda kept searching the distant landscape. "It's as though it knew we were talking about it, so it stopped following us."

Brimmelle showed little interest as he walked past them to the west. "Coincidence," was his only comment.

The other Nums followed Brimmelle as they continued to peer off to the side to see the red glow again. Their interest quickly died off as the foothills showed no signs of life.

Bryus followed Grewen, who was following the Nums through the desert as it slowly became littered with cacti, short desert trees, aloe plants, and jagged rock outcroppings. Wind had carved horizontal designs and holes into the unearthed large rocks. Even with a slight breeze, the holes caused an eerie whistling sound.

"Do you hear that?" Thorik turned his head to hear it better.

Avanda stopped to listen to the wind flowing through the holes in the rocks. "I think it sounds nice."

"No, not the wind." Thorik motioned his hand for everyone to stop moving. This worked for everyone except Brimmelle, who continued to lead them home as he walked around the next outcropping. Thorik waited for his uncle's footsteps to fade off so he could listen for the sound once again. "I thought I heard a rustling from an animal or something."

Grewen thought little it. "These parts are covered with snakes, scorpions, and rodents."

Shaking his head, Thorik didn't accept the explanation. "It sounded bigger than any of those."

Grewen's tiny ears couldn't hear anything moving. "How big would you say it sounded like?"

"I'd say the size of a man," Thorik answered as a man in black clothing stepped out from behind the rocks where Thorik had heard the sounds.

"Thorik Dain?" the uninvited guest asked.

Thorik immediately felt intimidated by the stranger's knowledge of who he was, but also by the weapons he carried. "Who wants to know?"

Sliding two thin, short swords from their sheaths, the man spoke in a bitter tone. "The Matriarch. She has a score to settle with you."

Thorik slowly stepped backward. "I've never met her. You must be mistaken. What is my crime?" Contradictory to his own words, he knew that escaping the Southwind Mines would eventually catch up with him. In addition, the Dovenar Knight had warned him about the Matriarch's assassins.

"Crime?" the man said. "I could not care less. The Matriarch ordered your capture. That is enough for me."

Glancing over the man's shoulder, Thorik searched for the man's ride. "You should know that we have seen you following us for days. We've had time to prepare for your attack. And, as expected, you've fallen into our trap." Thorik stood up straight and firm, hoping to bluff his way out of the confrontation. "I will give you only but a moment to turn and leave on the dragon you flew in on before we release our plans."

"Dragon?" The man chuckled at Thorik, causing the Num's square shoulders to soften. "I know not of who you have been watching, but I travel by land, which is how I plan to return with you." Stepping forward, he raised the tips of his swords toward Thorik in order to caution the Num from any unexpected movement.

Not his dragon? Thorik's demeanor sank as he questioned what he saw. Is there a second assassin tracking us?

"Leave us alone!" Avanda valiantly jumped in front of Thorik. "We won't allow you to harm him."

Now, with both of his blades near the female Num's face, the assassin grinned. "Extra casualties are not a concern of mine."

Her eyes watched the sharp points of the swords circle her nose and lightly touch against her cheek. Swallowing hard, she realized that her move may have not been her best option to help Thorik.

Grewen stepped closer to the Nums to intimidate the assassin with his massive size. But the act only caused the man to bolt forward, push Avanda to the ground, and then grab Thorik. In the same motion, he swung himself behind the Num and placed one of his sharp iron blades on the Num's neck and the other near his gut. The man was incredibly quick.

Avanda shot back up, only to see the blade pull tight against Thorik's skin as she approached.

"Stay back," Thorik told her to prolong his life long enough to find a way out of the situation.

She did as he asked, but it wasn't easy. Her instincts told her to lunge forward and knock the man on his backside. Nevertheless, she followed Thorik's instructions.

Bryus looked the man over, only to find nothing intriguing about his attire or weapons. The risk of losing Thorik from the party actually resolved the issue of the missing dagger secret, plus it provided an opportunity for him to retrieve the Spear of Rummon. Therefore, Bryus stood idly by to see what would unfold.

Vowing not to harm others, Grewen had only hoped to scare off the intruder. Instead, he had escalated the issue. This vow had often put him at a disadvantage, for a quick bit of violence from a giant his size could easily change the outcome. One advantage Grewen had was his height, and with it he could see Brimmelle working his way back around the outcroppings toward Thorik and the assassin. Grewen needed to keep the man's focus away from Brimmelle's path long enough for the Fir to show up and grab him from behind, assuming he had the courage.

"Do you plan on killing all of us?" Grewen asked the assassin.

"If you choose to protect Thorik. However, the Matriarch's purse of gold is awaiting only one head, and apparently I was the first to find you, so it will belong to me."

Grewen's eyes focused on the man, even though he was tempted to glance behind him at Brimmelle's approach. "Are there more coins for your purse if you should bring him back alive?" His voice was loud enough that the Fir should have been able to hear the conversation.

"There are, which is why I've allowed him to live this long. But if any of you try to stop me, I will gladly accept fewer coins for his dead carcass."

Grewen patiently waited for Brimmelle to jump out from the outcropping and tackle the assassin, but he hadn't seen any movement out of the corner of his eye. Raising his voice, he again tried to tell Brimmelle what was about to happen if he didn't act quickly. "So what you're telling us is that you're going to kill Thorik right here in front of us... right now?"

Darting his eyes between Avanda, Bryus, and Grewen, the assassin thought it was odd that the only one showing any interest in saving Thorik was the female Num.

"If you'd like to watch." An evil little grin rose from one side of his face.

It was at that time that Brimmelle finally jumped out from behind the large rock and grabbed the assassin from the back. The act nearly caused one of the blades to slice Thorik's head off, leaving a long cut along the side of his neck to remind him of just how lucky he was.

All three fell to the ground and rolled toward Bryus. Brimmelle clung to the man's back as Thorik turned to face the assassin and grab the man's wrists. Thorik's arms strained and shook in an effort to push back the sharp iron blades from piercing his face.

Avanda never thought twice as she ran over to help subdue the assassin, but she found it difficult to reach him since she was sandwiched between the two other Nums. This issue didn't stop her from trying. Collecting a hand-sized rock, she grasped it as a weapon and began swinging it. Unfortunately, most of her attacks hit Thorik and Brimmelle by mistake.

The three continued to wrestle as Bryus stepped closer and watched with concern. "Watch out for the spear! It's irreplaceable!" As he tried to avoid Avanda's wild swings with her rock, he attempted to pull the spear out from behind Thorik, but the incessant rolling prevented him getting proper access to it. "Brimmelle, hold him still!" he yelled as he made another unsuccessful attempt to grab the spear.

Grewen had stepped over to the chaotic mess of flailing body parts fighting for dominance. Wishing to pull the assassin off Thorik, the mognin realized he would have to peel away Bryus, Avanda, and Brimmelle first. It wasn't an easy task to do while trying to avoid injuring them.

Wrapping his three fingers around Avanda's waist with one of his mighty dual-thumbed hands, he pulled her out of the mix.

She responded with one last attack on the assassin as she threw her rock at his head. This, of course, hit Brimmelle square in the back.

Setting her off to the side, Grewen grabbed Brimmelle with his left hand while moving the Alchemist away with his forearm. His other mighty hand swung forward to scoop up the assassin. Before he could do so, however, Avanda jumped back toward the fight, causing the giant to reach out and stop her. Inadvertently, this allowed the assassin time to make an attempt on Thorik's life.

Rolling Thorik onto his front, the assassin swiftly pulled his sword over his head to make a fatal cut into the Num's back.

Eyeing the Spear of Rummon as it sat in jeopardy of being damaged during the attack, Bryus lunged forward to push the assassin off of Thorik as the hired killer swung downward.

It was too late for Grewen to stop the motion, too fast for Avanda to conjure a spell to disable him, and too close for Brimmelle to not visually remember this tragic end to his sister's son with his non-forgiving memory. It would assuredly play in his mind every day for the rest of his life.

Just as the sharp blade began to puncture the Num's skin, the unthinkable happened. Bursting out of the ground, a crusted-over molten mass flew up, striking the assassin in his torso and arms. The heat from the object instantaneously vaporized his flesh upon impact as it arched over Thorik's body. The assassin hadn't even had time to scream before he was devoured by the heated rock.

The trajectory over Thorik led the molten rock through the assassin as well as one of Bryus' arms. Falling to the same fate, the Alchemist's right arm dissolved into steam and liquid from the flying mass. The nerves and arteries were instantly cauterized, and Bryus' mind had yet to comprehend the pain as he tried to jump out of the way.

Landing and then rolling to a stop, the heated mass paused for a moment. As it did, Thorik and his party watched as the spherical magma-filled-mass opened its enormous mouth, spewing inferno-temperature heat as it surveyed the damage it had done. Long, thin teeth extended from the outside as well as the inside of its mouth, as the red fiery blaze inside dried the surrounding air. Its underbite allowed an enormous amount of heat to escape his mouth even when it was shut, causing the view of him to look blurred through the vapors.

"It's you!" Thorik attempted to block most of the heat from his face. The Num was only shocked and not seriously harmed.

Upon that one comment, the mass lowered itself into the solid rock below, leaving a black scorch mark on the desert floor. It departed as quickly as it had appeared, taking the heat along with it.

"What was that?" Bryus asked as he stood in awe from the experience, having one less arm than he had a few seconds prior.

"Bryus!" Avanda shouted as she stared at the stub of an arm remaining. "Your arm is gone!" She rushed to his side to help, but once there, she realized there was nothing to do.

The Alchemist looked down at his missing limb. "Damn!" The pain from the unexpected amputation began to overpower him. Falling to his knees from the wave of agony, he started giving Avanda instructions to help him reduce the pain. His words were hard to understand as he tightened up his jaw from the horrific sensations he was now feeling from the remaining stub of his arm.

Avanda quickly grabbed the needed components and followed his instructions. Slicing off a leaf from a local aloe plant, she collected an iron bowl from his pouch. "Bryus, where did you get these things?" She looked into his pouch filled with an hourglass, empty jars, blades, and metal plates, just to name a few of the items.

"Who cares!" he screamed. "I got them at Trewek, if it hastens your pace!"

Avanda ignored the items and quickly mixed the plant's juices with some pollen that they had collected earlier on their journey, per his instructions. She then quickly began applying paste mixture to the burnt flesh on the end of his remaining arm, just below the shoulder.

"Awww!" Bryus screamed as she applied it, causing her to stop. "Don't stop! It will be worse for a moment, but then it will quickly subside."

She did as she was told and continued to apply the aloe juice as he yelled from the liquid's touch. However, within moments, she could see the agony in his face quickly drop, and he began breathing normally again. Avanda sighed. "Bryus, your arm is gone. What are we going to do?"

With the pain reduced to a tolerable level, the Alchemist looked at his now stub of an arm. "Actually, my arm has been gone for years. The one I just lost wasn't mine to begin with, and it surely wasn't the best one I've had." A clenched teeth light-hearted chuckle over his obvious pain showed he was fighting his way through it.

"Not yours?"

"It once belonged to a blacksmith from Spiritwater." He glanced over at his still intact arm. "Why couldn't that beast have taken the one I retrieved from River's Edge?"

Brimmelle had finished dusting himself off from the fight as he watched Avanda and Bryus. "Your arm is missing, and you're upset about which one it is?"

"I'm not missing my arm. It was destroyed," he spit back as a facial tic pulled hard on his cheek. The aloe continued to reduce the pain, but Bryus' temper was starting to show through as he began to fully rationalize that he had lost a body appendage. "If I was missing my arm, then we'd all be walking around looking for it. Or I'd be having sentimental memories about it, causing me to miss it. The arm is gone, and now I need to look for a new one again."

Avanda tilted her head at his last statement. "Again?"

"Alchemy is a very dangerous profession, my dear." He stood back up and readjusted his balance, now that he was missing a limb. "You'll learn that the only way to succeed is to try, and sometimes that means causing a few painful attempts until you get it right."

Brimmelle coughed. "She's had plenty of painful attempts, for sure."

"It hasn't been that bad. I just need practice and guidance."

"Guidance?" Fir Brimmelle pointed at Bryus, who was looking for objects to temporarily replace his arm until he located a new human one. "You want to take guidance from a man who has blown both of his arms off?"

Bryus spoke up without looking toward the Nums. "Not true. I only blew one arm off twice. The other one was eaten away." Bryus shivered at the memory. "Nasty story."

A sickly look crossed Brimmelle's face at the thought.

Avanda, on the other hand, was intrigued. "How do you put on a new arm?"

Bryus picked up one of Thorik's cooking spoons and held it up to his stub to see how it looked, but he wasn't impressed, so he tossed it back down. "The same way you put on a new leg or eye."

"A new eye?"

Swiveling abruptly toward her, Bryus pointed at his eyes, one blue and the other one green. "You don't think these are my originals, do you? I lost my first one while casting a spell to achieve my mastery of enchantment."

"I'm sorry it didn't go well."

"What are you talking about? The spell went perfectly. In fact, I received special commendations for ingenuity."

Chapter Twenty-Two

PRATTLE BOX

After ensuring Bryus was going to live, Thorik and Grewen approached the scorched circle of earth left by the molten rock creature. Tenderly stepping out onto it, the area under the toe of Thorik's boot cracked and sank down an inch. It was unstable, much like how Thorik felt at the moment.

They both stood there and stared at the ground for several minutes before Grewen broke the silence. "Do you know what that was?"

Thorik had been holding his hand to his neck in an effort to stop the bleeding from minor cut caused by the assassin's blade. He also favored one leg because of the injury during the ordeal. "Yes, I've seen it before in Della Estovia. It's most likely the red light that we've been seeing following us."

"I see, our assumed dragon following us from distant hilltops is really a glob of lava," Grewen said.

Thorik corrected him. "Grub."

"A grub of lava?"

"No, Grub. I think it's the creature's name."

"You've met it?"

"It's Bakalor's son. He was born while we were trying to escape." Thorik rubbed his fingers against his forehead. "It's difficult to recall the details. It happened so fast."

Bryus continued walking around the area to find a temporary arm which would last him until he found a live donor. Meanwhile, Avanda bandaged Brimmelle's cuts from his confrontation with the assassin.

Grewen pushed one of his toes down onto the location of Grub's exit, only to find the ground brittle. The pressure broke off shards of glass-like fragments for several inches deep. "Why would Grub be following us, and why would he be saving your life?"

"Saving my life? He nearly killed me," Thorik replied.

"No. It was an obvious attack on the assassin. Bryus happened to be in the way. And once you showed signs of being alive, he vanished."

Thorik hadn't even considered the idea. "I have no explanation."

"Thorik, did you make some type of pact with Bakalor to save the lives of Avanda and yourself?"

"What? Why would you say that?"

"Well, I don't know anyone who has ever escaped from Della Estovia, yet you did without any powers of an E'rudite or an Alchemist. And then, when your life was threatened, one of Bakalor's servants shows up and saves you. It's a question that needs to be asked."

Thorik was shocked. "Grewen, how can you imply such things, after what we've been through?"

"I'm not implying anything." The mognin grinned. "It's a fair question, which you are now avoiding."

"Avoiding? I'm not avoiding anything."

Grewen's response was light-hearted and slow. "Then answer the question."

"I shouldn't have to. You're my friend. You should trust me."

"I never said I didn't. It's only a question, Thorik. You're reading too much into it."

"If you must know, we didn't make any pact with Bakalor, nor Ir-luk. I have no idea why they let us go or why they have Grub following us. I can't for the life of me understand why they would protect me. I'm no one special. I have no way to help them, even if I wanted to."

"How about if you didn't want to help them?"

"What?"

"What if you're correct and they don't expect you to help them?"

"Then they are fools to let us go."

"No. Think about this. What can you do that others cannot?"

"Activate my Runestones?"

"That's good. Anything else unique that you do that most others don't?"

"I record our travels in my coffer...or prattle box." He quickly corrected himself.

The term caught Grewen's attention. "Prattle box?"

"Yes, that's what Bryus said it was. He informed me that he gave a set to the king's twins."

"Ambrosius and Tarosius?" Grewen asked. "I would assume he would have given it to them before Tarosius changed his name to Darkmere."

"I don't know. Are those the only twins in the king's line?"

"As far as I know," Grewen answered after a moment of thought. "Is your coffer similar to the ones he gave them, or is this actually one of them? Does it have any magical abilities? How did you acquire it in the first place?"

"Slow down. I have no knowledge of any magic it may have. Years ago, a stranger to Farbank gave it to me during his visit. His name was Su'I Sorat."

Grewen looked up from the Num to the Alchemist who was tugging on a limb from a short, dead desert tree. "Bryus?"

"Not now." The man tried to snap off the trunk of the tree with his one arm. "I'm busy."

Grewen approached the Alchemist, reached down, and snapped the base of the stiff plant from its root system. "There. Now do you have time?"

"No." Bryus' candid responses often came off arrogant. "Break off all the side limbs so it's a single stick."

Grewen complied by snapping the limbs off a handful at a time.

"Be careful!" Bryus shouted. "That's my future arm you're recklessly ripping apart."

Grewen grinned at the statement as he continued trimming.

"A little more off from that side," Bryus instructed. "No, you fool. Leave that one alone. Take off the one next to it. I don't want to look like a freak with an odd curled limb at the end of my arm."

"Sorry. What was I thinking?" Grewen spoke with a straight face but in a humorous tone.

"Apparently you weren't."

"Here." Grewen handed the modified tree trunk to the spellcaster. "Now, we'd like to ask you about something you told Thorik, regarding a prattle box."

Bryus pushed the end of the thick stick up against his stub of an arm. The width of the stick was perfect, but it was made for the length of a mognin's arm as it dragged on the ground eight feet in front of him. "Hey, you big buffoon. Do you see an issue here?"

Grewen chuckled at the sight. "No, is there a problem?"

"Perhaps not, if I wanted to use my arm to plow a field! Listen, baby-ears, if you want my help on something, I suggest you shave a few feet of trunk off my arm."

Grewen began doing just that as Thorik arrived with his coffer. "I hear you gave the king's twins prattle boxes," Grewen said.

"Smooth out the base," he instructed the giant. "Yes. So?"

"Are prattle boxes common?" Thorik asked, hoping he would say no.

"They once were, but you don't see them much anymore."

"How about this one?" The Num held up his coffer.

Bryus reached for the wooden box with his right arm, only to recall not having a right arm. His left hand did a much better job in taking it. Opening it, he dumped the contents onto the ground before looking inside. "Ah, yes, here it is."

Grewen set the wooden arm near Bryus as he waited to hear his assessment.

"Here what is?" Thorik frantically picked up his papers and writing utensils from the desert floor.

"This is one of the prattle boxes I made for Ambrosius and Dark-mere."

"This is one of those boxes? Are you sure?"

Pointing inside, at the base of the box, he noted his name carved into the base.

"Um," Thorik mumbled. "No, this says Suyrb."

Bryus chuckled. "I know. It's an old game, but you know how tradition plays a role in games."

"What are you talking about?"

"Surely you know. It's the same for prattle boxes as it is for prattle bottles or prattle clay pots."

Grewen and Thorik looked at each other with confused faces before they both replied, "No."

"Alchemists have used prattle devices forever. I just thought it would be fun for the twins to each have a prattle box. It's all fun, you know."

"What's fun?"

"Writing a little note and tossing it inside."

"Yes, and then what?"

"Then the person with the other prattle box opens it up and the words flow onto their paper. That way, when the twins were separated, they could write back and forth from anywhere."

"So anything I write will be available to be read from any other prattle box?"

"No, of course not, only from its mate. They are made from the same material, and the spell is cast on both at the same time."

"It's always two at a time?"

"Well, doing one by itself seems pointless."

"What I meant was, are there some prattle boxes with three?"

"Perhaps, but I only made two of these."

"But again," Thorik was still confused, "it doesn't say your name."

"Sure it does. You see, the original inventor of the prattle spells signed his name backward as a joke so others wouldn't know who created it. Ever since then, it has been a tradition to do so. Call it an inside joke."

Thorik looked at the name carved inside the box. "Suyrb is Bryus backwards."

"You're a genius. How did you figure that out on your own?" the Alchemist sarcastically mocked.

Thorik had learned to ignore Bryus' patronizing tone. It was somewhere on the border of lighthearted teasing and condescending truth. Thorik brushed it off like normal. "Where is the other one?"

"How would I know? It was a child's toy. Most toys are destroyed or lost by the time their owners grow up."

"But what if someone has the other one, such as Ambrosius or Darkmere?" Thorik asked, now concerned about someone reading all of his logs.

Without any passion in his voice, Bryus told it like it was. "Then you have been telling them everything we've been doing: where we are going, when we expect to be places, and what we have done."

Thoughts rushed into Thorik's mind of all the information he had recorded since they had left Farbank. "It would make sense if it was Darkmere. That's how he's known how to always stay one step ahead of us."

Grewen agreed, but he gave another point of view. "Or perhaps Ambrosius has the other one, and Bakalor and Irluk are hoping you will call him into their trap. Maybe that is why Grub is following us, to keep you alive long enough to lure Ambrosius to you."

"How would we know?" Thorik asked. "Bryus, are there any markings on these to say which one you gave to whom?"

"Are you serious? I gave them to the king as toys for his children. Did I not already say this?"

Frustrated with himself over the information he had written down and placed in his coffer, Thorik wondered what to do with the wooden box going forward. "If I write something to bring Ambrosius out into the open, and he does, then we fall into Bakalor's trap. But if Darkmere has the other box, then we've alerted him that Ambrosius is still alive."

Grewen added an additional scenario. "You're also under the assumption that the other box still exists and that it is being used by someone."

Thorik nodded. "There's only one way to find out."

Chapter Twenty-Three

Avanda's Magic

Thorik's Log: 23rd day of the 7th month of the 650th year.

An assassination attempt has been made upon my life, and my understanding is there will be more. The Southwind Matriarch has ordered my death for crimes against her. I was lucky to survive this first attempt with only minor injuries, but Bryus lost an entire arm. I fear that we will not make it past the Squalid Waters as we seek safety beyond them in the Chuttle Fields. The next four nights will be sleepless until we pass this waterway. It's imperative that we survive, for I must deliver critical knowledge, which I obtained from Della Estovia, to Ambrosius. All will be lost if this information falls into the wrong hands.

The stage was set. Whoever would meet them at the Squalid Waters would be the one owning the twin to Thorik's prattle box. However, there were still assumptions being made, such as if they would take the bait, or if they could arrive within the time given.

If no one arrived at the destination, nothing would be learned. The other prattle box could be lost or destroyed just as easily as it may not be opened and checked within the next few days. This scenario would be the worst case, for it left all questions still open.

The travelers had set up camp within the rocky terrain to minimize the exposure of their campfire. As usual, Grewen collected the brush and limbs, Brimmelle stoked the fire, and Thorik set up the camp and beds. Avanda tended to spend the evenings with Bryus to learn as much magic as he could teach her.

"Hold still," Avanda said to Bryus. Her attempt to attach the arm-sized tree trunk onto the stub of his arm was not going well.

"You're still not pronouncing the words right," Bryus complained as he tried to keep the stub of his arm lined up with the moving trunk. "If you cast that spell while my arm isn't lined up, you're going to cause it to be lodged in my chest."

She balanced the new wooden arm on her shoulder, but the trunk swayed from side to side and up and down as she tried to keep up with Bryus' own corrections. "I'm going to lodge it into your chest without the use of any spell if you don't stop fussing!" Her words were firm but without anger.

With one arm steadying the thin trunk, Avanda grabbed the stump of his arm and forced the two up against each other. "There! Now, what's next?"

"I've told you three times already." Bryus reached up to cut a handful of hair from the side of his head, but despite the blade's sharpness, he simply couldn't cut it with one hand. "I don't know why you're making this so difficult. Both my wife and daughter have performed this spell on me many times with ease."

Avanda's arms and back were getting tired as she watched the old man attempt to cut off some of his hair to activate the spell. It was pointless. "Why didn't you tell me you needed some of your hair before we got your arm fit up?"

"Because you asked me to only give you one step at a time."

Grinning at the sight of Bryus wrestling with a blade in his hair, Avanda wondered how he ever became a master in Alchemy. "What else do we need besides the verbal commands and your hair?"

He looked at her with great confusion. His face twitched and his good arm lowered. "Are you daft? We'll need my new arm."

"I know that." She pinched the skin of his stub to emphasize her reaction to his ridiculous response. "I meant what else besides that?"

"Those are the only components."

To the relief of her back, she dropped the yard-long trunk on the ground, let go of his stub, grabbed the blade from his hand, and cut off a handful of hair from the side of his head. Tossing the blade to the side, she slapped the wad of hair in his hand before she picked up the trunk again and pressed it up against his stub.

"There." She thought for a moment before moving on. "Now, what do we do with the hair while I'm casting the spell?"

Impressed at her brashness, Bryus gave it away in his facial expressions. "Well, after we boil the hair for a while, we will—"

"Boil the hair?" Avanda interrupted.

"Well, of course. You always boil the hair to ensure it's pure for the joining of the arm, otherwise it may not take. Every third level student of magic knows that."

"How could I possibly know such a thing?"

Bryus' face twitched. "How do I know what you do and don't know?"

"Didn't you find it odd that we hadn't boiled up some of your hair prior to us lining up your new arm?"

"No. I assumed you would have already had some."

Avanda was perplexed as she dropped the tree trunk back to the ground. "And why would I have some of your boiled hair?"

"I have no idea. I wondered the same thing."

Not knowing how to respond, Avanda slapped her hands on the sides of her head and began shaking it as she talked to herself. "This is the person who's going to teach me magic? I'd be better off on my own."

He nodded. "You're probably right. But then again, how far are you going to get without even knowing about the basics of preparing your spell components?"

"Preparing? I've never had to prepare anything before casting spells."

With a smug look, he nodded again. "True. And how has that been working for you?"

Embarrassed by the obvious answer, she skirted the question. "We've done just fine with what I've taught myself."

"I'm glad to hear it. Then you won't be needing any of my help then."

Sighing, she knew this might be her only chance to learn the skills needed to cast spells that wouldn't cause Thorik and Brimmelle to run in fear. She grabbed the wad of hair out of his hand and headed over to the campfire to boil some water.

Bryus was quite pleased with himself as he watched her walk away. There was a satisfaction he received when he manipulated people into doing what he wanted without using any magic.

Sitting near the campfire, Grewen had taken a flaming limb out of the fire and began scrubbing the bottom of his feet, while Brimmelle took his usual nap before the evening meal.

Thorik had finished his camp chores and had begun working on something to eat. Pouring some of their water into one of his pans, he hoped to make a stew with the roots and fruit Grewen had collected from the desert plants.

Placing the pan over the fire, he looked down and noticed a grouping of small rocks in a smooth artistic pattern near his feet. It reminded him of his grandmother. She had a tendency to make various designs in the sand with her collection of gems and stones.

While he was smiling at the thought of Gluic, Avanda walked up next to him and tossed a wad of hair into his pan. Thorik glanced up in disbelief. "What are you doing?"

Avanda crossed her arms and stared at the fire with a pout on her face. "I'm fixing Bryus' arm."

"You just wasted good water for our stew." Thorik looked into the pan to see if it could salvaged by picking the hair out.

"Leave it in there. It needs to boil for a while."

"What's a while?"

Avanda hadn't asked. "I don't know. Could be a few minutes to an hour. Bryus will have to let me know."

"An hour? That will boil off most of the water. We can't afford to waste it."

She shrugged, accepting his statement as fact. "We'll get more to-morrow."

"I don't know if you've noticed, but we are in a desert, and there aren't a lot of fresh streams handy."

She turned to look directly at him. Her face was serious and her hands were firm against her hips. "Bryus is missing an arm, Thorik. Don't you think that is a little more important than us eating tonight?"

Grewen's eyebrows raised as he looked up from tending to his feet. "Can we vote on this?"

Thorik glanced over at Bryus, who was reaching for things with a hand that no longer existed. "Avanda, do you think it's a good idea for you to be spending so much time with him?"

"Why not?" A frown grew upon her face. "He can teach me how to be a great Alchemist."

"And why would you want to do that?"

"Why wouldn't I? The ability to cast spells to help all of us has to be a good thing."

"Is it?"

"Yes," she answered quickly. "Just think, Thorik, what if I could wield the power to stop people from hurting us, such as that assassin?"

"Or like Lucian?" Thorik frowned with concern. "Is this your way of preventing someone like him from ever taking advantage of you again?"

"It sure wouldn't hurt. I would have cleaned the world of his scum, and no one would have missed him."

"Avanda, I know how hard that was on you, but learning magic won't erase the past."

"But it can prevent it from happening again in the future. The next time a stranger lays a hand on me, I'll be ready."

Thorik sighed. "Don't go down this path with the intent to harm those who threaten you."

Realizing that she was painting herself into a corner, she tried a different angle. "Learning magic is more than protecting myself. Think of it. What if I could cast spells that could ensure we had plenty of food to feed everyone in Farbank? We wouldn't have to spend all year fishing, hunting, and farming."

Looking sad about the idea, Thorik paused before he responded. "Then what are all the farmers, hunters, and fishermen going to do? What would be the point of the Harvest Festival if we didn't have to work hard in the first place?"

"They could just enjoy the festival instead of having to slave all year long to prepare for it."

"But that's part of the festival. It provides us with a time to feel good about all the hard work we've done."

"But what harm is there in making life easier?"

"None. But if people don't struggle to achieve, then they also don't appreciate what they have once they receive it. There's a personal satisfaction that comes along with overcoming hardships. Never giving up and forging ahead to accomplish your desires, regardless of the obstacles, is one of the most powerful feelings in the world. I would never want to give that up."

Again, she felt he was cornering her, so she turned the conversation in a new direction. "Yet you have done just that."

"What?"

"Are we heading back to Farbank?"

Thorik's shoulders drooped a bit. "You know we are."

"Well, we're heading back there because you gave up on Gluic."

Thorik's face turned red at the accusation. "I didn't give up on her. Brimmelle asked me to leave his mother at peace."

"She's at peace? Gluic is trapped in a dagger which is lost in the desert."

Thorik's throat tightened. He couldn't respond.

"Would you have left me in the desert?" she asked.

"No. Of course not."

"Then why did you leave her?"

His eyebrows pulled in tight. "I already told you."

"Because Brimmelle told you to." She wanted to confirm his reason.

Thorik nodded.

Avanda asked her questions casually and without malice. "What happened to 'regardless of the obstacles' in your lecture to me? It looks to me like your biggest obstacle is Fir Brimmelle, and you gave up instead of forging ahead."

Using his own words against him hurt. His heart tightened at the thought of abandoning his grandmother. She had helped him in so many ways, and he gave up on helping her without much of a fight. But every time he needed the courage to stand up and fight for his beliefs, visions of Bakalor flashed through his mind and caused him to lose his edge.

He turned and stared at the fire as he crucified himself for his actions. He had abandoned Gluic and he no longer possessed the courage to fight for her survival. How would he ever live with himself?

Avanda realized she had gone too far in her efforts to turn the issue away from herself. However, she stood by her comments, even though they could have been conveyed with less sharpness.

Standing behind him, she reached up and placed a soft hand on his back. "I'm sorry. I didn't mean to hurt you."

"No, you're right. I shouldn't have given up on her. Now it's too late."

Her hand slowly traced his spine up and down as they softly chatted. "I didn't think I would ever hear you say that anything was too late to be fixed."

Thorik drew in a deep breath in response to her comment. "We can't turn back now. We have to be at the Squalid Waters in a few days. Hopefully, Ambrosius will be waiting for us. He can help us find Granna."

"Avanda!" Bryus yelled from his side campfire.

Turning her head slightly, she responded. "Yes?"

"That should be long enough. Let's get this over with."

Turning back to Thorik, she ran her palm across his back one last time. "I've got to go."

"I know." His voice was soft and appreciative of her comfort.

Avanda collected a fork to scoop the hair out of the boiling water, but when she peered over the pot's rim, she was surprised to find a dozen roots floating in the water along with the hair.

Grewen noticed her displeasure. "What?" Giving her his wide grin, he hoped to soften her obvious issue with his actions. "I figured we could do both things at once. It's getting late, and I'm hungry."

Avanda glanced back at Bryus to make sure he hadn't seen anything before she quickly scooped out the majority of the hair. She didn't believe the roots would affect the spell. At least she hoped they wouldn't.

CHAPTER TWENTY-FOUR

SQUALID WATERS

Two rivers merged into one at a city of filth and depression. The Fount River from the north and Hessik's Blood River from the east bordered the city of Corrock before joining. The northern river was fresh and drinkable, while the Hessik's Blood was stained red and caused illness upon consuming. Sewage from the city added disease and poisons, which would take over a hundred miles of river to clean out.

It was down this river where Thorik and his team had planned to cross. Nearing the only remaining bridge that still stood intact over the river, they slowed their pace as they watched for anyone emerging to meet them.

The bridge was many hours south of Corrock but still considered the property of the city. As the only safe crossing outside of the city's bridges, it had become a source of revenue for the city as it collected tolls from those who crossed. In addition, it allowed the Del'Unday to monitor all who traveled from the O'Sid Fields to the Volney Lake Valley.

Constructed of stone blocks, columns rose out of the water every dozen paces and arched up to a keystone. Long, thick timbers had been crudely placed along the row of wide columns to replace what had originally been built at the crossing. With the multitude of battles that had taken place in the area, it was surprising that the bridge was in as good a shape as it was.

Spanning over a half a mile long, the bridge included two-story guard towers on each side of the river, where guards were posted for taking tolls and protecting their land. The tops of the towers allowed for an easy view across the bridge to see if anyone was crossing.

Thorik looked up at Grewen with concern after spotting a blothrud standing on the tower closest to them. "Will he allow us to pass?"

The giant looked at the lone guard posted on the upper floor. "We won't know until we try."

"What if he doesn't?" Thorik asked.

"Then we will be forced to find another way across."

"Assuming they don't capture us and throw us in prison," Brimmelle grumbled.

Grewen grinned. "No such luck. Remember, Dels don't believe in prisons for criminals. The victim has the opportunity to retaliate with whatever force they feel necessary, or you will be tied up in public to have the locals decide your fate. Hopefully, if we pay the toll and quietly move on, this guard won't accuse us of any crimes."

"That's not their only option for crimes, you know," Bryus interrupted. "They've been known to hold your family responsible for your crimes against them. Blackmail is not against the law to the Del'Unday. In fact, it's an acceptable part of their culture."

Avanda kept an eye on the blothrud who was standing firm on top of the guard tower, watching the outsiders chat about their approach. "I think we're making him nervous. We should either approach or leave before he calls for assistance from the far tower."

She was correct. The blothrud stood like a statue, overlooking the eastern desert as the mognin, human, and three Nums stood just minutes from the crossing. Changing his grip on his long spear, the blothrud squinted his solid red eyes as he wondered why they had stopped.

Like most blothruds, the guard on the roof stood several heads taller than the average human, with thick wolf-like legs, muscular human arms and torso, and a head that resembled a hairless wolf crossed with a dragon. His attire was heavy and bulky to increase his size even further, while leaving open slots for his spikes to extend out of his skin from various locations on his back and arms. The metal helmet he wore had holes for his eyes and ears as well as studded leather strips running down his thick neck. The blothrud was in battle gear, making the simple guard shack seem more alarming than it should have been.

Bryus collected a few items from his small pack and began grinding them up in his hand. Once he had it massaged into a thin paste, he began plastering it all over his face, neck, and chest. "Shields my skin from the sun, as well as other things." He gave a wink to Avanda, who had watched him create it.

Even though Avanda had attached the tree trunk onto Bryus' arm, he continued to struggle with it. If all had gone right with the spell, he should have been able to control it and bend it by now. Instead, it was just a weight hanging from his shoulder. The spell had only been partially successful.

"There's only one way to find out what he will do." Thorik then started his walk toward the tower.

But before arriving, a second guard walked out from the first floor of the stone building. This one was a krupe, a two-legged human-size creature completely covered in thick, black, spiked armor. Krupes were the foot soldiers for the Del'Unday, obedient and silent.

In some way, the krupes made Thorik more nervous than the blothruds. At least he knew where he stood with the latter. Krupes never showed their faces or talked, so they were impossible to read.

Thorik approached cautiously. "Hello. We wish to cross."

The krupe stood silent as he watched the rest of the Num's group arrive.

"What is the toll for the bridge?" Thorik asked firmly, not showing any signs of being intimidated.

Again, the krupe was mute.

It was apparent that the creature was not going to talk, so Thorik decided to walk past him. He figured that he would enter the bridge without issue, or he would be stopped and then a toll would be discussed.

He was half right. The krupe's long spear sliced down inches in front of Thorik, stopping the Num in his tracks. But no instructions followed.

"Name your purpose," the blothrud guard said as he stepped out from the lower level of the tower. He had made his way down as the travelers had approached.

A shiver of fear ran up all the Nums' backs from the loud, rough voice. "Thorik Dain of Farbank." Thorik's voice was quick and in a higher pitch than he had intended to be.

The blothrud used his impressive size to walk up near the Nums and look down over his wolf-like snout at them. "I asked for your purpose, not your name."

Even though he had Grewen, Bryus, and the other Nums with him, Thorik felt extremely vulnerable and at a disadvantage. "We're traveling back home to Farbank."

Pushing his way through the group, the blothrud eyed each one to ensure each member had fear in their eyes. This was true until he found himself looking up into the eyes of Grewen, who was grinning at the posturing that so many Del'Unday do.

"Something amusing, Ov?" the blothrud said sharply.

Grewen knew all too well that a bad tempered blothrud could take down just about any foe, so he didn't wish to provoke him. "Just pleased to see that the Del'Unday are still the masters of intimidation and brutality."

Thorik closed his eyes at the comment, wishing he hadn't irritated the Del.

Lifting his shoulders back and his chest higher, the blothrud eyed the mognin hard. "We will always be the masters of such admirable traits." Grewen's comment had actually been a compliment to the Del'Unday, so the guard allowed the grin to go without ramifications.

Next, the guard eyed Bryus, who was busy scratching his skin where the flesh of his arm was attached to his wooden appendage. "You disrespect me by ignoring me?" the guard barked.

Bryus glanced up at him. "Listen, you sickly dog-faced mutant, right now my arm is more important to me than watching you boost your ego."

"Perhaps you will think differently after I rip your head off."

"Not likely," Bryus snapped back. "If you ripped my head off, I wouldn't be thinking anything, would I?"

"You would long enough to know you were defeated by the hands of a superior species, instead of a mutant."

"Nice retort. Did they teach that kind of misguided sense of importance in some arrogance lesson as a child?"

The blothrud's patience had run out. "Here's a lesson you should have learned a long time ago." His arm swung out at Bryus, clobbering the man square in the chest. The sound of cracking bones rang out.

Bryus was pushed back from the impact, but not as far as the others would have assumed.

The blothrud's fist had been destroyed upon the attack against the shield of magical lotion Bryus had applied earlier. Bones were snapped in half, and some were poking through the blothrud's skin. His fist was a mass of loose flesh instead of the weapon it had once been.

Howling in pain, the blothrud used his other hand to grab Bryus by his tree trunk arm in order to pull him close enough to bite his head off. Not an uncommon tactic for blothruds.

Bryus snapped his fingers and spoke a short phrase just prior to having his head encased in blothrud teeth. The spell which Bryus had cast was based on the beetle poison he had collected earlier in the desert. The snapping had released a spray into the air and into the face of the Del'Unday, causing extreme burning in his eyes and on the surrounding tissue as well as in his nasal cavities.

The blothrud reared back as the spray instantly blinded him. Swinging violently, he proceeded forward to attack Bryus, who had already calmly stepped off to the side. It wasn't long before the poisonous spray had made it to the blothrud's lungs, causing them to constrict and burn.

The blothrud coughed and struggled for air as he fell to his knees.

Bryus put his magical components away. "Brains will always win over brawn." His brazen attitude was apparent.

Avanda was in awe of his ability to take on such a powerful creature. In her mind, it validated the need to learn as much from this Alchemist as possible. He could teach her how to protect herself from all enemies.

Seeing the attack, the krupe lunged forward but was quickly stopped by one of Bryus' spells, which locked the creature into a frozen position before it crashed to the floor, stiff as a board.

"That's amazing!" She was visibly pleased.

Bryus, on the other hand, was disappointed. "That's not right. He should have gone up in flames. This new arm of mine is proving to be detrimental to my spells."

"Why did you have to do that?" Thorik shouted at Bryus while looking at the Del'Unday guards.

"Unfortunately, they won't die," Bryus responded. "In fact, they'll be healed in a matter of days. If my spells had worked properly, they would have been dust by now." Inspecting his wooden arm, he looked perplexed. "What went wrong?"

Thorik was visibly upset about his actions. "We could have made it past these guards without incident."

"He was a loud, pompous fool. I just taught him a lesson. No harm was done."

"No harm?"

"They're just a few stupid Dels. What's your issue?"

"One minute you're jumping all over the place with excitement about a rare insect or plant you found, and the next minute you're treating people like lesser beings."

"I treat people appropriately for what they deserve. Don't blame me if most are idiots."

"Why couldn't you have been respectful long enough to allow us to just pay our toll and move on?"

"Paying a toll on this bridge is ridiculous. They didn't even build the bridge. They use this as an opportunity to intimidate others and to collect finances for war. I have no interest in supporting either of them."

"I don't care if you have an interest in them. One of these days, your arrogance and personal interest are going to get someone killed, if you're not careful."

Bryus laughed. "Then be advised right now to stay out of my way while I'm helping you."

Thorik was frustrated and knew he wasn't getting through to the man. "I don't want your help!"

"Oh, yes, you do. You simply don't realize it."

"No, you aren't listening. You're making things worse for us. You treat us as fools and don't even try to get to know us and what we really need."

"I don't need to get to know you. Nums, humans, Del'Unday, Ov'Unday, you're all the same. You're all annoying. Most are unpredictable, savage, underhanded, and of false words. They talk of petty issues and fill their lives with menial work. However, enchanted items, such as the great Spear of Rummon you carry, are intriguing." Bryus' face lit up as he looked at the spear hanging on Thorik's back. "They are part of the larger scope which changes the world."

The unpleasant words bothered Thorik, even if he knew there were threads of truth in them. "You're entitled to your thoughts, but as long as you travel with us, you don't take action unless we menial people ask for it."

Bryus laughed again. "And you will eventually come asking."

Chapter Twenty-Five

THE CROSSING

Thorik led his followers onto the long bridge toward the distant bluffs just beyond the second tower. Sturdy and functional, the wide bridge had seen better days. Many armies had crossed here at some point since it had been built, and it appeared that some had actually fought directly on the bridge.

Avanda walked up front with Thorik and Bryus as she continued to question the Alchemist's knowledge of magic. She wanted to know everything that there was to learn about the subject.

Fidgeting with his wooden arm, the Alchemist continued to test the new limb with minor spells to no avail. "This arm is simply no good," he muttered to himself. "Why won't it take?"

Wanting to avoid the conversation about what went wrong with the spell used to attach his arm, Avanda changed the subject. "How did you know to cast a spell ahead of time to shield your chest from the blothrud?" she asked.

"It's a typical blothrud approach to issues. They strike out at any-thing that denies them what they want. It's usually respect." His tone was condescending and rubbed Thorik the wrong way.

"You don't have a lot of respect for most species." He had given up trying to be nice to the Alchemist.

Attempting to bend his wooden arm, Bryus realized that his spell-casting would be limited until he found himself a new arm to replace it. "That's not true at all. I find all species equally inept and annoying." He smiled, enjoying his own validation of thought.

It took Thorik a few seconds to accept what he thought he heard was really what was said. "How can you say that?"

"Simple, Num. It's easy to tell the truth when it's painfully obvious." Bryus smiled. He enjoyed a hardy disagreement with someone who stood up for themselves, and his respect had begun to grow for Thorik.

"Have you no admiration for the great accomplishments our people have made? The ability to create great cities, music, and art can't be dismissed."

"True, but they are few compared to the damage we have all done. The wars we have fought, the blood we have all spilled. We are like roaches that are slowly destroying the land. Your approval of great, beautiful cities is just another example of the destruction of nature. Music is played from instruments made only by the death of plants. We are all guilty of this. However, you wonder why I lack reverence for our own kind?"

Thorik responded quickly. "As much as I agree with you that war is usually counterproductive, using what the land provides to improve our lives doesn't seem wrong, as long as we only take what we need."

"But we don't follow that, do we? Unlike the Fesh'Unday, we take more than needed. We become greedy and careless." Bryus cleared his throat. "And because of this, I have more respect for Fesh'Unday than I do for the rest of us."

"And yet you marvel at objects of old."

"Without question, Num. You see, they don't create war or destroy resources. They can be utilized to do such things by us barbarians, but not by their own volition, for they are pure. Embedded into them are the raw powers that were used to create this land, untarnished by men, Dels, Ovs, or Nums. Good and evil do not apply to them. They are what they are, even if we label them as cursed, while others label them as a grand gift. Oh, we are a fickle lot, aren't we?"

"Although I do not share it, I can surely see your point, but you act as though these objects are more valuable than us."

Bryus nodded. "More valuable, and more trustworthy. I would easily give my life to prevent the destruction of Rummon's Spear, Varacon, or others with such a rich history and background."

"And yet," Thorik spoke slow and sharp, "you had no issue with us leaving Varacon in the desert, unprotected from the elements or future careless people who may stumble upon it."

Bryus stopped in his tracks, motionless and silent, staring forward instead of looking Thorik in the eye.

Turning to face the Alchemist, Thorik assumed there must be more to his statement than he had thought. "Do you care to explain why you left this enchanted dagger so easily?"

Bryus was staring at the bluff on the north side of the river. The grasslands, across the top of the bluff, broke away to layers of hard rock before leveling out in a dry flood plain next to the river. His eyes squinted while he focused on his thoughts. "I think there is someone waiting for us on the other side."

Thorik turned to verify. The prattle box had worked... but on whom?

Chapter Twenty-Six

Return of the E'rudite

Beyond the bridge and guard tower stood a cloaked man hunched over as he rested his weight on a wooden staff, while his left hand held his cloak tightly in front of him, keeping his identity concealed. He stood alone on the far side of the bridge, as though he had been waiting for hours for them to arrive.

A fully armored blothrud stood high on the second guard tower, watching the travelers cross the bridge. His muscles strained against the confines of the restrictive metal, leather uniform, and headgear. He was even more massive than the blothrud they had met at the first tower.

Standing on the end of the bridge were two krupes, one keeping a trained eye on the travelers and the other staring at the cloaked man beyond the bridge. Weapons in hand, they gave the impression that there would be trouble.

Cautiously, Thorik led his team toward the end of the bridge as one krupe kept his focus on them. The blothrud focused on the strangers as he modified his grip on the long, thin spear before him.

It was odd to Thorik that the man concealed his identity. If it was Ambrosius, why did he not just step forward and hold the Del'Unday at bay with his powers? Or had he lost some of his abilities in his fight for survival from being crushed in the Weirfortus Dam?

If it was Darkmere, why the façade? The Del'Unday from Corrock were at his disposal. Why not just allow the guards to capture the travelers and then step out of the tower for his attack?

Thorik's lips tightened as variations of these thoughts raced through his head. Why the charade?

Avanda walked alongside Thorik and noticed his pacing had changed as his body became tense. "What's the matter?"

"I don't know. I just feel like we're walking into a trap."

The feeling was spreading to the rest of the group. Something definitely felt amiss. Bryus was the only one not paying attention, as his focus was on repairing his wooden arm.

Stopping several yards short of the guard tower, Thorik scanned his environment one last time. From what he could feel, all eyes were on him to make the next move. Although he had never seen the actual eyes of a krupe and the helmet on the blothrud made it difficult to see its face, Thorik could sense their stares.

Avanda grabbed Thorik's hand and squeezed it tight.

He squeezed back to assure her that all would work out. But he had misunderstood her hand gesture.

Releasing and squeezing his grip several times, Avanda was alerting Thorik to a new threat, one they hadn't noticed yet. A subtle red flame appeared behind the cloaked man, up in the bluffs.

The tension in the air was thick as everyone waited for Thorik's next move.

Following Avanda's line of sight, Thorik instantly realized the pulsing light in the bluff was the lesser demon, Grub. He was here to attack Ambrosius. Thorik had played into Bakalor and Irluk's trap and had lured the E'rudite out from hiding and into danger.

Her voice stayed calm and soft. "He's here to attack Ambrosius."

Bryus finally looked away from his arm and noticed the man in the distance. "Ambrosius? Is that you?" he yelled.

Grub's light immediately vanished. The krupes quickly turned toward the cloaked man as the blothrud above them left his post and ran down the tower steps to join them.

The cloaked man removed his hood to show his face. And there stood the man Thorik had thought he had sent to his death so very long ago. His mahogany hair and beard covered his tanned face as he displayed his blue robes by tossing off the old cloak. Standing up straight, it was obvious that his arm and legs had been repaired since his battle with Darkmere.

Knowing that Grub would be attacking, Thorik raced forward to warn his old friend. "Watch out! It's a trap!" he screamed as he sped past the unsuspecting krupe guards.

His warning was just in time. Ambrosius leaped forward as the ground opened up and Grub shot out to hit him.

Thorik charged ahead, with the krupes on his heels. "Ambrosius! We're under attack! You've been set up."

Avanda ran behind the krupes as Brimmelle stood his ground on the bridge. "Avanda, get back here! You'll be killed!" he yelled. "Ambrosius can take care of himself."

Grewen made his way off the bridge to help but was slammed along the side by the blothrud, who had raced out of the tower to enter the battle. The impact knocked the mognin over and his bulky body hit hard onto the ground, stirring up a cloud of dust. The blothrud dropped his spear, fell to one knee, shook off the unexpected collision, and then bolted toward Ambrosius.

Bryus, standing near Brimmelle, pulled out several items from his pack and began casting a spell from the safe distance of the bridge. Brimmelle had seen enough spells go wrong that he instinctively moved back away from the Alchemist.

Meanwhile, Ambrosius and Grub were in a heated battle. The E'rudite held off the heat of the creature as it relentlessly attacked him. At one point, he literally caught the crusted-over glob of magma in his hands to prevent it from slamming into his face. He then used his powers to throw the creature high into the air over the bluffs.

Keeping his distance in front of the krupes, Thorik arrived to see Ambrosius' hands still smoking from his touch of the lesser demon. "Ambrosius!" the Num yelled as he tossed his body into his old friend for a strong hug. "I'm so glad you're alive. The Death Witch said—"

"Irluk? What does she have to do with this?" Ambrosius asked as he pushed Thorik back to look him in the eyes.

But there was no time to answer. Two krupes were arriving fast.

Reaching out with his right hand, Ambrosius used his powers to cause the ground at the two guards' feet to crumble away. With no time to react, one immediately fell and broke his neck on the far side. The other had enough momentum to launch himself over the hole, only to miss his footing and fall backwards into the deep pit. Krupes were sturdy front line attackers but had little talent for jumping and climbing.

Avanda arrived and made the leap over the crack in the ground with ease. "Ambrosius!" She quickly jumped into his arms.

Again, there was no time for a reunion. The blothrud had been on Avanda's heels and jumped over the hole without missing a stride. He was in a full attack run toward Ambrosius and had unsheathed his bastard sword for the pending brutal battle.

Raising his staff in his right hand, Ambrosius froze the air around the blothrud, causing the beast's lungs to restrict airflow. The blothrud grabbed his chest and tumbled to his side near the E'rudite's feet, stirring up dust from his crash.

"Thorik, tell me about Irluk," Ambrosius said quickly, knowing the blothrud would soon be back on his feet. "What does she have to do with this?"

"It's too late." Avanda watched a black mass of floating debris in the sky approach. Irluk was arriving to take Ambrosius once and for all.

"NO!" shouted Ambrosius. "What have you done?" he asked, looking directly at Thorik.

"I didn't know if you had the other prattle box."

Crashing out of the earth behind them, Grub flew into Ambrosius' back, knocking him forward toward the pit where the krupes had fallen.

Spinning around and using his powers, he held the magma creature at bay while screaming in pain from the fresh burns on his back.

Free of the E'rudite's powers, the blothrud rolled to his feet to return to his attack on Ambrosius.

Thorik grabbed the Spear of Rummon from his back and blocked the blothrud's path. "Get back!"

In one quick slap, the blothrud knocked the spear out of Thorik's hands and sent the weapon flying. He then quickly pushed the Num aside to make his attack on the E'rudite. Stepping forward, he thrust his sword into Ambrosius' arm.

The Death Witch slowly closed in on the battle, waiting for her revenge. "Grub, I want him alive. In pain, but alive. I will deal the final blow in front of Bakalor himself." Her airy voice sounded distant but clear.

Grub opened his mouth, displaying the fiery furnace within. The heat would have instantly killed any mortal, but this was an E'rudite. The lesser demon had hoped it would at least cause him to pass out from the pain.

Removing the thick blade from Ambrosius' arm, the blothrud kept as much distance from Grub as he could as he drove the metal tip of the weapon into the E'rudite's side.

Thorik returned to the battle with the Spear of Rummon in hand as he leaped into the pit and jammed the weapon into the back of the blothrud. "Leave him alone!"

The Del'Unday guard screamed in pain as he arched his back. The spear hadn't gone deep, but the essence of the dragon within it fought for his Num master and inflicted great pain on his victims. A mighty roar emanated from the spear, and the blothrud fell.

Thorik then turned the enchanted weapon to Grub. Wondering how it would affect a lesser demon, he had no other option but to plunge it into the creature if he had any hope of saving Ambrosius.

This time, there was no roar when Thorik stabbed Rummon into Grub. Instead, the spear shook uncontrollably, and Thorik could not hang on to the weapon as it violently thrashed about. Grub also began to vibrate and swirl recklessly. Heat blasted in every direction. The spear slapped against the ground and through the air as the two continued their fierce attack with one another.

Ambrosius was unconscious from the attack so Thorik leaped on top of him in order to protect him from any more harm as Grub and Rummon fought to the death. "I'm sorry I pulled you into this." Thorik looked the man over.

The E'rudite's skin was swollen and blistered from Grub's attack. His right hand still firmly clenched the wooden staff, which Thorik had made for him so long ago. He noticed the Runestone of Health was proudly carved near the top of the now-blackened burnt wood. Thorik recalled the day near Kingsfoot when Emilen and he had originally etched Runestones into the staff.

The memory caused Thorik to jump up to his feet and race off to the blothrud, where he proceeded to steal the guard's wide bastard sword.

The Death Witch quickly approached, floating just feet from the ground.

With the guard's sword in hand, Thorik stepped back to the E'rudite and raised it over his head, positioned to plunge the blade straight down into the E'rudite's chest. "You want him dead, then you shall have him!" he yelled at Irluk. "But I will not allow you the satisfaction of bringing him to Della Estovia alive to be tortured."

Thorik drove the sword straight down into the unconscious man's chest, causing the E'rudite's body to jolt from the pain.

Both Avanda and Irluk screamed, "NO!" as they rushed forward to stop the attack on Ambrosius. But they were unable to prevent it in time, and the sharp tip penetrated his chest and wedged itself deep inside of him.

Avanda pushed Thorik out of the way and uprooted the sword before being shoved to the side by Irluk. She could see that the E'rudite was still alive but fading fast.

"Thorik, what have you done?" Avanda turned to fight off the Death Witch.

Thorik grabbed her from behind and pulled her away. "I did what I had to do."

Without warning, an explosion rocked the ground and stopped all conversations as pieces of pumice rained down on them. The sound of the Spear of Rummon dropping to the ground followed. Grub had been defeated.

The swirling charcoal debris that made up Irluk's body intensified at the scene. With a quick unsettling gaze at Thorik, she increased the speed of the debris that made up her body and robes. Accelerating, the debris spread out and began collecting the steaming rock fragments of Grub.

Once all the lesser demon's parts had joined her chaotic mix of spinning fragments, Irluk lowered herself onto the E'rudite before lifting him up into the air and away from the bridge, back toward Della Estovia. Her mission was finally complete, in spite of the fact that Thorik tried to take the honor of the last blow from her.

Avanda was furious at Thorik. "How could you do that?"

But an explanation would have to wait, as he noticed the blothrud guard standing back up. Thorik ran past the blothrud to collect the Spear of Rummon.

"Thorik, hurry!" Avanda yelled.

Thorik quickly wrapped a cloth around the enchanted spear's handle and picked it up. Smoke rose from the cloth as it singed against the heat of the metal remaining from its battle with Grub. Swiveling around, he expected to see the blothrud attacking Avanda. However, he was surprised to see the Del'Unday right behind him.

Slapping the spear out of his hands for a second time, the creature twice Thorik's size roared at him in anger. "Sec, don't you ever strike me with the damn spear again!"

The words struck a moment of fear into Thorik before he abruptly thought it odd that the blothrud knew his spiritual designation was that of Sec.

"Next time you do that, I'll break Rummon over your head!"

The voice was familiar. Could it be? "Santorray?" Thorik asked.

Removing his helmet, the blothrud displayed his true identity. It was, in fact, Thorik's dear friend.

CHAPTER TWENTY-SEVEN

A BLOTHRUD'S POINT OF VIEW

Santorray pulled off the rest of his restrictive Corrockian guard uniform. Scars covered his body, and some scars, such as the angled one on his back, covered the entire length of his torso. Few areas were without wounds from swords, claw marks, arrows, dagger stabs, and countless other items. The freshest was, of course, the gash Thorik had given him with his spear.

Thorik put the Spear of Rummon in the holder of his backpack. "It's so good to see you." He couldn't help but give his friend a tight hug, even though the num was in the blothrud's way of tending to his own injury.

Grewen approached, limping from the earlier knock down by Santorray as the blothrud had raced out of the tower. "What just happened here? Did my eyes deceive me, or did Irluk finally gain Ambrosius' body?"

Avanda was still in shock. "How could either of you do this? Ambrosius is part of our family."

"True," Thorik said. "But Darkmere is not."

"Darkmere?"

"Yes, without question."

"How do you know?"

"I didn't at first, but then I noticed he was holding his staff with the wrong hand. But what gave it away was the staff. I carved a Runestone symbol into it myself, but it was the Portent Runestone, not the Runestone of Health. Darkmere wouldn't have noticed the subtle differences in the designs."

"And that is all you went on?"

"Yes." Pulling out some cloths to help bandage the blothrud, Thorik glanced up at Santorray. "How did you know?"

Santorray had been holding his palm over the bloody injury. "I was sent here by Ambrosius to meet you at the crossing. I replaced the prior guard with myself." He gave a confident nod. "Just in case it was a trap. Obviously it was. Darkmere arrived at the same moment you did."

"But," Thorik began to ask as he tried to make sense of it all, "how did Ambrosius know that we would be here?"

"He's been following your logs."

Thorik pulled the wooden box from his pack. "Did he take the notes from a coffer such as this? Did it have this inscription on the base?"

Santorray worked on his wound and never looked over. "I never actually talked to Ambrosius. His messenger pigeon, Draq, arrived and notified me of Ambrosius' findings. I then rushed over here to meet you."

"Ambrosius must have the twin to this prattle box."

"He's been watching after you for a long time."

"You mean, even before we destroyed the Temple of Surod?" Thorik asked.

"Long before that. He sent Captain Dare down to save you from the Palm Islands, and I followed Ambrosius' instructions to help you find Ericc."

"You knew he was reading my logs all this time and never told me?"

"If you had found out that he was alive, there was a high likelihood of others finding out as well. He needed to heal before Darkmere and his minions started hunting him down again. He couldn't risk letting you know; therefore, I couldn't."

"But now you can? What changed?"

"Apparently you have already been telling others that Ambrosius lives. His secret is out."

Thorik felt slightly guilty for foiling the E'rudite's plan. "How did Darkmere know about us coming here if Ambrosius has the twin coffer?"

Santorray shook his head at the naïve Num. "You've been traveling in Corrockian territory for many days. Do you honestly think that no one would have spotted you and alerted him?"

"But how would he have known to meet us here at this specific bridge?"

"It's the only crossing of the river in these parts, unless you pass at Corrock itself. It's easily determined where you would be forced to cross. I made the same assumption myself. You're a predictable creature, Sec."

"If I'm so predictable, then how is it I was able to stab the mighty Santorray without him being prepared for it?"

"You're right. I should have assumed you would backstab me while I was saving your life." A smirk grew upon the blothrud's face after speaking.

Thorik apologized again for the misunderstanding.

Avanda still wasn't satisfied with their answers. "Why would Darkmere arrive disguised as Ambrosius?"

"Perhaps he was after information," Grewen speculated. "If he had wanted to kill us, he would have just sent a small troop of warriors to wipe us out. But this tactic smells like an attempt to gain our trust to find something out."

Thorik pulled the bandage tight around Santorray's waist. "Well then, he has succeeded."

Santorray sucked his stomach in slightly for the bandage to be tied off. "What do you mean?"

"The only information I have was obtained from Bakalor and Irluk," Thorik answered. "Darkmere will now have plenty of opportunities to ask them both questions once he arrives there.

Avanda looked back toward the bridge, but there was no sign of Brimmelle and Bryus, so she headed back to see where they had gone.

Grewen chuckled at the thought while looking at the recent battlefield. "I would love to see the faces on the Death Witch and Bakalor when they realize their prisoner is actually Darkmere."

Santorray considered the situation at hand. "If it were me, I'd come back to take my revenge. We should stay alert."

"Yes, but we are small ripples in the waves of this pending war," Thorik replied.

Grewen found the comment enlightening and entered his own comment. "You never know what ripples will be the final blow to dislodge a shoreline boulder."

Thorik rolled his eyes at the thought. "Trust me, they have more important issues at hand than to take revenge on a Num trying to travel home."

"Travel home?" Santorray jerked his head with surprise. "I thought you were going to the Govi Glade in order to save your grandmother."

The words took an emotional toll on Thorik. "I... well, I lost the dagger."

Santorray was stunned. "This is not the Sec I remember. You look older, but you are not acting wiser than the last time I traveled with you. You have given up on Gluic, just as you did with Ambrosius' son, Ericc."

"I haven't given up!" Thorik fired back.

"Then why aren't you out searching for it?"

"Because we had to be here in time."

"In time to what? To spring your trap? To see who had been reading your precious logs and notes?" Santorray's voice carried. "This was more important than finding your grandmother?"

"It's not that simple. Brimmelle asked me to leave his mother at peace."

"When did you start listening to him?"

"Hang on. When we traveled with you, you wanted to leave her behind in River's Edge, and then you ended up stabbing her. Why would you care about her?"

"I don't," Santorray barked back sharply. "It's your decision whether you try to save your grandmother. But an actual warrior would fight for what he believes in long before he would be concerned about himself or who was spying on him. A warrior stops at nothing to achieve what he wants. You fought for Gluic then. Why aren't you willing to fight Brimmelle for her now?"

"I don't know. Ever since Bakalor attacked us, it's been different. His curse upon me has softened my courage and made it difficult for me to stand up for myself and fight with confidence."

"That's an excuse!"

"No, it really happened. And I've never been the same since."

"I don't care if it's now harder to fight for what you believe in and what you desire! All that means is that you have to want it that much more. Your curse is an excuse to not have to try harder. It's a crutch that you flaunt in order to justify why you're not willing to do what it takes!"

"No, it's not. It truly has affected me."

"I never said it didn't affect you. It happened! It hurt you! Accept it and stop allowing this excuse from preventing you from getting what you want. Bakalor can't stop you from achieving your goals, only you can! If you want to save her, tell me you are going to turn around and find Gluic! Send Bakalor a message that you are victorious over his attempts to weaken you!"

"Santorray, I wouldn't even know where to start looking for Granna."

"That's Fesh talk!"

"No, it's not. It was somewhere between Lagona Falls and Trewek. That is an amazing amount of desert to search through."

"So, you're going to quit. Yes? Say it, Sec. Say that you are going to quit on your grandmother!"

"I can't just turn around and start marching back the way we came."

"Why not?"

"Because we've come so far."

"Then say it out loud. Say you're quitting on Gluic. At least be proud of your actions, like an actual warrior, regardless if they're right or wrong. Take a stand and make a move," Santorray yelled. "Tell me you're quitting on your grandmother. I want to hear it."

"I could give you a hundred reasons why I should leave her out there."

"There will always be a hundred excuses why not to struggle to accomplish something great. Greatness is only achieved when you follow your beliefs despite your reasons not to. So, tell me right now, are you going to quit on her, or are you going to find her?"

Thorik's voice was now nearly as loud as Santorray's as the two shouted back and forth. "Obviously, I want to find her."

"That's not an option! Either you are going to find her or you aren't."

"I could try for a year and still not find her."

"That's because you haven't decided beyond any doubt that you will find her."

"What?"

"A warrior determines the results they expect first, and only afterward do they determine how to achieve them. You, on the other hand, want to plan your way and hope it results in success. And because of that, every obstacle can potentially throw you off course. A warrior finds a way, regardless of what is thrown at them."

"Failure to plan usually results in failure of a goal," Thorik snapped back.

"But planning only comes after you determine exactly what you want to accomplish. You need a goal so firm and real that nothing will draw you off course. Once you have it burning down in the pit of your stomach, nothing can stop you from achieving it, plan or not. You must become a driven man to be a warrior."

Thorik felt the fire within him growing again. He had lost it ever since they had been in the underworld. His passion for what he wanted had been less than what it once was. But now, with Santorray's words, he was feeling empowered over his own life once again.

"Shout it out, Sec!" Santorray roared. "I am giving up on Gluic!"

"NO!" Thorik shouted back.

"You don't have the desire anymore. Give up!" He taunted the Num.

"I will not give in. I refuse to give up," Thorik screamed at the blothrud. "I will find my grandmother! And I will release her from Varacon!"

"I don't believe you!"

"I don't need you to. I'll find her with or without you!"

Santorray stepped back, as though a wave of energy from Thorik's words had pushed against him. Ambrosius had ordered Santorray to ensure that Thorik make his way to the Govi Glade. The blothrud had not only succeeded in changing the Num's course, but he had strengthened the Num's character. Pleased with his mission, he nodded approval. "And that, Sec, is what a warrior sounds like."

Searching for Brimmelle and Bryus, Avanda arrived back at the tower at the base of the bridge spanning the Squalid Waters. The last time she had seen them was when Grub was spotted and she had chased Thorik into the battle. But now they were nowhere to be seen. "Bryus? Fir Brimmelle?" she called out.

She heard a distant complaining from Brimmelle.

"Brimmelle? Is that you?" she yelled.

"Down here!"

Peering over the edge of the bridge, she found the two missing members within the top of a tree. Bryus' arm had flourished into a robust tree, rooted in the water near the shore. His arm was at the top of the central trunk, locking him into an uncomfortable position as he hung from his shoulder at the peak of the tree.

Laughing at the sight, she struggled to keep a straight face at the scene. "What happened?"

Wedged between two large limbs, Brimmelle didn't find the humor in the situation. "Your friend used his magic. And we all know how that usually turns out."

Bryus glared at Avanda. "Are you sure you cast the spell correctly to attach my new arm?"

Avanda knew exactly what he meant. "You instructed me. You were there."

"True. How about the boiling of my hair? Was there any contamination during the boiling?"

Avanda wanted to avoid that specific step. "Why, what happened to you and Brimmelle?"

Bryus didn't allow her to change the subject. "By now, I should have some flexibility in the new arm, but I don't yet. I should have also started being able to feel sensations with it, but all it does is itch toward the upper end." Bryus was going step by step through every possibility where the error could have occurred. "I'm not sure what went wrong."

"Something always goes wrong," Brimmelle complained. "Avanda, have Grewen get over here and pull me out of this tree!" Brimmelle shouted.

Bryus grumbled to himself, "I've replaced limbs many times with splendid success." The Alchemist gave a nod of reassurance. "Even my daughter has performed this spell with no issues."

"What exactly happened here?" Avanda called down to them.

"Avanda! Go get help." Brimmelle ordered.

"I will." She replied as she waited for Bryus' answer to her question.

"I gave it plenty of time to adjust onto my arm," Bryus said to himself before glancing up at the female Num. "I simply cast a spell to root the wood deeper into my arm. But instead of rooting deeper into me, it pulled me off the bridge, rooted itself in the river, and then grew like crazy."

"And in doing so, he knocked me over with him," Brimmelle said. "Now go get us some help."

Chapter Twenty-Eight

UNCOVERED

A lone tree stood in the Squalid Waters River near the shore and almost underneath the long bridge which spanned the waterway. Flower blossoms sprang to life on its branches as a giant mognin walked away from the beautiful tree and back toward the shoreline. Grewen carried Brimmelle and Bryus back to the base of the bluffs from this tree after snapping the Alchemist's arm off nearly a yard from his shoulder, giving him the same ugly wooden arm he had had prior to the incident.

With the day nearing its end, the travelers decided to utilize the guard tower as their shelter for the night. After removing the stench left from the krupes' beddings, Thorik lit a fire in the fireplace to cook dinner while Bryus cut off new leaves and branches that had grown on his wooden arm.

Thorik stoked the fire. "So what you're telling me is that, while we were fighting off Darkmere, you were casting a spell on your arm instead of utilizing those great powers of yours to help us?"

Bryus sat on a bench across the room from Thorik. "Yes, that's correct." He appeared to have no issue with his actions.

Thorik was baffled by the candor of his responses. "Did you not see the life or death situation we were in?"

"Oh, without question. I wasn't sure if you were going to survive or not on several occasions."

Thorik was awestruck by the lack of caring for his fellow men. Tossing another log into the fireplace, he continued his discussion with the Alchemist. "If you saw that I was in trouble, then why didn't you at least try to help?"

"Oh, no, I couldn't do that."

"And why is that?"

"Because you specifically told me not to, on the far side of the bridge."

"That was a unique situation." Thorik stepped back from the fire and paced around the room in frustration. "You obviously don't have any interest in helping us, so why are you traveling with us?"

"To take you to the Govi Glade."

Thorik was shocked. "Govi Glade?"

"Yes, you know, where the book of magic is. Vesik awaits." Bryus' smile beamed with intrigue.

"We're not heading to the Govi Glade."

"What? Why not?"

"Because we don't have need for Vesik if we don't have Gluic's dagger."

"Well, no one ever notified me that the plans had changed."

"How could they not change?"

"I don't see what one has to do with the other. Vesik is by far a better relic than the dagger, Varacon."

"But I don't need the book without the dagger."

"That's because you don't know of its powers. It can help us in ways you've never dreamed."

"Can it help us find Gluic?"

"Oh, I have no idea."

Thorik grimaced at the nonchalant attitude. It was driving him crazy. He simply couldn't continue the conversation and found himself sitting back next to the fireplace. Looking down near the burning logs, he noticed a few dozen small rocks placed in a swirling pattern near the fire.

Thorik looked around the room. It was only Bryus and himself. "Has anyone else been in here?"

"More than a few krupes, from the smell of it."

"No, I mean while we were talking?"

Bryus looked at Thorik as though the Num was losing his mind. "If we aren't heading to the Govi Glade, then I will depart tomorrow morning and go my own way."

Thorik leaned down and placed his hand near the small rocks. The air that hung over them was cold, in spite of being near the fire. "We will be going to the Govi Glade."

Bryus now knew the Num was losing his mind. "Collect your senses, Num! You just told me we weren't."

"No, I said we weren't heading there. We will search for Gluic first. Once we find her, then we will head there."

"But what if you don't find her?"

"That's not an option. We will find her." He was firm on this stance. "I'll start by calling out to her like I did once before. I think she is still following us."

Bryus was amused at the idea. "How do you plan to do that?"

Thorik grabbed the Runestones out of his backpack and pulled out the Runestone of Courage. Closing his eyes and opening his mind, he waited for the flow of energy to stream out of the stone, through his body, and then back into the stone.

Amazed by the sight before him, Bryus leaned forward with interest at the new arrival to the room.

By the time Thorik opened his eyes, a semi-translucent figure was forming next to him on the bench. Gluic had returned.

"Granna?" Thorik spoke softly. "Can you hear me?"

"Well, of course, dear. I listen to you every day."

"You do?"

"Yes. I've also had a chance to catch up with so many others that I've lost. It's been a delight."

Thorik smiled. Nothing ever bothered her. "Do you know what happened to you?"

"Surely. As a child, I grew up in Longfield. Then I moved to Far-bank when—"

"No, I mean, do you know that the dagger, Varacon, has captured your essence?"

"Yes." She showed little interest. "I told you I would be changing. It's time for me to spread my wings and enjoy an existence with new heights and fewer limitations. I certainly can't do what I needed to do with my old, worn-out body."

"What is it you need to do?"

"Help free those who are forever captive."

"I don't understand."

"I know, dear. Sometimes I don't either." A shallow laugh followed her own comment.

"Granna, I need your help."

"No, you really don't. You've just become dependent upon it. It's an unfortunate fate we give to those we wish to protect."

"I'm not the leader you think I am. I'm constantly second guessing myself, and I don't have all the answers."

"All the answers? Leaders discover the answers. They don't presume to know it all. Leaders show up for the adventure instead of shying away from it or ignoring it all together," she said. "You'll do just fine as a leader. You don't need my help."

Thorik shook his head. "No, this is different. I need to find Varacon so I can free you from it."

"Oh, won't that be pleasant?"

"What? No. I don't know where the dagger is, and without it, I can't free you."

"But I feel free already. What's so wrong with this? We can still chat when you need to."

"It's not the same, Granna. I need to bring you back."

"Why is that, dear?"

The question surprised Thorik. "Because you are my grandmother, and I love you. I miss you terribly."

"Well, I miss you too, but we must let go at some point. Wasn't it nice while it lasted? I did so enjoy our outings."

"But it's not your time yet. Santorray stabbed you by mistake. You shouldn't have been killed."

"Mistakes will happen, dear. Did you know your mother is here? She is very proud of you."

"My mother? Where?" Thorik whipped his head around to spot her.

"Not in this tower. She has better taste than to be hanging around in these types of places."

Disappointed, he turned back to her. "But how do I find her? How do I talk to her?"

"You don't have to find her, but she hears you each time you speak. She waits for you back in Farbank with your father."

"They're both there?"

"I would assume so. They tend to stay in the village."

"So, how is it that you are not attached to the dagger?"

"Oh, I am, dear. I can only stray so far from it."

"But we are a long way from where I lost it in the desert."

"Dear child, I've been lost most of my life," she said with a grin. "You, on the other hand, are but a few feet from the dagger I reside in."

"What? How can that be?" Thorik asked, searching the room with his eyes.

"Go to the Govi Glade and obtain the book of spells. You will need it before your work here is done."

"Therefore, we were correct. There is a spell to release you."

Gluic smiled kindly at her grandson. "You, my dear, will release me, and we shall free those imprisoned." She then stood up from the bench, walked across the room, and stopped near the Alchemist. "Bryus is protecting Varacon for you."

Thorik's eyes grew large, and his jaw drifted down. "What?"

"Enjoy the journey, dear. That's what life is all about." Turning, she walked through the far wall. And with that, Gluic was gone.

The moment of silence afterward was filled with emotions from Thorik as he stared at Bryus.

The Alchemist had little emotion in his glance at Thorik, as though there was no issue at hand.

"Bryus, is this true? Have you had the dagger the entire time?"

"No. You and Brimmelle have both had it from time to time. In fact, Santorray actually had it prior to us, seeing that he activated the spell by stabbing her in the first place."

Thorik stood up and came closer to the sitting man. He struggled with being in shock and becoming outraged at the possibility of this treachery being done by people he had trusted. "Do you have the dagger, Varacon, in your belongings or on your person right now?"

"Now that is a completely different question. If you had asked me that the first time, we wouldn't have had to go through this series of unrelated comments."

"Yes or no!" Thorik shouted.

"Yes."

Thorik bit his lip in anger. "How could you steal her from me and make me think she was lost?"

"Again, that is a completely separate question. I did neither of those."

"You've already informed me you had the dagger."

"True. The rest you assumed."

"Assumed?" Thorik's cheeks flushed with emotion as his anger grew. "If it wasn't you that performed the other actions, then who did?"

Just then, Brimmelle walked into the tower, rubbing his hands together. "Do you have our meals ready?"

"YOU!" Thorik announced.

Brimmelle didn't know what he had walked into. "Me?"

"You stole the dagger from me and told me that I had lost it!" Thorik had fury in his voice that he himself didn't expect.

Brimmelle gazed a nasty stare at Bryus. "You had to tell him, didn't you? Did you also happen to tell him that you threatened to toss me over a cliff if I didn't give it to you?"

Thorik's view changed back to Bryus.

Bryus grinned. He obviously liked this game. "And by doing so, I saved the dagger from being lost forever. If I recall correctly, you were about to throw it over the Lagona Falls ridge."

Brimmelle didn't care any more about the secrecy. In fact, it felt good to get it all out in the open. "Which is why I stole it back from you at the Trewek pyramids. She deserved better than to have her fate in your hands."

"Is that why you tossed her down into the farmlands while entering Trewek? You'd rather have her lost in mounds of mud and manure?"

"Better there than to be with you," Brimmelle protested. "At least now she is at rest."

Bryus reached into his pack and pulled out Varacon. "Apparently not!"

With the horror at the thought, Brimmelle was momentarily speechless. "You found it?"

"What was your first clue?" Bryus asked with an overly theatrical curious expression.

"You lied to me. You told me you couldn't find it."

"You don't know how bad I feel about that." Sarcastic tones filled Bryus' speech.

"Stop it!" Thorik shouted as he reached over and snatched the dagger from Bryus. "I'm furious at both of you!"

Bryus nodded. "Good, it's about time you give us your honest opinion. Let it out, Num."

Thorik's hands shook as he spoke. "And especially you, uncle. I shouldn't have to worry about trusting my family."

"He's right, you know." Bryus pointed at the older Num. "Damn shame he couldn't trust you."

Thorik whipped back around to Bryus, catching the Alchemist off guard. "And you! You have been nothing but a thorn in our side ever since we met you."

"Glad I could keep things lively," he retorted.

"If I didn't need you so much..." Thorik had reached the end of his anger limit and struggled to finish his sentence.

"Ah, but you do." Bryus' smile just added to the issue at hand.

"And you're lucky I do!" Thorik's clenched fist raised toward the man.

"Odd. I don't feel lucky."

Throwing his hands in the air, Thorik knew he couldn't get through to Bryus.

Turning back to Brimmelle, Thorik struggled to know how to convey his anger and distrust. "Why would you do this to your own family?" Thorik asked as his voice trembled with emotion. "Brimmelle, why have you done this terrible act?"

"Because my mother is dead, Thorik. I don't want her memory tarnished any further. Let her rest! She has done her part in this world."

"No, she has one last thing to accomplish, and she can't do it without my help. We must proceed to the Govi Glade and find the spell to release her. And neither of you two can be trusted around this dagger again." Thorik stormed out of the room, furious at his uncle's betrayal.

Bryus raised a single eyebrow and looked at Brimmelle. "I didn't realize they trusted me around it in the first place."

CHAPTER TWENTY-NINE

DEMONS

Thorik's Log: 12th day of the 8th month of the 650th year.

The days are hot and the nights are cold on the dry grasslands. I have attempted to reach out and contact my grandmother several times since we left the guard tower. Regardless, she has chosen not to show herself to me. I am relieved that she is safe and is here with us, but I feel cheated that I can't spend time with her. I suppose she has her reasons. I don't know if I can ever forgive my uncle for his betrayal. We aren't speaking at this time. Perhaps that's best. Our next step is to travel to the Govi Glade so we can collect the book of magic, Vesik, to find the spell to free Granna.

Extreme tension remained between Thorik and his uncle over the following weeks. They had hardly spoken to one another after the incident at the tower near the Squalid Water's bridge, and he could hardly look at Brimmelle without becoming angry. The man had crossed a line, and they both knew it.

Thorik and Santorray had led the group across the grasslands, while Grewen and Brimmelle followed several yards behind. Bryus and Avanda continued to stop and collect various plants and insects as they trailed far behind.

"I don't know if I can ever forgive Brimmelle for his treachery against Granna and me."

Santorray didn't speak as his eyes continued to scan the horizon for danger.

"Have you ever had anyone betray you in such a way?"

Santorray growled at the question. "You have no idea."

"No, I mean someone very close to you, such as a family member."

"Your displeasure in Brimmelle pales in comparison to my past."

"How did you handle it?"

"Like all Del'Undays are trained to do. We take action and then move on."

"Take action?"

"When we are wronged, we take it upon ourselves to take vengeance or allow it to pass. This decision is made and lived out. Once complete, we move on with our lives without the continual emotional ties to it."

"You mean once it's over, you forgive them?"

"We do not forgive, nor do we forget. We move on."

"As though it never happened?"

"Not exactly, but that's close enough for you to understand."

"But how could you look them in the eye again if they had killed a family member, such as your grandmother?"

"My vengeance would cleanse me of my pain. Afterwards, assuming I allowed them to live, we would greet each other as normal."

"I don't know if I could do that."

"As a Num, I wouldn't expect you to live to these standards. These are the demon's teachings that have been embedded into our culture for thousands of years. We are Del'Unday. This is who we are."

"Demons?" Thorik asked with concern.

"You're not familiar with the Del'Unday culture on this?"

"No," Thorik answered. "I know of the demon Bakalor. Is this who you speak of?"

Santorray nodded. "There are actually three demons which the Oracles created for our lands. Rummon, the dragon, ruled the air, the wind, and the storms. He brought rain when he was pleased and drought with lightning when he was angry. Bakalor was created to rule the underworld. He shakes the earth and blows fire from the mountaintops when he is not fed properly. However, he provides us with metals to build weapons and caves to shelter us from Rummon."

"And then there is Ergrauth, ruler of the land and all that rests upon it. Ergrauth's shovel cleared the way for water to flow to our rivers and crops. His axe cut down the forest so the Fesh could graze on the grasslands, and his breath allows life to exist or be taken."

Thorik was amazed at the story. "These three demons took care of all Australis?"

"Offspring helped. Rummon and Ergrauth would often breed with mortals to create trusted henchmen and servants to carry out their needs. It is believed that Bakalor creates his children by cutting off one of his toes, which then takes a decade to fully grow back."

Recalling Bakalor's creation of Grub, Thorik nodded in agreement with Santorray's story. "But if Rummon is a demon, how did he get trapped inside my spear?"

"Ergrauth ordered the making of the most powerful weapon ever, one that could protect the skies above his battlefields. It was decided to send the blind E'rudite, Schullis, in disguise as a peasant to the dragon's lair. As a mighty demon, the dragon underestimated the maliciousness and underhandedness of the meek requester sent by Ergrauth. With his guard down, Rummon's spirit was extricated from his flesh. His body instantly froze in time and forever waits until his soul is returned."

Thinking about the story, Thorik began questioning it. "For all this to be true, the sky and the wind would cease to move until Rummon returned. However, we know this not to be the case. The wind blows, storms come and go, and he has no part in it, so this must be a fable."

Santorray's eyes never left the distant hilltops. "You would be correct if I hadn't already explained that his children took on many duties. Each of the demon's offspring plays a role, and when they argue, like siblings inevitably do, lightning flashes, thunder roars, and the sweat of their battle falls to the land as rain."

Chapter Thirty

CHUTTLE RANGE

The airy grasslands of the northern Chuttle Range were sporadically marked by large vertical rock formations, that towered over the landscape. Sometimes in clusters, but more often standing alone, the upside down cone-shaped black rocks stood out against the green and gold colors of the tall grass. The thin, rocky points reached hundreds of yards into the sky while the bases bulged out to a meager dozen yards across.

Ignoring the odd scenery, Avanda spent most of her time with Bryus as he taught her the magical properties of weeds, roots, insects, stones, and anything else they could get their hands on. With each passing day, she became more knowledgeable about spellcasting and its few limitations.

As she listened to his explanation of how the legs of some insects can be used as a primer for illusions, she noticed odd stitching in the collar of his shirt. "What's that in your tunic?" she asked, interrupting his lecture as she pointed to the stitching.

Bryus recoiled slightly and covered it up with his hand. "Nothing."

"Well, it's obviously something. What is it?"

Bryus traced the odd thread with his fingers and his facial expression became sad from his thoughts. "It's a memory."

Avanda leaned in closer. "They are hairs sewn into your clothes."

"Yes. My wife's hair." He traced the one on his left side. "And a lock of my daughter's." His hand trembled while touching the one on his right. "This is all I have left of them."

His sadness infected her as well. "I'm sorry to hear that. Is there no way to help save them?"

"I don't know where they are being held." A small tear filled one of Bryus' eyes.

Avanda looked up into the sad man's face. "I'll help you find them. I promise."

He quickly wiped his eye and sat up straight, slightly embarrassed that he had allowed himself to show any emotions. "Thank you, Avanda. I may just take you up on that someday."

Smiling, she reached over and gave him a warm hug before returning to listening to his lecture.

Thorik watched as the girl he had become enchanted with was now drifting away. No longer was she clinging to him and wanting to hold his hand. Instead, she seemed happier around the Alchemist, who had something to teach her.

Unexpectedly, Thorik had missed her soft touch. He found himself spending several hours a day looking back over his shoulder to make sure she was still there. A flicker of panic ran through his chest each time she wasn't in view. These usually only lasted a few minutes, only to find Bryus and Avanda had fallen behind while digging up worms or chasing grasshoppers.

Santorray walked up front with Thorik to scout their path. "She is not in danger."

"Who?" the Num replied in the most innocent way he could muster.

Santorray snorted. "You've been bitten, and the poison will always be in your veins."

"Poison? What are you talking about?"

"Sec, I can see the way you look at Avanda. You have been compromised."

"I don't know what you're talking about."

"Don't lie to me. You're not good at it."

Thorik looked back again, past Brimmelle and Grewen, at Avanda as she laughed after turning a pebble into a frog. "We're good friends who have been through a lot together. Of course we're going to be concerned for one another."

"Now you're lying to yourself."

"Okay, so let's say you're right, which I'm not saying you are." Thorik was absolutely serious. "How does that compromise me?"

"It compromises your mission. Having loved ones always does."

"I disagree. It makes you stronger to fight for them."

"Agreed." Santorray noticed Thorik's surprised reaction. "However, if it came down to choosing between completing your mission or saving someone you care about, which do you select?"

There was no hesitation from Thorik. "If it were between a loved one and a goal to accomplish, it is an easy answer. I would choose the loved one."

"And that is how your mission has been compromised."

"It doesn't have to be that way. We can do both."

"Perhaps. But most great successes require you to give up something equally valuable to you." Santorray scanned the horizon for life.

Several Chuttlebeasts roamed in the distance. "If it came down to you saving your grandmother or Avanda, who would it be?"

"I don't like this game," Thorik said flatly.

"Sometimes life places you in circumstances where these situations occur."

"It would be different if you asked me if it was between my own freedom and a loved one."

"Really?" Santorray scuffed. "And you would be so quick to surrender your freedom in order to save another?"

"Of course. Wouldn't you?"

"Thorik, I have had my freedom taken from me. You have no idea what you're committing to."

"Yes, I do. The other option would haunt me for the rest of my life. I could never be happy again knowing that I allowed someone to die when I could have saved them."

Without warning, an explosion erupted a dozen yards behind them. Smoke billowed up from around Bryus, leaving a gray charcoal color over his entire body. His incorrectly attached wooden arm had fouled up yet another spell. His hair smoldered, and one eyebrow was now completely burnt off. Bryus was looking in worse shape than ever.

Laughing at the spectacle, Avanda handed him a cloth to wipe his face clean.

Santorray watched for a response from the local Chuttlebeasts from the blast. As he expected, the explosion caused them to start a stampede. "Pick up the pace. We need to leave these fields before we are trampled and become permanent residents."

CHAPTER THIRTY-ONE

CUCURRIAN RIVER

Another night had settled in on the land, and the campfires were in a full blaze as Brimmelle made a makeshift fishing rod to catch some of the Cucurrian River's fine selection. The river, as well as the forest they had just entered, was full of life. It had been a long time since Brimmelle had fished, but it kept him busy and helped him avoid Thorik's gaze. The two Nums hadn't spoken in several weeks.

Northeastern Lakewood Forest was much like the southwest part of the forest, but far less spoiled. Few traveled here, and the Fesh'Unday population had grown heavy. Deer, wild boars, wolves, and grazers had not yet learned to fear travelers. In many ways, it felt more at peace to Thorik than his home village of Farbank.

After prepping the camp for the night, Thorik sat near the riverbank, upstream from his uncle, as he watched his unique extended family. Grewen was busy eating an endless supply of plants, while Santorray ensured there was enough firewood for the night before scouting the perimeter for danger and food.

Avanda was busy at Bryus' secondary campfire, rubbing various items together and speaking in odd tongues to evoke spells. Some changed wood into water, while others sent pulsating lights into the air and around the camp. Other spells allowed her to communicate with ground squirrels and other rodents.

Thorik listened as Bryus complained about his wooden arm still not allowing him to do spells correctly, making it difficult to show her the desired results. Avanda, on the other hand, was so mesmerized by the effects she achieved that she didn't really care. Her only issue was the time it took to plan and contrive a spell. She constantly wanted to take shortcuts, to speed up the process. However, when she did, something inevitably went askew.

"Not so fast," Bryus shouted at Avanda. "Instead of this spell allowing us to stay awake without the need for sleep, it could just as easily put us fast asleep if done wrong."

But it was too late, for she had rushed the mixing of components. The spell instantly knocked them both out cold, and they fell softly to the ground.

Thorik's instincts were to rush over, but he had overheard Bryus' comments and thought it was most likely best that they received a good night's sleep. Traveling in the forest would be more difficult than in the grasslands. They would need their strength.

Breathing in the fresh, moist air of the forest, Thorik could almost smell his distant village of Farbank. The sounds of the river lapping along the shores and the wind rustling through the trees were all pleasant and familiar.

The one element that corrupted his cheery memories was the sight of Brimmelle; he sat facing away from camp, fishing by himself. It hurt Thorik to even look at his uncle after his plot to steal Gluic from him. It tore at his heart each time he thought about it.

The two Nums hadn't spoken since that fight, and Thorik didn't know how to repair their relationship, or even if he wanted to. Dropping his head down as he thought about the dilemma, he noticed several dozen small river rocks placed in a spiral pattern near his feet.

The sight inspired Thorik to pull out the Runestone of Courage. Closing his eyes, he concentrated on the Runestone until he felt a presence near him. Opening one eye at a time, he was pleased to see a ghostly spirit sitting next to him.

"Granna?" His voice was gentle.

"Isn't it pleasant here?" she said instead of a greeting.

"Yes, it is. It reminds me of our home."

"And where would that be, dear?"

Taken slightly aback by the question, Thorik answered, "Farbank."

"Oh, I see. You still see that as your home/"

"Well, of course I do. Shouldn't I?"

"If it grounds you, dear. But the entire world is your home." Motioning toward Grewen, who had his feet up against the roaring fire, she continued, "Home is wherever you feel comfortable. Sometimes it may or may not be where you grew up."

"My cottage in Farbank always made me feel comfortable."

"That's nice." She gave an agreeable smile. "Doesn't this place make you feel content as well?"

Thorik glanced around and nodded. "It's very nice, but I think I would get lonely out here."

"I see. So your home is based on being near friends and family."

"I guess you could say that."

Gluic glanced over at her son, Brimmelle. "Do you understand my son is part of your family?"

"No, not anymore." Thorik was clearly being defiant. "He has betrayed us both. You wouldn't be here right now if he had had his way."

Gluic smiled. "True, but he has saved your life more than once."

"And I his. My debt is paid, as well as any debt you had to him."

Gluic laughed. "If mothers began a tally of all the debts their children and the grandchildren owed them, they would run shy of paper to keep track."

"But he tried to prevent me from saving you."

"Thorik, dear." Kindness filled her voice. "This is not always about your journey to grow, but it is also about his as well. Have you not seen the changes in him? He is learning from you every day you're together."

"Learning from me?"

"Is it so odd for someone with more years about them to learn from someone with less? To be honest, you were born an older and wiser soul than he will ever achieve during this lifetime. You are helping him reach what's needed so he can move onto his next life."

Thorik was visibly confused at what she was saying.

Gluic leaned over and moved a few of the small river rocks that Thorik had accidentally kicked. "Be patient with him. He will make you proud in the end."

"But he's so difficult. I can't change him."

"You can't blame a hog for being a hog, and you can't change the hog from being a hog, but you can teach a hog to come when it's time to eat." She followed her statement with a giggle.

"But how can I think to teach him anything when I don't even have my own soul-markings yet? Children half my age have theirs, and Avanda's continue to flourish upon her skin. Fir Brimmelle's markings are so solid and thick; surely his soul is much stronger and more mature than mine."

"Oh, I see. Your lack of soul-markings is holding you back from being the person you want to be?"

"Yes. No. Well, in a way. I just don't feel that others see me as they should."

A soft, warm smile grew on Gluic's face. "It's not your skin or any other physical feature that holds you back. Only your mind can prevent you from achieving greatness."

Reluctantly nodding in agreement, he still felt bad about not having soul-markings like all the other Nums did. "I know, Granna, but when will I get them?"

"When you don't need them anymore, and only after you become the person you want to be by having them." Gluic began fading away.

"Wait, when can I call upon you again?"

"When you are in a room surrounded by death and life as you wait your turn for both."

"Granna?" Thorik looked to see where she went. Asking a few more times, he realized that she had said what she wanted to for now.

Mulling on her words, Thorik eventually stood up, slowly walked over, and sat next to Brimmelle along the shoreline. "Anything biting?"

Brimmelle took a quick glance at his nephew before looking away. "No."

And so they sat for nearly an hour with one and two word questions and answers. Their subjects for discussion were unemotional and unrelated to the events around Gluic or the dagger. No issues were resolved, although the stress and friction between them had begun to clear away.

The camp remained still, aside from the two campfires and Bryus' snoring, until Santorray walked back into camp from his hunt for dinner. He had a dead wild boar over his shoulder, which he had caught with his hands before breaking its neck. He had returned to skin it and feed the travelers.

Walking past the smaller of the two campfires, he kicked Bryus' wooden arm away from the flames. "Wake up. Your arm's on fire," he growled as he continued on toward the main campfire.

Bryus woke from the abrupt kick and quickly noticed the end of his wooden arm was fully ablaze. He had swung it into the campfire during his spell-enhanced slumber. Jumping up from the campfire, he attempted to put it out, but his own spells continued to fail him.

Hearing the commotion, Avanda woke to view the excitement as Bryus ran around in a state of panic. Thinking quickly, she got behind him and began pushing him toward the river to extinguish his flaming arm. The two raced to the shoreline, where Avanda stopped and gave one last shove to the Alchemist.

Thorik and Brimmelle turned in time to watch Bryus fly through the air with a flaming arm and then splash recklessly into the water.

"Done fishing?" Thorik asked in an even tone.

Brimmelle nodded. "I am now."

Chapter Thirty-Two

BAKALOR'S NEXT MOVE

Rivers of lava coursed through the cavern like arteries supplying fresh blood to a body. The intense dry heat filled the air as Bakalor slammed his fist on the armrest of his throne. "This is unacceptable!" The demon growled at Irluk. "Where is my son, Grub?"

Floating nearer to the demon, the swirling coal-colored debris of the Death Witch hovered over the demon's hand for a moment before dispensing fragments of rocks which once had been the lesser demon, Grub.

Watching the pieces of his son drop into his open hand, Bakalor was momentarily speechless. "What could have done this?" He pondered the question until the final rocks fell from Irluk. "Was it Ambrosius? Has he returned?"

Moving back from the enormous throne, Irluk landed on the cavern floor in front of him. "We thought it was he, but it was Darkmere in disguise. Our trap was sprung on the wrong E'rudite."

"How could you make such a mistake?" Closing his palm on the remains of Grub, he squeezed his fist so tight that heat and light from the extreme pressure escaped from between his fingers. "I want this to be over! Bring the Nums back to me."

Standing next to the spinning burnt fragments of the Death Witch was the white-cloaked Darkmere. Looking out from his solid white eyes, Darkmere had already healed his own wounds from the attack near the Squalid Waters Bridge. "You have interfered with my plans!" he shouted. "I could have had information out of Thorik about our enemy's war plans and a prisoner to lure Ambrosius into my trap."

The swirling of Irluk's debris increased as she took offense at his comment. "This was not my mistake. Changing your form to look like the one we are all hunting was a foolish idea. My only mistake was believing Grub when he informed me he had found Ambrosius."

"Stop bickering!" Bakalor squeezed tighter on the nearly liquid rocks of Grub and grabbed his mighty mace with his free hand, pointing it at Irluk and Darkmere. "Movement toward war has begun. Someone must ensure that Ambrosius will not interfere."

"Where do we start?" Irluk backed away slightly from the demon and lowered her eyes. "We no longer know where Ambrosius' friends are heading."

The demon slammed the mace into the cavern floor, releasing a massive quake that erupted around them. "Irluk! You promised me you wouldn't let Thorik escape."

She had no response to his accusation. He was correct, and they both knew it.

"I can tell you where he is." Darkmere's statement was clearly a surprise to the others.

With the earthquake fading, Irluk hissed at Darkmere's arrogance. "And do tell, how you know this?"

Darkmere opened a side pouch and pulled out an old, battered wooden box.

Irluk laughed at the absurd item. "A child's toy? You're using a prattle box?" Overjoyed at the stupidity, she waited for Bakalor to lash out at the E'rudite.

Bakalor was not impressed. Opening his palm, he dropped the red glowing magma glob onto the cavern floor. His eyelids narrowed over his diamond eyes, and his teeth began to grind.

"Yes." Darkmere was obviously irritated at Irluk's lack of respect. "It was given to me as a child, to be used as a toy." He confirmed the witch's comment. "However, many years ago, my master, Deleth, instructed me to give it to Thorik."

Irluk watched the steaming ball of magma start to cool and crust over. As it did, she could start making out features of legs and arms. "Then how did you gain its mate?" Irluk snapped back to Darkmere.

"I never did." Darkmere smiled at the confusion. "However, the Dark Oracle, Deleth, also informed me I would need Thorik's prattle box, which will be buried in the future, even though it will show up in the past. Deleth did not explain how, but he provided me with a map of its location near Farbank. The search caused the death of Thorik's parents. I don't know how the Oracle knew my prattle box would end up in a northern canyon, but it did. There are only two boxes. Ambrosius has one, while the other box exists twice; one from my past, and one from the future."

Now fully crusted over, a mouth opened in the center of the round glob, exposing the liquid inside. Grub had returned, and he stood ready for his master's orders.

Irluk avoided staring at the lesser demon and kept to her conversation with Darkmere. "If you knew Thorik and his parents, how come the Num doesn't recall you?" She was more than a little skeptical.

Suddenly, Darkmere used his E'rudite powers and changed his body to look like a typical human traveler. "Because..." He gave a slight bow. "... I was Su'I Sorat at the time."

Irluk scoffed at the name. "A child's toy and a child's game?"

Bakalor looked confused. "Explain!" He struck the cavern floor again with his weapon, causing the ground to vibrate uncontrollably, loosening rocks from the walls and ceiling.

Irluk glanced over at Darkmere before providing the answer to the demon in order to stop the quake from dropping more rocks from the cavern's ceiling. "It's a foolish tradition that the maker of prattle boxes sign their name backwards on the box. Darkmere removed the original name and added his birth name of Tarosius as Su'I Sorat before delivering the box to Thorik."

Bakalor shook his head in anger, causing the ground's shaking to increase again. "I don't care about this! I want to know where they are headed!"

"Their travels lead them to the Govi Glade..." Darkmere changed his form back to his normal white robes, eyes, and hair before smiling at Irluk as he finished his sentence. "... in search of Vesik."

Irluk was shocked. "That's my book! How dare they venture to its hiding place?"

Darkmere didn't allow her complaints to derail his conversation. "They most likely will die in their efforts to find your book, but if they should be so lucky, I need a spell from within it for myself."

"Out of the question," Irluk hissed. "It's mine. It is bound to me. Only I should have access to it."

"The spell I need will allow me to swap locations with my brother, Ambrosius." Darkmere could tell he had their curiosity. "How convenient would this be for the two of you to have him suddenly show up here in Della Estovia?"

Shaking her head, Irluk argued the point further. "You can't perform that spell without possessing a piece of his body."

A thin, evil smile crossed Darkmere's face. "Which you do not have, but I do. Which is why I am now taking control of the hunt for him."

Irluk knew that the Dark Lord had played the game better than she had in front of the demon. The charred debris that made up her body violently swirled as her anger at Darkmere's comments grew.

Bakalor grinned at the idea, and the remaining earth tremors ended. "What do we need to do?"

Darkmere plotted for a moment before glancing down at the lesser demon awaiting his orders. "Send Grub to kill them after they have possession of Vesik. Then Irluk can make haste to bring the book back here."

Bakalor glared back and forth between Irluk, Darkmere, and Grub as he considered the E'rudite's idea. "And what will you do in the meantime?"

"Return to Corrock. I have business to take care of there, just in case Grub fails to perform the simple task of rolling onto a frail Num."

Grub's heat intensified at the backhanded comment.

"Agreed," Bakalor replied.

CHAPTER THIRTY-THREE

GOVI GLADE

Thorik's Log: 29th day of the 8th month of the 650th year.

We have reached the edge of the Govi Glade. The open land, surrounded by the thick forest, is far different than I had expected. Then again, this entire journey has not gone as planned, so why would I expect this to be any different? Brimmelle and I are starting to talk again, but I still harbor a lot of anger from his actions. We are so close to freeing Granna and returning to the safety of Farbank that I can't put my excitement into words.

The open glade had suffered from the ravages of war between the E'rudites and the Alchemists. Over a thousand years of mystical powers and spells had been unleashed into the mile-wide swath of land coated with grass, clumps of bushes, boulders, and a few trees.

Translucent spheres of energy floated in the glade like room-sized bath bubbles, slowly bouncing off one another as they passed through trees and rock outcroppings, and even into the ground.

The spheres were the remnants of the powerful magic gone astray during the battles. Some provided a view of the glade from another time; others lingered about as a captured spell waiting to be activated. Still others had deeper, darker secrets within thick vapors.

As the travelers reached the glade, they started noticing the signs of the deformities caused by the war and the remaining spheres. The most noticeable was the giant spheres' ability to change the time of the field months and years prior to or after the current date. As each sphere floated along, it erased whatever was there and replaced it with what existed at a different time in history, based on what time that specific sphere was caught in.

Trees were warped, some with branches a decade older than the rest of the tree due to where a sphere had brushed by them. Snow rested upon branches on half of a tree after a sphere engulfed that section before moving on. Twisted and bent by the spheres, few things looked right.

Rock outcroppings were cut away by the spheres, only to be replaced with a layer of tree bark or a frozen snowdrift. Patches of green grass would suddenly turn brown and dead as a sphere raised out of the ground. Dead became alive, the living became warped, and the warped became dead in a never-ending cycle.

"Fascinating." Grewen gazed at the odd formations caused by the spheres. "Past, present, and future all overlapping in our view. What an amazing sight."

Santorray stood next to the giant and sniffed the air. "This smells of a trap that waits for some fool to spring it." Squinting his eyes, he thought of just the right person. "Send in Brimmelle."

Fir Brimmelle shot Santorray a disgusted glance, while the blothrud grinned at the Num's expense.

"Where is Vesik?" Thorik asked Bryus, as the entire group stood just outside of the glade's grasp.

"How would I know?" Bryus stretched his neck and looked about for the book.

Throwing his hands in the air, Brimmelle sighed overly loudly. "I knew he didn't know."

Thorik's face turned two shades of red as he addressed Bryus. "This is the reason we brought you here. You told us you knew where Vesik was."

"Well, of course I do. The book of magic is in the Govi Glade."

"But where within the glade?" Thorik asked.

"That's a wonderful question to ask." Bryus was clearly excited to find out the answer. "The Govi Glade is an ever-changing place. Even if I set Vesik down in one place, the book could be in a different time or place when I looked for it again."

"Different place?"

Bryus' eyes grew like a child who was given a treat. "Yes, a different place or time."

"Then how will we find it?"

"The real question is, do we need to make any efforts to find it?"

"Yes, we do. I need it to save my grandmother."

"Seeing that all things in this ancient battlefield constantly change and move, then it's just a matter of time before Vesik moves right here before us." The Alchemist pointed to a spot just a few yards in front of them as an example.

Brimmelle's patience had worn thin with the entire idea. "Are you suggesting that we just stand here and wait for the book to appear?"

Bryus laughed. "No, no. It's best if we sit down and relax. This will most likely take some time. To be realistic, it would be wise to build some type of shelter for the winter."

Thorik's face tensed up. "We aren't staying here through the winter in hopes that it will appear."

"We aren't?" The Alchemist seemed genuinely surprised by Thorik's comment.

"No, you're going to tell us a faster way to find it."

"Faster? That's easy. Just walk through the glade until you find it."

"It will just be lying there? In the grass?" Thorik was in disbelief.

"Or on a rock, or in a tree."

"How do we know it hasn't already been distorted and shredded apart by the spheres or animals, or weathered away by time itself?"

Bryus laughed. "Vesik is the primary book of magic. It has a spirit of magic all its own that rivals all living things. It's protected from aging and weathering. Even the infamous Wyrlyn couldn't destroy Irluk during the E'rudite and Alchemist War... so the legend goes."

"So, Vesik has been tossed around this field for thousands of years. If it's been just lying in this field, why hasn't anyone else come here to find it?"

A devious smile rolled up Bryus Grum's face, ending at his twitching eye. "Oh, many have tried, and their remains are scattered throughout the glade. The risk has just been too great."

"The risk seems low as long as you watch what you're doing. The spheres are sluggish at best."

Bryus nodded. "True, until you enter the glade. Then the energy of your body affects them, causing the orbs to speed up. The longer you stay, the faster they go. The battlefield stripped this glade of its own natural powers, so it becomes energized once an alternative source enters."

Thorik took a deep breath, wondering what his strategy would be. "I've come this far. I must try."

"Let's get this over with," Santorray announced. "I'll start on the far end and begin working back toward you."

Avanda helped Thorik remove his pack. "I'll go with you as well. We can cover three times as much ground at the same time."

"True," Thorik said, "But the spheres will speed up that much faster with the presence of all three of us in the glade at once." Looking to Bryus for confirmation of his logic, he received it in the form of a nod. "It would be best if I go alone to minimize the effects of the spheres. I'll make a path straight across, move over a bit, and then come straight back. That way, I can eventually cover the entire field."

Growling at the idea of Thorik going in alone, Santorray reluctantly agreed to stay out of the glade. "I'll sweep the perimeter and then follow you from the far side, just in case you need help."

"Avanda and I will monitor you from this side of the field," Grewen noted.

Bryus' cheek twitched. "By your presence being in the glade, the likelihood of Vesik being in one place the entire time is unrealistic. Your scouring of the field will quickly age this land. It could show up directly behind you after your first pass and you would never know it."

Frustrated, Thorik realized that there would not be an easy way to solve this. He would have to do the best he could and rely on some luck to be in his favor. "Just wait here. I'll keep making passes back and forth until I can't keep up with the spheres. At that point, I'll rest outside the glade so they slow down." Removing all of his gear from his pack, he strapped on the empty backpack, hoping to fill it with the book, Vesik.

Meanwhile, Santorray made his way around the edge to the far side of the glade as he searched. He also kept an eye on Thorik, just in case he fell prey to anything in the open field.

Watching the mostly transparent spheres slowly bounce off of one another, Thorik waited for a clear opening before entering the field.

He had only made it ten yards before he noticed the slight increase in sphere speed. He had underestimated how difficult it would be to look through the tall grass for a book while simultaneously watching out for nearly invisible spheres coming at him from every direction. Running too fast increased the risk of not seeing the book. Going too slow increased the danger and the speed of the giant spheres.

Jogging through the glade, he came upon a tree trunk. The upper half had been cut off, and embedded in the bark was a human arm. The flesh had been infused into the wood, preventing it from deteriorating.

Next was a patch of grass that changed colors as a sphere lifted from the ground directly in Thorik's path. The view inside the sphere was distorted, but it was distinctly the view of a raging battle, perhaps from the very war that caused the spheres in the first place.

Avoiding the giant orb as it rose and lifted over his head, Thorik watched the chaos of the battle continue before running underneath it to finish his first pass of the glade.

He had completed one row. At this pace, it was going to take most of the day to complete enough rows to search the entire field.

Thorik moved over a few yards and waved to Avanda on the far side, and she enthusiastically waved back. The spheres were now at a quicker pace than they had been before leaving on his first trip across.

Jogging a little faster this time, he hoped to reduce his influence on the spheres; however, he was wrong. Nearly halfway across, the ground broke free and opened up below Thorik's feet into a hole created by an underground sphere which had removed the soil. The sphere had passed, but the hole remained, like an air bubble floating just below the water's surface. Rolling to the bottom, he tumbled into the top of a tree, which had been relocated to its new home by the sphere. Thorik couldn't tell if the entire tree was buried below him or if just the top had been misplaced, but he wasn't going to stick around long enough to find out.

Quickly scrambling up the side, he pulled himself up to the grass and rolled to his feet. It was then that he noticed a large leather-bound book sitting in the high grass. A thin leather strap held the overlapping leather covers from opening up and exposing the pages. Symbols had been burned into the leather work, which was old and worn but not damaged. It was not fancy, nor did it glow or emanate any magical lights. But then again, it had survived the Govi Glade, so it must be the book he was after. *Could I be this lucky?*

But before he could run for the book, a sphere lowered itself onto the book and the grass around it.

Thorik jumped back to prevent the sphere from taking one of his arms with it.

The book had been taken underground with the sphere.

He was suddenly torn between disappointment over missing a great opportunity and excitement, knowing that this was achievable. He now knew what they were looking for and he just needed to be prepared.

Returning to his mission, he decided to keep moving forward instead of retracing his steps. It could reappear anywhere, but it seemed demotivating to start all over again each time it was seen.

There was no giving up. Thorik was bound and determined to race this field until he was lucky enough to be in the right place at the right time. He would not fail his grandmother.

The spheres continued to speed up as he spent more time inside the glade. Spheres seemed to come out of nowhere and collide with one another, causing additional small distortions and cracks in the ground. The faster they moved, the harder they crashed, and the more likely these new effects created problems.

Rifts in the ground rose, gale force winds blew out of nowhere, and snowstorms and hail sprang forth from some of the faster collisions. This new uneven glade was now wet and slippery as Thorik fought his way back and forth, working his way across the field.

Time and time again, he had no luck as he raced back and forth across the glade, until fortune fell upon him for a second time. He noticed the book just as it began to slide into one of the new rifts in the ground.

Thorik jumped for it, sliding his upper body into the small crevasse. His hands were wet and cold as he reached out and grabbed onto the spine of the book with one finger and a thumb. But before he could pull it up, a fast-moving sphere rolled itself along the grass toward him.

There was no time to think. Thorik instinctively pulled his arm out of the way. But in doing so, he dropped the book.

Now, with nearly the entire glade done, the sun was starting to set, and many of the spheres were starting to be more difficult to view. A few of them had raging fires or electrical storms within them, and they lit up the glade. Nevertheless, it was the calm ones that Thorik now feared the most, for they were becoming increasingly harder to see in the darkening evening hours.

Racing against the lack of light, Thorik continued with his quest. The grass changed from dry to wet as he ran down the last row for the night with tired but determined eyes. Slipping more than once, he finally fell, slid off his planned path, and crashed into a tree trunk. He had seen this trunk in the glade before. This time, however, the arm was not embedded as far, nor was it protected. Insects were having their way with the fleshy pieces that still clung onto the bones. The remains fell onto the Num upon impact.

Thorik didn't have time to think about the sight before a stray sphere approached and removed it just as he leaped away. By this point, the giant spheres were flying in every direction at a quick pace, and with the sunlight dwindling, they were nearly impossible to see. Suddenly, Thorik was no longer looking for the book. He was trying to stay alive in the minefield of magical distortions.

Jumping to his feet, he bolted for the side of the glade but was blocked. The crashing of the spheres sounded like thunder, and the waves of energy dramatically increased, causing rips in the earth to snap open unexpectedly. Thorik was trapped. His only option was to continue to evade. Each time he focused on an exit, it nearly caused his death.

Diving under a collision caused a wave of energy to flatten him onto the ground. He could feel his body sink into the earth from the force, knocking the wind out of him. Fortunately, it only lasted a second.

Once it passed, Thorik heard Santorray's voice ordering him to run his way. Looking up, he saw the blothrud waving the Num forward as he stood near the edge of the glade. Taking the chance, Thorik sprang to his feet and made a mad dash for safety. Spheres tumbled toward him as though they were consciously trying to block his path, but he slid, rolled, jumped, twisted in the air, and weaved back and forth in this attempt for freedom.

But then it happened. Just a few yards from the edge of the glade, two more spheres rose from the ground and closed in on his path. He reacted without thinking and ran in between the two spheres. Then, just as they prepared to crash and squish him between them, Thorik jumped as high as he could. Unfortunately, the jump was not enough to carry him over the spheres.

As he fell, the spheres clashed, sending out a shock wave which pushed the Num back up into the air, past the edge of the glade, through the trees, and into the arms of Santorray.

He was safe, but he had failed to capture Vesik. They had nothing to show for their efforts.

Chapter Thirty-Four

CAMP CHORES

Returning to the campsite with Santorray, Thorik held his head down low as he listened to the loud crashes of spheres from the glade. Flashes of light helped him see his way, now that the sun had set, and the cool winds cascaded down from the Cuev'Laru Mountains into camp.

"Congratulations!" Grewen's typical baritone voice bellowed forth once he noticed Thorik walk into camp. The mognin was busy twisting a thick flaming log into the sole of his foot. Sparks flew as he moaned from the enjoyable feeling it gave him.

"Not now, Grewen. I let Granna down and am not ready for an argument."

Turning his foot, the giant began working the fiery end of the log between his toes. "I was being serious."

Thorik sighed and picked his head up to view the camp. There, on the far side of the fire, Bryus and Avanda were reading through the book of magic. "How did you find it? I searched all day and nearly had it twice, but I wasn't able to hold on."

Bryus glanced up at the Num and smiled. "I simply stood on the edge of the glade and waited for it to appear. When it did, I just walked out, picked it up, and brought it back to camp before the next sphere took it away. It was a lot easier than I thought it would be."

Avanda looked at Thorik and winked at him. She was glad to see that he had returned to camp but was at the moment very enthralled with what Bryus was teaching her from the book, Vesik.

Thorik was slightly disheartened by her lack of excitement over his return. Even if she hadn't known how perilous his adventure had been, he still had hoped for her to run over and welcome him back. But she didn't, and for some reason it made his chest feel tight and his stomach churn. He found himself missing her attention.

Santorray patted Thorik on the back. "It doesn't matter how it was achieved. Success of the mission is what's important. The book has been found, and now your grandmother can be freed."

Grewen placed his log back into the fire and straightened his legs so the flames would work their way between all his spread-out toes. "Oh, Bryus makes it sound simple. But if you hadn't stirred up that hornets' nest of spheres, it could have taken months or even years before it would have appeared for him."

"To be honest, I nearly didn't make it." Thorik glanced about to see if anyone was willing to listen.

"But you did," Brimmelle said without any empathy toward his nephew. "Now that you're here, why don't you start cooking supper? We haven't eaten yet."

All of the gear from Thorik's pack had been piled up near the main roaring fire. Bryus had created his own smaller second fire, like usual. No beds had been created, no herbs had been gathered, and no one had even gathered water from the nearby stream. "You waited for me to return to cook for you?"

Brimmelle raised one of his thick eyebrows at the young man's tone. "Don't be ungrateful. We could have eaten hours ago, but I insisted we wait for you."

"I don't know how to thank you enough." Thorik made no attempt to hide his sarcastic tone.

"Well, you can start by making us something to eat," Fir Brimmelle shot back at him.

"I'm not your servant, nor your cook. Everyone needs to share some responsibilities around camp." Thorik stomped the rest of the way into camp and threw his empty backpack down on top of his gear, knocking the pile over. "What would you have done if I hadn't survived? Would you have even noticed until you became hungry? Would you have all ended up starving to death?"

Grewen cleared his throat. "Um, Thorik, not to change the subject, but—"

"No! I don't want to change the subject. I've had enough of this. I'm tired of carrying more than my fair share of weight around here."

Grewen cleared his throat again and pointed toward the fire. "Thorik, your backpack is on fire."

"What?" Thorik yelled and jumped for the pack, dragging it to safety before stomping out the flames. Flushed with adrenaline, he continued to stomp on his pack to take out his frustrations.

Once he had relieved himself of his anger, he looked up from his sorry excuse for a backpack, knowing he would have to apologize for his overreaction. But instead of the glares he expected, he saw Bryus teaching Avanda magic. Several yards away, Grewen was lying on his back, slowly chewing on a shrub and getting ready to fall asleep. Apparently, everyone had ignored his outburst.

Brimmelle sat next to the fire, waiting for dinner. "I'll start reciting our nightly Mountain King readings while you make us something to eat. Perhaps I'll discuss controlling one's temper."

Once he cleaned up after they ate, Thorik sat next to Grewen, who was also sitting while chewing on local vegetation. Leaning his back up against the giant's side, he watched Avanda, who had been listening intently to what Bryus was saying for nearly two hours. Thorik finally commented to the mognin, "She's really grown up, hasn't she?"

Grewen swallowed a handful of local weeds before answering. "You both have. Your stint in Della Estovia appears to have stolen several years from each of you."

"No, that's not what I mean. Not what we look like, but how much she's matured since we left Farbank."

Grewen had underestimated how much time he had before he would need to talk again, and had tossed half a shrub into his mouth while Thorik was talking. "Yes," was all the mognin managed to say before food tumbled out of his mouth and down his chest.

"We nearly died in Della Estovia."

Grewen gave a quick swallow but wasn't able to get it all down. "If you had, your spirit wouldn't have had to travel far afterward." His little joke slipped past Thorik's ears but caused the mognin to chuckle uncontrollably, spraying leaves and small branches into the fire.

Thorik's focus was not to be swayed away from Avanda. "We became very close in the underworld."

Choking on a limb, Grewen pounded his chest. "I noticed."

"Sharing such trauma can strengthen a relationship, you know." Thorik leaned slightly forward as he watched her.

Pounding his chest again to dislodge the branch, the mognin nodded his head in agreement.

"But I think something existed between us before we went through all that suffering. And I'm concerned that I want to be closer to her." Thorik looked up at his companion. "Would it be wrong to fall in love with her? After all, she was once my student."

A loud snap could be heard in Grewen's throat as the limb finally busted and slid down into his stomach. After a quick sigh of relief, the mognin glanced over at Avanda. "It looks like she is Bryus' student now. She hasn't been your student since I met you."

Thorik's eyebrows raised at the observation. "You're right. She's my equal. But I have another concern."

Pulling another shrub from its roots, Grewen decided to wait until his conversation with Thorik had ended before filling his endless hunger. "And what would that be?"

"Em."

"What about her? Emilen has been gone a long time."

"I know, but I still dream about her."

"Thorik, she led all of us into Darkmere's trap and nearly got us killed. How can you possibly have feelings for her?"

"I'm still not certain if she had control over her own will. Darkmere's amulet controlled his followers. How could she be held responsible for her actions? Instead, we should be concerned that she is still being held under his powers."

"Little man, I know how much you cared for her. But I also know that no matter how strong of an enchantment someone may have over another, you cannot cause anyone to do something that is against their core values."

"You don't know that."

"I do know that. People and events are going to influence you all the time. Some are going to entice you with power or seduce you with lust, while others will enchant you into believing you are doing the right thing. Life is full of temptations. But none of these can force you to do something that you are hard-fast against. They can only play on your existing desires in order to push you further."

"Maybe that's what happened. Darkmere's amulet enticed her."

"To commit murder? To kill her own family? To lead us into a Darkmere's trap? I think not. She had to have accepted these actions in some way to help carry them out."

Thorik's head lowered. "Perhaps you're right. She's just difficult to get out of my head. I still miss her."

"Was she your first love?"

Fending off some embarrassment, Thorik looked at the ground while answering. "Yes."

"Good."

"Good?"

"Yes, now that you have your first out of the way, you are ready to get your head out of the clouds and see what is really available to you."

Thorik peered up from beneath his eyebrows at Avanda. "I think you're right, Grewen." A long pause followed before continuing. "To be honest, she may have been right for me all along."

Grewen waited for the Num to continue and patiently held another shrub ready to eat. He didn't want to talk with a mouth full again.

Thorik stayed silent and watched her from a distance.

The giant finally placed the plant in his mouth and started chewing.

"Should I talk to her and let her know that I'm over Em?"

With a mouthful of limbs and leaves, Grewen sighed. He nodded his answer instead of trying to swallow fast this time.

Thorik stood up and patted his hand against Grewen's thick skin a few times, partially out of nerves and partially out of respect for the giant's wise words.

While walking over to the second campfire, Thorik continued to convince himself that he was finally over Em and it was time to move forward with Avanda. Bryus and Avanda stopped talking as soon as he approached. Both looked up at him and waited for him to speak. Uncomfortable about talking to her in front of Bryus, he rubbed his hands together as his throat felt like it was swelling up. "Avanda, I love…"

Oh no! Why did that come out? Thorik's thoughts raced with emotions. He had panicked and became flustered. Sweat bubbled up from his skin as his audience of two sat in front of him, looking perplexed. His mind raced on how to finish his sentence before it became too awkward. All he wanted to do was tell her he was in love with her and not Em.

"… Em…" Oh no! What am I doing? That's not what I meant. I didn't want to say I'm in love with Em. How can I change this? Can I just run away? Would it be safer to run back into the Govi Glade? "… Embracing new things to learn," he corrected himself.

Rolling her lips up on one side, she squinted her eyes in confusion. "What?"

"Your lessons." Thorik smiled while hiding his panic. "I love to see you have embraced what Bryus is teaching you."

"I thought you didn't like me learning magic."

"Oh no, that's not what I meant. I… um, just don't like you using it. It's very dangerous."

Avanda crossed her arms and scowled. "What's the point of learning it if I can't use it?"

Thorik continued to paint himself into a corner and needed a way out. "So you can recognize magic when others are using it against us," he blurted. "Just thought I'd let you know." He pivoted and walked away before she could ask him another question.

Returning to Grewen, he fell forward onto Grewen's thick arm and placed his hands over his own head in an attempt to bury his face out of the light of the campfire.

Grewen chuckled at the sight. "It could have been worse."

"How? How could it have been any worse?"

"I don't know." The mognin laughed at the situation. "You're probably right. That's about as bad as it gets."

Thorik's face pressed harder into the mognin's arm.

Chapter Thirty-Five

GHOSTLY STRUCTURE

The stars slowly moved across the sky as the travelers slept near the fire. Distant howls from wolves and other Fesh'Unday echoed softly in the glade. The glade itself had returned to normal as large clear spheres slowly floated out of the ground and then back below, each time modifying the landscape.

Thorik was the only one awoken by the sound of a wooden door slapping against its frame in a soft wind. Its hinges gave off a soft squeak each time they moved.

Opening his eyes, Thorik saw a wooden shack standing a dozen yards inside the Govi Glade. It hadn't been there before, and he wondered how long it had been sitting there.

The shack was old and worn, its shutters hung askew, and holes could be seen in the roof. The front door and one window faced the campfire.

Thorik wiped his eyes to make sure he was seeing what he thought he was. Watching the shack for a few seconds, he noticed a shadow move behind the window, causing the Num to sit up straight and question himself. "Did I just see someone in there?" he mumbled to himself.

His answer came in the form of the front door slamming shut.

Startled, Thorik jumped slightly from the event before standing up to take a closer look.

As he approached the edge of the glade, he was surprised at the sight of a tall figure leaning against a tree, staring at the shack with his arms folded in front of him. It was Santorray. "There's been movement inside for several minutes now." The blothrud watched the small structure for any threats to the travelers.

Thorik crept his way closer to the shack. "Why would anyone build a home here?"

Leaving his scouting position, Santorray walked over to follow the Num in case he needed protection. The glade was anything but safe, and he knew it would only be a matter of minutes before their presence would affect the spheres of magic that floated within it.

Thorik's pace slowed as he entered the glade and crept up toward the front of the shack. "Hello?" He then made his way closer.

As he approached, the wind picked up, and he could hear movement from inside. Thinking it best to look inside first, he walked up to the window. It was dirty and difficult to see through, so the Num placed his face up against it and blocked out as much campfire light as he could with his hands.

Inside the single-room shack sat a table and chairs, and a fireplace was on the far side. Footsteps could be heard from within, but no one was seen. At least until a hand print slapped against the window, directly across from Thorik's face, from an unseen hand.

Thorik jumped back. His heart raced as he tried to make sense of it. He had seen the shack to be empty, yet the impression of a hand could not have been made by itself. Staring at it, he tried to figure out what he was missing.

Santorray unsheathed his sabers and scanned the area for anything hostile. He found nothing.

But then a single invisible finger pressed against the window from the inside. It moved sideways before it pulled back. A few vertical lines were added as well as a horizontal. Next to that, a circle was drawn, and a backward letter "R", and another two vertical lines, ending with two angled lines stemming from the last vertical one.

Shivers ran up the Num's neck as he looked at the word in the window. His name, Thorik, had been spelled facing inside. Was it a call for him to enter? How did they know his name? Who are they? Questions raced through his head as he stared at his name.

Stepping forward, Thorik peered into the window again, this time without placing his face so near. Again, it appeared empty. "No signs of life," he whispered to Santorray. Regardless, something had written Thorik's name on the inside of the dirty window.

Thorik moved from the window to the door. Taking a deep breath and holding it, he grabbed the handle and pushed it open. The hinges whined as the door opened to unveil the room, with trash piled in the corners. The walls were covered in writings on top of writings, so much so that it was difficult to read any of them. What he could read made little sense, but he still heard scribbling on the walls.

"Hello?" Thorik asked, still standing in the doorway, knowing that there wasn't anyone in the room to answer.

"Hello?" It was a soft faint voice that had replied.

Thorik's body froze. Had he imagined that he had heard the voice, or was it really there? "Watch my back," he said to his blothrud friend.

"As well as the rest of you," he replied.

Stepping cautiously into the shack, the Num asked a different question. "Who are you?"

The pause was long enough to make Thorik feel he had imagined the original greeting, so he stepped farther into the room.

Santorray took one last look around before leaning down to enter the small doorway.

Without warning, the door pulled away from Thorik's hand, slammed shut, and locked, smacking Santorray square on his nose in the process.

Grabbing the door handle, Santorray attempted to thrust it back open. Unsuccessful, he pushed it with his shoulder to dislodge it. Again, it didn't budge the lock. He'd have to break it down. Stepping back, he prepared to use his body as a ram to bust through the door as he howled a warning cry, alerting Thorik to jump clear.

"Stop!" Thorik yelled from inside. The blothrud's attempt to open the door was causing the shack to nearly collapse on top of the Num as beams cracked and ceiling boards fell. "I'm not in danger!" he shouted, just in time to stop his companion from knocking the entire shack down.

Santorray halted his attack and scanned the area before moving to the window, but even with his strong night vision, it was difficult to see through the dirty glass into the dark room. Growling at the situation, he kept his senses on alert for approaching danger. Spheres would soon gain speed and could approach from any angle.

Thorik's eyes adjusted as the falling debris subsided. Only traces of the campfire light now worked into the room through the soiled window. Coughing from the unsettled dust, he stepped toward the table in the center of the room. As he approached, a chair pulled out from the table by itself, as if to invite the Num to sit down.

His options were simple; either he leaves now, or he stays and finds out what is going on. Thorik took in a deep breath before sitting down.

"Get out!" said a low, shallow voice. This one differed from the original voice he had heard. "Leave us alone..." The sound of writing became more intense on the walls, and symbols were added on top of other writings. None were legible to the Num.

Thorik was confused. "You called to me. My name is Thorik. You wrote my name on your window."

The table pushed away from Thorik, and trash in the room began flying about. It suddenly became cold, and when Thorik tried to stand, he found himself held down in the chair by an unseen force.

"... Warning!" the softer voice said near Thorik's ear.

Thorik pushed with his hands in an attempt to get up from the chair as a dark shadow materialized and stood before him, pushing him back down. Papers and trinkets continued to be thrown about the room, and more writings were etched onto the walls. "What warning?" Thorik asked. "What do you want?"

"... Vesik..." The voice faded in and out, often preceded or followed by other words that were too faint to hear.

Thorik didn't like the sound of a warning relating to the book they needed to save Gluic.

"... Avanda..."

"Avanda? What about her?" The idea of her being pulled into this warning struck a nerve of fear down Thorik's neck and back.

A second, larger shadow moved toward the center of the room. It was then that the table next to Thorik exploded into pieces, knocking Thorik onto the floor and freeing him from the grasp of the first shadow.

Thorik rolled to his feet and moved to the back wall, near a small window. Outside of the window, Thorik could see an approaching Govi Glade sphere. His time was up; the sphere would soon take the entire shack away just as fast as it had appeared. "What about Avanda? Is she in danger?"

"... danger..."

The back wall began to disappear as the sphere rolled into its space.

"Thorik," Santorray shouted. "I'm getting you out of there!"

"Not yet!" Thorik shouted back as he jumped from the wall and toward the front door. Halfway across, he was struck with the chair he had been sitting on earlier, and he fell to the floor. "Danger from what?" Thorik asked the shadowy mass after pushing the pieces of the broken chair off him. "What can I do to stop the danger?"

"... Vesik..."

Over half the building was now erased from sight as the sphere filled it in with a boulder. The remaining walls shifted and bent under the pressure of the changes being made.

"What about Vesik?" Thorik yelled as he ran to the door.

"... must prevent..."

The ceiling was now gone, and a thunderstorm raged overhead when looking into the sphere. Thorik unlocked the door and grabbed the handle to pull it open in order to escape the shelter, but the shifting of the walls had jammed the door and prevented it from moving. Thorik pulled again and again, but he was trapped.

The shack was nearly gone. Only the front wall remained as Thorik stood on the few feet of floorboards that still existed. Jumping into the sphere could end his fate inside of the boulder. If it allowed him to live, where would he actually be? Would he ever see his friends again?

Thorik then spotted the handprint on the window and realized his last option. Taking a few quick steps, he launched himself into the air and toward the front window. Unfortunately, the floor buckled from the sphere's pressure, causing him to miss his mark and slide to a stop under the window.

Torrential rain pounded hard from the open roof as the sphere rolled up close to him, making it impossible for him to stand up and jump through the window. He had stayed a few seconds too long and screamed in terror for help.

Crouching down to maximize the time he had before the sphere rolled on him, Thorik heard an explosion as shards of glass and wood sprayed his body. Two large hands reached through the wall and grabbed the Num, pulling him out into the glade, free of the sphere's stormy destruction.

"Are you insane?" Santorray released the Num in the calm night air of the glade only feet away from the nearly destroyed structure. "You could have been killed."

The front of the shack was being replaced with the large boulder as the sphere continued to roll toward Thorik on its way back down toward the ground.

Thorik was far too appreciative of the blothrud's assistance to argue with him. "Thank you." He was still catching his breath from the ordeal between his words. "Let's get out of this glade while we still can."

"Agreed."

Thorik quickly led the way to safety. "Did you hear the warning? Did you experience the voice?"

"The only thing I heard was a helpless princess voice calling for help. That wasn't you, was it?"

"Yes, that was me. That must make you my prince who came to save me."

Passing the Govi Glade's boundaries, they both had a good laugh as they returned to the camp.

Chapter Thirty-Six

ORDERS TO KILL

Heading back out of the Govi Glade before their presence caused the spheres to speed up any more, Thorik and Santorray carefully watched all sides for danger. And danger is what they found, only this was not in the expected form of a rogue sphere.

"Stop!" Santorray ordered. "I sense a new trembling... different from the spheres we have evaded so far."

Lifting out of the ground just outside of the glade, a red glowing mass of liquid rock formed arms, legs, and long teeth. The creature stood between the sleeping travelers back at camp and the two still in the glade. Fire escaped from cracks on the creature's motionless body while its outer surface cooled to a crusty black. Bakalor's son had returned.

"Grub?" Thorik's eyes widened and his mouth opened as he stood speechless for a moment. "But... Rummon killed him."

Santorray stepped in front of Thorik to protect him. However, doing so meant Grub could tell exactly where the blothrud was. Without eyes, the lesser demon used the vibrations in the ground to determine his enemies' locations.

Opening his gaping mouth, which spanned his stomach, intense flames rolled out of Grub as he faced toward Santorray. Then, without hesitation, he charged at the two travelers in the glade.

"Run!" Thorik swiveled around and followed his own advice.

"Split up," Santorray said. "He can't follow us both."

Grub ran halfway before folding up his arms and legs and rolling after them. The massive heat pouring out of the lesser demon scorched a path in the earth as he increased his speed.

Thorik veered off to the left, and Santorray to the right. Spheres increased their speed from the energy of three beings within the glade perimeter. Lightning struck inside some, while others were completely black. Nearly a third of them had sunshiny days within their barrier's grasp.

Looking back to see which one of them Grub was chasing, Thorik had mixed feelings about finding the molten mass rolling behind him.

Banking to the left and then tumbling to the right, Thorik used every trick he knew to lose his chaser. Unfortunately, the small gains he made were quickly lost when he ran straight.

"Get him near a sphere!" Santorray followed from behind, carrying a large branch he had pulled from one of the deformed trees.

The Num turned and dodged a near-fatal attack from Grub. "Why?"

"Get as close as you can and I'll knock him into it."

It may not have been a good plan, but at least it was a plan. Thorik knew he couldn't keep running forever. Seeing a cluster of spheres all rising up near each other, he figured it would increase the odds of Santorray being able to knock Grub into one of them as they ran near them.

Darting off in a new direction, Thorik added a few feet between himself and the lesser demon as they both raced toward the spheres, with the blothrud following behind with his bulky wooden weapon. By the time they reached the cluster of spheres, Grub was on Thorik's heels, and his heat started to burn the Num's back.

Struggling to catch up to them, Santorray leaped forward with all his might and swung at the lesser demon while still flying in the air.

He smacked the fiery mass with the end of the thick branch, causing the wood to immediately ignite into a huge torch as Grub went rolling into one of the winter spheres with an ice storm coating everything in sight.

Crashing to the ground, Santorray nearly impaled himself on the other end of the tree limb.

Thorik skidded to a halt before running back to his friend. "You did it!"

"Not so fast. We're not safe yet." Santorray peered up to witness a few more spheres emerging on their other side. They were now surrounded by them. They were trapped.

A flash from within one of the darker spheres caught Thorik's eyes. He looked inside of it to witness a battle of magic. "The spheres are moving faster. We'll have to make a quick escape once an opening presents itself."

"No time!" Santorray yelled as Grub launched himself back out of the sphere he had rolled into. His crusted-over mass flung through the air, striking and igniting the branch that Santorray quickly pulled up in order to block the attack. The thick wood had prevented Grub from touching the blothrud, but the impact knocked him backward.

Santorray's fall pushed Thorik and himself into the sphere the Num had been looking at. They fell backward in time and into the actual events which had carved the glade into a place of danger. They were now in the middle of the Alchemist and E'rudite War, and the night air was electrified with magic.

Grub followed them through the orb into the glade of the past.

Seeing him arrive, Santorray rolled to his feet and swung his flaming club, knocking the glowing mass out of the glade toward one of the two battling sides. In doing so, his branch exploded into a thousand splinters. His weapon was destroyed.

"We need to get back out of this sphere before it closes," Thorik yelled over the pounding noise of the battle.

It was a strange statement, seeing that their surroundings had no resemplence to a sphere. The only noticeable sight of their passageway back to their time was a slight hue change to what appeared to be the inside of a piece of concave glass, a section of glass which was getting smaller by the moment. The gateway home was unnoticeable to anyone not specifically looking for it.

As they raced back toward their exit home, a battered old man appeared before them, blocking their way. "Death to all those who refuse to join us!" he yelled before clapping his hands tightly together. Waves of energy sprung forth from his single clap, knocking Santorray high in the air and into the front lines of the battle.

There wasn't time for Thorik to run all the way over to his friend and back as the sphere continued to close.

"Thorik! Run!" Santorray shouted as he became engaged in the battle. "Don't wait for me!"

Thorik tried to determine exactly how far the blothrud had been thrown, but all he could see were the bodies he was tossing up in the air as he attempted to make his way back.

"A Num?" laughed the battered old man. "I'll melt you down where you stand." As the man raise his bracelet-filled arms to perform a spell, Thorik felt his feet become stuck to the ground, preventing him from escaping.

Thorik could see the sphere continuing to close. Attempting to jump, he found that his feet were rooted to the ground, causing him to fall forward. In doing so, he felt a ball of extreme heat roll past his back.

Grub had returned. His flying attack on the Num had missed. When the Num fell, the lesser demon had shot past him and hit the old man by mistake, instantly killing him instead of Thorik.

The spell holding Thorik's feet to the ground was immediately released, because of the spellcaster's death. Freedom to reach the exit was available again. However, Grub now stood in front of the Num, as he breathed a furnace of heat toward the Num.

"Off with you!" came a voice from the side. It was followed by Grub's body being crushed in midair. As he was squeezed tighter and tighter, the lesser demon shrank from the pressure building around him until a bright flash of light blazed outward, leaving nothing but a large diamond floating where he once was.

The E'rudite, who had turned Grub into the gem, grabbed the diamond, blew on it to cool it off, and then handed it to Thorik.

Thorik looked up to see a friend he had missed for a very long time. "Ambrosius?"

"Thorik, get out of here! You don't belong here."

"The sphere is nearly closed." The Num pointed to the small section of floating color distortions hovering in the air. "And Santorray is out in this battle. I can't leave him."

"Get back to where you came before you make things worse. I'll take care of your friend."

Thorik took a step toward the sphere and then turned back to his dearly missed companion. "I have so much to ask you." He hesitated as to his next action. "Come with me!"

"Go!" The E'rudite held out his hand, forcing the Num into the air and back into what remained of the sphere before it closed up.

Thorik rolled out of the sphere just before it went under the ground. Several more continued to float about, and he waited for Santorray to appear from one of them. He knew that the longer he stood in the glade, the more danger he put himself in. But he refused to leave. In fact, he was hoping to increase the frequency and number of spheres in order to increase the chances for Santorray to appear in one of them. It was a risk he was willing to take.

Dodging his way from one sphere to another, he kept on his toes and hoped one wouldn't open up directly below him.

This went on for a while before he heard a loud scream of pain. Looking up, he witnessed a massive creature fall from a sphere above him. The two-headed creature had two arms, four legs, and a tail that had a sharp hook on its end. Long, sharp horns rose from its heads while shorter ones traced down both of its long snake-like necks. Blood from recent cuts and bite marks coated parts of the beast's body and splattered upon the blades of grass. The creature had fallen out of an overhead sphere and into the glade, nearly landing on the Num.

Thorik fell backward from the shock. This was not what Thorik was hoping would appear.

Shaking off the unpleasant landing, the creature stood up and looked down at the Num. Reaching out with both of its arms, it leaned forward to scoop Thorik up as he attempted to crawl away.

But before it reached the helpless Num, Santorray fell from the same sphere and landed on the creature's back. With a bloody saber in each hand, he stabbed the creature deep in its back.

Three times the size of Santorray, the creature arched its back and tried to grab the blothrud.

Bracing his body, with one saber deep into the creature, Santorray used the other one to slice one of the creature's long necks. Blood sprayed from the new gash, glazing the grass and the Num with thick red liquid.

Jerking from the cut, the creature attempted to buck the blothrud off its back. It thrashed back and forth and swung its tail violently to crush its attacker.

Even with his best grip firmly holding onto his saber, the speed and mass of the creature's tail knocked Santorray off its back. Sliding down the beast's side, he dug his arm spikes into the creature's skin, ripping a long, gaping cut down its shoulder and chest.

Flailing about, the creature reached over and finally caught Santorray in its grip.

It was at that moment that Santorray reached up inside the fresh wound with his saber and struck the creature's heart.

A sudden moment of silence followed as the creature realized what had happened. An instant later, it fell forward, while Thorik scrambled to get out from under it before being crushed.

With a thunderous crash, the lifeless body stretched out across the field.

Pulling his arm and weapon out of the creature, the blothrud stepped back from it and wiped his sabers clean.

"Santorray!" Thorik shouted.

"Thorik, what are you still doing here? Did you accomplish your mission?"

"What? We haven't even finished sleeping the night away."

"This is the same night we fell into the sphere?"

Thorik looked baffled. "Of course. Why would you think differently?"

"Because I've been fighting in battles for months. It could be a year for all I recall. Then I saw the inside of this sphere."

"And that creature prevented you access to the sphere, so you had to kill it?"

Santorray shook his head as he sheathed his sabers. "No, he and his two bigger brothers were in my way. He made a run for it once I taught the others a lesson." A hint of a smile crossed his face at the joke as tears pooled within his eyes from a deeper personal meaning that was unknown to Thorik.

During their discussion, a sphere emerged from the ground near the two and covered up the location of the creature's left shoulder and head. As it moved past, those segments of its body vanished and were replaced with grass and shrubs. The parts had been precisely carved away from the rest of the creature's body. It wouldn't be long before the entire body was replaced with the glade at other times in history.

"We need to get out of here." Santorray turned toward the nearest edge of the glade.

Thorik jumped to his feet and followed Santorray, exiting the glade boundary. He didn't understand why the spheres couldn't pass the perimeter, but it was obvious where the boundary was by the row of undistorted trees and brush.

Rounding the perimeter of the glade, the two returned to camp. No one was the wiser that Thorik and Santorray had nearly vanished into the night after speaking to ghostly spirits and falling into a sphere. But what haunted the Num, more than the disembodied voices and not having a chance to speak with Ambrosius, were the words of warning he had received about Avanda and Vesik.

Once they arrived, Santorray began healing his wounds while Thorik woke Grewen and told him of the shack and the adventure that followed. It was important that he didn't forget any details by sleeping on it prior to discussing it.

Grewen sat quietly and listened before responding. "Are you sure you weren't sleeping?"

"Yes, I'm sure. Santorray was with me."

Grewen stretched his long arms out and twisted his head to work out the kinks in it. "You saw Ambrosius? Are you sure it was him?"

"Yes, but he was different somehow. His face... it wasn't burnt. I never met him prior to Darkmere's attack on the Grand Council, when Ambrosius was severely burned across the side of his neck and face. But I know it was him, and he knew me as well. He called me by name."

"Did he tell you how he survived Weirfortus or what his plans are to prevent Darkmere from destroying our lands?"

"No, there was no time to talk. He simply saved me from Grub and then sent me flying back through the sphere. Look, I even have what remains of Bakalor's son." He pulled out a large diamond from his pocket.

Grewen nodded. "We know nothing more about him or what we need to do to help in this pending war."

"No, we will have to carry on as we were. The question I have is whether this is tied to the warning about Vesik."

Grewen's bald forehead bunched forward at the thought. "So, a haunted shack shows up out of nowhere to warn you that Avanda is in danger from Vesik?"

"You make it sound ridiculous."

"I didn't make it sound like anything more than a summary of your story." Straightening out his legs, he hung his toes over the campfire flames. "Would you say it's a fair statement?"

"Yes, mostly. The problem is that I couldn't hear a lot of the words. There was a warning, and Vesik's name was said. And so was Avanda's. So it seems pretty clear."

One of Grewen's large eyebrows raised up. "Perhaps. But could it be a warning that Avanda will destroy the book?"

Thorik hadn't considered that. "Why would she destroy it?"

"I didn't say she would. We're just guessing the meaning of this riddle... we may not even have enough clues to properly perform this task."

"We know enough that Avanda needs to stay away from Vesik. That we know for sure."

"We do?" Grewen wiggled his toes in the lapping flames.

"Yes. I heard it say, 'Warning,' 'Vesik', and then 'Avanda.' What else could it be?"

"I don't know, but that doesn't imply there isn't another option."

"Well, until you think of one, I'm going to make sure Avanda keeps her distance from Vesik."

"That may be a little harder than you think." Grewen pointed toward the second campfire that Bryus had established farther from the glade than the original camp.

Vesik was snuggled up under Avanda's arms as she slept next to Bryus and his campfire. Her face was content and relaxed as she cuddled the large book.

Thorik had no idea if they had fallen asleep naturally or if one of her spells had knocked them both out again. "You know, Grewen, I just get a bad feeling about her having that book."

Grewen yawned and stretched. "You might still be spooked from the shack you saw. See if you feel differently in the morning."

"I doubt it. The book could be dangerous. It might be best if we keep it away from her, perhaps even tonight. At least until we know what the warning is about."

"We may never know. Besides, doesn't this sound like Brimmelle's reasoning for taking Gluic's dagger from you?"

"No, this is completely different. When we first met Ambrosius, he warned us to stay away from magic. Then he suddenly appeared right after I received this warning. Let's face it, Avanda's spells are usually more dangerous than they are helpful. And now we have just given her more power."

Raking his fingers back through his hair, Thorik knew that pulling the book away from her would only end in a fight. "I'll address this with Bryus in the morning. Do you think he would help me with this?"

Looking back to Grewen for approval, he found the mognin already lying back down and falling asleep. Apparently, Grewen didn't feel it was his decision to make.

Chapter Thirty-Seven

Open Book

B ryus and Avanda woke up early and began searching through the book of magic while everyone else still slept. A leather strap was untied and the overlapping leather cover opened up to reveal pages and pages of handwritten notes, drawings, and symbols. Avanda carefully turned Vesik's large, old pages in order to preserve their delicate appearance and to ensure none of them would be bent or torn. Bryus allowed Avanda to handle the book, seeing that he feared he would damage it with his defective wooden arm.

Within its pages, red and black ink explained the world's most powerful spells in great detail. Most of them were so complicated that the book would need to be present while actually performing the planned enchantment, summoning, or evocation. Divinations and illusions also filled the pages with instructions on hand and body gestures, vocal commands, and physical components such as objects and plants. Some included blood of various species, while others required tears. Vesik was a mixture of the Alchemists' spells used before the E'rudite and Alchemist war.

The vast powers listed between the rich overlapping leather covers caused the book to have a life of its own. The pages they read would glow in the dark of the night, causing the writing to look etched into the pages.

Gazing upon the magical pages, Avanda's fingers gently traced the soft material that held the writings. "We should write these spells down, just in case we lose the book."

Bryus shook his head, but retained a smile. "It won't work. Even with all that this enchanted book has to offer, the book hides one key element from every spell to ensure you don't attempt the spell without Vesik being involved. In fact, Vesik is often one of the components in order to control the use of the spell. Sometimes the book hides writing on entire pages with the most dangerous powers until you can be trusted."

Gently, Avanda turned another page. "Can we try one of the spells?"

Bryus was nearly giddy as he watched the pages of spells unfold. "Absolutely. I'd like to try them all."

"Which one should we do first?"

Bryus closed his eyes and touched a page with the end of his fingertip. "Open it to this one."

Avanda watched the pages fall one after another until she reached the page his finger was holding back.

Bryus smiled. "Very interesting."

"Really? What is it?"

"It's a summon swap spell."

Smiling at the sound of it, Avanda waited for an explanation.

"Who sleeps the most soundly?" the Alchemist quietly asked.

Scanning the group, she quickly responded, "Brimmelle and Grewen."

"Excellent. Let's try Brimmelle. Collect a few hairs from his head and bring them here."

"Hair, again?"

"I'd gladly take a toe or finger, but I have a feeling he'd wake up from such an amputation."

"Good point," she replied as she took a blade. Quietly walking over to him, she gently lifted a few hairs from the back of his head. Pausing, she became concerned about her actions, but a quick glance at Bryus' smile prompted her to complete the mission. After a quick cut, she had half a dozen pieces of hair in her hand, and she quickly maneuvered her way back to Bryus, who had been reading the spell in the book.

"Here they are," she said. "Do I need to boil them?"

"No," he responded, as though it was a foolish question. "Not for a summon spell."

"Sorry. I didn't know."

"You have so much to learn." He took the hair from her. "Now cut some of your own hair off."

"Mine? How about Grewen? He's a sound sleeper."

"He's also bald."

Nodding, she agreed and then reluctantly cut off several hairs from her own head before handing them to Bryus.

"Grab that hourglass I obtained from Trewek."

"Obtained?" she asked, skeptical of how he ended up with a pouch full of items with no way to trade for them.

"Well, I didn't have it prior to arriving in Trewek, and I had it before I left, so yes, I obtained it during that time."

"Did you steal it?"

"Listen, I'm not going to sit here and allow you to call me a thief," he said in a raised voice.

Avanda backed down but still questioned the thought. "Just tell me what I'm supposed to do."

"Reality is, you shouldn't be doing anything with your limited knowledge. However, seeing that I am currently unable to perform spells correctly, you will do exactly what I tell you to in order to make sure nothing goes wrong."

Avanda nodded and searched for the hourglass in the large pouch. Moving several jars and brass hooks out of the way, she found an hourglass with a metal frame to keep it from breaking.

Bryus watched her pull it out. "Excellent." He then tied Brimmelle's hair onto one end and her hair onto the other. Following the instructions in the book of magic, he had Avanda utilize various verbal and physical commands to prepare the spell. It was at that point that the final verbal commands appeared on Vesik's pages.

"Can you read these?" Bryus asked.

"Yes."

"Good. Now, go cuddle up against Grewen and say those last few words as you flip the hourglass over. Just relax. It will take a while, so you must be patient."

Patience was not one of her strengths, but she would do her best. Reciting the last words to the spell over and over in her mind, she walked across the camp and snuggled up to Grewen, who naturally tossed an arm over her to protect her. She had felt the need for protection before, and he instinctively moved when he felt her body.

Bryus watched with excitement as she spoke the last words and flipped the hourglass over.

She waited for the spell to take effect, but she couldn't see anything happen. Looking over at Bryus, he nodded to her to give it more time, so she did. However, lying still and waiting silently only lasted a few minutes before she fell asleep.

"Avanda?" Bryus whispered in order to wake her without alerting everyone else in camp.

Rubbing her eyes, she sat up next to the main campfire. "Bryus?"

"Yes, it's me." He helped her up to her feet as he escorted her to his smaller campfire.

"Why didn't it work?"

"Why do you say that?" he asked as he sat her down on a log, facing the other travelers.

With her eyes finally coming into focus, she could see Brimmelle cuddled up against Grewen, with the mognin's large arm over him to protect him. Avanda and Brimmelle had swapped locations.

Thorik yawned and stretched and stirred as he struggled to sleep. He was so close to releasing his grandmother and ending his journey. Every minute seemed to drag out. Drifting in and out of his slumber, he was nudged awake by the sound of Avanda cheering.

His eyes popped open, and he immediately sat up. Thorik could see the delight on Avanda's face. Bryus was pleased as well.

Tossing off his blanket, Thorik lifted himself to his feet, wiped his eyes clean, and stumbled over to Bryus' campfire. "Did you figure it out?"

"Yes!" Avanda was filled with great happiness. "We did it!"

"That's wonderful." With a grand sigh of relief, Thorik removed the dagger Varacon from his belt and held it carefully in front of him. "Let's get this over with."

Avanda and Bryus looked at each other and laughed. "We didn't figure out that spell," Bryus said.

Thorik was shocked. "You mean to tell me you haven't been working on freeing Gluic? What have you been doing?"

"Are you insane?" Bryus was clearly annoyed. "Asking Vesik for a spell of that magnitude would be improper before we showed her that she could trust us with something less extensive."

"Showed her? It's a book."

"Perhaps, but if not treated properly, she may not provide us with any spells." Using his good hand, Bryus opened the book up to several blank pages. "See, now look what you've done! The spells are gone. You've offended Vesik and possibly lost our opportunity to save Gluic."

Thorik glanced at Avanda and then back at Bryus. "Are you serious? The book has emotions?"

Bryus showed him a few more blank pages. "Every time you open your mouth, the more we lose the chance to see her spells."

"I apologize," Thorik said half-heartedly. It all seemed a bit ridiculous.

Bryus watched the blank pages stay blank as he shook his head. "You will have to do better than that."

"What?"

"You've offended the most powerful and sought-after enchanted item in all the land, and you think a casual apology will suffice?"

"What would you have me do?"

"Indeed, what would I have you do... Ah! First of all, you must lower yourself to one knee and bow to her."

"How would it know if I'm bowing?"

"It? You continue to call Vesik an 'it?' Do you want to save Gluic or not?"

Thorik quickly backed down and lowered himself onto one knee before bowing forward.

Bryus let the Num stay down several moments longer than Thorik would have liked. "Excellent. Now place your hand near Vesik without touching her and apologize for your insensitive comments."

Thorik did as he was told. "I am sorry, Vesik. I was wrong to call you a book. I will treat you with more respect.

Bryus nodded. "Keep going. I think it's starting to work."

"I will never again assume that you or any other enchanted items are without feelings. I meant no harm by it. I have been on the receiving end of such insults and should know better."

Aside from the rustling of the campfire, the camp was quiet. Thorik slowly lifted his head to see Avanda and Bryus holding back their laughter. It had all been a ruse. "Well played." Thorik got back on his feet and dusted himself off.

The other two released their laughs at Thorik's expense.

"Now that you have humiliated me, have you found the spell that we need?"

Bryus had Avanda turn a few pages before he instructed her to stop. "Ah, here it is."

"A spell to release Gluic?"

"Yes," Bryus said sarcastically. "The spell is named 'Releasing Gluic'."

Thorik was not impressed. "Did you find one or not?"

"Understand, Thorik, finding the right spell is difficult. We must combine a spell such as this one, which reverses an enchanted object's spell with one that safely relocates a soul."

"What does that mean?"

Bryus kept his attention on the notes from the spell. "It means, Num, that we will find the spells we need in here."

"Excellent. How long before we can free her?"

Bryus stroked his chin as he continued reading. "How far is it to Ergrauth Valley?"

Thorik thought it was an odd question to ask, but that wouldn't be the first one from the Alchemist. "I have no idea. The Guardians block the entrance, and they are a week or two of travel from here. Why?"

"This spell requires Ergrauthian Spice."

It meant nothing to Thorik. "Can't we purchase some in Woodlen?"

"No, you can't just purchase this spice from your local market. It is special and has natural magical powers. In fact, it's actually two spices that, when mixed together, can negate any spell. We will need this to reverse the flow of the dagger."

"Is this another one of your jokes?"

"I wish it was. We'll need to travel to the Guardians, if not beyond, to obtain the components for this spell."

By this point, the sun had started to rise and Brimmelle had begun to wake while cuddled up to Grewen, under the mognin's protective arm. "What?" He then realized that he was snugging with the giant. "By the powers of the Mountain King himself, what's going on here?"

CHAPTER THIRTY-EIGHT

CULTURAL DIFFERENCES

Thorik's Log: 30th day of the 8th month of the 650th year.

Our journey to save Gluic has changed course. Now that we have the spell required to release my grandmother from the dagger, it has become apparent that we are in need of a critical component to perform it. The only location that holds this component is beyond the Guardian Towers, in Ergrauth's Valley. We will head out this morning, once I have informed everyone of the news. I doubt they will be pleased to hear it.

Morning came, and the discussion of the new destination was not well received. Not only was it one more delay for their return to Farbank and away from any plans to help stop the pending war, but it was also leading them into the most dangerous part of Terra Australis. Only Del'Unday were permitted beyond the Guardians, which stood at the entrance to Ergrauth's Valley.

But Thorik had come too far to give up now and he would travel there by himself if need be. His determination trumped the concerns that any of the others had. Eventually, they all agreed to follow him to the valley to help free Gluic.

"Santorray, I don't understand why you're against this trek. Aren't you originally from the Ergrauthian lands?" Thorik asked as they walked out of the forest that surrounded the Govi Glade.

"It's not a place for you. Outsiders are immediately found guilty of trespassing and are enslaved or taken to the city of Ergrauth."

"But we have you with us."

"I may not be able to save you."

"Why can't we pretend to be your slaves, like we once did in Corrock?"

"The two cannot be compared. Corrock is a far easier place to get away with such deceptions."

"Is that why you left?"

Santorray didn't answer at first, as his eyes squinted at the memories. "I was exiled for crimes against my father."

"Your father? What did you do?"

"I disobeyed him."

Thorik waited for further explanation, but received none, so he coaxed the blothrud for more. "It had to be more than just disobeying him."

"Your culture differs from ours. I'm fortunate to be alive after disobeying my father."

"What? Surely you're exaggerating. He wouldn't have murdered you for such a thing. Your neighbors and local authorities would have never stood for such an atrocity."

"He had full right to kill me where I stood, and no one would have batted an eye. Disrespecting my father in public is one of the worst things I could have done to him. If word had gotten out that he didn't dispense immediate, severe punishment, then he would have lost face, and respect toward him would have been lost by all. He did the right thing by unleashing his fury at me."

"How horrible. What a terrible place to grow up and live."

"No, it was a grand place to live. Everyone knew the rules. Life was very cut-and-dry. You cross the line, you receive punishment. You do what you are told, you are rewarded. Knowing boundaries keeps things in order and reduces unnecessary stress. Many cultures could learn from our structured ways."

"But..." Thorik thought a moment before continuing. "The Ovs in the city of Trewek live just the opposite, and they seem to be happy."

"I'm sure they are, considering they run around without any ramifications to their actions."

"But it seems to work for them."

"That's because the Ov'Unday are pacifists and avoid dealing with real issues. This allows others to take advantage of them very easily."

"I didn't get the sense that any of them were taking advantage of one another."

"And you won't. They will turn the other way and allow the minority of the culture to have their way. Warriors like you and I could never live in such places."

Thorik found it odd that Santorray would place them both in this category. "Why do you say that? I felt very relaxed there."

"You and I could never sit idly by once we started witnessing some individuals get away with murder. They allow their victims to suffer as the city officials try to help the criminals understand that what they did was wrong. Instead of taking swift action to eliminate the bad eggs, they allow them to continue to spread their poison, all the while hoping the offenders will change for the better."

"You don't think individuals can change?"

Santorray growled at the idea. "Few do."

"I hope you're wrong."

"I wish I was. Look at your fellow Nums. Brimmelle hasn't changed much since I have met him. He's still prejudiced against all Altered Creatures and most likely always will be, even though he relies on several to travel with and keep him alive. And then there is Avanda."

"What about her?" Thorik's voice was defensive.

"She will never take the time to get things right. She likes shortcuts and quick results. Her magic is chaotic and risky and always will be. Despite knowing this, you have provided her with a book that provides her with more of these dangerous powers. Your mission to save your grandmother has put our safety in jeopardy by giving her the book, knowing in your heart that she will never change."

"You don't know that she can't change."

"I know that as long as you keep feeding her what she wants, there is no reason for her to change and become more responsible. Pain is a needed part of the Del'Unday culture. People don't change until they feel they are forced into doing things differently in order to survive. As long as you protect Avanda and give her what she wants to learn more magic, she will never grow less dangerous."

Thorik looked back behind them at Bryus attempting to get Avanda to practice a spell, with little luck. As normal, she continued to want to move on to other spells that were more enjoyable to perform.

The Alchemist was sweating from the heat, which was increasing as they traveled southeast toward the Guardians. The sun continued to drain his strength as Avanda tested his nerves with her obsession with studies that were of more interest to her. Worn and tired, he continued to explain the basic elements to her.

"Excuse me," Thorik said to Santorray before he walked back to Bryus. Once he arrived, he asked Avanda to walk up front with Santorray for a while to help him scout for danger while he chatted with Bryus. She was always looking for something different to do, at least until she became bored with it.

"Bryus," Thorik said, once they were alone. "Is Avanda ready to cast the spell we need to free Gluic?"

"Absolutely. I've had more than enough time to explain decades of knowledge to her on how the fundamentals of the components work."

Thorik bit his tongue, knowing that Bryus' condescending tone was just how the man talked to everyone. "Will you be able to perform it?"

"Not with this oak tree growing out of my arm."

"But if we fixed your arm, you could save her?"

"I'm more than capable of purging her from Varacon."

"Okay, so all we need to do is find a new arm for you. Then you can cast the spell once we collect the spice."

"New arm? It will take a year for my body to heal after I remove this one because of the compromised magic used to attach it in the first place. Then, and only then, can I add a new one."

This was not what Thorik was hoping to hear. "I'm not willing to wait that long. You need to find a way to focus Avanda's training just on this spell so she can perform it."

"What do you think I've been trying to do, teach her to plant a garden? I've tried, but she just won't slow down. She has no discipline or fucus. I'm better off teaching her the basics and seeing what she makes of it."

"No, I need her to learn this spell."

"It's a complicated series of movements, words, and components. She doesn't have the patience. And I think I'm just about out of the patience I have. I surrender! I don't need this aggravation."

"Please don't. I need your help on this and am willing to make it worth your while."

The words caught Bryus' attention and caused him to stop walking. "Go on." He quickly exposed a devious smile.

"After she has successfully completed the spell and released my grandmother, I will give you Vesik."

"Avanda thinks the book of magic is hers. She will not be pleased."

"I know, but I will give it to you under one condition."

"Which is?"

"You leave with it, so she no longer has access to it."

"Odd request from someone who is so fond of our little lady Num."

"Not at all. I want her to be safe, and I fear the book will only cause her to harm herself in the end."

Bryus nodded. "That would be a logical conclusion for anyone who has seen her cast spells." He grinned at the idea of not having to steal the book after the spell occurred, which is what he had planned to do anyway. "I accept your offer." He then held out his thin dirty hand.

Thorik unexpectedly paused before reaching out to shake the Alchemist's hand. As he did, it felt wrong, as though he had made a pact with Bakalor himself. Even though he knew what he was doing was best for Avanda, he didn't like the emotions he was starting to feel.

CHAPTER THIRTY-NINE

THE SPELL

Bryus grabbed Avanda's arms in order to stop them from waving around in front of her. "Don't flail your arms about. You must move them in a gentle flowing pattern to the beat of the words. It should feel natural and smooth, not chaotic and sharp."

"I know. I'll do it properly once we retrieve the Ergrauthian Spice. Until then, it doesn't matter." Avanda went back to practicing spells during their midday rest.

Bryus shook his head. "You will only have one chance at this after we gather the spice, so you need to have every movement and word precisely in place and perfected, or else."

"Or else what?"

Bryus lifted his wooden arm that had caused him nothing but trouble since the moment they attached it. "We don't want anything like this to happen again, do we?" Several newly sprouted leaves and limbs had grown since the last time she had looked at it.

"Are you blaming that on me?"

"Avanda, I've performed over a dozen limb attachments, and all of them took. In fact, my head is the only original body part I have left.

And in all the spells used to attach these various parts, this is the first time the spell hasn't worked. Care to tell me why?"

"No, I don't," she said honestly.

"And why is that?"

"Because you'll get mad at me."

Bryus actually appreciated her candor. He would much rather have her be honest than to lie or play word games with him. Pointing to his wooden arm, he spoke in clear, crisp words, "This can't happen again."

"It was an accident."

"It was carelessness."

"You rushed me."

"You could have told me you weren't ready." Bryus shook his head with disappointment. "These are the types of mistakes that give Alchemists a bad name."

"What do you mean?"

"Unlike E'rudites, anyone can perform spells if they are taught properly. Therefore, a poorly trained Alchemist can perform a spell and end up doing more harm than good. You know the type, they'll cast spells first and see how they work later."

"I hate those kinds of people." She knew that he was teasing her, so she played along.

"In order to make sure you don't get labeled as one of them, we will continue to practice the mixing of components, the proper pronunciation of verbal commands, and the physical movements required to carry them out."

Taking a deep sigh, she knew he was right. There was just so much to learn, and his desire for her to understand the details seemed to slow her down from learning so much more. "Can we at least practice the explosion spell you taught me? I do so enjoy that one."

Recalling the pain from the last time she had performed it, he declined. "No. We're nearly out of powder, and it takes too long to prepare more. You need to continue learning the spell needed to cleanse Varacon of Thorik's grandmother."

"Cleanse?" "Yes, Varacon was virgin and pure until Gluic was stabbed. In doing so, she has tainted the dagger."

"Tainted? That's rude to say."

"Perhaps, but the truth is more important to say than worrying about someone's feelings."

"I don't know if that's true."

"Would you rather have the facts or have someone lie to you to make you feel good?"

"Can't you do both by telling me the facts in a way that doesn't make me feel bad?"

"Why waste the energy? The fact is, Gluic must be removed so Varacon can be the priceless enchanted blade about which so many stories have been written."

Avanda ears perked up. "What stories? Do tell."

Bryus had an audience of one, eager to hear him speak of his favorite subject. Excitement gleamed from his face as he prepared to tell his story with all the theatrics that he could muster.

Thorik interrupted their conversation. "Time to go. I want to get past that next ridge by nightfall. We should be at the Guardians within the next few days.

Bryus grabbed his items and stood up, never losing his excitement to tell the tale as they walked. "Long ago, there lived a beautiful princess..."

Avanda smiled as she listened to the story of two lovers, each fighting to free the other. Their day's trek went by quickly as she dreamed about his fable, when they weren't practicing her spells.

CHAPTER FORTY

SUMMON SWAP

Night arrived on the grass plains like it did most nights. Wolf howls and the ramming of heads by Chuttlebeasts fighting for dominance carried across the soft hills of the prairie. Lightning from the southwest sparked across the sky in a show, with a backdrop of blue and green ribbons of light adrift in the night sky.

Another long day had been spent walking, and the Nums were exhausted and quickly fell asleep after eating.

Grewen typically was more hungry than tired, but he had dragged his hands in the tall grass during their walk and pulled up handfuls of the plants every few minutes to chew on. With a full stomach, he dozed off halfway through his normal foot cleansing in the campfire.

Santorray never showed signs of being tired. He always ensured that the camp was safe and the surrounding area was secure before retiring for the night. But before doing so, he would often crouch down on his hairy wolf-like legs and stare his dragon-like eyes to the east for several minutes. Periodically, he would sniff in the air before returning his gaze. Eventually, even he would fall prey to the need for sleep.

"Avanda," Bryus whispered as he shook her shoulder to wake her.

Squinting, she looked up and saw Bryus' face, with one eye missing.

Bryus quickly placed a hand over her mouth to prevent her from screaming. "Shhhh. It's me, Bryus. Stay quiet."

The distant lightning added a dreadful look to the man's thin face with his missing eye. Sweat ran down his forehead and down the sides of his face as he apprehensively glanced around. It took her a few moments to fully wake up and realize she wasn't in danger. As his wet and clammy hand released her, she could taste the bitterness of the salt from his wrinkly skin. "What are you doing? Where is your eye? What happened?"

"Keep it down. Everyone is sleeping."

"Bryus, what's going on?"

"Let's perform that spell one more time."

"Spell? Which one?"

"The summon swap spell."

Scrunching up her face, she obviously didn't think that was a good idea. "Listen, it was funny once, but next time we're going to get in trouble."

"Shhh, keep your voice down. Listen, just one more time. I'll never ask you to do it again."

"I don't understand why you want to do this. Everyone is tired. I'm tired. I don't feel like any games right now."

"How would you like to learn a charm spell? Perhaps even a love charm?"

Avanda's eyes gave away her interest.

"Good. We can barter. Cast this spell for me one more time, and I'll teach you a charm spell."

Nodding her approval, she still questioned his motives. "Why now?"

"Trust me, you'll understand later."

Sighing at his lack of forthcoming information, she agreed to perform the spell. "Where is your eye?"

"Never mind. Get started on the spell."

"Whose hair should I cut?"

"No need," he replied, handing her the hourglass with two different types of hair tied onto each end.

"Four people? We're swapping four of us?"

Bryus nodded for her to continue as he pointed at the instructions in the book.

She waved her hands appropriately and said the words needed to prepare the spell before the final words appeared upon the pages.

"Go on, say them," Bryus urged her in a nervous voice.

"Something doesn't seem right about this."

"It soon will. You were nervous about it last time as well, if you recall." Bryus' voice gave signs of anxiousness as he prodded her to complete the spell.

"I suppose. Where do you want me to sit?"

"I don't give a damn where you sit. Just start the spell." His nervous smile had changed to a look of anger.

"Hey, what's gotten into you? Why are you acting this way?"

Grabbing her shoulder with his one hand, he strongly encouraged her to stop asking questions. "Say the last words to activate the spell!" His sharp words were exiting through tight teeth, and sweat poured down his face and his arms.

"No!" She tried to pull away from him, but his grip was too strong.

Raising his hand to slap her, he stopped himself just prior to the act. "You don't understand! You need to finish this spell right now!"

"No, she doesn't!" Thorik announced from behind Bryus. The Alchemist's conversation had obviously been louder than he had hoped.

He quickly turned to face the Num. "Thorik, you don't know what's going on here."

"Get away from her, Bryus."

The Alchemist grabbed her throat and shook his head in defiance of the Num's demand. "Thorik, if you take a step closer to me, I'll kill her. Her blood will be on your hands."

Thorik slowly stepped back, showing his palms to suggest he would obey the old man's wishes.

Wiping the salty sweat out of his eye with his upper arm, Bryus loosened his grip slightly on Avanda's neck.

Seeing this, Thorik decided to take advantage of the opening. "Now!"

Before Bryus could turn around, Santorray rushed forward and knocked Bryus off his feet. Flying eight yards, the man landed and rolled to a stop.

The blothrud wasn't through. He leaped forward, picked the man up, and then slapped him hard to the ground, flat on his back. "You like picking on little girls?"

"It's not like that!" Bryus began spitting up blood from the violent attack.

"Don't kill him," Thorik announced as he walked over to the Alchemist. "I want to know what he's up to."

Shaking his head, his body was held down by one of Santorray's mighty legs. "Nothing. It was just a spell."

"What kind?" Thorik asked.

"Same one Avanda and I did before." He spit up more blood. "Avanda, tell them we were just playing a joke. It was a game."

"Grabbing her throat was no joke!" Santorray growled.

"I was frightened by Thorik's arrival and I panicked."

Santorray looked at Thorik. "He's full of Fesh lies. I should just kill him now and salvage the rest of the night for our sleep."

Thorik raised his hand to prevent the blothrud from killing Bryus. "No. I want to know what he was really up to. Perhaps you can help him recall."

"Gladly." Santorray extended his claws from his paw and began to drive the sharp tips into the man's chest.

"Awww!" Bryus screamed from the new pain.

"Thorik." Grewen had stood up and was walking over to the scene. "I don't like the idea of torture, and I'm surprised that you are condoning this."

"Grewen, you didn't see what he was doing."

"What was he doing when you first approached him?" the mognin asked.

"He nearly hit Avanda for not performing a spell."

"Nearly?"

"Yes, he stopped himself, but he then grabbed her by the throat."

"Should we not give him the right to speak without threatening his life?"

"No!" Santorray was unsatisfied with the suggestion. "His reasons for the crime don't justify doing it, regardless of what they are."

Grewen attempted a different approach. "Even among your Del customs, dear Santorray, it is the victim who selects the response, not an outsider such as yourself. Based on your traditions, Avanda is the one who selects his fate."

Grinding his claws slightly deeper into Bryus' chest, Santorray smiled before looking for Avanda to step forward. "What would you have me do to this Fesh in a human's skin?"

Avanda walked up quietly, tears in her eyes. "Why? Why were you like this to me? I trusted you."

"You don't understand," he coughed out.

"Then explain it to me. Why force me to cast this spell?" She held the hourglass before her and noticed the hair on each end. "Whose hair is this? I recognize Santorray's coarse red leg hair and Brimmelle's black hair, but not the ones on the other side."

Bryus was silent, grimacing at the situation.

"And where is your eye? What does this have to do with it?"

Brimmelle walked up behind her with a cloth wrapped around a small sphere. "I think I found it."

"NO!" Blood shot from Bryus' mouth. "Whatever you do, don't open that cloth!"

"And why not?" Thorik asked.

He received no answer.

Santorray pressed harder onto the man's chest, achieving no results except additional pain for the Alchemist, which Santorray enjoyed watching.

"Open up the cloth," Thorik announced.

"No, please, anything but that," Bryus begged.

Thorik raised his hand to Brimmelle to stop the action. "Tell me why. I shall not ask again."

The Alchemist finally broke down and cried. "Because if you do, my family will die."

"How so?"

"Darkmere has my family in one of his prisons." Bryus struggled to get the words out.

Motioning to Santorray to have him reduce the pressure he was placing on Bryus' body, Thorik was impatient about wanting more information. "What does that have to do with this spell?"

"Darkmere allows my family to live under one circumstance: I must lead him to Ambrosius."

"I knew it!" Brimmelle announced. "I told you he was working for the Dark Lord. Santorray, kill the traitor!"

As much as the blothrud would have enjoyed finishing the battle, he didn't take orders from the likes of Brimmelle.

"I agreed to do this for him in order to save my family," Bryus insisted. "I meant you no harm. If I had refused, he would have killed my family as well as myself. This way, I had time to plan their escape."

It still made little sense to Thorik. "I thought you didn't know where they were being held."

Spitting blood to the side, he took a few needed breaths before answering. "I don't. Which is why I needed the spell."

Avanda held the hourglass up and looked at the hairs on the bottom. She then noticed the unique stitching in Bryus' collar was gone. "These are the hairs of your family?"

Bryus nodded. "Yes, my wife and my daughter."

She squinting as it came together. "You wanted me to cast this spell so your family would appear here with us?"

"Yes, where they would be safe from Darkmere."

"But then Santorray and Brimmelle would have awoken in their place, in some prison."

Santorray scowled and added some weight back on the man's chest.

Brimmelle was outraged at the idea. "You mean to tell me I would have woken up in Darkmere's prison in a distant land?"

"Yes." Bryus squinted at the added pain on his chest. "But you would have had Santorray to bust you out. The two of you would have had a fighting chance to escape. A chance that my family never would have had."

"How could you violate our friendship?" Thorik asked. "We trusted you. I trusted you."

"Why do you think I avoided trying to become friends with you people? I didn't want a relationship. I didn't want there to be any bonds. Every time I found myself getting closer to you, it made it all the harder to complete this task."

Avanda then asked, "How did you choose?"

"Santorray had the best chance of escaping Darkmere's prison, and Brimmelle just annoys me."

Brimmelle stepped forward after hearing the comment and raised the cloth-covered eye as he prepared to uncover it. "I'll show you how I can annoy you."

"No! Wait!" Bryus shouted.

"What does this eye have to do with your family?" Brimmelle asked.

"Darkmere sees through it. He thinks I am asleep right now. If you reveal it, he will see you and know I have been exposed as a traitor. He will murder my wife and daughter."

Avanda considered his point of view. "Have you been plotting against us all this time?"

"I've been trying to save my family all this time. Surely you, of all people, can understand what measures you would take to save family."

Thorik sighed. "And this is why you were persistent in wanting to help us find the book of magic? You needed to find this spell in order to save them."

Glancing over at his wooden arm, Bryus nodded again. "I hadn't expected to lose the power to properly perform spells."

"Which is why you needed Avanda," Thorik added. "Why didn't you come forward so we could help you?"

"There was nothing in it for you. Without a reason for you to get something from it, why would you have helped?"

Thorik motioned to Santorray to free his prisoner and lift him up. He then walked over to the man. "Because we are family. And once you are part of our family pod, we help you out, even when we may disagree with your decision."

Bryus was confused. "You mean you're not vengeful after what I attempted to do?"

"Oh, I'm furious with the danger you put us in, the fear you gave Avanda, and the position you nearly put Santorray and Brimmelle in! I'm disappointed in you as well. So let's make this clear. You are walking a fine line with this family pod, and you have a lot of rebuilding to do."

"And my wife and daughter?"

"I can't guarantee we can help your family out of their situation, but we will try our best once you have proven yourself by helping us save Gluic from Varacon."

Bryus nodded one last time.

"Santorray, escort Bryus back to his bedding. Brimmelle, keep that cloth tight around that eye and give it back to Bryus. The last thing we need is for Darkmere to know we are on to him."

CHAPTER FORTY-ONE

GUARDIANS

Thorik's Log: 12th day of the 9th month of the 650th year.

Last night we camped just west of the Guardians and the entrance to the Ergrauthian Valley. The Guardians remind me of giant gateposts, as our path sits between the two pointed mountainous peaks. The air is hot and vegetation is sparse in this region. The dry riverbed that leads up to the mountain pass looks like a long tongue extending from two mountainous teeth of the range. I'm feeling less optimistic about our success the closer we get to this eastern valley as we prepare to walk into what appears to be the mouth of an evil beast.

Two light gray masses of solid stone pierced the sky on either side of the travelers' path. A thick wall of clouds hung onto the mountain range behind the rock towers as stray wind-gusts forced long streams of clouds down toward the earth, giving the appearance of an upper set of teeth. Thorik and his friends felt as though they were walking into the mouth of the foreign land itself. Adding to this, the sun painted the underside of the clouds with a red glow, as though the valley's mouth was preparing to blow fire toward them. The ominous scene produced a heightened feeling of apprehension for the Nums.

Long cracks raced up the smooth sides of the main two cone-shaped towering rocks as water stains coated the areas beneath them. Beyond these two gigantic teeth, the wide path flowed around the various bends in the desert foothills of the mountains. The dirt road and dry riverbed were filled with bristle bushes, while the foothills were covered with red cacti of various sizes. Most were thin and tall with a few arms at their sides, and nearly a fifth of them had black flowers crowning their highest point, giving the travelers a feeling of being watched by an audience.

"It's like being in the Woodlen coliseum, with thousands of spectators standing in silence." Avanda was in awe of the number of cacti.

She was correct; the initial small valley that lay ahead was bowl-shaped as they walked into the center dirt arena. The assembly of deep red cacti stood eerily silent as they seemed to watch the group walk past them. Silent, at least until a buzzing caught the attention of all three Nums.

"Do you hear that?" Thorik asked. Something was alerting him to danger as the hair on the back of his neck stood on end.

Brimmelle dismissed the noise. "It's the wind." But he himself was too uncomfortable to look up at the hillside audience.

Grewen corrected the Num. "There is no wind."

Scanning back and forth, Avanda watched the foothills for movement. "I heard it as well." The idea of the cacti coming to life was magical, and she looked forward to seeing how they would uproot themselves to walk.

Santorray raised his muzzle and sniffed the air. "Quiet."

The group came to a halt. Brimmelle kept his head low to avoid seeing anything unpleasant, whereas everyone else was on the lookout for movement. As the only one hoping to see something happen, Avanda struggled to stand still.

Breaking off some new small branches from the end of his arm, Bryus was more interested in looking for Ergrauthian spices. "That should do nicely." He then headed for the hills.

"Bryus, wait for me." Avanda immediately followed his lead.

Santorray kept his position as he allowed his senses to determine his surroundings. "The Guardians are coming. We need to move quickly."

Thorik was confused. "The Guardians? I thought the two stone teeth we walked between were the Guardians."

"No, they are the Guardians' gate, where none shall pass."

Thorik chuckled to himself. "We had no trouble entering. It wasn't much of a gate."

"It's not to keep us from entering. It is to keep the Guardians from escaping and destroying everything beyond this point. Long ago, a spell was cast to prevent them from leaving this narrow passage within this mountain range."

"How do the Del'Unday cross into the Lake Valley then?"

"They don't. That is what has held Ergrauth back from attacking and destroying the humans and Ovs for so long. There have only been a few times that he has been willing to risk this journey."

With his body becoming numb, Thorik suddenly realized the danger he had put everyone in. "You mean even the demon, Ergrauth, is afraid to pass by the Guardians?"

"He's not afraid. He just understands the casualties that are likely to come along with doing so. It must be a major play for him to risk the lives of so many of his troops to leave his home valley."

Filling the foothills, the buzzing became loud enough for everyone to hear.

Bryus ran up to the nearest cactus. "Defend yourself, or I shall run you through," he jested as he stabbed his wooden arm into the thick stalk of the red cactus.

Avanda skidded to a halt as she witnessed a thick plume of red dust spray out from the hole in the plant and onto the Alchemist. Avoiding the cloud, she could hear Bryus cough from within it.

"Don't let the spice hit the ground," Bryus choked out as the cloud slowly faded. "Grab the glass jars from my pouch."

Red spice poured out of the cactus as Avanda collected the glass containers and placed the open mouth of one under the stream. A fragrance of fruit accompanied the spice, which poured out over Bryus' wooden arm and into the jar.

Avanda completed her fill, pulled the jar back, and turned to face the Alchemist. In his face, she could see the pain from his ordeal, but she didn't know where it was coming from. "What's wrong?"

His face was turning red as he attempted to pull his arm out of the cactus. It had punctured the plant easily but was now caught inside it. To make matters worse, the hole was reducing in size around his arm. Soon after stopping the bleeding of red spice, the cactus repaired itself and began squeezing his arm.

Even though his vision was nearly useless, due to the spice in his eyes, Bryus quickly cast a spell to open the hole back up. But nothing came of it, for the spice had protective properties. He then performed a spell on his arm. It too was coated by spice, preventing any success. The man was trapped as his arm continued to be squeezed.

Without thinking, Bryus placed a sandal up on the cactus for leverage to force his arm out. But instead of pushing the cactus away, he screamed in pain from the sharp needles that stabbed through his sandal and foot. Unable to pull his leg free, he panicked, for he was now at the mercy of the others in his party.

Avanda had closed the top of the glass jar and set it inside her purse before running behind him. Hugging him from the back, she pulled him as hard as she could as Bryus screamed in pain.

"It's not going to work," Bryus yelled. "We need to mix some of the black spice with the red spice to neutralize it so my spell will work."

"Where do I get the black spice from?"

"The pollen from the flowers on top of the cactus."

Avanda looked up at the desert plants, which had crowns of flowers at their peaks. Bryus' cactus had none, but others nearby did. The shortest ones were easily three times her height. She wouldn't have given it a second thought if it had been a tree, but the thick needles on these cacti provided her with a greater challenge. "Grewen!" she yelled to the mognin.

Meanwhile, Thorik had been standing with Santorray as they watched the other hillside. "The buzzing is getting louder, but I can't tell from where."

Just as the words sprang from his lips, movement could be seen coming over one of the hills. It was a dark tornado growing toward the sky as its base climbed the foothill on the gray, cloudy day. However, this tornado was not connected to the clouds themselves as it moved over the terrain directly toward the travelers.

"The Guardians approach," Santorray growled.

A second tornado appeared behind it, followed by a third from the opposite side of the road.

Not willing to stay long enough to understand exactly what was approaching, Thorik yelled out to his team, "Grewen, pull Bryus free! We're making a run for it!"

As the closest tornado approached, it became clear that the dark flowing mass was actually tens of thousands of fist-sized flying insects, all using the heat from the desert floor to swirl around in a collective group around a larger insect which stayed in the center.

Swarming around their queen, each insect rapidly flapped its wings in order to stay in formation. Red and black external skeletons covered their thin bodies and long, thin legs, and each appendage came to a sharp point.

The queen in the center of each gathering was easily ten times the size of those that protected her. Marked with bright yellow streaks, the red insect had extra pincers in front to help her slay her victims, assuming anything could make it past her army.

A fourth tornado of insects was spotted as the first three closed in on them.

Grewen had already arrived and wrapped his oversized hand around Bryus' wooden arm, tugging it slightly to free it from the cactus. It wouldn't budge.

"Stop playing with it and give it a quick yank," Bryus ordered.

Following his instructions, the mognin made a swift pull. Bryus' body folded up around Grewen's hand from the violent thrust, which freed the cactus from the ground instead of the wooden arm from the cactus.

"You idiot!" Bryus protested, nursing a bloody nose from his face slapping into the side of Grewen's hand. "Can't you do anything right? Put me down." One of his feet dangled in the air, while the other was still pinned to the cactus.

"My apologies." The giant chuckled as he let go of the man's arm. The weight of the uprooted cactus catapulted Bryus forward as the plant tumbled to the ground. "Anything else?"

It was at this point that Thorik and Brimmelle arrived. Anxious to escape the mountain pass before the Guardians arrived, Thorik whipped around to keep a bearing on their advancement. "What's the holdup?" Thorik asked quickly.

Bryus looked up from the painful predicament and noticed the swarms. His face twitched at the sight. "Avanda! Get the black spice. Hurry!"

"No, we have to free you first," she said.

The Alchemist was appalled. "Are you insane? We may only have one chance at cleansing Varacon of Gluic's soul. We must restore him."

Avanda disagreed and moved toward him, but was stopped by his thrashing about with his free arm. "You can't free me without the black spice. Get the spice first," he ordered her.

"Spice?" Brimmelle complained. "We need to make a run for it."

The swarms were closing in; there was no time to argue. "Grewen." Avanda handed the mognin an empty glass jar. "Put some pollen from those flowers into this while we help Bryus."

Delicately taking the small container between two of his massive fingers, he stepped over to a cactus with a full crown of black flowers. Each had long, sharp needles protecting it, and the access to the flower itself was too small for the mognin's thick fingers. Trying anyway, the needles pricked his fingers time and time again. Even with his thick skin, the suffering was tremendous, for each needle gave off a painful poison.

Thorik and Avanda continued to pull at Bryus' wooden arm to free it from the fallen cactus. But without any leverage to hold the cactus in place, they ended up dragging the heavy plant nearly a foot before realizing it was pointless.

The first swarm was now in striking distance as it approached the group.

Brimmelle had been keeping his attention on the Guardians. "They're coming! Drop what you have and run!"

"Avanda," Grewen said, "my fingers are too large. I will have to lift you to do this."

Looking down at the lack of progress with Bryus, she saw the Alchemist's nod of approval to leave. She didn't think twice as she bolted from her position and over to Grewen.

She had climbed up on Grewen so many times in the past that they knew how to get her up high in the least amount of time. Plucking the jar from him, she began scooping out black powder from the center of the flowers.

The Guardians attacked.

Testing their opponents, only a few dozen insects flew from the swirling swarm. The first attack was on Grewen and Avanda as they used the sharp ends of their legs to stab their victims.

Grewen received most of the attacks, as his free hand swatted away any that came close to Avanda.

The insects' abrupt diving at her nearly caused Avanda to drop the jar more than once, but her confidence in Grewen kept her focused on her task.

Thorik and Bryus were also now under attack as they swung their arms out to protect themselves. Thorik rolled away from the attacks and kicked the giant insects off of Bryus, but the Nums simply couldn't keep up. More showed up. One firmly landed on Thorik's back and stabbed the Num deep into his shoulder. Another landed on Bryus and drove a sharp leg into his side.

Brimmelle was not immune from the attack, and he fought off one of the insects by swinging his hands wildly in front of it to shoo it off.

Grewen struggled more and more to fend off their attacks on the little Num, as he held her near the cactus. He had sustained extensive injuries, since he spent no time trying to protect himself. Over a dozen had landed on his body and begun to dig into his thick skin. "I think it's time you get down now. It's getting too dangerous for you."

"Just a little longer." She attempted to scrape off enough black spice from the flowers to fill her jar.

A second wave of Guardians were launched from the swarm.

Brimmelle screamed at the sight. "We're doomed!"

Thorik knew they couldn't possibly defend themselves from this new threat. Bryus was immovable, while Grewen and Brimmelle simply couldn't outrun them. He and Avanda had the only chance of survival, assuming they abandoned their friends, and he couldn't fathom them doing such a thing.

SNAP!

The sound caused Thorik to turn and see Santorray stepping on Bryus' wooden arm. He had snapped it in half and freed the Alchemist from the cactus. "Use Rummon!" he barked at Thorik. Holding the cactus at bay with the broken-off piece of Bryus' arm, he tore Bryus' foot from the needles which held it.

Bryus screamed in pain. Ignoring the Alchemist's agony, Santorray tossed him over his shoulder. "Grewen, take her down this instant!" the blothrud bellowed.

His powerful voice was enough to rattle Avanda and cause her to lean back from the cactus, indicating to Grewen that it was time to take her down. In doing so, he turned and lumbered down the hill back to the road with her in his arms, swatting the attacking insects along the way.

Thorik pulled out the Spear of Rummon and grasped it in both of his hands while pointing it up at the swarm. Feeling the heat radiate from within the spear, he knew the dragon's soul was ready to do his bidding. To his relief, the insects began breaking off their attack.

Brimmelle fell to the ground as his single insect opponent dove toward his face and grabbed onto his head. Its back legs lifted into the air, preparing to thrust down into the Num's throat.

Reaching down with his free hand, Santorray grabbed the insect on Brimmelle's face and squeezed it tight, popping it in an explosion of black pus. The insect's forelegs fell as the Num's mouth, nose, and eyes were coated with the insect's remains.

Brimmelle was horrified. In some way he almost wished the blothrud hadn't helped him.

Picking up Brimmelle and tossing him over his other shoulder, Santorray ran down the hillside, back to the dirt road.

Following his friends, Thorik too made his way to the dirt road, but not to safety. The swarm had followed them down the hillside and blocked their path. In addition, the other three tornado-like swarms had also arrived and blocked any other path to escape.

Thorik lifted the spear up toward the swarm in front of him, causing them to withdraw. But in doing so, the other three swarms moved in from behind. Pulling the spear back, he then pointed it at another swarm. It too, withdrew. But again, the others advanced.

Every second that went by, tens of thousands of Guardians moved closer to their prey. Thorik glanced at Grewen and Santorray for options. They gave him none.

Chapter Forty-Two

CAPTURED

Four tornadoes of flying insects surrounded Thorik and his party in the desert mountain pass, blocking them from any escape. Only by Thorik's use of Rummon was he able to keep them at bay, but even that was short-lived as the queens within each tornado swarm worked together to attack from behind Thorik and the direction he held the spear.

The yellow stripes on the back of the queens flashed brightly in order for them to communicate, and the frequency of the light show was intensifying. It was just a matter of seconds before the Guardians would work in complete unison to launch a full attack and destroy them.

Without warning, the flashing lights from the queens stopped. Thorik could hear a moment of silence from the extreme buzzing, as every insect stopped for a moment to change flight paths. The only sound he heard was the thumping of his own heart against his chest as he looked out at the towering endless supply of attackers. His decision to come here had not only failed, but it had cost them all their lives. What had he done?

The quarter-mile high towers of insects dove onto the travelers to carry out the orders of their queens. The sheer weight of all the insects smothered everyone's bodies, and the travelers were quickly covered.

Grewen fell to his hands and knees, sheltering Avanda and Brimmelle from the weight of their attackers, but could not stop the attacks themselves.

Santorray remained standing as his powerful arms and hands continued to destroy the insects. But even he would have to relinquish eventually, and there seemed to be an endless supply of insects.

Thorik turned and faced his friends, launching Rummon's power up in the air and frying dozens of insects every second with the spear's heated breath. But the insects were replaced so quickly that it was barely even noticed by his companions.

A dozen insects landed on Thorik's back, forcing him to the ground with the spear trapped underneath him. The weight quickly loaded on, preventing him from pulling the spear out to use it. He was defenseless.

Continuing with the attacks, the Guardians pounded the travelers until suddenly, there was a second lapse in wing beats. Immediately afterward, all the insects abandoned the attack.

Injured and bloody, the travelers looked up to see the four tornadoes reform above them. In addition, dust was being kicked up from the dirt road as an army approached. A Del'Unday army. Ergrauth's army. As if the Guardians needed help, Thorik thought in dismay.

The army of Del'Unday had come around the bend unnoticed by the Guardians, who had been preoccupied with the travelers. Thousands of Del'Unday warriors filed in around the valley walls, armed with catapults, battering rams, counterweight trebuchets, and wagons filled with weapons and supplies.

It was only moments before the Guardians reacted to the approaching armored troops and quickly launched their attack on the Del'Unday with all four swarms flying toward them.

Fortunately for Thorik, he had assumed wrongly. The Del'Unday army and the Guardians were adversaries, which had provided a reprieve from their attack on the travelers.

"Thorik," Santorray said with haste. "Cover up that spear."

"Why?"

"It once was Ergrauth's spear. If he reclaims it, there will be no stopping him."

Thorik quickly covered it up. "How about Vesik and Varacon?"

"He knows not and cares not about these things. The spear was a special gift given to him, long ago."

The Del'Unday army continued to approach as various Del species came around the bend carrying weapons while some rode Fesh'Unday creatures. Other Fesh pulled wagons and the larger warfare equipment. Flags flapped in the breeze as their masses seemed to grow.

Standing several heads taller than the other blothruds in the ranks was the one that led them. He was a towering blothrud of massive muscles and sharp spikes who had giant red wolf legs, the hairless body of a human, and the head of a red dragon. His red skin dripped with sweat, and his veins pulsed with heated blood. Thick black battle blades and spikes extended from his body across his shoulders, down his back, and on his elbows and knees.

This was the great demon, Ergrauth, and he walked with a confidence of victory, leading his army of Del'Unday warriors toward the Guardians. Each powerful stride slammed onto the ground, causing the earth to shake. Ergrauth was the ultimate Del'Unday. He was the most superior blothrud, or any Del'Unday for that matter. He was the demon of the land and all that rested upon it, and he showed his pride with each massive step.

Seeing the clouds of insects attacking, Ergrauth launched his own forces to intercept them by giving off a deep howl which shook the hillsides. The order had been given, and his army lurched forward.

Smashing with maces and shields, an assault by armed Dels immediately started wiping out the insects near the ground. One after another, they made a path forward past the cloud of bugs.

However, it wasn't long before the rest of the invading insects arrived. By sheer numbers, they changed the tide of the battle as hundreds of thousands hovered over the road, diving and attacking the backs of their victims.

Ergrauth easily swatted them away from his face. He was a master of war and knew when to use the right weapon for the right enemy. Grabbing a horn from his side, he blew into it.

The high-pitched noise was hard for most to hear, especially in the heat of battle. After the long blast into the horn, he placed it back at his side and swatted away the insects near him as though they were nothing more than flies.

The battle raged on as two more tornadoes of insects arrived to help dominate the battle.

Ergrauth watched his army to observe their abilities in this difficult situation. Seeing one of his warriors recoil from an attack by a dozen insects, Ergrauth stomped over and killed the Del'Unday himself. "I will not have cowardice in my army," he announced as he watched his men fight. But his army couldn't possibly hold up against the numbers of its enemies.

He then looked up and saw what he was waiting for. Two dragons were diving toward them.

Covered in blue and white scales, the lead dragon headed in from the back of the battle. Grazing the air just above the soldiers, it opened its mouth and sprayed a fan of deadly frost into the air, killing thousands of the insects that then rained down to the ground.

The second dragon approached at a higher level and sent a series of lightning bolts showering from his mouth as though heat-lightning had occurred without the clouds. Again, thousands of insects were instantly killed and fell to the earth.

The tide of the battle quickly changed to Ergrauth's advantage as the dragons continued to destroy legions of insects with every attack.

Free from defending against the insects, Thorik hobbled himself around to ensure his friends were alive. "He has dragons in his army? I thought they belonged to Rummon."

Santorray shoveled handfuls of dead insects away to free the others as well. "It would appear that he has freed Rummon's children, the Winds of Conquest."

"Those dragons are the Winds of Conquest?"

"Yes." Santorray pulled Bryus up to his feet.

Grewen stood up from his hunched-over position and stretched his back. Standing about the same height as Ergrauth, he was far less threatening. "Trewek's elders must be informed."

"It won't help them. Nothing shy of a demon can stop them," the blothrud said.

Thorik thought about it for a moment. "I have Rummon. Therefore. I am the only one who can stop them."

Santorray scoffed at the idea. "Don't even think about taking that weapon out. Besides, even if Rummon was here in the flesh, he would still have his hands full, taking on both of his children at the same time. His presence inside that spear has no chance, brave Sec."

"Then Grewen is correct. We must at least notify the Trewek elders of the pending invasion."

"We won't have that opportunity," Santorray growled.

Thorik looked down the path at the unguarded rock towers, where they had entered. "And why is that? We can run back to the Chuttle Range before we are spotted."

Heavy footsteps approached the travelers from behind Thorik. Turning, the Num gazed upon the mognin-sized blothrud demon, Ergrauth, only twenty-some yards from him.

The demon stopped and inspected the small band of injured travelers. One of his eyebrows raised at the sight before him. "Santorray? Is it possible?"

Santorray growled at the demon. "More than possible, father."

"Father?" Thorik was louder than he had hoped.

"You are returning to my valley?" Ergrauth asked.

"It would appear so."

"It has taken you many years to finally return and stand at my side. Your timing is of interest, considering I move to destroy the land you have called home for so long."

"You are walking into Bakalor's trap. He is using you to launch this war and sacrifice your troops to do his bidding. He plans to take over the land once you are finished."

Ergrauth grinned on one side of his mouth. "I fully understand what he plans on doing. But I haven't given him all the facts. I will be ready when he comes to the surface. I will be victorious in the end. And with you at my side, I have no doubts about our easy victory."

Blood dripped from the insect cuts across Santorray's body as he stood strong and defiant. "I am not here to stand at your side."

"You have been, and always will be, an Ergrauthian Elite. You have no choice but to fight for me."

"Living for so many years on the terrain you plan to destroy, my destiny is now chosen by myself, not others, and especially not by you."

As the battle raged on behind him, with victory nearly at hand by the Del'Unday, Ergrauth stood motionless for a moment. "You have learned nothing," he growled in disapproval. "You're just as disobedient now as you ever were."

Santorray spit on the ground between them. "I will not blindly follow anyone, including you."

The demon's lips quivered with anger. "I would kill you here and now, but you would not suffer sufficiently for this crime against me. Instead, you shall suffer for all eternity inside of my city."

"You may wish it, but I will not go. You will have to attempt to kill me where I stand."

"Attempt? You are nothing to me. I made you. I can destroy you."

"You can try." Santorray crossed his sabers onto his chest and pierced the sharp ends into his skin before slowly dragging them down, forming a bloody X on his front. He was ready for war.

Ergrauth was not accustomed to being treated in such a way. The disrespect toward him fueled his emotions and heated his body with fresh blood. "You challenge me?" he yelled, staring at the cuts his son had just given himself. "No one challenges Ergrauth!"

Stepping out, the massive demon violently rushed toward the travelers to slay his son. His eyes narrowed, and his teeth seemed to grow larger as his skin tightened and pulled back from his mouth. Using his claws, he ripped into his own biceps to signal his willingness to forgo pain to win his battle.

Santorray also charged forward, as blood dripped from his chest, and spotted the dirt road. With sabers tightly gripped, he howled the war cry of the Elites, which he once led.

His father growled at the sound that he himself had taught his son in his youth, when he had believed that his son would be his finest warrior. Instead, his son turned out to be his greatest disappointment, as he had betrayed him so many years ago.

Ergrauth's thoughts affected his attack by taking his mind off the task at hand for a split second. The two collided, and he had underestimated the skill of his son.

Santorray leaped up and swirled in the air, slicing his sabers deep into the demon's arm and torso before landing firmly on the road, ready for his next attack.

Yelling from the unexpected pain, his father slid to a halt just before stomping upon the Nums. A dust cloud of sand covered the travelers as Grewen pulled Avanda and Bryus to a safer location. Brimmelle and Thorik followed Grewen as the demon turned around toward his son.

Santorray didn't provide his father with any time to realize his son's abilities. He again leaped forward, into the air, thrusting his muscular shoulder and sharp blades into his father's stomach. His weight and speed knocked Ergrauth off of his feet and down into the dirt with a sound that rocked the canyon's walls.

"Not only am I still an Elite, but I am now much more!" Santorray used his fists to hammer a solid blow to his father's chest, cracking a few ribs.

However, Ergrauth's long mighty arm sprang upward, tossing Santorray a dozen yards away from him, giving him some time to recoup. Clutching his chest in pain, the demon revealed to Santorray that he actually was injured.

"You can cut me all you want, boy. But you will never be able to defeat me." Ergrauth kept a keen eye on him as he stood back up. "You know it in your head that you can't win. And as long as I'm in there, you will always lose."

Santorray fought to ignore his father's words. "Go back to your city and give up this war, or I shall be forced to slay you."

Ergrauth coughed out a painful laugh before standing up straight and tall with his shoulders back. "Let me see what my little boy has learned."

Santorray hated his father calling him boy. The degrading tone his father always used had festered into his dreams and nightmares. "More than you think." He then raced back toward his father with his sabers spinning in his palms.

The demon stood like a statue as he watched his son charge at him. Raising his arms straight out to his side, he invited his son to end this once and for all.

Blood sprayed from Santorray's self-inflicted cuts on his chest as he raised his weapons to impale his father. Again, jumping at the last moment, he flew through the air at his target. Ergrauth's chest had no protection. He was vulnerable.

With lightning-fast reflexes, Ergrauth violently swiped one of his enormous arms forward, crushing Santorray's side and sending him straight into the ground. The attack had come out of nowhere, a blow that would have easily killed a Num and most likely disabled the blothrud.

Momentarily clutching his own chest from the pain of the prior attack, Ergrauth quickly grabbed the blades along his son's back and lifted Santorray up in the air before his son could recover. This was an insult more than a tactic, for parents would pick up their children in this manner when they misbehaved.

The demon then ran back toward his army before launching Santorray into the side of one of the military catapults. The wooden weapon shattered upon the impact as splinters and dust shot in every direction.

Before the dust could settle, Ergrauth stepped over, brushed the debris off his arms, and surveyed the damage to his son. Expecting to see a lifeless body, he was astonished to find a large wooden beam from the catapult come flying out at him, striking him in his face.

Ergrauth crumpled backward from the impact, which lacerated his face and broke several of his teeth. He couldn't recall the last time he had tasted blood from his own wound.

Leaping from the catapult, Santorray landed a solid kick to the demon's stomach, followed by a two-handed strike on the back of his neck after Ergrauth bent over from the first attack. The two quick assaults knocked the demon to his knees.

Santorray quickly gathered his strength and lifted the demon up by his back blades. His arms and legs shook from the weight as he attempted to run with him in tow before tossing him head-first into a wagon of supplies.

The wagon burst into pieces as the wheels popped off, and the supplies tumbled out. There was a moment of silence as Santorray waited for his father to leap back out. Instead, Ergrauth slowly stood back up from the far side of the wagon and laughed.

"You still are an Elite. And you have retained everything I have taught you. I'm impressed."

Santorray stood up straight, still waiting for an attack.

The demon smirked. "You are a valuable asset to me. Therefore, I will ask you one last time to join me."

There was no hesitation. "I will not."

"Understood. Nor would I give up what I believe in. But we are at an impasse. And my army will stop at nothing to be victorious."

From his right, Santorray glimpsed several warriors charging him. Pulling out his sabers again, he fought them off. He disabled one, and then another would take their place. He would slay two more, and then three would move in. He simply could not fight the entire Del'Unday Army.

Ergrauth laughed as he watched his son sidestep his way back to his companions as his warriors continued to test his skills. Even with the loss of the demon's men, Santorray was slowly being beaten down with blades and blunt weapons.

By the time Santorray had backed up all the way to the other travelers, he was a bloody mess. It was amazing that he could still stand, let alone fight. It was at this time that the fight stopped and the soldiers backed off, giving way to Ergrauth's approach.

Santorray stood wobbly on his legs as he held out his sabers toward his father. "This is what you call honor?"

The demon laughed. "This is what I call victory. Winning is what matters, not how you do it. Winners write the history to their own favor and tell the tale of victory they want others to know. No one remembers the tales of those who lost."

Santorray spit on his father's foot in defiance. "You are what's wrong with this world. I've known Fesh that I respect more than you."

The phrase struck a nerve, as Santorray knew it would, but the blothrud was too injured to stop the demon's attack as he pounded both of his fists into the side of his son. Santorray crumbled and went tumbling into the pile of insects, which had been killed earlier by the travelers.

Santorray was definitely hurt as he struggled to shake off the powerful blow to his side. Clearing the pain from his brain, he could tell his father was approaching. The thunderous footfalls closed in on him, but he hadn't cleared his vision yet.

Knowing his back was exposed, Santorray rolled to his side and grabbed whatever he could find to use as a shield until he could stand.

The first object he grabbed was a large book, which he held up to stop the demon's blow.

"Vesik!" Bryus yelled in horror. His desire to protect the book of magic far outweighed his interest in preserving his own life. Running toward the fight, he screamed for them to stop.

But it was too late; Ergrauth's mighty fist came crashing down onto the book, forcing it into Santorray's chest and knocking the wind out of him.

Thorik frantically called to the Alchemist, "Bryus! It's not worth your life."

But he was wrong. Bryus felt it was worth much more than his or anyone else's life. Ancient magic was history, while each person was only a blink of time. He would do anything to save Vesik. Besides, he believed he needed the book to save his wife and daughter.

The demon stomped a heavy foot onto his son's chest. "You will never defeat me as long as you believe you can't."

Bryus arrived in time to see the book pinned between the demon's foot and the blothrud's chest. Stabbing his broken wooden arm into Ergrauth's other leg, he quickly cast a spell while the demon was taken by surprise.

The spell was intended to liquefy the demon's leg, but because of a failed arm replacement, as well as the red spice still on his wooden arm, it backfired. Instead, moisture from the demon's leg was pulled toward Bryus' wooden appendage, causing it to spring roots into and around the demon's leg. The Alchemist was now attached to Ergrauth.

Removing his foot from Santorray's chest, Ergrauth began kicking his leg in order to knock the Alchemist off, but the roots continued to expand and tighten their hold.

Thorik and Avanda came running to his defense.

"No!" Bryus yelled to Avanda. "Save Vesik!" he pleaded to his young apprentice. "Use it to save my family!"

Watching the Alchemist flail around on the side of the demon's leg, she knew any magic she attempted could easily hurt her teacher. Accepting his request, she stopped at Santorray and Vesik.

Thorik refused to change course. Holding his hunting daggers out in front of him, he charged at the demon to save Bryus.

Santorray tossed the book off of his chest and rolled to his hands and knees, clutching his side in pain. But his father's attacks would not be enough to stop him.

Avanda grabbed Vesik and helped the blothrud to his feet, just in time to see Ergrauth reach down and snap Bryus' arm from his thick demon leg.

"Is this what you fight for now?" the demon asked harshly to his son. Holding the battered Alchemist in his huge hand like a rag-doll, he spiked Bryus back and forth between his hands. "This is what you're fighting for instead of your own people?"

"This is between you and me," Santorray told his father. "Leave him be."

"What interests you about these lesser beings?" Ergrauth looked at Bryus' limp body in his palm. "They are so weak." To display his thoughts, he firmly held Bryus in one hand and used his other hand to pull on the human's arm. Muscles and flesh stretched and ripped as the demon snapped off the man's arm. The bone of the limb was exposed as blood ran down the flesh that had been torn off with it. Holding the arm out toward Santorray to view, he eventually flung it at his son, and it hit him in the chest before it fell to the ground.

Somehow Bryus remained conscious as he screamed in pain, while his left eye jerked from his eye socket due to the demon's abuse. Falling to the ground, it was inadvertently stepped on and crushed.

Looking at the man flailing about in his hands, the demon grabbed him tight again and ripped his right leg from his pelvis, and then followed it with removing his left leg. Each limb hit Santorray after being torn from the human, in an attempt to get the lesser demon to realize how frail his companion was. Tossing the head and torso of Bryus violently at Santorray, he shouted, "They are weak. We are the dominant species!"

The Alchemist was unrecognizable as the mound of body parts splattered on the desert floor. The sight caused Brimmelle to jump and fall back in fear of the demon's strength, while Thorik finished his charge toward the demon with even greater fervor. They had lost a companion who, despite what he had done, was still a part of their extended family.

"No!" Avanda screamed as she attempted to race forward to save her mentor, Bryus. She simply couldn't accept that his journey was over. In addition, her desire to learn new magic had just been crushed by the hands of the demon. Somehow, she had assumed that Bryus' powers could protect them from anything. She turned to charge at Ergrauth and cast whatever spells she could think of.

Before doing so, she heard a soft cough from the mound of flesh and body parts.

To her surprise, Bryus had somehow remained conscious, at least for a short time. She had to assume he retained enough magic to keep himself alive after being ripped apart limb by limb.

"Avanda," he sputtered as he saw her approach. "Perform the summon swap spell. Quickly, I haven't much time left."

"What?"

"Place my hair on one side, the talon from my belt on the other." He struggled not to fade away.

"Why?"

"Let me see my family one last time."

"Then who will appear here? Who will you swap with?" Grabbing the components, she cried as she waited for him to have enough strength to answer her.

"Our family pet. Take care of her."

"We will be long gone by the time the spell is completed."

Coughing and spitting out blood, his words were slurred and difficult to hear. "Keep my rags with you. She will follow my scent to you."

Avanda did as she was told and began the spell, wiping the tears from her face to ensure they didn't fall on the components and corrupt the magic.

"Thank you," he said softly, "... for letting me into your family." Then Bryus fell unconscious.

Meanwhile, Ergrauth had already selected his next victim, which was Thorik. As the Num raced forward to stab him with his hunting daggers, the demon simply leaned down and scooped him up. Thorik never had a chance. He was now being squeezed by the enormous hand of the land demon and would end up as a pile of limbs on top of the late Bryus.

This time Santorray yelled out. "STOP!" The word echoed against the valley walls, causing everyone to pay attention.

Ergrauth was intrigued by his son's stance against the killing of the Num. "You really care about these little creatures, don't you?"

Santorray could see that Thorik was in pain. To continue this fight would only cause the death of all of his companions. "Release him."

With a shallow laugh, he did nothing of the sort. "Why? What purpose could this Num have?"

"I cannot see his fate any more than you." Santorray then gave off a deep growl as he planned his next statement. "But I will succumb to your punishment if you let my fellow travelers live."

"Santorray, save yourself and the rest!" Thorik shouted.

Ergrauth shook his head with disappointment at his son. "You have become weak, boy. Never would I have expected to see the day when an Ergrauthian Elite would forgo his freedom to save a Fesh. You, my son, have been compromised."

Santorray stood firm as the emotional impact played with his mind. "Do you accept my offer?"

By this point, the Del'Unday army had chased the Guardians away and had filed into rank behind their leader. Keeping their eyes forward, they never looked directly at the demon, for fear of swift repercussions.

Tossing Thorik down in front of Santorray, the demon then spit on the dirt near his son's feet. "Santorray, you could have had the world. Instead, you choose eternal pain. You're a fool."

"General!" Ergrauth ordered. "Take these traitors and have them absorbed into my city."

Nearly fifty soldiers stepped forward to surround the travelers. "Drop your weapons," the general ordered Santorray and his friends.

"No," Ergrauth corrected. "Let them keep them. If there is any of my blood left in my son, allow him a chance to die fighting for his life. Just ensure you have enough guards to make his life end quickly should he choose to give up his Fesh ways and be a blothrud once more."

The general nodded. His troops then led the travelers east through the mountain pass.

Chapter Forty-Three

DEATH MARCH

Thorik walked between Santorray and Grewen, while the mognin carried Brimmelle and Avanda. Brimmelle's feet bled from the harsh conditions, and both he and Avanda had become overwhelmed by the heat. It was best for them to be carried, and Grewen didn't mind it a bit.

Thorik felt misled by Santorray as he walked alongside him. "I don't understand. How can you be the son of a demon?"

"What's there not to understand?"

"Well, first of all, how is it that you failed to mention this bit of information in our travels?"

"It would have only complicated things."

"Yes, because things weren't complicated prior?" Thorik asked with a bit of sarcasm.

"My relationship with Ergrauth would have prevented you from trusting me, as it has so many others."

"What is your relationship? If he is your father, why the bad blood? What did you do?"

"No one disobeys Ergrauth on anything and lives to tell about it."

"Apparently that's not true, seeing that you did both."

Stopping, Santorray turned to show Thorik his back. "Do you see this scar?"

"I see a lot of scars."

"The largest one. The one that cracked and broke several of my back blades."

The thick deep scar ran from his left shoulder down across his back to his right hip. The blades in its wake were remnants of the powerful weapons that once were.

"Yes, I see it."

"He split me open and left me for dead."

"Just because you disobeyed him? Who would have known?"

"Everyone. I held a position of great power here. I was the general of the Ergrauthian Elite, a force designed to destroy anything and everything in its path. We were not directed to keep order or to ensure citizens were faithful to Ergrauth. Our missions had a single result: death to whomever Ergrauth wished to be removed from the living."

"And you refused to kill someone?"

"Yes."

"Who?"

"A family member."

"He wanted you to kill one of your own kin?"

"Yes."

"That must be the most horrible crime."

"No. Not supporting Ergrauth is the ultimate offense to all Del'Unday. Our punishment will take place in his namesake city."

Thorik realized that something still didn't add up. "But Santorray, you once told me that the Del'Unday don't take prisoners. Will we be executed once we arrive?"

"We will not be that fortunate, Sec. Ergrauth's enemies are utilized to expand the city's size."

Thorik sighed. "If we are to spend the rest of our living days constructing streets and buildings, Brimmelle will not last long in this heat."

"The heat will be the least on his mind, for as soon as we enter the city, they will lead us to the Gateway of Schullis. This passage will strip your flesh from your body and absorb your bones, your muscles, as well as your spirit. By entering the gateway, your willpower will be muted and your obedience will be rectified."

Thorik's eyes had grown large during the blothrud's description, and his face had tightened as though he was going to be sick.

Avanda and Brimmelle had been quietly listening, but now they shot each other looks of concern as they continued to listen to the discussion.

Grewen's stomach groaned from hunger as he grinned at Santorray's comments. "Leave it to the Del'Unday to strip a man of his flesh and bones and then still expect him to follow orders."

Santorray growled. "You disrespect my culture?"

"Far from it," Grewen said in a light-hearted tone. "I find it fascinating that an entire culture is based on fear. Whether it be fear of disobedience or fear of some superstition giving you bad luck."

"You will find out that this is no superstition. The gateway pulls you into the city's walls and streets and roofs. You become part of the fabric of our towers and the building blocks for our statues. The city of Ergrauth is a combination of sand, water, and living tissue. The city is alive with tens of thousands of spirits following a single one who serves Ergrauth himself."

"The city is living?" Avanda asked, trying to understand.

"Yes. The city grows and changes based on the Del'Undays' needs. The crystal structures of the city expand when fed. But unlike anything you've seen crystallized, the spirits can move them slightly, making them appear to be fluid solids. You will understand when you see the lost people press their faces against the walls and scream for mercy. But there will never be any for them."

CHAPTER FORTY-FOUR

ER'QUE DOOMA BADLANDS

Days passed as they marched to the east toward the city named after the demon, Ergrauth. Their trek through the badlands was uncomfortable, at best. Aside from the sparse vegetation, packs of wild Del'Unday roamed these lands. Periodically, these packs were spotted standing motionless on the top of a mesa, watching the travelers pass below.

"They are called kewtalls," Santorray informed his companions. "Mutated and insane Dels. They stand up there on those ridges to mark their territory and intimidate outsiders."

The Ergrauthian guards frequently tried to tempt Santorray to fight his way out, to no avail. They simply couldn't get him irritated enough to attack. The guards also offered the Nums and Grewen the opportunity to escape for freedom if they wished to attempt to travel on their own in these lands.

Santorray shook his head at the Nums, assuring them it was a foolish choice. "The wild kewtalls are like pack animals. They wait for a few individuals to break off from the main group, and then they attack. You'd never survive half a day out here on your own."

"But if we all escaped together, we could make our way back past the Guardians." Thorik looked up at another kewtall on the ledge above them.

"I could, but you Nums wouldn't stand a chance. These aren't Fesh'Unday. They are tribes of Dels who hunt travelers for survival. They are skilled and savage warriors."

Disappointed in his response, Thorik grimaced at the blothrud. "Haven't we proven ourselves to you yet? I think we can support our own." Glancing back up to see the kewtalls, he found they were no longer there. A quick scan back at the other mesa tops showed that all the recent kewtalls had disappeared. "Where did they all..."

Grewen glanced back at the ledges above them and noticed the same thing. "We're just being watched."

"Or hunted," Thorik said.

"They're stalking. Waiting to see a weakness. Looking for a wounded member, or a smaller one they could easily drag off from the rest of the group," Santorray replied.

Thorik swallowed hard and took a quick inventory of his group's whereabouts. "Perhaps you're right. Maybe we don't want to take the guards up on their offer for freedom."

Periodically, the captive party would spot more kewtalls on the upper flats of the desert badlands. They would be under their watchful eye until they had left their lands.

After hours of walking in the blistering sun, Avanda thought her eyes were playing tricks on her. One of the motionless kewtalls swung about, but by the time she pointed it out to Thorik, it was gone.

It was nearly an hour later when she noticed it happening again. This time, she monitored it and watched it thrash about as some type of bird attacked the mutated Del and pecked away at it. This kewtall moved away from the overlooking ledge as well, but the bird remained as it watched the travelers walk past.

Avanda struggled to see the bird high on the ledge. The sun burned her eyes when she looked up, but she could view the bird lift off and fly above them. Circling for several minutes, it slowly lowered itself closer to the marching prisoners.

Nudging Thorik to look up at it, she noticed the bird had disappeared. Thorik wasn't in the mood for games as he attempted to develop a plan of escape.

Frustrated that no one else had seen the bird except her, Avanda scanned the skies to see where it had flown. She watched for kewtalls, as well as the possibility of it resting on a ledge, but found no evidence of it.

"Idiot!"

Avanda heard the voice of Bryus and looked over at Thorik. He had heard it as well.

"Leave me alone," Bryus' voice said again.

Brimmelle heard it and spun around. All three Nums were looking for Bryus after hearing his voice in his typical condescending tone. But he was nowhere to be seen.

"I have to do everything myself." It was clearly Bryus' voice, but this time Avanda saw where it was coming from. The bird she had seen earlier was now waddling along with them as it blurted out comments it had obviously heard Bryus say more than once.

Bright red and orange colors coated its feathers except for its orange and white face. With eyes way too large for its head, it looked like someone had squeezed its neck so hard that its eyes had popped out of their sockets.

Abrupt swipes of the bird's head back and forth nearly caused it to lose balance as it limped along with a talon missing from one claw. "Idiot! Out of my way," it said as it walked past Brimmelle and up to Avanda.

Brimmelle grimaced at the comment. "Great. I was just getting used to the idea of Bryus not being around."

"It's Bryus' pet." Avanda knelt down and showed the bird a piece of rag with Bryus' scent on it.

"How is that possible?" Brimmelle asked.

"I performed the summon swap spell on Bryus and his pet before I left him at the Guardians. He told me that his pet would find us by following his scent." She reached out to pick the bird up. "I wonder what her name is..."

"Idiot!" the bird blurted out.

Brimmelle smiled. "Good enough for me."

Thorik laughed. "What use could this crippled bird be for us? Why would he send her to us?"

Lifting the bird up, Avanda began to pet it. "I don't know if she has a purpose for us. I think the idea was just to get Bryus back to his family. I hope he made it."

"Hi, Idiot." Brimmelle then reached over to pet it.

Idiot snapped at Brimmelle's fingers, nearly taking one of them off. "Leave me alone!" it squawked.

Chapter Forty-Five

CITY OF ERGRAUTH

Weeks of chilly nights and hot desert days had taken their toll on the travelers. Guards had provided just enough water and food to keep them walking, but not enough to have the strength to escape or fight their way out. Nevertheless, this day would be different, as they grew closer to what appeared to be a distant gathering of enormous red crystals under a thick cloudy sky. But as they traveled closer, it became obvious that it was the namesake city of the demon, Ergrauth.

Dark red monoliths of the city grew out of the pristine white sands of the desert floor at the shore of the Ergrauthian Lake. Dozens of the monolithic towers sprang up from the dune floor as though a growth of natural crystals rose from the convergence of the sand dunes and lake's blue water. Reflecting the sun's sporadic rays off these tremendous towers, the white dunes near the city took on a bloody red hue.

Waves lapped at the ivory dunes surrounding half the city. It had no moat, no drawbridge, and no protection from outside invaders. There had never been an attack on the city, nor could anyone ever imagine one happening. This was the namesake home and the living place of the demon, Ergrauth.

At the entrance was an impressive marble statue of Ergrauth standing victoriously in the center of a fountain, surrounded by a herd of Del'Undays charging along with the demon out toward the desert. Water sprayed out from the feet of the herd as though they were kicking up sand and dust in their rush to fight opposing forces.

The statue depicted the demon with a sword in one hand, showing strength, and a vessel with three spouts in his other. Water poured from one spout, landing on crops carved out leaning against his leg. Red liquid poured from the second spout, which sprayed at the demon's feet, in honor of the blood he had spilled and walked upon to create his empire. The third spout gave a free falling of sand into a vat to symbolize the earth over which he ruled.

Beyond the fountain, the walls and streets of the buildings were made from the flesh and bones of those who died in the city, combined with the desert sands and the lake water. But it was not constructed. It had grown over the years, infused with the physical bodies and the essence of those who were under each step and along every path.

Ergrauth had designed a city that wasted nothing. Those not faithful to him would be absorbed into the city and become part of it. No prisons were needed, for the endless existence as part of a collective that made up the entire city would be the punishment for those who did not obey.

Thorik and his friends were led up to the city. The hard crystal surfaces were glossy and red, and the walls appeared to move slightly as though they were breathing as the travelers entered between two enormous towers. The wall's surface moved and faces and hands appeared to be pressing out from within it, looking at the new captives with whom they would be spending eternity.

The ground had been hardened from the sun's powerful rays, turning it into a sandy and gritty red glass filled with bone fragments. These streets were in use by the locals who went about their business. Various types of Del'Unday pushed carts and moved goods from place to place. Things were orderly, unlike the chaotic streets of Trewek. Residents of this city had clear intentions and rarely stopped to chitchat in the streets.

Pulsing with red fluid, veins clung to streets and towers like vines of ivy. Thin at first near the edge of the city, they grew in girth as the travelers moved toward the center towers.

A low background moaning could be heard from every direction as the dead suffered. It was clear that the locals didn't pay any attention to it. But for the Nums, the entire sight was horrifying.

Even Santorray was uncomfortable, but for different reasons. The traitor, the son of Ergrauth, had returned home. There was a time when all Del'Unday respected his position and his lineage. He was admired and feared, just the way he had meant it to be. But now it was different.

The locals lowered their eyes when they saw Santorray as they went about their daily business. It was a disgrace to see their once mighty hero fall to be a captive.

Few of great strength and stature remained in the city, for the demon had taken most of them to war. What remained were the weak and crippled, as well as the old and the very young.

Ushered into the center of the city, the travelers could see how the city had grown from the center tower, much like a patch of clover expands from its single root. This tower was much larger than the rest and had angled offshoots to all the surrounding towers. Thick veins pulsed fluid from this central location.

Upon this center tower was a great mural of Ergrauth looking over his domain. Words of respect and punishment littered the walls to remind those in the city of how disobedience would not be tolerated. A clear list of rules was carved into front of the tower for all to see, starting with 'Ergrauth's words are law,' and followed by 'Never compromise the mission.' These were just the first two of the many rules for all to obey.

Santorray led his companions in a display of strength, followed by Grewen and the Nums. Even in the face of condemnation and certain death, the blothrud held his head high and was proud of his accomplishments. None of those who looked upon him could say they had stood up to Ergrauth for their own rights.

The city amazed Grewen. He had only heard about it in legends. "It's cleaner than I had expected," he said to his blothrud friend.

Walking behind them, Brimmelle dragged his feet on the streets. Parched and sunburned, the elder Num was struggling to go any further. His eyes glazed over and his breathing became shallow as his legs gave out from under him.

Collapsing onto the street, Brimmelle was kicked by one of the Del guards, who ordered the Num to stand back up. Brimmelle was exhausted and simply couldn't go another step.

A second kick was made by the guard, but it was stopped short. Grewen had reached down to pick the Num up, and his mighty hand had taken the impact of the attack. Grewen flinched slightly from the kick, but it was the guard who felt the pain of several broken toes and claws upon the strike.

"Come on, Brimmelle." Grewen lifted the Num to carry him the rest of the distance. "Stay with us."

Avanda stood defiantly and glared at the guard who had kicked her fellow Num, as though she was going to take him on herself.

"Idiot!" the bird on her shoulder shouted.

As another guard approached, Avanda felt a tug on her sleeve. It was Thorik.

"This won't help us," he informed her.

"What will? We're doomed anyway. Let's at least go out fighting," she replied.

Several guards now approached the two Nums.

"Leave me alone." the bird squawked.

"Avanda, please. I don't want my last memory of you to be during a bloody battle."

"Then fight alongside me."

Thorik softly placed a firm hand on her shoulder. "I've always been fighting at your side, and I always will. But I don't want us to end as dead Nums on the streets of this city. Trust me, we'll find a better way. And when we do, we'll do it together."

"I should turn them into frozen statues." Her voice was intentionally loud enough for the guards to hear.

Bryus' bird flew off from her shoulder and up in the air.

"I'd like to see that, but then the rest of the guards will unleash their rage upon us." Thorik pulled together a half grin for her before being escorted back in line behind Grewen.

"I don't want to die, Thorik." She had finally given in and lost her anger at the guards as her eyes filled with tears. "I miss Bryus, and there is still so much I want to learn and do."

"I know," he said as they walked to the center tower. Wrapping his arm around her, he pulled her in tight. "The opportunity will come, and I'll be there for you."

Avanda leaned her head against him as tears flowed over her cheeks. "Promise?"

Thorik sighed and nodded. He hoped he would be correct.

White droplets splattered on one of the guards from above. Bryus' bird squawked, "I have to do everything myself." Continuing to fly above the prisoners, the bird finally landed back on Avanda's shoulder just prior to them entering one of the structures.

Changing guards at the entrance, four elaborately dressed blothrud guards guided the travelers through two massive doors at the base of the center tower and led them inside, down a few corridors, and then into a large room in the heart of the tower. They were now in the exact center of the city in a room with nothing except a gateway which would absorb them into the structure for all eternity. A dozen massive veins across the ceiling and walls came together at the edges of the gateway.

Two executioners stood near the gateway with long, multi-bladed spears. All four guard escorts remained at the doorway of the room while the executioners managed the events within the room.

Santorray could take out any blothrud, but attacking six at once was a major risk, especially after minimal rations for the past several weeks. He turned his attention to the gateway instead to see if he could destroy it.

Several elder Del'Unday were already standing in line as they waited to be corralled into the gateway. They looked up at Thorik and his friends with desperate eyes. Age had made them unproductive, which was a crime against Ergrauth and his people. Their punishment would be never-ending; the executioners in the room, armed with spears, prodded those on death row to move forward.

Realizing her own mortality, Avanda clung onto Thorik as they entered.

Chapter Forty-Six

GATEWAY

The gateway was more of a thick, golden-trimmed doorway with detailed etchings. Inside the doorway was a dark mirror, reflecting the room without the person standing in front of it. To stand in front of it made one realize one's lack of worth.

The travelers stood in line as they waited their turn to walk into the mirror. Thorik and his friends were three from the front, as they watched the process unfold. Santorray continued to stand up front with his chest and snout held high and proud.

Grewen had set Brimmelle back down next to Avanda so he could take the last few steps on his own. Stepping in front of the Nums, the mognin would go before them, hoping his enormous mognin body would break the device before the Nums had to try.

"Idiot!" Bryus' bird yelled out as it stood on Avanda's shoulder and stared at the pulsing veins across the ceiling.

Brimmelle flinched at the bird's yell, since it was so close to his ear.

The executioners gave Brimmelle a scowl, as they assumed the comment came from him.

Brimmelle put his head down to avoid their attention, and Avanda attempted to quiet the bird.

The bird's large, independently moving eyes rolled around and scanned the room. "Fesh face!" the bird squawked.

Brimmelle's eyes opened wide at the remark and then glanced over at the executioners.

Walking over, one of the executioners prodded Brimmelle with his spear to move up in line, right behind Santorray. "Sooner we get rid of your mouth, the better."

"But..." Brimmelle didn't have the opportunity to explain that he hadn't said anything.

The blothrud moved the short Num between Grewen and Santorray. "I don't want to hear it."

It wasn't a position Brimmelle had ever wanted to stand in, for he was half Santorray's height and a third of Grewen's. His view forward and behind was repulsive, so he stared at the floor. But the view was the least of his worries at the moment.

One executioner used his spear to prod the first elder Del'Unday in line to remove his belongings and walk toward the gateway. Reluctantly, the old Del dropped his gear to the floor and walked over to the mirror, stopping a yard in front of it. He gazed at his non-reflection, knowing that he was doomed for all eternity. Stepping away from it to calm his thoughts, he felt the blothruds pressing their spears into his back, forcing him forward.

Once he was within a few feet, his body slid violently against the mirror, as though gravity had changed directions. Tight against the dark reflection of the room behind him, he screamed in pain. Pulling his head back away from the mirror, flesh could be seen dissolving wherever his body touched the flat surface, as though the mirror was comprised of acid.

With the sideways gravity pulling him, he continued to press against the inside of the gateway as he dissolved away inch by inch.

Clothes lit on fire and quickly burned away, while flesh melted off. As the skin was removed, the man's muscles and fat broke down into a liquid and boiled away, followed by his bones sinking down into the darkness of the mirror. Fresh blood and flesh pulsed through the veins in the ceiling overhead.

The entire event only lasted a minute, but the horror for those who witnessed it would last forever. The victim, however, would now add to the city's walls and structure, expanding it just that much more.

The scene struck Avanda with overwhelming fear. This was finally hitting her as her end. There was no escape. They would end up as lost souls floating among these halls forever. "The walls are filled with the lives of so many prisoners. Could this be a worse fate than Della Estovia?"

"When we are in a room surrounded by death and life as we wait for our turn for both," Thorik mumbled to himself.

Avanda wiped her tears from her face. "What?"

Thorik let go of Avanda so he could remove his pack and the Runestones within it. He then pulled out his Runestone of Courage. "Granna had warned me of events such as this. I am to call upon her when it should occur." Not seeing anything to lose, he moved between Grewen and the wall to concentrate on the stone as the next old Del'Unday in line was prodded toward the gateway. Now, out of the executioners' and guards' view, he unsheathed the dagger Varacon as he called to her.

Avanda hugged Grewen's giant hand as she waited for someone to save them. Looking up into the giant's face, she could tell he hadn't given up hope yet.

"Every moment is precious," Grewen said to her. "Even if it's your last. Revel in what you have, instead of focusing on what you don't."

Avanda repeated the statement to herself as she tried to determine how to use his words to help. "What do we have?"

In the dim light behind Grewen, Gluic's ghostly appearance flowed from the dagger. "It is time, Thorik."

Glancing back to make sure he wasn't being seen, he questioned her. "Time for what? I've done what you've asked, but we have failed. We are about to be sentenced to a place without life or death. I have fallen short of your request."

"Nonsense. You have succeeded."

Thorik listened to the second man scream in horror and pain as he looked at his friends standing in line. "Only in the deaths of my loved ones."

"This is not your destiny, Thorik."

"I would love for that to be true, but unless you can convince the executioners of this, I'm afraid it is."

"Do you recall what I told you before my death, when I had seen my future?"

Thorik remembered the event. In fact, he had thought of it often, ever since she first touched Santorray with a memory crystal and saw his past and her future. "Your death provides you an opportunity to move into a new body to fulfill a new purpose," he said softly. "But now I can't even give you time to fulfill any purpose."

"But you are wrong. This is what I was meant to do."

Thorik watched the third person in line toss his belongings to the floor and move into position. "You're meant to be heaved into a pile of garments and travel supplies? I think not. I would use you to fight for our freedom, but I fear I would lose you in the process if Varacon were to be scratched."

"No, my grandson. My dear courageous boy. You will not do this. Instead, this is my time to do what has been needed for thousands of years. It is my destiny to free these people."

Thorik held the Runestone in one hand and Varacon in the other as he listened to another brutal death and watched Avanda and Brimmelle cry in each other's arms. "I don't know how to help you save these people."

"Yes, you do."

"Granna, please. No more games. Tell me before there is no time left for us to speak."

"What do you wish to do?"

"Me? I wish to stop these deaths, save ourselves, and release you from this dagger." Thorik thought of what else needed to happen. "And free all those enslaved inside the walls of this city of death."

"Exactly."

"Granna? What does that mean?"

"You must be willing to let go of something you cherish in order to make all of those things happen. Can you do this for me?"

The executioners moved over to the next person in line. It was Santorray.

"Of course, name it! Quickly!"

"Stab Varacon into the vein in this wall."

Santorray unsheathed his sabers and hesitated before dropping them on the pile of gear from the prior victims.

Thorik was sure he misunderstood. "Use the dagger?"

"Yes." Gluic's voice was soft but clear.

"But we have the spell and the components to free you."

"I don't require them. They aren't for me."

"Then why did you have me collect them to free you?"

Gluic smiled. "You must promise me to travel north to the dragon's lair and use them to save Rummon. He will require them for you to be successful in your future journeys."

Santorray walked over in front of the mirror and saw a reflection of the room without him in it. He no longer would exist except in the walls of this city.

Thorik peered back and forth between the blothrud and Gluic. "I can't. I promised to save you."

Santorray bit hard against his lip to draw blood for one last battle.

"You have, and many more. But it is now time." Gluic touched his cheek with her translucent hand.

Santorray stepped up to the gateway, roared with a mighty force, and then attacked, slamming his fists into the mirror as he attempted to pound his way through the gateway to see what was on the other side.

"Granna. No," Thorik stated firmly.

"Courage, my brave little hunter. I will always be there for you."

A howl of pain filled the room as Santorray's fists began to bleed and his flesh started to strip off the muscles on his hands. He hadn't even made a dent in the mirror as it attempted to drag his body toward it. His paws were losing grip and sliding toward the mirror.

"Granna!" Thorik shouted.

Gluic's journey was complete. "Goodbye, my hero."

Santorray continued to pound his fists as pieces of flesh flung off his knuckles as he shouted his last battle cry. Santorray was losing this last battle. He was about to die. His paws slipped, and his body slapped hard against the mirror.

"NO!" Thorik yelled as he plunged the dagger, Varacon, into the wall next to him. The shiny dark red wall immediately turned a dull ivory with a rough texture of sand. This change spread out from the dagger across the room and into the next, like a rapid plague as the veins carried Gluic's essence in every direction. The mirror in the gateway froze solid, its acids neutralized and its ability vanished.

The following powerful thrust of Santorray's fist slammed right through the mirror and the wall it leaned against as shards of glass sprayed the room. The blothrud stepped back to see the sight of the damaged gateway as he raised his arms in the air and roared in victory before smashing both fists one last time, destroying the gateway and the wall behind it.

But his victory was short-lived. The walls were losing their strength, as the city was becoming a giant sandcastle, and it was falling apart under its own weight. Using this to his advantage, he grabbed the spear from a nearby executioner and used it against him before taking out a second executioner as by driving the spear into his gut.

The four guards at the door were confused as to the reaction of the structure around them, but they refused to leave. They had been ordered to stay with the prisoners in the chamber until they had all been through the gateway. To change plans would be to disobey Ergrauth. Ergo, they blocked the exit to stay loyal as parts of the room's ceiling crumbled down on all of them.

Using the chaos to her advantage, Avanda grabbed Bryus' bird and tossed it at the guards near the doorway. "Attack!" she yelled, hoping the bird would respond.

Panicking from the confusion, the bird flew toward the exit and the guards. Instead of trying to attack the blothruds, it was simply attempting to escape the room. In doing so, it recklessly flew toward the face of one of the blothruds.

One guard swung at the bird, knocking it into the face of the other guard, while it flapped and squawked uncontrollably.

It was the distraction that Santorray needed. He quickly grabbed his sabers and headed for the exit. By the time he arrived at the doorway, the guards had knocked the bird to the ground, but they hadn't been ready for Santorray's sabers. With a few swift moves, he cut the blothrud guards down, freeing those in the room.

"Everyone out!" Santorray commanded.

Avanda scooped up Bryus' bird from the floor on her way out of the room. Limp in her hands, she hoped it was only knocked out.

Racing out of the room, just as it fell in on itself, the group ran down one hallway after another. Each one crumbling under its own weight, each one breaking down into its raw elements of sand and bones.

Reaching the exterior, they could see the influence of Gluic, turning the glossy red towers pale. The central region was fully ivory by now as it spread outward.

Santorray led them through the streets crowded with locals screaming from the chaos. They ran for their lives around corners and under archways just prior to their collapse.

A large red section of a tower gave way and fell from its lower ivory sand walls, crashing against one of the streets. The exploding walls sent red blood spraying in every direction.

Dodging around a corner, they avoided the spray as they approached the last row of red towers, which hadn't been affected yet.

The sound of towers crashing and sand raining down on the streets pounded against their backs as they rushed to exit the city limits, passing the fountain statue of Ergrauth. Even with all of that, Thorik thought he heard a familiar voice calling to him.

Thorik stopped and looked around for the owner of the voice, unable to find it until he heard it again.

"Thank you, dear boy," the voice said again. This time Thorik spotted it. It was his grandmother's face, pressing up against the side of the base of the fountain. "I am now free, and so are these victims."

Thorik's eyes swelled with tears. "Granna!"

"You have done the right thing. Now, go become what you were born to be."

"But Granna."

"Become the leader you desire to be and do what you wish others would." Her face faded as the short wall, which surrounded the fountain, was turning ivory. "Goodbye, dear boy."

"I'm not giving up on you, Granna!" Thorik yelled over the roar of the city falling in on itself. But the surface he reached out to was now solid sand. Rough and dry, it no longer showed the face of his grandmother.

"Thorik!" Avanda yelled as she grabbed his arm. She had turned around and come back for him. "We have to leave this place."

A section of wall crumbled into the street, blocking their escape route with over ten feet of rubble made of bones and sand. But it failed to pull Thorik from his state of mind.

"No, not yet." Thorik refused to believe it was over for her. "Granna is right here. It's time for the spell!"

Looking dumbfounded, Avanda jerked her head around at the sights of the city falling in on them from every angle. "There isn't time. We have to leave, Thorik. You have to trust that Gluic knew what she was doing."

"Trust?" Thorik said while the fountain statue of Ergrauth began to crack apart and lean toward the Nums. "The Runestone of Trust!" Thorik quickly tossed off his backpack and dug inside for the Runestone.

Avanda tried to pull him away as she watched the giant statue lose its strength in its base and started falling toward them. There was no time to talk, or even run for that matter; the statue came crashing down upon them.

To her amazement, however, the statue froze in midair. In fact, everything in the city had stopped moving. Everything except Thorik and Avanda.

Thorik concentrated on the Runestone he had once tried in the caves of Della Estovia, after climbing out of the underground river. He had recalled that time stood still when it was activated. "Avanda, quickly! I don't know how long I can hold this." It was taxing to his mental fortitude.

Unnerved by the free-floating statue of Ergrauth hovering above them, Avanda didn't understand what he wanted her to do. "What's happening?"

"I'll explain later. Perform the spell to release Gluic before I can't hold this any longer."

"I can't."

"Yes you can. You have the components and the spell book. Perform it, now!"

Realizing she hadn't practiced as much as she should have, she questioned her ability. "I'll mess it up! I don't know it well enough."

"I trust you. Hurry!" Every second that went by made it more difficult. And as he strained from controlling the Runestone, the objects outside a yard from his position began to slowly move again.

"You shouldn't."

Thorik removed one hand from the Runestone long enough to grab something out of his pocket and hand it to her. The motion outside of his control moved slightly faster until he placed both of his hands back on the Runestone of Trust. The statue hanging over them was nearing their heads.

Avanda looked down in her hand at the object Thorik had given her. It was a blue tinted crystal shard from Bakalor's attack on them. The one she had given to Thorik while on the bridge, while looking over the Lagona Falls. The one that caused her to remember how much they trusted each other and themselves. It was the perfect item, and perhaps the only item, that caused her to straighten up and believe in herself.

Grabbing her components, she prepared her spell as quickly as possible.

"Hurry!" Thorik shouted as he saw the movement increase outside their barrier of safety.

"I'm ready!" She announced. "Wait! We need a body for Gluic to be absorbed into."

Thorik realized he hadn't thought that far ahead. "Have her go into mine."

"No, you could die!" she responded. Looking overhead at the statue just above them, she added, "And if you go, so shall the two of us."

"We have to try!" Thorik yelled, straining to keep time frozen. His muscles trembled from the major toll it was having on his body. Closing his eyes, he used everything he had to keep the Runestone working as he heard Avanda performing the spell.

The statue began to breach the dome of Thorik's time control bubble, causing fragments of the stone to chip away and rain down upon the Nums. With each second that passed, the pieces became larger.

Words were spoken, motions were made, and components were used as Avanda waited for the last steps from Vesik. She sighed with relief as they appeared in the book, as Bryus foretold they would.

Performing the final elements, a misty figure pulled out from the base of the fountain and wafted into her new host. The transition was complete, and Avanda finished the spell.

Thorik squinted his eyes from the pressure of controlling the Runestone. "Make haste!"

"It's over, Thorik. Now we need to get out of here."

"Over? But it didn't work," he said through tight teeth. "I don't feel any different."

"That's because I found a different host for her body."

Squeezing one eye open to see who she was talking about, Thorik watched Avanda tossing her items in her pack before collecting Bryus' bird under her arm.

The bird squawked as it tried to clear its throat, and then it winked at Thorik. Wiggling her digits and claws, Gluic rotated its large, bulging eyes in opposite directions. Gluic tested out each part of her new body, including her voice. "Well, this is different."

"Bryus' pet was dead, anyway." Avanda gave a quick half grin before returning to business. "Now we need to get out of here."

Pulling Thorik out from under the falling statue allowed him to maintain his focus on the Runestone. And not a second too soon, for once they were out from under it, Thorik's trembling from the stress caused the Runestone's powers to fade and the statue to crash down behind them.

A loud crack from above caused Thorik and Avanda to look up as the side of the tower near them had broken away and was heading straight for them. The red surface near the top reflected the light from the sun into their eyes as it slowly rotated and plunged downward.

Running back into the city would only put them in more danger as more towers fell and crushed the local Del'Unday. Their only choice was to climb over the pile of bones which blocked their path to safety, but the likelihood of doing so before the tower crushed them was slim to none. Regardless, they would try.

Thorik and Avanda jumped onto the pile and climbed with every ounce of strength they had. Gluic leaped from Avanda's hand and flew up in the air, only to land on top of the pile as she casually waited for them. But the loose bones rolled out from under their feet, causing them to slide back down with every step forward. It was pointless. Every foot forward resulted in a half a foot backward. They knew they would never make it past the crest in time.

Just as they recognized it was over, Gluic flew up in the air and the section of bones they were climbing suddenly fell away, causing them to roll forward, away from the city.

Grewen had used his oversized hands and arms to grab a section of the bones from the far side and pulled it back away, opening a path for them. Gluic had led him to just the right location to dig.

Santorray then leaped forward and grabbed the two Nums from the pile. Placing one under each of his arms, he ran for safety as the tower crushed the location where the Nums had been blocked.

CHAPTER FORTY-SEVEN

UNEXPECTED VISITOR

Bones, flesh, and blood shot out from the violent crash of the tower, pelting the backs of Grewen and Santorray. Screams of the trapped souls echoed in the Nums' ears as the blothrud tried to protect them from the flying debris. But they had been too close when the tower had crashed, and the force of the bloody muck knocked Santorray over, causing Thorik and Avanda to tumble out of his arms, far from the blothrud's reach.

A large chunk of another tower twisted and rolled toward the fallen blothrud and Nums with extreme speed. Attempting to stand and run out of the way, the thick, wet debris caused them to slip and fall. They had lost momentum, and only the blothrud was able to grip the ground with his rear wolf-like claws to get started again. Unfortunately, the Nums had slipped too far away for him to save before the tower would crush them. His options were to either save himself or die trying to save Thorik and Avanda. Gripping the blood-saturated ground with his claws and fingers, he leaped toward the Nums.

Red liquid rained down on the white desert sand and bones fell from above as the city continued to destroy itself. But out of the chaos, a tall, blood-covered human ran from the city and scooped up the Nums on his way to safety. Chunks of flesh from the collapsing buildings coated the muscular man's shoulders, back, and head as he continued his escape without skipping a beat. The lifting of the Nums had been a small deviation to his running, as though it was of minor inconvenience.

Santorray was both relieved and angered by the man who had just saved his friends. Not knowing who he was, the blothrud could only assume his motives were not good. He quickly changed his course and followed the man out to safety just as the tower arrived and liquefied into a red mess of body parts.

Once they were at a reasonable distance from any more harm, the man set the Nums down and fell to his knees in order to catch his breath.

Santorray would have done the same if he weren't concerned about displaying any weakness in front of the stranger. "Who are you?" he barked at the man.

The man quickly spun to his feet and pulled out his sword. It was obvious that he was well trained and knew how to handle his weapon. "Stay back, blothrud, or I shall slay you like I have too many of your kin before you on this day." Thick strips of red flesh still coated the man's head and shoulders.

Pulling out his sabers, Santorray grinned at the idea. "I am not like any blothrud you have ever met. I am Santorray, general of the Elite forces, son of Ergrauth, and the only lesser demon of his lineage still alive. A human presents no threat to me."

Standing an impressive height for a man, he was still over a head shorter than Santorray. But he refused to back down. "And I am not your typical human. I am Asentar, the last Dovenar Knight of our great kingdom. How poetic that such great warriors of our two lands finally meet in combat again, for my blade has tasted your blood once before."

"Not poetic. Just unfortunate, for you." Santorray stepped forward to launch his attack.

"Stop!" Thorik shouted as he jumped in between them. "Asentar is our friend. I sent him here to collect the urn for the Winds of Conquest," he told the blothrud.

Scooping a handful of thick, bloody flesh from his head and face, Asentar kept his sword firm in his other hand.

Thorik turned to the man. "And Santorray is our friend, as well as Ambrosius' close ally."

Neither of them looked down at the small Num as they continued to eye each other. Both still expected the other to strike first. But the long delay served to reduce the stress.

Thorik thought it best to keep talking to ease the tension. "We met Asentar in the City of Trewek. He came here to Ergrauth to find the urn in order to prove to the elders of Trewek that the dragons had been released and that war was coming. The urn must be returned to them before Corrock launches its attack."

As Santorray and Asentar squared off with each other, a large multicolored bird with oversized eyes recklessly flew between them before landing on Thorik's shoulder. Glancing over at it, the two warriors noticed the Num smiling.

Panning back to the Dovenar Knight, Thorik cleared his throat. "Asentar, I don't believe you've met my grandmother, Gluic." It was obvious to the Num that everyone assumed his comment was a joke, as they watched the bird fall backward before spreading its wings and flying away.

Still, Santorray and Asentar stood silent, waiting for the other to back down first.

Thorik continued. "Listen, you two are fighting the same battle and need to work together. Ergrauth's army has passed the Guardians and is heading toward Doven's wall. Darkmere, in disguise as the Terra King, has convinced the Dovenar army to move north into Woodlen, away from Doven. This will make an easy path for Ergrauth."

Asentar lowered his weapon, but kept it ready to rise quickly if needed. "Then I must travel to my people and warn them." Glancing down to Thorik, he added, "You will have to take the urn to Trewek." Reaching into a sack at his side, he pulled out a cracked urn covered in markings and paintings and then carefully handed it to the Num while eyeing the blothrud.

"Thank you." Thorik glanced up to see the bird with Gluic's essence flying overhead in clumsy circles while testing her new abilities. Thorik thought it best not to attempt to convince Brimmelle of his mother's fate, knowing how he reacted the last time she changed form. "But I cannot travel there. I have made a promise to my grandmother to travel north across the lake to Rummon's lair in order to release him."

Brimmelle blurted out his first thoughts about the new plan. "There is no way I am going to climb a volcanic spewing mountain to release a demon that will most likely eat us the first chance he gets."

Asentar's eyebrow's lowered. "Your companion is correct. Nothing but death awaits you in Rummon's lair. In Trewek, however, you can save the lives of many."

"Perhaps, but it is a promise I must live up to nonetheless," Thorik said. "Brimmelle can travel with Santorray and Grewen to the Ov'Unday city. They will have to take this on without Avanda and me."

"No." Santorray's tone was as sharp as his blades.

Thorik turned in surprise at his response. "No? But we need your help."

Santorray began cleaning the remnants and debris from the city off of his blades. "Grewen and Brimmelle will have to perform this task on their own. I must travel to gather Del'Unday who are tired of my father's wrath. We must meet his forces in combat before he rules all of Terra Australis."

"Hold on," Brimmelle said. "I'm not traveling with Grewen. How will we survive?"

Santorray sheathed his clean sabers. "You won't travel to Rummon's lair, and I'm not going to put up with you. Your options are slim if you choose not to travel with Grewen."

Brimmelle looked at Asentar as an option.

"Your little Num legs and wide waist would slow my travels. I cannot risk the delay."

Brimmelle looked at Grewen and wondered how he ever put himself into a position where he would have to travel alone with an Altered Creature.

The mognin grinned. "Looks like you're stuck with me."

"Looks like it," Brimmelle muttered under his breath.

Thorik handed the urn to his uncle. "It is now your responsibility to ensure the elders of Trewek receive this in time to prepare themselves for the upcoming war."

Asentar glanced back at the city as the last few structures fell and countless Del'Unday wandered around in confusion. "We must leave this place without time to heal our wounds. Chaos from this destruction still provides us with a small window of freedom." Taking in a deep breath, he turned back to Thorik. "May your journey be safe and all of our missions be successful. I will see you on the battlefield as we fight for the future of our world."

"Let Ovlan guide our ways," Thorik added.

"Have the courage and desire for freedom to overcome our fears," Santorray added.

Avanda was not to be left out. "And the love of our friends and family give us strength to do what we need to do."

Grewen added his final thoughts to the collection. "As we live within the teaching of Trewek.

All eyes turned to Brimmelle, awaiting his words of wisdom. Everyone else had already spoken. "This is hopeless without the Mountain King's guidance," Fir Brimmelle said flatly.

The group showed obvious signs of disappointment at his comment.

Clearing his throat, Brimmelle added, "Let's be honest here. We have six of us against Ergrauth, Bakalor, Irluk, Darkmere, and all of their armies. We don't even have a crew to carry supplies and a flag for us yet."

Obviously, his words did not stimulate excitement in the group.

Thorik nodded in agreement. "He's right. As much as we don't want to hear it, those are the facts. But in spite of them, I am more confident than ever that we will succeed. For we are an oddity of sorts. When, in history, has a team of this many species come together and put their prejudices aside to fight for the greater good of our land? Never in the minds of evil would they conceive we would work together against them, and that is their greatest weakness. They feed off our intolerance toward one another. But for this moment in history, we shall dismiss these long-taught urges and pull together to take back freedom and our own destiny."

Looking directly at Brimmelle, Thorik straightened up his uncle's shirt. "You are right about our chances of success. But I would rather die in the fight against them than become their slaves."

Brimmelle was struck with a newfound respect for his nephew. He had no idea he had such deep thoughts. Perhaps he had something more than he had given him credit for.

"We all have our missions. We must all do our part." Thorik ended his speech and concluded the discussion.

"I am off to Woodlen!" Asentar shouted as he turned and began running to the west.

"And I am off to stop Ergrauth once and for all." Santorray spit into his hand and shook Thorik's own hand, dripping with saliva. They nodded to each other with respect as a slight grin crossed one side of the blothrud's face. "Goodbye Sec, my little warrior friend. Never forget, it's not the size of the warrior that wins the battle, but the size of their passion and conviction to win." He then turned and ran to the west as well, quickly catching up to Asentar.

Grewen nodded that it was time for him to leave as well. "Every moment I wait here is another moment that could cause the people of Trewek harm. It is time for us to go." Reaching down with his enormous hands, he picked up Thorik and Avanda and lifted them up to his chest and shoulders. They hugged each other tightly. Tears from the Nums ran down the mognin's leathery chest.

"We will see you at the battle," Thorik said.

"I hope no battle is needed." Grewen then set the Nums down, stepped back, and turned to walk southwest.

Brimmelle stood motionless. "You're making a mistake. You should be traveling with us."

"Perhaps, but it is my mistake to make, Uncle."

Avanda gave Brimmelle a hearty hug goodbye.

"Speak the words of the Mountain King. They will help guide you," Fir Brimmelle told her.

Avanda smiled as tears dripped from her cheeks. "I will. You take care of Grewen. Don't let him eat any plants if he doesn't know what they are."

He nodded.

Now it was just Thorik and Fir Brimmelle left to say their farewell. They stood there for several moments, waiting for the other to speak.

Thorik broke the silence. "Take care of yourself."

"I always do."

"I know."

Brimmelle bit his lip slightly as he struggled to say anything worthwhile. "Don't go getting yourself killed. I won't be there to save you."

A light smile crossed Thorik's face. "I'll miss you too." It was followed by a nod and quick slap on the shoulder for luck. His uncle returned the same gesture.

The two parted; Brimmelle followed Grewen, and Thorik returned to Avanda's side as the two Nums watched all of their friends leave them in the middle of the Ergrauthian desert, just outside of the destroyed city.

Misty vapors rose from the fallen city, but instead of fading off, these vapors separated into thousands of individual pieces and roamed the ruins. Moans and screams could be heard from them; they were the freed souls released by Gluic. This continued for several minutes until a dark mass appeared and began tearing through the city, collecting the vapors behind it.

Avanda gasped. "Irluk?"

Thorik nodded as they watched the Death Witch capture a new batch of souls for Bakalor. There was nothing they could do to stop her, and the sight caused them both to feel helpless.

Raising her hands to cover her mouth, Avanda watched as the recently released souls were captured for Bakalor. "Is there no hope for the dead? Are we all destined for this?"

As Irluk collected her bounty, the dark clouds in the sky parted, and intense beams of sunlight pierced down into the city. A sense of calmness filled the air. Vapors quickly moved into the beams of light, immediately disappearing out of Irluk's wrath.

Collecting the last few souls that hadn't reached the beams, Irluk left with her load in tow toward Della Estovia.

Thorik smiled as he noticed how the light appeared to resemble the glowing columns in Della Estovia. But as quickly as the beams of light had appeared, they fell behind the clouds once more.

The trapped souls of the City of Ergrauth had been freed.

Avanda's hand reached over and intertwined with Thorik's fingers. They were now on their own. From this point forward, they had to rely on each other. "Thorik, I know we are fools for doing this on our own, but I believe our trust in one another and our love will allow us to accomplish anything we set our minds on. As long as our hearts are forever together, we are invincible."

Thorik smiled and turned back to look at her lovely face. Somehow he saw past the dirt and debris from their adventure and saw a lovely woman that he had fallen for since they left Farbank. "I can't think of anyone else I'd rather be alone with than you, Avanda."

As they gazed into each other's eyes, it quickly became apparent that they were not alone. There were now thousands of prior residents standing just outside of their destroyed city, many of them spreading out and nearing the Nums. The vast majority of them were Del'Unday, which made sense. But there was also a small band of humans and Nums that had escaped the collapse of the towers as well. They were being led by a Num.

The Num leading the group was a female. Her clothes were ripped and bloodstained, like the rest who followed her. Her long, curly hair was red and golden blonde, and her face looked familiar. "Thorik?" She ran up to him, leaped up into his arms, and knocked him onto the ground. Planting a massive kiss onto his lips, she finally gave him room to breathe.

Thorik was flabbergasted at what he was seeing. "Em? Is it really you?"

"Yes! Darkmere left us in Corrock, and days later, we were all released from his spell." Emilen palmed her necklace, which had held her in a spell under Darkmere's control. "The Del'Unday that worked for him eventually decided to bring us here to be absorbed into this city. However, just as we showed up, the city started falling apart. I don't know what happened, but I'm so thankful to see you. I've missed you so much."

Thorik laid on the ground in shock. He was sure that his eyes and ears were deceiving him.

Standing but a few feet away, Avanda crossed her arms and glared at Emilen's unexpected return. If looks could kill, the murder of a female Num would have just taken place.

MORE STORIES

Read **'Rise of Rummon'** to find out how Thorik and his friends attempt to resurrect the dragon lord to prevent the Demon War from happening.

Read "Outraged' to find out what happened to Santorray when he fell into the Govi Glade sphere.

www.AlteredCreatures.com
The epic adventures continues...

Nums of Shoreview Series (Pre-teen, Ages 9 to 12)
Box Set: All 6 Short Stories of the Nums of Shoreview books in one

Thorik Dain Series (Young Adult and Adult)
Treasure of Sorat (Prequel)
Fate of Thorik (Book 1)
Sacrifice of Ericc (Book 2)
Essence of Gluic (Book 3)
Rise of Rummon (Book 4)
Prey of Ambrosius (Book 5)

Plea of Avanda (Book 6)

<u>Tilli of Kingsfoot Series (Adult)</u>
Hidden Magic (Book 1)
Final Days (Book 2)

<u>Santorray's Privations Series (Adult)</u>
Betrayed

Hunted

Outraged

Look for other upcoming stories of
Santorray's Privations
Ambrosius
Tilli of Kingsfoot
Myth'Unday
Dragon & Del'Unday Wars
and more...

www.ingramcontent.com/pod-product-compliance
Lightning Source LLC
Chambersburg PA
CBHW070201120726
47909CB00001B/207